# The Lesbian MILFs

## Complete Collection 3

# The Lesbian MILFs

# Complete Collection 3

by

Reed James

Naughty Ladies Publications

All characters depicted in this work of fiction are over the age of eighteen (18).



Naughty Ladies Publications

www.NaughtyLadiesPublications.com

ISBN-13: 9798396295773

# Table of Contents

# Ms. Demeter's Sultry Room Service

## MILF CEO's Lesbian Cutie 1

## A Lesbian MILF Tale

by

Reed James

## Ms. Demeter's Sultry Room Service

The wish is spreading far and wide. So many naughty, young girls are discovering the joys of women at the hands of gorgeous and sensual MILFs. The world is beginning to notice the changes as more and more women turn to each other.

The world is becoming such a wicked delight.

* * *

### Ms. Xandra Demeter – Friday, Day 5 of the Wish

I smiled as I rode in the limo with my new personal assistant, Kelly.

And I do mean "personal." She was my naughty and kinky little lesbian slut. I had met her today or yesterday—travel could be such a chore on the concept of time—when her step-mother brought her into my office to give a presentation. I was the founder and CEO of Secret Delights, a lingerie company. My business had grown over the years. We now had our own stores selling our delights to women across the world.

When I met Kelly, the playful little cutie had turned me on. I just had to take her with me on my trip to Milan to meet with the models who would be showing off my newest line of lingerie. And what a trip it had been so far. I had played a naughty prank on her going through TSA that ended up with us in a wonderful menage with a Black woman who worked security at the airport. She had been a pleasure. Then on the plane, we had more fun with the all-female flight crew of my private jet.

Kelly had serviced the pilot and co-pilot with her mouth and toys. The flight crew kept finding excuses to come back and have their pussies eaten out by the nineteen-year-old cutie. And Kelly had been more than eager to do it. She ate pussy with enthusiasm.

Now she sat cuddled up against me, her hand beneath my skirt petting my pussy as the limo drove us through Milan. We were in northern Italy, a gorgeous city. You could see the Alps from here, rearing over the delicious place.

I loved Milan. It had a zest, a vibrancy, that American cities lacked.

Kelly's blonde hair spilled across my shoulder. She sometimes kissed it as her hand worked beneath my skirt. I groaned, savoring the stroking touch of her digits. This felt so incredible. I savored the feel of her touch. The way she caressed me and teased me. This heat swept through my body. I groaned at the wicked tingles her contact she gave me.

Her fingers thrust into my cunt now. I gasped, my twat squeezing around the playful girl's naughty digits. She giggled and pumped them in and out of me. I licked my lips, my toes curling in my stockings and heels.

"We are almost to the hotel," I groaned.

"And, Ms. D.?" she asked with that impish tone to her voice. Her nose ring glinted as she smiled at me. She thrust a third finger into my cunt. I gasped at that. My breasts rose and fell, stretching out my top.

She knew how to please an older woman.

"I'm going to do such naughty, naughty things when we get to the hotel room," moaned Kelly. "I can't get enough of your MILF pussy."

I never would have thought being called MILF would turn me on. But it did. This young girl loving my mature pussy was such a treat. A delight that I would enjoy. I quivered as her fingers stirred up my cunt. Her thumb swept out and found my clit.

I would have so much fun with her while we were in Milan. A wild time with my sexy, young lover. I had to give her step-mother a promotion for bringing this cutie into my office. Expelled from college, Kelly was working as an intern at my company now.

I had to thank her college for expelling her.

"What naughty things are you going to do to me?" I asked.

"Give you a tongue bath," she moaned into my ear. She licked my lobe, sending a shiver that ended at my pussy clenching around her three digits. "Just lick all over your gorgeous body. I'm going to soak you in my spit."

"That sounds so wicked of you," I moaned. "Mmm, but what if I have other ideas?"

"If they're as much fun as getting strip-searched by a sexy, Black woman and punished for having a vibrator in my cunt, then I'm down for it." Kelly licked her lips, her fingers pumping faster. "My ass is still sore from being spanked by her."

I laughed. "You were so naughty. You deserved to be spanked."

"You think I was naughty then?" she asked and then pulled her fingers out of my twat.

I gasped at the sudden withdrawal. Kelly brought her digits to her mouth, her blue eyes sparkling. She licked at her cream-coated fingers. Her tongue stroked up and down them, gathering up my juices from them. I shivered at the wicked sight. She looked so kinky doing that.

My pussy clenched, aching to be filled again. My breasts rose and fell. The heat swelled through my body. My fingers flexed as she lapped each one of her digits clean. I bit my lower lip at the teasing sight.

I wanted those digits back in me. I was so horny. I was about to order her to finger me again when the limo pulled off the street. I glanced out the window to see the Armani Hotel rearing over our heads. It was an elegant building, old-world charm stamped all over it. I shivered as the valet, dressed in the red livery that you would never see in the U.S., stepped up to the door. He looked from another age.

An elegant one.

He opened the door to the limousine and spoke first in Italian and then English, "Welcome to the Armani."

I nodded and stepped out, my pussy on fire. My naughty little cutie crawled out after me, gaping in that way of youth at seeing something impressive. Something their limited, though jaded, view of the world had never encountered. Her small breasts quivered in the boob tube she wore, her short skirt flashing the valet an eyeful of shaved cunt.

He hardly reacted.

"Wow, Ms. D.," she gasped and grabbed my arm, clinging to me. It was clear that she was my lover. Maybe a powerful woman with a beautiful, young cutie on her arm wasn't common, but an older and rich person bringing a young companion was a frequent sight. "This is incredible. We're really staying here."

"In one of the suites," I added. "No place finer to stay in Milan than the Armani."

The valet grinned at as I strutted to the doors. There, two more men in livery opened them for us and gave smooth bows. Kelly giggled in utter delight. She practically bounced with her giddiness at the continental service.

The interior was breathtaking. The lobby of the Armani Hotel in Milan was a work of art. Polished marble floors. Chandeliers above. Everything had elegance save my assistant and the trashy outfit she wore.

I liked that about her. The way she dressed, showing off her body and not caring what others thought. She looked around with that awe on her face. I wanted to just pin her to the wall and kiss her. Ravage her body and let all the guests see.

On the couch, an older woman sat beside a younger. Both were dressed elegantly. Their hands were clutched, fingers playing in such an intimate manner. I smiled. It was spreading. Wherever this headlong plunge into lesbianism had come from, it was changing women.

It made us open with our affections for each other. It was like we no longer cared what others thought of our desires. We felt free to share in our love for each other, no longer shackled by male expectations.

It was such a liberating thrill.

The concierge looked up and smiled. "Ah, Ms. D., what a pleasure to have you stay with us again."

"They know your name," Kelly whispered in awe.

"You know I just love staying in the Armani," I told him. "Where else can I get such rest and relaxation in Milan?"

The concierge gave a polite laugh. "We have your suite ready for you and your companion." He didn't bat an eye to the cutie on my arm. "Our bellhops shall bring up your luggage." He produced a key —not a keycard, but an actual key—with a bronze disc attached with the room number stamped on it. "Is there anything else I can get for you, Ms. Demeter."

"Have a bottle of champagne sent up," I said. "We're celebrating young Kelly's first time in Milan."

The girl grinned. "Just so eager to be here with Ms. D."

"Of course," he said. "Enjoy your stay. If you need anything, the staff shall provide."

I nodded and took the key. I glanced at the room number. 914. I had stayed in that suite before. It was a delightful one. My heels clicked as we crossed the lobby. Kelly clutched to me, this look of awe on her face.

"What?" I asked her.

"You didn't even have to sign paperwork," she said. "Or put a credit card down as a deposit."

"Like a plebe?" I asked and laughed. "No, no, this is Europe. They know how to treat the rich. They will have all that taken care of in the background. They no which accounts to charge."

"Do you even think about the cost?" the girl asked as we reached the brass doors to the elevator. They had an old fashion arrow indicator that slowly worked down as the elevator approached.

"Do you think about the cost when you go into Starbucks to by your latte?"

"No. But this must be expensive."

"Expensive is all a matter of perspective." I smiled at her. "That's all. That's what life is. People have different perspectives on the world, but it's easy to forget that. To think that yours is the right one or that everyone should see things your way. Now, do not worry about the cost. We are going to have fun. Ever had champagne? The real stuff?"

"No." She grinned at me. "I'm nineteen. You think I'm having champagne. I'm drinking whatever beer or wine coolers or whiskey my friends and I can get. It's not like we can buy it ourselves."

"We're not in America. We're in Europe. The drinking age in Italy is sixteen, I believe."

"I love this country," she groaned.

The elevator arrived, the inside mirrored silver. An attendant stood inside, giving us a bow. A pity. I wanted to shove my tongue into Kelly's mouth and tickle her tonsils. She was such a ravaging thing. She leaned against the wall, looking so coquettish as the attendant hit the button for the ninth floor (which would be the tenth floor in America, but in Europe, the ground floor didn't count).

The elevator rode up while the attendant had a polite smile as he stood there, his hands covered in elegant gloves. The elevator creaked to our floor. The doors opened, and we swept out. I sauntered down the hallway to the room and thrust in the key. I flung the door open onto an elegant sitting room.

"Where's the bed?" gasped Kelly as she strode in, her head snapping around. "There are couches here, Ms. D."

"It's a suite," I said, staring at the old-world decoration. The elegance of the Gilded Age on full display. An expensive pattern of fabric clad the couch, cream with gold accent. It matched the drapes at the windows. "The bedrooms are off of it."

"Bedrooms?" she gasped in shock. "Plural?"

"I know, a waste since we only need one," I said.

She grinned. "We could break them all in."

"You wicked and naughty girl," I purred and sauntered to her. I cupped her chin and lifted her head. I kissed her hard on the mouth. I thrust my tongue in deep.

She tasted so sweep, faintly minty from brushing her teeth right before we landed. She clung to me with hunger, her tongue dancing through my mouth. The heat rippled between us. She was such a treat to enjoy.

I wanted to rip her naked when the knock came at the door.

I sighed and broke it. That was the bellhop with our luggage.

He brought it in and placed it in the bedroom I directed. I gave him a fifty euro note for a tip. He grinned at me, promised me the world if I asked, and headed out.

"Now, strip," I told Kelly. "I want to see that delicious body of yours naked."

She grinned. "Such a naughty MILF. Did you bring me all the way to Europe to take advantage of me? I'm just so shocked that you would do that."

"I brought you out here to enjoy that body in every way possible," I purred. "You're going to be my little toy."

"Such a wicked MILF," she moaned. "Tricking a cute and naive little girl into such a lewd act."

"Naive?" I snorted. "When have you ever been naive?"

She gave me a big grin and peeled off her boob tube. Her small breasts came out. They were little mounds. Firm and gorgeous. She had a lean body. She thrust her arms over her head, her hips wiggling back and forth. She looked so gorgeous.

My pussy clenched at the sight of her. I bit my lip, so eager to enjoy my cutie. I would do such naughty things to her. My blood pumped hot through my veins as her hands swept down her body to her swaying hips.

She turned around as she danced, her hips rocking from side to side. Her skirt flared, barely covering that rump. She threw a coquettish look over her shoulder as she hooked her skirt's stretchy waistband with her thumbs and pushed it down.

I groaned as her welted ass came into view, still red from being spanked the TSA agent. Kelly bent over, thrusting her rump at me. She had a butterfly tattooed on her right butt-cheek, a playful creature just taking flight. I loved the sight as she pushed her skirt down off her thighs. It dropped down to her feet. Her shaved pussy gleamed between her legs, slit tight, vulva plump with her excitement.

"Now finger that twat for me," I moaned, my own cunt still juicy from her teasing.

"Yes, Ms. D.," she said in a breathy and girlish voice. "This is so exciting. I can't believe I'm doing this for you. But you're just so sexy, I can't help myself."

I shook my head at her girlish tone. She turned around, a look of innocence on her face even with her nose ring. She sank down on the couch, her legs spread wide. She bit her lower lip and slid her hands down her stomach to her shaved pubic mound.

"You want me to rub myself?" she asked. "That's so naughty of you. But it makes me all so tingly to do this."

"I bet it does," I moaned as the fingers from both her hands reached her pussy. She slid them over her and rubbed at her hot cunt. She shuddered as she rubbed at her juicy flesh.

She moaned and stroked up and down her cuntlips. Her digits traced her naughty flesh. Her juices stained her digits. I groaned, loving the sight of the cute blonde masturbating for me. My pussy rippled juices that leaked down to my thigh-high stockings. Her eyes stared at me with such passion in them. Blue depths I could get lost in.

I couldn't believe how much this girl was turning me on. How much she excited me. I rubbed my thighs together, my pussy growing hotter and hotter. I squeezed my tits through my blouse, watching her rub at her twat.

"That's it," I cooed. "Mmm, just rub yourself. Yes, yes, just like that. You're going to cum for me, aren't—"

KNOCK! KNOCK!

"Room service," a woman's voice said in accented English.

I grinned and said, "Don't you dare stop rubbing yourself."

"I won't," Kelly moaned, her excitement thick in her voice.

I sauntered to the door, my pussy on fire. I hoped it was a sexy, young maid bringing up the champagne. Another barely legal cutie for me to play with. I craved them so young now. Women my age were still gorgeous, but nothing like the vibrancy of youth to make my mature body ache.

I opened the door and groaned at the sight of the Italian beauty holding the champagne chilling in an ice bucket. She was a tall girl, had an inch or two on me, and possessed an adorable face framed by wavy-black hair. She had tan skin, that Mediterranean look of Italy, her eyes large and dark. I loved her plump lips. She wore a gray uniform, not a sexy French maid outfit, but a smock that went down to her mid-thighs. She had white nylons on her legs. Tied around her waist was a white, half-apron, a towel half-tucked into the pocket in the front.

"Your champagne, Ms. Demeter," she said.

"Mmm, put it on the coffee table," I said, stepping aside.

She stepped in and then gasped at the sight of the masturbating Kelly on the couch. The maid's eyes widened. A shiver ran through her as I closed the door behind her. Color blushed across her pretty, young cheeks.

She couldn't be much more than eighteen.

"Don't be shy," I purred. "Kelly is just relaxing after our long trip. I'm sure you can understand that need."

"I... That is..." She rushed forward to the coffee table and set the bucket down on the marble surface, her eyes flicking to Kelly who had two fingers buried in her twat now, thrusting them in and out. Her little titties jiggled. "D-do you need me to open it?"

"Of course," I said as she pulled two glasses out of her apron's front pocket and sat them down.

She swallowed and then picked up the champagne bottle with the towel. She had skill. In moments, had the champagne bottle popped, her cheeks blazing red. A bit of foamy liquid spilled down the side only to be wiped clean with her towel. Then she went to pour it.

I took the bottle from her and said, "I think I'd rather drink it from Kelly's tit."

"Ms. Demeter?" she asked as if she hadn't understood me correctly.

The blonde had a wicked grin on her face as I settled on the couch beside her and tipped over the bottle. The golden liquid splashed on her tit, coating her nipple and running in a fizzy rush down her body. She gasped.

I ducked down and lipped up the champagne off her tit. Dom Perignon. A good year. I savored the dry flavor as the exciting carbonation burst across my tongue. I licked up to her nipple and sucked it dry with hunger.

"Mmm, this is where champagne belongs," I purred, glancing at the shocked maid. I tilted the bottle over and spilled more champagne over Kelly's breasts. "What do you think?"

"I... I..." The maid squirmed as I ducked my head down and licked up more of the delicious drink.

Kelly cooed in delight as I caressed her tit with my tongue, lapping up the champagne. It poured over her stomach. Some had even pulled in her navel. My mouth salivated for that treat even as my tongue swirled around her nipple. The scent of champagne filled my nose. It buzzed across my taste buds.

"Care for a taste?" I asked the maid.

"M-me?" The maid clutched her hands to her chest. Her eyes were so wide.

"Yes, you," I said. "You're cute. And tell me it doesn't look hot to drink champagne off her tit." I tilted the bottle and spilled more on Kelly's other tit now. It spilled over her right mound and pink nipple. "Isn't that just a succulent sight?"

The maid quivered there.

"I was promised the staff would be ready to fulfill my wishes," I purred. "Aren't you...? What's your name?"

"Ferdinanda," she answered, her name musical.

"Lovely," I purred. "Ferdinanda, you're here to serve. So... start serving. This naughty girl is covered in champagne. She needs you to lick her clean. Like this." I dumped some of the golden drink on Kelly's left nipple and darted down, sucking the bubbly wine and her nub into my mouth all at the same time.

Kelly moaned. "Yes, yes, I'm all wet. You have to clean me up, Ferdinanda. You can't disobey Ms. D. She's a MILF. Young girls have to obey MILFs. They know what we need."

The maid let out a groan. I watched her stumble around the coffee table in a daze. Her hands rubbed at her apron. Her smock rustled about her thighs. She sank down to the couch on the other side of Kelly. Such confusion spread across the maid's face as she leaned down. Her wavy, black hair spilled about her cheeks.

*"I can't believe I'm doing this,"* she said in Italian.

*"I know,"* I said in her tongue. *"Wicked, yes? Just suck on her. Sharing a woman is a treat you'll remember forever, Ferdinanda."*

"Oh, god, that's hot hearing you two speak Italian!" moaned Kelly. "Now suck my titty clean. You're going to love it!"

Ferdinanda licked her tongue around the cutie's nipple. She

caressed over Kelly's tit, lapping and licking at it. The girl whimpered in delight. Her entire body trembled. I spilled a bit more champagne on my side of the cutie and then ducked down.

Kelly whimpered as the sexy maid and I attacked the girl's tit. My lesbian cutie moaned as our tongues caressed over her breast. I splashed more champagne across her chest, letting the amber liquid run down to her tits where our hungry tongues licked it up.

Ferdinanda's pink tongue flicked out again and again. The maid moaned as she gathered the liquid as she caressed over my lover's tit. The Italian cutie nuzzled her plump lips into Kelly's pink nipple. Sucked on it.

"Yes!" Kelly moaned.

I latched onto Kelly's other nub, nursing on it, loving the taste of champagne lingering on her nipple. The taste felt so incredible to enjoy. It was a wild pleasure. I was so thrilled to get to nibble and suck on her tit. I swirled my tongue around it, dancing and caressing her.

She gasped and moaned, her body squirming as we nursed on her. My pussy grew hotter. Having two barely legal lesbians to play with was even more exciting than one. I sucked hard on Kelly's nipple, loving every moment of it.

"Oh, that's making my pussy so hot," moaned Kelly. She was still masturbating herself.

"Is it?" I purred. I ducked my head down and sucked the champagne out of her bellybutton.

Kelly squealed.

"Yes, yes, it's making my cunt just drip. Ooh, Ferdinanda, I love your mouth on my nipple. Is this your first time sucking on a girl's nub?"

The Italian girl moaned and nodded. She kept doing it.

"Well, I think I know what you need," I said. "Something more than your fingers."

"Yes!" howled the naughty girl. She squirmed on the couch as she ripped her fingers out of her cunt. She held them up. They gleamed with her pussy juices.

I sucked one into my mouth, savoring the tangy flavor of her pussy cream. She shuddered as I nursed on her bud. As I did, I brought the bottle of champagne right to her pussy lips. I nuzzled the tip into her.

"Oh, fuck, yes!" she moaned as I pushed forward. "Fuck that bottle into my cunt!"

Ferdinanda's head snapped up. Her wavy-black hair danced around her face. She gasped as she watched me push the bottle into Kelly's twat. I slid my mouth off her finger to watch her pink cuntlips swallowing the slender neck of the bottle. The girl moaned and then gasped as the bottle widened to its shoulder.

*"You can't fit that in her,"* Ferdinanda gasped in Italian. *"The bottle is too big."*

*"My dear, pussies stretch,"* I purred and kept pushing.

Kelly moaned as her pussy lips spread across the widening shoulder. She squirmed and moaned. I gripped the bottle's base and pushed harder on it. I worked it into her pussy. She groaned, her body trembling.

I pushed harder and harder, watching her pussy lips stretch to engulf that dick. Then she gasped as her they swallowed the body. I pushed it deeper, the champagne sloshing around inside the bottle. The barely legal cutie shuddered.

"Fuck, yes!" Kelly moaned. "Oh, Ms. D., fuck that bottle in and out of my cunt. This is so fucking hot!"

"Mmm, you like this?" I asked her and worked the bottle in and out of her."

"I do!" she moaned, her pussy clenching around it. "Oh, yes, yes, I fucking do. This is hot!"

I grinned at her and thrust the bottle in and out of her snatch. I plunged it in deep. I buried it over and over into her. She groaned, her snatch squeezing around it. her body squirmed on the couch. Ferdinanda leaned down and licked at her nipple again.

Then she sucked it. The maid's cheeks hollowed as she nibbled and pleasured Kelly's nipple. My own cunt was on fire. My pussy clenched. The heat swelled through me. Juices stained my thighs as I fucked my lover.

"Yes, yes, yes!" gasped Kelly. "Oh, I'm going to cum on this bottle. The champagne's pouring into my cunt. I can feel it!" I jammed the bottle in deep. The liquid sloshed. "Yes!"

"Mmm, then you're going to give us a treat, aren't you?" I purred.

"Yep! Pussy-flavored champagne. You're going to love it, Ferdinanda."

The maid popped her mouth off Kelly's nipple. "You want me to lick champagne out of your pussy?"

"Fuck, yeah!" Kelly grabbed the front of the maid's uniform and attacked the buttons of her smock. "I want you and Ms. D. just drinking it. Oh, yes, yes, it's going to be delicious."

"Best bottle of champagne ever," I agreed, hungering for it. "So you need to cum!"

"I'm getting there," she moaned and thrust open Ferdinanda's blouse.

The Italian maid had large tits. Her smock and tight sports bra hid just how big they were. They were squished against her chest, just needing to be freed. They would be magnificent. I shuddered, staring at those boobs. My cunt clenched.

Kelly pulled off the blouse, letting it fall down around the maid's waist. Then she peeled up that sports bra. Those large, young breasts pilled out. They were perky and firm despite their size. I stared at them with envy, fucking the bottle in and out of Kelly's cunt.

"Big boobies!" she squealed in delight and grabbed them. She squeezed Ferdinanda's tits and kneaded them.

Ferdinanda shuddered and moaned as the blonde cutie dug her fingers into them. Pleasure crossed Ferdinanda's face. She whimpered, her eyes squeezing shut. She must have such sensitive tits. I loved it. I kept fucking Kelly as I watched the fun.

Then Kelly hefted them and tugged. Ferdinanda moved, shifting onto her knees and pressing her boobs into my lover's face. Kelly moaned in delight, her face clearly buried into the heaven of the maid's big breasts.

Lucky her.

I thrust the bottle faster and faster. Kelly moaned into the cleavage, her body shuddering and moaning. The maid moaned, too. She gasped, her smock rustling around her hips. It fell over her rump. I licked my lips.

"Ms. D.!" moaned Kelly as I plundered her pussy with the bottle. "Ooh, she's got such wonderful boobies. You're going to love them!"

"I bet I will," I moaned and leaned down.

I attacked Kelly's clit. I licked at her pink bud thrusting out of the folds of her pussy. I kept jamming the bottle into her cunt, working it in and out. The scent of champagne and tangy cream filled my nose.

I sucked on Kelly's clit. Nibbled on it with my lips. She groaned and gasped, voice muffled by a magnificent pair of tits. The couch creaked as she shuddered. Ferdinanda trembled. Her dark hair fell down her supple back.

I flicked my tongue. I swirled and danced around Kelly's clit. I wanted her to cum. I sucked it back into my mouth. She moaned, her body twitching. Her pants were growing louder. Throatier. I jammed the bottle hard into her cunt.

"Yes!" she moaned. "Oh, god, I'm about to cum, Ms. D. Keep sucking on my clit! Oh, yes, yes! Fuck that bottle in and out of my cunt. Make me cum."

Such a demanding girl. But I did it because she was so cute. I loved making Kelly cum. She was such a surprise to meet. Such a treat to bring on this business trip. My tongue danced around her clit. I stroked her. Stimulated her.

Loved the gasps and moans and cries of ecstasy that burst from her lips. She shuddered and whimpered. Her body trembled. It was so delicious to hear. It made me so excited to deliver this bliss to her and make her explode.

She would have such a huge climax. It would be amazing to give that delight to her. Just the best. I thrust the bottle into her twat hard and deep. She squealed into the maid's big breasts. Her body bucked on the table. She gasped out in rapture.

"Yes!" she howled. "Oh, yes, yes, that's it! Oh, I'm cumming."

I pulled my lips from her clit and tilted the bottle up so the contents poured out into Kelly. Her body bucked as the champagne bottle plugged up her cunt. Her moans echoed through the suite. It was such a delight to hear. My own cunt clenched. I needed to cum hard.

I knew just how I wanted to.

I massaged Kelly's clit as she thrashed through her orgasm. Ferdinanda pulled her tits away. She had a look of awe as she stared down at Kelly's pussy stuffed full with that wine bottle. She licked her lips, dark eyes sparkling.

"Mmm, get down here," I moaned, massaging Kelly's clit. "You're going to want to be in position to drink the champagne."

Ferdinanda bit her lip. She glanced at the door. Then she groaned and settled down between Kelly's legs. I smiled at the maid. At how cute she was. I rubbed harder at Kelly's clit. She gasped and bucked, her face contorting with bliss.

"You're going to make me cum again, Ms. D.!" gasped the girl.

"I know," I purred.

She shuddered. Bucked. Her wet titties jiggled. I jerked the bottle out of her cunt. Ferdinanda and I buried our faces into my cutie's pussy just into time for the champagne and pussy cream to gush out. A flood of bubbly wine and hot juices bathed our faces.

I opened my mouth wide and gulped down the treat. Kelly thrashed in delight as her pussy poured us such a wonderful drink. The champagne spilled down to my neck, soaking my blouse. I didn't care. I just kept drinking it down. Her tangy juices flavored the bubbly wine, giving it this wonderful zest.

My tongue licked out, brushing Ferdinanda's. She was moaning beside me, drinking the same treat as us. Kelly thrashed, her orgasm still raging through her. Another gush of champagne and pussy juices, though more cream this time, flooded out of her nethers.

"So fucking good, Ms. D.!" howled the cutie. "Oh, yes, yes! That's amazing. Just drink it all down! Oh, god, that's good!"

We gulped it down. We feasted on that wonderful treat. Drank down all that champagne that gushed out of my assistant's pussy. After a moment, the flood became a trickle. The taste of champagne dwindled to just that of yummy pussy.

Our tongues stirred through her. I knew it was Ferdinanda's first time licking pussy. It was so exciting to share this with her. Our tongues brushed and danced together. Hers caressed over mine as we lapped up that treat.

"Oh, god," panted Kelly.

"My breasts are soaked," moaned Ferdinanda. She sat up and her big tits were covered in champagne.

"Yum!" Kelly pounced, pushing the maid onto the coffee table to attack those breasts. My blouse was ruined.

As Kelly lapped up pussy cream and champagne off Ferdinanda's heavy breasts, I stood up and unbuttoned my designer blouse. I slid out of the sleeveless affair. My breasts, clad in a lacy black delight sold in my stores, quivered. The champagne had soaked through my brassier, soaking my flesh. I freed my large breasts and dropped my bra. My tits swayed, not nearly as perky as young Ferdinanda's.

Her eyes flicked up to me and she gasped in awe. *"You're beautiful, Ms. Demeter. Like the moon rising upon the world."*

*"Aren't you a delight, my dear,"* I answered. *"A poet?"*

She shrugged, looking a little embarrassed. Or maybe that was just the delight of having Kelly licking at her tits. The girl was bathing those big breasts with her tongue, sweeping over every square inch of jiggling, feminine flesh.

I shuddered and pushed my skirt off, my pussy on fire. I wasn't wearing panties beneath. I stroked my landing strip down to my juicy pussy lips. I needed to cum so badly. The cutie's eyes were locked on me. She licked her lips.

"Want to play with my MILF pussy?" I asked and sank down on the couch like it where my throne. I spread my legs wide for my supplicants. "Kelly, don the strap-on. It's in my carry on bag."

"Yes, Ms. D.!" The girl bounded to her feet, short, blonde hair swaying. She darted around the couch and raced to the bedroom.

"Oh, my, her butt," gasped Ferdinanda. "Did you have to..." She frowned. *"Did you have to spank her for being a naughty slut?"*

*"Someone had to,"* I said, smiling. *"Now, my dear, come here and finger my pussy. And don't be afraid to use your tongue."*

*"Yes, Ms. Demeter."* The maid licked her plump lips as she slid off the coffee table. Her smock rustled about her waist. Her large breasts swayed as she moved between my thighs. I shuddered in delight as she placed her hands on my knees.

She slid her palms up my thighs. Her black hair rustled about her face as she leaned in. This look of feverish heat spilled through her dark depths. It was so exciting to usher her into lesbian passion. Such a thrill to show this young thing the joys of womanly love.

Of sapphic pleasure.

She kissed at my landing strip, her lips nuzzling into the line of brown pubic hair. She kissed lower and lower, smooching to my pussy lips. I gasped as she brushed my labia. Then my clit. Her tongue flicked out, dancing over it. Sparks burst from me.

"Ooh, that's nice," I groaned. "Oh, that's real nice. Mmm, that's delicious. But as nice as your tongue is, I need your fingers."

"Yes, Ms. Demeter," she moaned and flicked my clit again with that naughty tongue of hers.

She rubbed the digits of her left hand up and down my cunt. She stroked my shaved flesh. I groaned, savoring her touch. This wicked sensation swept through me as she worked her fingertips up and down my folds. She teased me.

I needed this so much. Her tongue pressed into my pussy lips. She caressed up and down them. I shuddered. Whimpered. My back arched. My large breasts jiggled as she teased me with her digits. Her eyes were hot as they stared up at me.

Then she slipped her fingers into my pussy.

"Yes!" I hissed at those two digits entering me. They felt so different from the teasing fingering that Kelly gave me in the limo. These fingers were probing me with passion. Ferdinanda wanted to make me cum. "You delicious thing. *My dear, you are going to make me explode."*

*"Like Mount Vesuvius?"* she cooed in Italian. *"Pompeii?"*

*"Yes! Keep fingering me, and I'm going to bury you beneath my molten passion!"*

"Ooh, you're speaking that sexy Italian again," Kelly said, sauntering out with a large, fleshy dildo thrusting out from her crotch, a clear harness holding it to her body. "Hot! So, am I fucking our cute maid."

"Have fun."

Ferdinanda gasped at the sight of the strap-on while Kelly pushed back the table to have room to pound the Maid. My pussy clenched around the two probing digits while Kelly fell to her knees. Her firm titties had just a delightful amount of jiggle. With a wicked grin, she flipped up the maid's skirt and then tore down white pantyhose and panties.

"Ooh, she's got a bush," Kelly said. She guided her dildo forward. "A wet bush. You need my big girl-cock to fuck you, don't you, sexy?"

"Yes!" groaned the maid, her fingers pumping in and out of my pussy. She nuzzled into my clit and nibbled on it with those plump lips.

Kelly grinned at me. I gave her a wink.

She thrust.

Ferdinanda moaned around my clit.

I groaned as she sucked on it, my pussy squeezing around her digits pumping into my twat. She stirred up my cunt with those digits, teasing me as Kelly pumped away. The enthusiastic blonde didn't hold back. Her short hair swayed about her mischievous face, nose piercing gleaming. The slap of flesh on flesh echoed through the suite.

Ferdinanda sucked on my clit. She pumped her fingers in and out of my cunt. She teased me. This wonderful heat swept through me. It was delightful. I groaned, savoring every moment of her digits thrusting into my pussy and stirring me up.

I needed more.

"Use three fingers!" I gasped. "I need to explode. You won't make me erupt with two."

"Sorry, Ms. Demeter!" she moaned and thrust a third digit into me.

I groaned as she stretched out my pussy even more. She worked those delicious fingers in and out of my cunt. I gasped, my back squirming against the couch. Her tongue flitted around my clit, stroking my bud as she reamed my twat.

Kelly pumped away at the maid's pussy. My lesbian cutie moaned and gasped, driving her hips forward. She fucked without holding anything back. She gave her all into plundering the maid's pussy. Ferdinanda responded.

Her fingers thrust faster and faster in and out of my cunt. My flesh drank in the friction. The pleasure swelled through me. A delightful swell that would have me cum. But not explode. Oh, no she would have to really ream my cunt for that.

"More!" I moaned.

"More?" Ferdinanda moaned, looking up at me with confusion in her eyes. "More licking? Sucking?"

"Fingers!" gasped Kelly, thrusting away hard at the maid's cunt. "She wants more fingers! Put that pinky in her twat! Do it! Ms. D. wants to cum!"

*"Oh, my, that's so naughty,"* gasped he maid in Italian. *"You're pussy can take that? All four of my fingers?"*

*"Yes, my dear!"* I moaned. *"Kelly took the bottle. Now do it! I want to erupt and gush my cream all over your face."*

The girl licked her lips and thrust her pinky into my pussy. I gasped as I had four of her digits stretching me wide open. She pumped them in and out of me while her tongue played with my bud. She stroked it, sending sparks rippling through my body, building and building me towards my orgasm.

I groaned, clenching down on her fingers, anticipating the real fun to come. The true joy. Ferdinanda moaned into my pussy as she plundered me. She took Kelly's strap-on like a slut, the smock rustling around Ferdinanda's waist.

"Oh, yes, yes, you love that!" moaned my lover. "You love my girl-dick plundering your cunt."

"I do!" Ferdinanda moaned. She licked my clit. "It's such a treat. Ooh, Kelly, keep fucking me. I'm going to cum!"

"You better!"

SMACK!

My lover's hand cracked down on the maid's rump. Her butt-cheek jiggled. She gasped, jamming her fingers deep into my cunt. I groaned, squirming on the couch at the sudden rush of bliss surging through me.

"You better cum hard!" moaned Kelly. "I'm not fucking you for the fun of it."

"Yes, you are," the maid moaned, her voice flirty. "You are fucking me to cum, too. Yes, yes, you want me to make you cum!"

"I do!" Kelly slammed her hips forward, burying the dildo into the maid's depths. "But I also want you to make Ms. D. cum. She needs you to fist her."

"Fist?" The maid looked confused.

*"Yes, yes, ball up your hand into a fist and thrust it into my pussy!"* I moaned. *"That's how you're going to make me erupt, my dear."*

*"Yes, Ms. Demeter!"*

She pulled her fingers out of my pussy. They dripped in my cream. She formed a fist and pressed it against my pussy lips. She pushed on my labia. I groaned as my cuntlips widened and widened, stretching to take her fist. I squirmed and groaned. My body shook and jiggled.

Then her hand popped into my cunt. She sank into my pussy with her big fist. She worked it into my depths, sliding it deeper and deeper into me. I groaned, my pussy squeezing down on the intruding hand. She reached deep in me. I shuddered, the pleasure flowing through me. It was incredible to enjoy.

"Yes, yes, yes!" I moaned, squeezing down on her. "Ooh, that's perfect. Just like that. Don't stop. Mmm, you're going to make me explode."

Awe spilled over Ferdinanda's face. She stared up at me as my pussy swallowed her wrist. She reached my cervix, filling my MILF-pussy up. I groaned as she drew back and slammed into me. The pleasure rippled through my body.

It was incredible. My orgasm swelled faster and faster now as she punched her fist into my cunt. Her knuckles massaged my pussy walls. She stretched me out. The volcanic pressure built and built inside of me. My large tits jiggle and swayed as I squirmed.

"Just like that!" I moaned as she pumped her fist in and out of my cunt.

"Yes, yes, make her cum!" gasped Kelly, slamming the dildo hard and fast into the maid.

Ferdinanda churned up my pussy with her fist. She plunged fast and hard into me, staring up at me with such hunger in her eyes. She whimpered as she buried her fist hard and deep into me. Her own pleasure built and built in her youthful expression.

She jammed to the hilt in me. Her knuckles caressed me. My pussy quivered. The volcano erupted inside of me. I gasped. My cunt spasmed wildly around her fist. Juices gushed out around her arm, bathing her skin. She ducked her head down as I screamed out in bliss.

"That's it!" I gasped, the pleasure slamming into my mind.

Stars exploded across my vision as the rapture burned through my thoughts. I gasped and bucked, the couch creaking beneath me. My pussy spasmed around her fist. Her tongue licked around her wrist, gathering up the juices. I heard her squealing. Heard Kelly moaning.

They were cumming, too. Their gasps joined mine. The hotel suite reverberated with our sapphic passion. Rapturous lava buried my mind. I bucked and shuddered. I reveled in the bliss. It smothered my thoughts. Ecstasy coated every bit of me.

I hit that wonderful peak, my pussy convulsing around her fist. Kelly and Ferdinanda moaned out their passion, their words lost to the pleasure buzzing through my thoughts. It was so intense. My big boobs heaved. I squeezed my eyes shut.

"Yes!" I howled as my orgasm died into panting euphoria. "That was incredible!"

"I'm so glad to please you, Ms. Demeter," panted Ferdinanda, her own voice throaty with her climactic release.

As she pulled her fist out of my pussy, I found myself trembling on the verge of exhaustion. The flight and the fun was catching up to me. I wanted to sleep. I panted as I watched Ferdinanda lick her fist clean of my juices. She savored them, her eyes bright.

"Thank you," I panted. I grabbed my purse and pulled out two one hundred euro notes for her. "Your service was exquisite, but I need some sleep."

"Yeah." Kelly yawned. "Mmm, we were fucking the entire plane ride. That jet's going to smell of pussy for years to cum."

I smiled and rose.

"If you need me again..." the maid said.

I winked at her and then left her to dress and clean up as I stumbled into my suite's bedroom. The curtains were drawn. It was dark. I fell on the bed naked and buzzing from my orgasm. My cutie crawled up beside me. She snuggled into my tits.

"Tomorrow," I purred as sleep pulled me down, "we'll see the models."

"More barely legal cuties for you to play with?"

"Yes," I groaned.

My breathing slowed. I held Kelly to my tits, luxuriating in this bliss as I sank down into sleep. Tomorrow would be such an interesting day. I couldn't wait to get my hands on the models now that the world had changed.

They were such gorgeous things. But did they know about lesbian love? I'd have to teach them. It was so wonderful being a sexy MILF in a world full of cute, young things needing my touch. I fell into dreams full of nubile delights.

To be continued...

# Ms. Demeter Sapphic Photoshoot

## MILF CEO's Lesbian Cutie 2

## A Lesbian MILF Tale

by

Reed James

# Ms. Demeter Sapphic Photoshoot

## Ms. Xandra Demeter – Saturday, Day 6 of the Wish

"Mmm, that looks delicious," I purred the next morning when Ferdinanda brought in our breakfast.

"Ooh, sliced oranges," cooed my lesbian cutie. Kelly had a mischievous grin on her face. Something wicked and wanton that sent a fiery rush through my body. She always had this playful aura about her. I recognized it the first time I met her just the other day when her step-mother brought her into my office to give a report on my company, Secret Delights, venture into selling sex toys.

There was a whole new market opening as this wave of lesbian seemed to be sweeping the world. It had swept over me. I had been utterly consumed by this wicked need to seduce young women and show them joys of lesbian sex.

Especially barely legal delights like Kelly.

It was why she was with me in Milan. The moment I met her, I just had to make her my personal assistant. Within hours, she was on my private plane flying out to Italy. I had a meeting with the models who would be showing off my new line of lingerie in an upcoming fashion show. And to attend their next photoshoot.

Young women who needed my mature hand making sure everything went correct.

The Armani Hotel in Milan was a thing of Old World beauty. The majestic delights of a bygone era. My suite had all that Gilded Age charm. Excess oozed through the sitting room where I sat in an open robe of silk, my naked breasts being ogled by the Italian maid. She set down the silver tray, holding a fruit platter, onto the marble coffee table.

Ferdinanda licked her lips with hunger. The young thing, eighteen or nineteen, had learned all about lesbian delights yesterday when she brought a bottle of champagne to my room. She looked delicious in her gray smock and white apron, her wavy, black hair falling around her tanned face. She had such exciting and plump lips.

She'd fisted me so hard after we licked champagne off Kelly's body and out of her pussy.

"And what naughty thing do you plan on doing with those orange slices?" I asked my young lover.

Kelly was naked and kneeling on the couch beside me. The barely legal cutie had short, blonde hair that swayed about her adorable face. A nose piercing gleamed on her right nostril, adding a wild charm that went along with the butterfly tattooed on her right butt-cheek. Small breasts, the opposite of my large and mature tits, quivered as she squirmed in delight.

"Mmm, feed them to you," she said. "Ferdinanda, if you could take care of Ms. D.'s pussy while I attend to her breakfast."

"I would love to, Kelly," moaned the Italian maid. She glanced at me and said, in her native Italian, *"I will enjoy my own breakfast of strawberries and cream."*

*"Enjoy, my dear,"* I purred, spreading my legs and showing off the landing strip of black hair that led down to my pussy. I always liked to be shaved for my male lovers. Now, I was glad to share this with my female lovers. This wave of lesbianism was such a delight. I used to make lingerie so women could look stunning for their men.

Now, I wanted them to melt the hearts of their women. For Secret Delights to be known as the lingerie brand for lesbians. This photoshoot would be the perfect time to demonstrate that. To put out a catalog full of the delights my clothing would deliver to young women.

Ferdinanda knelt before me, her black hair swaying about her face. The naughty maid grabbed a strawberry from the plate. She had a naughty grin on her lips. She had fallen into lesbianism with such a plunge. I hoped she found a lesbian MILF to seduce last night. An older woman, a step-mother or perhaps the head of housekeeping, on whom to unleash the skills I'd taught her.

To fist her.

I shuddered as the strawberry nuzzled into the shaved folds of my pussy. The naughty girl rubbed it up and down my folds, coating the tip in my juices. She brought it to her lips and bit off the tip while staring at me with such hunger in her eyes.

A hot shiver ran through me. A wave of heat that washed through my body. I groaned, loving the sight. I would have such an amazing orgasm from her. She would make me explode. I couldn't wait for that delight.

She pressed the strawberry into my cunt as her tongue flicked at my clit. I groaned and quivered at the pleasure coursing through me. Her tongue swirled around my nub while the strawberry stretched open my pussy lips before it popped into me.

"Ferdinanda," I groaned. "Yes! Yes! Such a dedicated maid."

"Isn't she?" Kelly said. She

crouched on the couch beside me and spread her knees apart. Her juicy pussy gleamed with her excitement. She grabbed a slice of orange and pushed it up inside of her snatch. As Ferdinanda licked my clit and my twat squeezed down on the strawberry, I watched the wedge vanish into Kelly. She groaned as she pushed it all the way in her.

I licked my lips as she grabbed another slice and worked it into her cunt. She shuddered. Juices, both hers and from the citric fruit, gleamed on her finger. Her small breasts jiggled as she pressed the fruit deeper into her self.

Ferdinanda's tongue dived into my pussy. I gasped as she scooped out the strawberry. I shuddered as she pulled it into her mouth out of my pussy and chewed it, moaning as she savored the flavor of my cunt cream mixed with the berry.

"Good?" I asked.

She nodded, a look of ecstasy on the maid's face.

"You're going to enjoy this," moaned Kelly as she thrust a third slice into her pussy. She gasped, her head throwing back. She let out a whimper of delight. She pressed that slice of fruit up into her pussy. Her cuntlips were already gaping open, the tips of the orange wedges peeking out of her. "Going to make you such a treat."

"A messy treat," I purred, so hungry for it.

Ferdinanda thrust another strawberry into my pussy. I shuddered at the chill of it and the bumpy texture. It spread open my pussy lips. I gasped in delight, a shiver running through my body. My fingers flexed as this wicked heat rushed throughout my flesh.

My pussy soaked it. My juices engulfed it while Kelly pressed a fourth slice of orange into her pussy. She whimpered now, her pussy stuffed with the wedges. Ferdinanda licked at my cunt, her tongue sliding around the fruit she'd inserted while her right hand slid along my taint.

*"Oh, you wicked thing, my dear,"* I cooed at her in Italian.

*"I thought you would like this,"* the maid said. *"Mrs. Barbieri, the head housekeeper, did when I fingered her bum last night."* Her digit reached my asshole and stroked it.

"God, it's hot when you two speak Italian," Kelly moaned as she finished inserting her orange slice in her pussy.

*"And what naughty and nasty things are you going to do with those orange slices?"* I asked my lesbian cutie.

"I have no idea what you said, but it sounded so fucking hot, Ms. D.!" she moaned. No one had ever called me that before her. She had such an impudence around her; I couldn't help but let her get away with it. "You ready for your orange juices. It'll be freshly squeezed."

"Mmm, yes," I moaned then gasped.

Ferdinanda's finger wiggled into my asshole. She worked her digit into my bowels. My toes flexed and curled. The pleasure soared through me. My anal sheath gripped her digit as she went deeper and deeper into my bowels. Her tongue scooped out the strawberry from my pussy. I heard her chewing on it as the delight flowed out of my asshole.

Then Kelly stood up on the couch and straddled my face. She

grinned at me, her shaved pussy sliding over my face. I tilted my head back and opened my mouth right beneath her pussy. I could smell the citrus and the tangy aroma of her pussy all mixed together. The heat from her cunt bathed my lips. A drop landed on it.

Her face contorted. She groaned and then a rush of tangy-flavored orange juices poured into my mouth. She quivered there, squeezing my morning drink straight from her cunt. It was so hot. I pressed my lips against her cunt, my mouth sealing around her opening.

I drank down the pussy-infused orange juice. She moaned, her head throwing back as a final gush of juices poured into my mouth. I gulped it down, savoring the warm treat. It poured into my stomach, sending a wave of heat washing through my body.

My bowels clenched down on Ferdinanda's finger. My pussy savored the next strawberry she pressed into my twat.

"Mmm, yes, yes, drink it up," moaned Kelly, her body trembling.

I thrust my tongue into my lesbian cutie's pussy. I scooped out the pulp. The citric flavor mixed with her tangy delight. I pulled it into my mouth and swallowed it, savoring my breakfast. Sticky juices ran down my chin and cheek.

We were making a mess and I didn't care.

Kelly moaned as I licked out more of the orange wedges from her twat. Ferdinanda's tongue played with the strawberry into my own pussy while her finger pumped in and out of my tight asshole. The velvety delight she stirred in me melted to my twat.

She pressed a second finger into my asshole. I groaned as it pushed in beside the first digit. My anal ring stretched more. My entire body shuddered. My large breasts jiggled and heaved as this wicked delight swept through me.

"Mmm, you like that, huh, Ms. D.?" moaned Kelly as my tongue probed deeper into her cunt, scooping out more orange and her pussy juices.

"Yes," I moaned.

Ferdinanda sealed her lips around my pussy and sucked. I gasped as she drew the strawberry out of my depths. It popped out of my cunt and into her mouth. Her lips moved against me as she chewed on it, moaning as she savored her own breakfast.

I grabbed Kelly's rump, squeezing and kneading her ass. My tongue thrust into her pussy's depths. I didn't find any more orange, though that citric flavor lingered. I danced my tongue around in her, savoring the way she groaned and gasped. How she ground her cunt on my mouth.

The sticky mess spilled over my chin and cheeks. I reveled in it. My nose pressed into the top folds of her pussy. The wonderful musk filled my nostrils. I gulped down her cream. It warmed down to my pussy and asshole, mixing with the delight Ferdinanda gave me.

"Ms. Demeter," she moaned and thrust only her tongue into my pussy now. "Mmm, you taste like strawberries."

I shuddered as the naughty thing licked at my MILF pussy with the same hunger I feasted on Kelly. My asshole clutched about her twin digits plundering away at my bowels. Her tongue swiped around my pussy lips; brushed my clit.

Sparks flared.

I bucked and moaned, my fingers digging into Kelly's pussy. I stared up her body. Her hands played on her stomach, rubbing her toned flesh as she moaned. Her nose piercing flashed as she panted, her orgasm building and building.

I wanted to drink more of her cream. I flicked my tongue to her clit and sucked hard on it. She gasped and squealed. Her head swayed. Pleasure built in my own body. Ferdinanda swirled her tongue around my clit then thrust it into the depths of my pussy.

She had gotten skilled at pussy licking. I was so glad.

She worked her tongue in and out of my cunt. She thrust it in fast and hard. She swirled it around inside of me. It was incredible. I groaned, squirming on the couch as the bliss swept through my body. My toes curled.

"Ms. D.!" squealed Kelly. "Oh, fuck, I'm going to cum. I'm going to drown you in more juices. Just the sort you love."

"Mmm, barely legal cunt cream!" I moaned and then sucked on her pussy itself, my fingers gripping her toned rump.

"Yep!" squealed my lover.

My own orgasm swelled faster. Ferdinanda's tongue rapidly

plunged in and out of my pussy. She teased me. Delivered such wild delight to me. My bowels clenched around her fingers, the added anal stimulation surging me towards my climax.

I nipped Kelly's clit with my teeth. A quick and soft bite. She gasped. Bucked. Her head threw back and then her pussy juices gushed out of her. They spilled across my lips and chin. I opened my mouth wide and drank them down.

"Ms. D! You fucking rock!"

Gulping down her tangy cream, flavored with citric delight, sent me over the edge. I bucked on the couch. My bowels convulsed around Ferdinanda's naughty fingers. Juices flooded out of my pussy. They rushed out of me while I quivered on the couch, moaning my delight. My digits curled. The bliss swept through my body.

The naughty maid licked up my flood while she jammed her fingers deep into my asshole. I moaned and bucked, the pleasure drowning my mind. It felt incredible. It spilled over my thoughts. I quivered through the rapture, savoring every moment of it.

My breasts jiggled. The bliss swept through my body. It was an exciting rush of ecstasy that spilled through me. I groaned, my tits heaved as I trembled through bliss. Kelly moaned her own, hitting the peak of her climax.

"Ms. D.," she panted as she wiggled her hips, grinding her cunt on my mouth. "Mmm, you're such a sexy MILF."

"She is," cooed Ferdinanda. "Now I hope you enjoy your breakfast, Ms. Demeter and Young Kelly, but I must be off to my other duties. Mrs. Barbieri will spank me hard if I don't."

"And I bet you want that," giggled Kelly. "It's hot getting disciplined by the naughty MILF."

She would know.

Ferdinanda kissed us both with strawberries and cream on her lips and then departed. Kelly and I savored the rest of our breakfast. And, yes, those bananas did end up in my pussy and they were delicious. Then we showered and I got some work done. I was the CEO of a company. I had several calls to make while Kelly played around on her phone, looking so sexy in the process.

Near noon, our limo arrived to take us to the photoshoot. Kelly bounced with excitement to see the models. I was eager for it, too. I wondered how Fabiana, the photographer, would react. I only employed women in my company. Secret Delights made lingerie for women by women. From my executives down to my designers down to even my IT department, were all women.

Now I was thrilled that lesbianism had swept through the office last Monday.

The limo arrived at a fairly nondescript building. It was old, made of white stone with decorative frames around the windows. It reeked of the old, the architecture so beautiful and permanent. It had withstood centuries. It was an apartment complex with the top floor holding Fabiana's home and studio for her shoots.

We rode an elevator up, something added in the thirties. It was old and creaked, laboring to climb up to the seventh floor (eighth in America). It opened onto her loft. She had it open the entire length of the building, her kitchen to the left all neat and orderly. She had a bed before the windows and a small living room in another corner. The rest was her studio. She had all sorts of equipment. Lights set up. Her cameras. She had an assistant moving around. There were several triptychs screens for the models to change behind. Each one had a Japanese watercolor painted on the panels. Scenes of herons wading in pools and birds perched on cherry trees with Kanji writing out whatever *haiku* inspired the work.

"Ms. Demeter," Fabiana greeted as she turned from her camera.

"Mmm," Kelly purred in approval.

Fabiana was a woman in her late thirties, mature and gorgeous. She had her black hair cut short in a bob that framed her narrow face. She wore a halter top that cupped her round breasts. The dragon tattoo she had wound around her right tit peeked out, scales crimson. A tight pair of jeans hugged her hips. She padded over on bare feet, several toe rings gleaming.

"I'm so glad you could make me," Fabiana said, her accent musical and Italian. She swooped and we kissed each other on the cheeks, brief, fluttering affairs. "And you brought an assistant. How unusual."

"Kelly Lorde," I said. "Her step-mother introduced us. I took a liking to the girl. She's my new personal assistant."

"Yep, that's me," Kelly said with her brash assertiveness. "I take care of all of Ms. D.'s personal needs."

"Wonderful," the photographer said. "I'm Fabiana." She went in for the European cheek kisses only for Kelly to go for the woman's lips.

My naughty assistant planted her lips right on the mature woman's mouth. Fabiana shuddered. A mother herself, a MILF, she quivered as the girl thrust her tongue into her mouth. A shiver ran through me, my pussy clenching in delight.

Fabiana broke the kiss and stumbled back. She panted, her hand pressed to her chest above her breasts. She shuddered while her tongue flicked across her lips. She glanced at me, a look of shock on her face.

"She is... a friendly one," Fabiana said. She swallowed. "Models should be here shortly. I have to... have to get ready."

The MILF photographer rushed to her equipment. Kelly flashed me a wicked and impudent grin. I couldn't help but chuckle. I darted in and gave her a quick kiss on the lips, so glad I brought her. Fabiana was a tyrant while taking pictures, but she had become as flustered as a school maid from Kelly's action.

I sat down on a couch and had more phone calls to make while Kelly flipped through a photo book left on the coffee table. Prints of Fabiana's work. The girl was cooing over all the gorgeous women as I made sure the arrangements for tomorrow's fashion show were well underway.

The models arrived about a half-hour later. The elevator dinged and they stepped out of it, both underdressed. One girl had yoga pants and a sweatshirt on, her blonde hair spilling about her face. She had Slavic cheekbones and a slender build. Even in the loose top, she had a beauty about her, a ballerina's grace. The other model wore jeans and a t-shirt, her breasts large and bouncy beneath her top.

Kelly ogled her, watching the black-haired, Eastern European cutie stroll past us to be greeted by Fabiana. They exchanged kisses and the photographer ushered them to the dressing screens so they could get changed. A dark-haired assistant, eighteen and perky, brought them bottled waters. It was casual and relaxed.

"Mmm, that big booby one is hot," Kelly moaned. She knelt on the couch and looked over the back to stare at the models. "I can't wait to see her in your lingerie."

"That's Beata, I think. She's Hungarian. The other should be Katarina." I glanced over my shoulder. "It's they're first time modeling for me, but Fabiana has used them before. They have the right builds. Your step-mother selected them for this shoot."

"She chooses sex toys and models, huh?" Kelly asked. "No wonder she's always fucking her secretary with strap-ons."

"And what does your father think of that?"

She shrugged. "He seems fine. He's busy suing my college for expelling me. He doesn't even mind sleeping in the guest room so Mom and I can have our fun before bed. He just... accepts it. We're lesbians now."

"Yes, yes, it's strange. Not normal at all."

"Who cares." Kelly wiggled her hips. "I just want to suck on Beata's big boobies."

I smiled. I had a feeling she'd get her chance before too long.

The models moved behind their changing screens as I had a call with a supplier over some small issue that came up in quality control checks. They promised to get it taken care of while I threatened to find a new supplier. I wouldn't put up with shoddy products. Secret Delights was a brand that represented quality.

The models emerged from behind the changing screens looking gorgeous. I hung up the phone as a rush of heat for these nineteen-year-old goddesses surged through me. They had such perfect bodies, flawless in every way. I groaned, my pussy melting.

Blonde Katarina wore the strapless, purple bra, part of my Dream Lover's line. It cupped her small breasts, giving them some extra shape. With it, she wore a Y-backed thong. It emerged from her butt-cheeks in two sweeping arms that hugged the contours of her rump as they wrapped around her waist. The front was a thin strip that hugged her body and had the same flower design worked into the fabric as the bra. Purple stockings held up by a garter belt completed the outfit.

"God, she's gorgeous," moaned Kelly. "Beata! Beata! Beata!"

I smiled as I turned to the black-haired, Hungarian model.

Beata wore a pair of black, French cut panties also from my new Dream Lover's line. They were an elegant pair of panties trimmed with black lace. They cupped her bubbly rump. Her large breasts were in a matching, black push-up bra with pink straps. The same lace accented the cups lifting her tits into a jiggling shelf of delight. She had a black, silk shawl that went with it, though she hadn't donned it yet.

"I want to play with those boobies so much, Ms. D.!" Kelly glanced at me, her blue eyes wild. "Thank you for bringing me on this trip."

"Trust me, you have made this a delight." My smile grew. "The fresh-squeezed orange juice alone was worth it."

She winked at me.

The two models sat down and the makeup lady went to work on them. She was a motherly woman with dark hair held back by a flowery kerchief. She worked fast, transforming their faces into sensual beauty before styling their hair to have an effortless look, like it naturally fell in that silky tumble about their youthful faces.

In all, it was another thirty minutes before they were ready for the photoshoot.

I drifted over to the camera to watch it up close, my pussy on fire for what would come. The two women stood before Fabiana's bed. While the makeup was being applied, it was transformed to have a silk canopy, pink drapes hung from it but died back to make it appear soft and inviting.

"Okay, give me sultry looks," Fabiana said and began snapping away. "Yes, yes, like that. Now some pouting. Ooh, just like that Beata."

FLASH!

"And Katarina, you can give me more pout. Thrust that lower lip out. Perfect."

FLASH!

"Now hand on your hip, Katarina. No, no, your other hip. Bend that leg, and Beata, get a little closer and bend over just slightly. Let me see those tits dangling. Perfect."

FLASH!

The models went through their poses. They were sexy women,

but they weren't what I wanted. They weren't sexy enough. They needed to be provocative. They were hardly touching each other. They needed to be lovers. To show off their passion.

But Fabiana wasn't getting that out of them. She was having them turn and pose and show off their gorgeous bodies, but where was the lesbian desire. The lust. Where were the looks that they shared that brimmed with their awakened passion for each other?

"No, no," I said, marching up to Fabiana. "I want you two closer. Touching. You're lovers. I want to see that!"

"Lovers?" Beata asked, her voice confused.

"Ms. Demeter," Fabiana said, rounding on me. "I'm in the middle of my photoshoot."

"And you're not getting the shots I want." I pointed at them. "Katarina, lean in like you're about to kiss Beata. Put your hand on her side. Go on."

"Fabiana?" Katarina asked, confusion on her face.

"Do it," the photographer barked, shooting me another angry look. "What are you trying to get them to do?"

"To be passionate! To show women that their dream lover is not a man, but another woman. I want to see sapphic beauty. Lesbian passion!"

Fabiana blinked. A shiver ran through her. She glanced at Kelly and then back at me.

"Fine, you heard her. passion."

"Okay, Fabiana," Beata said.

Katarina placed her hand on her fellow model's side and leaned in like they were about to kiss. She held it, looking stiff.

FLASH!

I frowned. Too stiff. That didn't look like passion at all. Their heads moved closer. Katarina's hand slid up. But it was so mechanical. Stiff.

FLASH!

Had neither of them been with a woman? Where they nervous about this type of modeling?

FLASH!

Their lips were almost touching, but they were both shaking. And Katarina's hand had stopped right below Beata's breast.

"No, no, sensual!" I said. "Kiss each other. Grab her breast. Show me passion!"

"Okay," Katarina said, her voice tight.

"They're not porn models," muttered Fabiana. "I could have got you girls that do softcore porn not *real* models."

"I want real models who can kiss and love each other," I snapped. "They can do it."

Katarina landed in. Beata swallowed. Their lips touched. Barely. No passion. No depth to it. Katarina put her hand on Beata's breast, just lightly cupping it. Not squeezing it. Not pushing her towards that inviting bed behind them.

FLASH!

Frustration rippled through me. How could these models demonstrate the lesbian seduction I wanted? When women saw these photos, they needed to feel the eroticism that only another lady could give them. Whether it was a MILF with a young girl or a nubile cutie with an older woman, they had to feel it. This had to be fixed.

"Katarina, come here," I said. "Kelly, take her place and show her how to kiss Beata."

"What?" Fabiana hissed. "Kelly is cute, but she's not a model."

I waved a hand. "This is just a demonstration. That's all."

Kelly, wearing a tennis skirt that barely covered her rump and a belly shirt, darted out while Katarina came to me, looking confused and embarrassed all at the same time. There was emotion shining in her blue eyes. The elegant model's lower lip quivered. Her body shook in my gorgeous lingerie.

"I'm trying, Ms. Demeter," she said, her voice thick with a Russian accent. "I am."

"I know," I said and cupped her cheeks. "Don't cry. You don't want to ruin your makeup. Just watch Kelly and do what she does, okay? You can do that for me? Mmm, you're so beautiful. You make me so wet, you know that."

She gasped.

Kelly sidled up to Beata, my blonde assistant a little shorter than Katarina, but she had the same build. She put her hand on Beata's side. The Hungarian girl flinched for a moment and then resumed that stiff, uncomfortable stance.

To my shock, Katarina put her hand on my side in the same spot, caressing me through the M. M. LaFleur strapless sheath dress I wore. The black fabric clung to my body and hugged my large breasts.

"Relax, cutie," purred Kelly as she leaned in. "I'm going to kiss you, not bite you."

"I just... never kiss girl," Beata said, her English broken. "It is not something... I wanted."

"That's okay." Kelly's hand slid higher. "I'll show you. It's easy. Nothing simpler than kissing a girl. Just kiss me the way you like to be kissed."

A heat swelled through me as I felt Katarina's hand sliding up my own body. She was watching even as she leaned her own head towards me. I shuddered, realizing she was about to kiss me. This wave of heat swept through me.

Kelly's hand reached Beata's breast, squeezing her through the push-up bra.

"You see how she's clutching to her tit?" I whispered to Katarina as her hand cupped my boob through my dress. "She's showing passion."

"Yes, Ms. Demeter," Katarina moaned. Her fingers squeezed into my tit. She gasped. "Oh, my. You're soft."

Kelly planted her lips on Beata, kneading the model's breast. The tension relaxed out of the Hungarian beauty. Her black hair swayed as Kelly kissed her. Their lips moved together. Beata's eyes closed.

"Just like that," I said. "You turn, Katarina."

The blonde's lips neared mine. Her blue eyes closed moments before our mouths touched. Her kiss was gentle, at first. I let her guide us, responding to her as this thrill rippled through me. Her fingers kneaded into my breast, digging deeper into my flesh. This wave of excitement washed through me. A heat that blazed across my thoughts and rippled out of my cunt.

A hot and delicious ache that had me moaning into the model's mouth. Her waxy lips worked with more hunger. She kissed me with more passion. I surrendered to it, loving the way she smooched me.

Her fingers dug into my breast. The heat rippled out of my cunt.

Then her tongue thrust into my mouth. My pussy clenched at her enthusiasm. I kissed her back with an equal passion. This was so exciting. Our tongues danced and dueled. The pleasure surged through my body as we shared this delight.

Her thumb brushed my nipple. I groaned.

"Kelly," Beata moaned.

Katarina broke our kiss and glanced over to see Kelly nuzzling her face into the model's generous cleavage. My blonde cutie kissed back and forth, smooching those delicious breasts, making them jiggle.

Katarina kissed the top of my right tit. I gasped at the heat of her lips. Her hands held my sides now as she smooched across my own cleavage. She even licked, her tongue stimulating my skin. My pussy clenched as this young and sexy model awakened to her desires for my MILF delights.

"That's it," I groaned, my heart pounding hot blood through my veins. "Mmm, you're doing great."

FLASH.

The camera went off.

I glanced over at Fabiana. She had one hand rubbing at her crotch as she watched Kelly push up Beata's bra cups so her large tits spilled out. My lover cupped those young and firm boobies, digging her fingers into them. She then buried her face between them, rubbing her head back and forth.

The top of my dress ripped down. I gasped as my large and naked breasts popped out, nipples throbbing from the caress of fabric. Moaning, Katarina buried her face between my large breasts. She squeezed them into her cheeks as she wiggled her face back and forth. She kissed as she did it. She smooched at my flesh.

"Mmm, yes, yes, just like that," I moaned. "Mmm, that's how you love a woman's big tits."

"Yes, Ms. Demeter," the sweet thing purred into my cleavage.

FLASH!

Fabiana kept snapping pictures as she rubbed at her pussy through her jeans. She wiggled her hips, staring with such hunger at the lesbian sight unfolding before her. I smiled, so glad that I had awakened such passion in her.

It was so exciting.

FLASH!

And she wasn't the only one. The motherly makeup artist and the young assistant were kissing, discovering their own delights. A MILF and a barely legal cutie coming together in awakened passion was such a beautiful thing to witness.

"Kelly!" Beata moaned.

My naughty assistant kissed up to Beata's right breast, nearing her wide, dusky-pink areola. I shuddered as Kelly's tongue danced out and then swept around the fat nipple. The model gasped, shuddered, then cried out in ecstasy when Kelly latched on to the nub and sucked.

My pussy clenched in envy. I stared down at the cutie nuzzling into my breasts. The model's blue eyes stared up at me as she rubbed her face back and forth against the inner slopes of my big boobs. I grinned at her.

"Now kiss up to my nipple and suckle."

"Yes, Ms. Demeter," she moaned and turned her head to my left tit, the one closest to Beata and Kelly.

I shuddered as Katarina kissed up my inner flesh, her blonde hair brushing my right nipple. Pleasure tingled through me. Her fingers dug into my flesh as she climbed higher and higher. She reached my areola, kissed at it. Her lips brushed my nipple. Tingles raced through me.

Then she latched on. Sucked. I gasped in delight, my pussy clenching hard. The camera flashed as this sexy model suckled. She nursed with hunger that shot pleasure straight down to my pussy. At the same time, hr hands slid down from my tits. Joy surged through me.

She was acting on her own.

This excitement rippled through me as she grabbed my dress and pushed down my skirt. I shuddered at the heat her touch swept through me. My body trembled as she worked my tight dress off my hips. It fell down my body.

My pussy clenched. My twat throbbed with an aching heat. I groaned, my tongue dancing with hers. The heat swept through me.

She kissed me back with such hunger. I shivered in delight, savoring the way her tongue played with mine.

She stroked my naked sides as she nursed on me. Kelly suckled with hunger on Beata's nipple, the Hungarian model gasping. Her black hair swayed about her face. Her green eyes sparkled in delight. She quivered there, the camera's flash painting her body in silvery highlights.

"Kelly!" she moaned. "That's good. Bassza meg*!*"

I loved it. "Mmm, Katarina, you're making me feel just as good as Kelly is Beata."

The model moaned in delight. She sucked harder on my nipple. I gasped, my pussy drinking in the heat. A wave of delight washed through my body. My juices soaked my twat. My nub throbbed in her hungry mouth.

Katarina's blue eyes flashed up at me as she suckled at my nipple. Her hands slid down and brushed the waistband of my panties. They were a red affair from my Sensual Everyday Line of comfortable yet sexy panties and bras for women to wear as they went about their day. I shuddered as her thumbs dipped into them.

"Yes, yes, you're getting it," I groaned. "All the things you have to do to please a naughty MILF.

Katarina shoved down my panties even as he popped her mouth off my nipple. I gasped as the beauty sank to her knees before me. She quivered there, staring up at me with fire in her sapphire eyes while she dragged my panties off.

"I love having pussy eaten," she moaned, accent thick. "My pussy, I mean."

"Yes, yes, I bet you do," I groaned. "Do it. Eat me."

Kelly's head shot from Beata's nipple to glance at us. She gasped and then fell to her knees, clearly not to be outdone as the novice was quickly surpassing her tutelage. Katarina nuzzled her face between my thighs, all her nervousness gone. She boldly pressed her young lips against my pussy.

Licked.

I gasped as that sweet, young thing fluttered her tongue up and down the folds of my pussy. My hot flesh drank it in. Kelly ripped Beata's panties to the side and buried her face into her pussy, licking, lapping.

FLASH!

Fabiana had her free hand down her jeans, frigging herself as she took pictures of the lesbian passion. Beata's big tits heaved, her bra still shoved up and over them. She groaned, grinding her pussy on my cutie's hungry mouth. Just like I did with Katarina.

"Oh, yes, yes, Katarina!" I moaned, pleasure rushing through me. The cutie was giving me just the right amount of bliss.

Her tongue danced over my pussy. I gripped her blonde hair. My naked breasts heaved as I ground my cunt on her. I threw back my head, my black hair swaying down my back. My moans echoed through the studio, mixing with Beata's. And with the makeup artist. The assistant went down on the motherly woman, feasting on her.

Sapphic delights echoed through the studio apartment. I groaned, savoring it. My pussy clenched. The heat washed through me. It was incredible. I whimpered, my heart pounding in my chest. I bit my lower lip and groaned. I smeared my cunt across the model's hungry mouth.

"Yes!" I gasped as Katarina feasted on me.

*"Bassza meg!"* moaned Beata. "Kelly! Kelly!"

I groaned, my orgasm building and building as the young model feasted on me. My large breasts jiggled. The passion swelled with her every lick and lap. She slid her tongue through my folds and brushed my clit.

I gasped at that.

"Mmm, I like that, too. Bud. Little, um... I do not know word." She licked my clit.

"Clitoris!" I moaned. "Clit! Yes, yes!"

"Clit," she cooed and sucked on it.

I gasped and trembled, my big breasts heaved as the pleasure shot through me. My cunt clenched, juices leaking out of me. I swayed, my boobs jiggling from side to side. Beata moaned nearby while my own orgasm hurtled at me so fast. I was so excited by having this sexy lingerie model sucking on my clit.

Loving me. Devouring me. I threw back my head and cried out in ecstasy. My pussy convulsed. My juices gushed out of my twat and bathed her mouth. I bucked at the cream rushing out of me. My entire body buzzed from the rapture of this. My head swayed. Stars danced before my eyes.

"Oh, yes, yes, that's it!" I moaned. "Mmm, that's so good. Yes, you're feasting on me. You're making me feel so good. Oh, you naughty thing!"

She sucked on me with hunger. Her tongue danced around my clit. I squeezed my eyes shut as the pleasure rushed through me. My hair rustled as it danced over my shoulders. The pleasure spilled through my mind while she devoured the juices gushing out of me.

"Katarina!" I moaned. "Oh, god, get on the bed. I have to love you!"

She pulled her face away and moaned, "Yes!"

She rose, still clothed in the purple lingerie. She spun around, her curvy rump clad by that Y-backed thong's spaghetti-thin straps reaching out of her crack to hug her waist. She hurried to the bed while I darted for my purse and what was in it. I pulled out the silver vibrator and grinned.

Katarina knelt on the bed, her thong-clad ass facing me. She looked so sexy in her purple thigh highs. I passed Kelly devouring Beata with hunger, the busty, Hungarian model moaning out her bliss. I slid onto the bed and turned on the vibrator.

"Ooh, you brought toy!" groaned Katrina. "I have toy. Buzzing toy. Is vibrator, yes?"

"Uh-huh," I said and ripped the thin fabric of her thong to the side exposing her shaved pussy and her asshole. A deviant hunger shot through me. I had my orgasm, now I wanted to make her cum.

I still buzzed from my orgasm.

I pressed the tip of the vibrator, the edges fuzzing indistinct, against her pussy folds. She gasped, her head tossing and butt-cheeks clenching. She had such a beautiful pussy, her slit nice and tight. Her juices leaked out, such a wicked and wanton sight to see. I licked my lips as I worked the vibrator up and down her slit.

Then I pressed my face between her butt-cheeks. I kissed right on her asshole. She gasped as I tasted that sour flavor. My tongue swirled out, rimming the supermodel's butthole. She tasted so wonderfully dirty.

"Ms. Demeter!" she moaned, her butt-cheeks clenching on my face. "That is... You are..."

"I know," I moaned into her asshole. I thrust the vibrator into her cunt.

She gasped.

A wicked thrill ran through me as I worked the vibrator in and out of her pussy. My tongue darted around her asshole. I caressed her puckered sphincter, drinking in the dirty flavor of her while I feasted on her, my ass wiggling from side to side.

*"Elélvezek!"* Beata gasped. "Kelly! Kincsem*!*"

The sounds were so naughty to hear. I pumped the vibrator in and out of Katrina's pussy while my tongue caressed her butthole. I fluttered against it as I listened to her moan out in delight. Her passion echoed through the studio, joining the cumming model behind me. The camera flashed while Fabiana groaned herself.

It was so exciting. I pushed my tongue against Katarina's butthole and thrust the vibrator deeper into her cunt. Her asshole relaxed. My tongue slipped into the model's bowels. I swirled around in her, savoring the earthier flavor coating my tongue.

That nasty, dirty taste of a woman's ass.

I reveled in it as I fucked the vibrator in and out of her pussy. I savored her moans. The buzzing shaft grew slick as her juices ran down it. Her tart musk rose in my nose. She groaned and gasped, her bowels clenching about my probing tongue.

"Ms. Demeter!" she gasped. *"Ye-bat'!* Ms. Demeter. You make butt fill so naughty. And humming toy—vibrator!—it feels well. Very well in me."

I loved hearing that. I danced my tongue through her bowels and plunged the vibrator in and out of her pussy. Her moans grew louder and louder. More of her juices soaked my hand. I loved the sounds she made as I drove this sweet, young thing to her own orgasm.

She deserved it. My pussy simmered as I pleasured her. It was a delight to teach this sexy model how to make love to a woman. I couldn't wait to make her cum now. To shower her mind in sapphic delight.

I swirled the vibrator around in her sheath. She gasped. Her butt-cheeks clenched around my face. Her asshole squeezed about my tongue. I fucked it in and out of her backdoor, savoring that dirty flavor.

"Ms. Demeter! You make me erupt. Cum. Yes, yes, you make me have orgasm. Big orgasm."

"Good," I moaned and then sucked on her asshole.

She gasped. Her moans echoed through the room. They joined the makeup lady gasping and cumming on the young assistant's mouth. The camera flashed, Fabiana whimpering through her own orgasm.

"Such hot pics!" the photographer whimpered.

"Yes, they are," purred Kelly. "Go, Ms. D., go!"

CRACK!

The naughty model spanked my ass. I groaned and jammed my tongue deep into Katarina's bowels and the vibrator into the depths of her cunt. The model gasped out in delight. Her body bucked. Then she cried out in Russian, the words spilling fast.

Universal words.

I made her cum.

Juices gushed out around the vibrator and soaked my hand. I ripped the toy from her cunt and moved my lips down to bathe in her tart flood. Her juices splashed over my face. I licked them up. I lapped and feast on the model.

I gave her this pleasure. This joy. I reveled in it, taking such satisfaction in making her climax. The bed creaked while the camera flashed, recording this beautiful moment. Katrina's hips wiggled. She smeared her shaved flesh across me.

Then she collapsed on her belly, panting, "Thank you, Ms. Demeter. I understand now. How to please women."

"Good," I purred and rose, my large tits heaving. I left Katarina whimpering as I turned to Fabian and told her, "Now they know what to do."

"Yes," the photographer panted, her body trembling through her own orgasm. "Let's get them ready again. Annunziata and Isotta, come on."

I sank naked on the couch. Kelly hopped up and grinned at me. She went to snuggle up to me when my phone rang. I picked it up, shuddering as the cutie latched onto my nipple and suckled on it with impish delight.

"Hello?" I asked.

"Ms. Demeter," said Dorotea, one of my local employees, "we have a problem. We're about to have our show protested by a feminist group for 'enabling the male gaze to flourish.'"

I groaned. This could ruin everything. Bad press. Terrible PR. I had to fix this. Spin it fast.

To be continued...

# Ms. Demeter's MILF Seduction

## MILF CEO's Lesbian Cutie 3

## A Lesbian MILF Tale

by

Reed James

# Ms. Demeter's MILF Seduction

## Ms. Xandra Demeter – Saturday, Day 6 of the Wish

Annoyance flared through me as I talked to Dorotea, my employee managing the fashion show here in Milan tomorrow. I was unveiling the new line of lingerie that my company, Secret Delights, was releasing. My own design.

Encouraging the male gaze? It was such an irritating accusation to have leveled at me. Why was there this strain of feminism that wanted to put women in trash bags and pretend that they didn't have beauty they wanted to show off? A protest could ruin everything, and once you capitulated to one group, the blood was in the water. They would swarm you. Feast.

"Who?" I asked as my lesbian cutie, who put the "personal" in personal assistant, suckled at my naked nipple. In the background, Fabiana readied the models to resume the sensual and sapphic photoshoot.

"Valentina Giovanni's Feminism in Fashion," answered Dorotea. "She just yelled my ear off objecting to our fashion show being held in Milan. That it's not progressive, that it's denigrating, and that you make clothing that lets men turn women into objects."

I rolled my eyes. As if women didn't do the same with men. Look at any romance cover and the buff, shirtless man on it proved that.

"Set up a meeting with her," I said, standing up and pulling my nipple from Kelly's mouth. My large breasts swayed as I turned around and stared at the two models having their makeup redone after the naughty fun.

I still could taste Katriana's sour asshole on my lips.

"Yes, Miss Demeter," Dorotea said. "Let me call you back."

"Problem, Ms. D.?" Kelly asked as I hung up. The impudent blonde stared up at me. She was young, a barely legal cutie that made me boil. I was old enough to be her mother, had a son her age, and that made this so exciting to play with her.

She called me a MILF. I liked that. A sexy, lesbian MILF running one of the fastest-growing clothing lines in the world. A decade ago, having a fashion show in Milan was my dream. Now it was reality.

"Yes," I said. I was not letting a screeching group of harpies destroy my dream. With these sort of people, it was always about control. They wanted to own you. Make you do things there way. It didn't matter what the cause was, they sought out whatever would give them power and shape their beliefs to fit them.

But this Valentina would be a hypocrite. For the right reason, she would compromise. True believers were fanatics and zealots. They would be shouted out in the metaphorical desert, unheard by most. People like Valentina were the ones who carved power and used such zealots to grasp it. Once they seized it, they would hold it at all cost, even if meant betraying their own professed values.

In short, Valentina was a politician.

I studied Kelly as she asked, "What's the problem?"

"We're enabling the male gaze with our fashion show."

Kelly blinked and then said, "What about the female one?" She turned around at the two models getting in position. Blonde Katarina and busty Beata were cuddled up, no longer stiff but relaxed with their lesbianism now. "I mean, my female gaze is drooling right now."

I smiled. "Let's get you dressed."

* * *

An hour later, Kelly and I were sweeping into a small office building on the outskirts of Milan to meet with Valentina Giovanni. I wore my black, sheath dress, no bra on beneath so my large breasts jiggled. It was a designer dress, M. M. LaFleur. I bought it in Paris last year and loved it. My hips swayed in it, my heels clicking. Kelly marched at my side in a trench coat, the luxurious, black affair hugged her body.

She looked mischievous in it. Her short, blonde hair and bright smile were at odds with the noirish outfit she wore. And that nose ring glinting in the Milan afternoon sun stood out. But she would be perfect for my idea.

She grabbed the glass door and pulled it open for me. I swept into a lobby. I glanced at the wall, reading the directory. Feminism in Fashion, or *Femminismo nella Moda,* was located on the third floor. I swept to the modern-looking elevator. This was a new building, probably at most thirty years old. The elevator rose smoothly up to the third floor (the fourth if we were in America).

A quick scan down the fourth-floor hallway led me to the office of Feminism in Fashion, its name printed in gold on the frosted window set in its office door. I threw it open and marched in on a small reception area, a few chairs, a coffee table, and a handful of Italian magazines. They looked like tabloids or gossip rags.

"Ms. Demeter," a young woman said in accented English, "I am Mirella, Valentina's assistant."

My eyes flitted to the round-faced and curly-haired woman. Her brown locks tumbled down to her shoulders. She wore a baggy t-shirt and a pair of jeans, casual wear for coming in on a Saturday. She extended a hand to me.

I took it and didn't shake it, but stroked the back of her hand and brought her knuckles to my lips to kiss them. She gasped at that. A look flitted across her lips, the first sign of her lesbian awakening. There was nothing like introducing a young woman to sapphic delights. The world had changed this week.

Why? I had no idea, but I was enjoying my new life as a lesbian.

"Is she ready for us, my dear?" I asked Mirella.

She swallowed, her look struck dumb. She flicked her eyes up and down my body, seeing the large swell of my breasts in my delicious dress. A shiver ran through the cutie, her curly, brown hair swaying about her cheeks darkening in a blush.

"My dear?" I repeated, still holding her hand and stroking her.

"S-sorry. She is. She's this way." Mirella whirled around, pulling her hand from mine.

"Mmm, someone's being a naughty MILF," Kelly whispered. "After some young, Italian pussy?"

"Why else are we in Milan?" I asked.

Kelly giggled something wicked as we followed Mirella through a door that led to an office area. There weren't cubicles, but there were desks. An open floor plan that let the workers see and talk to each other while they went about their tasks. One desk was covered in various Italian newspapers, another with international ones in English, French, German, and Russian. They were all stacked neatly as if awaiting the desk owners come Monday morning. A small kitchenette had a stove with a tea kettle resting on it.

Then we were at the doors to Valentina's office. In Italian, the words, "Managing Director" were printed in brass characters. Mirella knocked on the door, a soft rap. Then she opened it up and poked her head in. I heard muffled Italian before she swept the door all the way open.

Valentina Giovanni rose from behind her desk, a fancy affair made of glass, a computer monitor on the right side, a wireless keyboard before her. It had that artistic flair in its design that came from Apple. She had stacks of papers on the other side.

She smoothed the tight, scoop-neck blouse she wore, the dark-maroon setting off her tan skin. She had a large pair of breasts that had that perkiness silicone provided. A diamond necklace draped over her cleavage, sparkling as they jiggled. A mature woman, my age, with her black hair pulled back in a bun and narrow-rimmed glasses perched on her nose. She smoothed the black pants she wore. They fit tight.

She was in good shape and proud of it.

"Ah, thank you for meeting with me, Xandra," Valentina said.

I arched an eyebrow at that. It was a rare person who addressed me by my first name. It was unusual for Europeans to be that familiar. That casualness was almost exclusively an American thing.

Was she being condescending? Insulting.

"What do you want, Valentina, to make your group go away?" I asked as I stepped in and took the seat. Kelly stood to my side, drawing Valentina's attention.

The woman didn't comment. Instead, she said, "Mirella, is the tea ready?"

"It is. I'll go get it," she said and whirled out of here.

"My group has concerns," said Valentina, sounding like it was all reasonable, "about the messaging that your product line sends to women." She reached into the stack of papers and pulled out an advertisement for the fashion show tomorrow. She flipped threw it and shook her head. "Your models are so thin."

"They're beautiful," I corrected. "Sensual. Sexy, even."

Valentina pursed her lips. "Sexy. That's the problem. You are objectifying them and allowing the male gaze to just ravage their body. Look at this." She pointed to a picture of the Y-backed thong that Katarina had been modeling. "There's nothing to this. She might as well be naked."

"My lingerie is designed to be worn beneath the clothes or in the bedroom with a lover," I said. "Not walking down the street. I fail to see what the problem is."

"You don't? How man men will see her with this Y-backed thong appearing out of her jeans and think that means she is a slut and they can hit on her. Wolf-whistle and make her feel vulnerable."

I pursed my lips. "Women dress how they want. I merely give them the options to feel sensual and sexy. Appreciated even."

Mirella reentered. She placed a glass mug before me full of steaming, herbal tea. A spicy blend, almost African in its sensibilities. She put another one before her boss and then set down a small tray with sugar and a small bottle of organic honey.

"What you need to do is include plus-size models in your show," said Valentina. "None of these women with impossible figures."

I gave her a hard look.

"And your women are showing too much flesh. They should wear shawls or—"

"Too much flesh?" I demanded and stood up. I turned to Kelly and ripped open the front of her trench coat.

Beneath she wore a scarlet bra that cupped her small breasts, the straps thin lines of black. The panties were a playful cut, the same red hue but with a thin skirt of white lace that fluttered around the waistband. The silky garment hugged her rump tight, making her ass a gorgeous thing even if it hid that butterfly tattoo she had flapping on her right butt-cheek.

Valentina gaped at Kelly in her lingerie. The blonde struck a sensual and provocative pose. She knew how to carry herself, her lips pursed just right, her blue eyes brimming with a sensual invitation. She ran her hands over her flat belly.

"What are you doing?" Valentina gasped, her large breasts jiggling.

"This lingerie is for women to enjoy," I said, stroking the bra strap down to the cup. "So that they can feel sexy and sensual. So they can look amazing in them. I choose the models I do so that they can be inspired to reach the best selves they can be. It takes work, of course. Nothing worth doing doesn't come without effort. And you want to cover up my models? You want women to be ashamed of their bodies?"

"Ashamed!" gasped Valentina. "Of course I don't want women to—"

I threw the trench coat at her, the black cloth fluttering across her desk and striking her torso. "Then why do you want to cover them up with that?" I squeezed Kelly's breast through her bra. "Why do you want to cover up something as beautiful as young Kelly here."

Valentina spluttered, struggling to untangle the trench coat which had half-wrapped around her body.

"You stand there in your tight, low-cut blouse showing off your fake tits and hourglass figure, and you rail against me for having models just as beautiful?" I demanded.

Valentina glanced down at her blouse and then snapped her head up. "We're not talking about what I'm wearing."

"No, you just want to control what other women wear!" The fires burned inside of me. Censorship was never a beautiful thing. Always full of hypocrisy. I grabbed Mirella by the arm and pulled the young woman to me. "You want to control what she wears, don't you?"

"I have a dress code for my employees," Valentina muttered, on the defensive.

"That's not what I mean." I grabbed Mirella's t-shirt and hauled it up and over her round breasts. She had a nice pair of plump C's constrained in a disgusting, white bra. So boring and unimaginative. I clucked my tongue in irritation. "Look at this bra she is wearing. It's so ugly."

Mirella gasped in shock.

Then I shot my hands down to the fly of her jeans. I unsnapped them. The zipper rasped down and I groaned. Just seeing the waistband of her panties made me shake my head in disgust. They were cheap panties. The type that came in a pack of twelve for a handful of dollars. I shoved down her jeans, exposing her toned thighs.

"Look at how unsexy your assistant's bra and panties are," I said. "This is the sort of underwear you want women to wear. Things that make them look frumpy. She could be wearing something gorgeous beneath her clothing and *know* it. So that she could always feel like a woman no matter what she has to wear.

"So she can always feel sensual and feminine and attractive." I glanced at Valentina. "And don't you deserve her to have those delights to show you. A delicious bra and panties that she can unveil in the privacy of this office and set your heart racing."

"What?" Valentina asked. "Is my English not as good as I think. You did not just suggest that we are lovers."

"Why not?" I asked, sliding my hand around the befuddled Mirella's waist. "She is a young, sexy woman. Just the perfect thing for a mature beauty like you to enjoy."

Valentina sank down into her seat, stunned by what I was saying. She glanced at her assistant and seemed to be seeing her for the first time. Whatever was causing this lesbianism was spreading through the room. The change was beginning.

Kelly sauntered around the desk in her lingerie, the two-inch "skirt" of lacy white on her panties' waistband fluttering. She had such a coquettish look on her face as she reached Valentina and smoothly draped herself across the older woman's lap. Her left arm went around Valentina's neck. Kelly leaned back, making sure that her small breasts thrust up at the woman.

"Don't you like that I look sexy?" Kelly asked as she squirmed.

"I..." Valentina stared down at my cutie's breasts and flat stomach. The older woman swallowed. Her chair creaked from her trembles.

"Don't I look so hot?" Kelly jiggled her breasts in her bra. "Scrumptious? Just so delectable? Don't I make you wet?" She leaned her head up to whisper loudly, "Because you make me so wet."

"W-what?" gasped the MILF. Her eyes were wild as she faced the temptation of young Kelly.

"I have a vibrator in my pussy," moaned the naughty girl. "Don't you want me to use it on you? Make you cum so hard?"

*"A fanabla,"* groaned Valentina, the curse making me smile.

"Mmm, I think you do," Kelly said, raising her head. She brought her lips closer and closer to Valentina's. "I think you like that Ms. D. is making lingerie for women to see the beauty of other ladies. We're here to turn on the female gaze to the delights of sexy cuties like me and hot MILF's like you."

Before Valentina could answer, Kelly kissed her. My pussy clenched as that young and sensual thing glued her mouth to Valentina's. Their lips worked together. Heat rippled through me as they shared their passion.

Mirella gasped beside me, squirming.

"Mmm, and let's get you out of that unflattering garb," I told Mirella. Then I switched to Italian. *"I'm going to love you and your beautiful body, my dear."*

*"What does that mean, Ms. Demeter?"* she answered, her voice musical in her native tongue.

*"That I'm going to make love to you with the strap-on dildo I brought,"* I purred and grabbed her t-shirt bunched up and over her breasts. I tugged.

She lifted her arms up into the air, looking dazed. I pulled her shirt off, her curly hair tumbling about her face and dancing about her shoulders. I threw it to the floor, loving the awe that gleamed in her eyes.

"You are gorgeous, Mirella," I purred while Kelly devoured Valentina's mouth. Their kiss grew increasingly passionate and sloppy. "Let's see it."

She bit her lip as she let me reach behind her and unhook the unflattering bra. It did nothing to properly shape those breasts of hers. They didn't cradle her plump mounds to show them off to their best effect. She might as well have wrapped a breast band around her chest and squished her tits to them. She had a body she should be proud of.

Her breasts spilled out. I cupped them in my hands. My fingers dug into her youthful flesh. She gasped in shocked delight. She quivered as I kneaded her breasts. A flush spread across her cheeks. She flicked her tongue across her lips.

"You like that, don't you?" I purred. "A woman touching your breasts. Not rough and pawing, but gentle. Knowing."

She nodded, her dark eyes growing glossy.

Her pink nipples thrust hard from her areolas. I swept out my thumbs across her silky skin to reach them. I massaged her nubs, loving how she quivered. The heat swelled in my pussy at the delight rippling across her face.

"First time having a woman touch your breasts?" I asked.

She nodded, her hair swaying about her face.

I pressed her nipples into her areolas, my fingers rubbing around them. She quivered there. "How much do you like it?" I massaged faster, smiling at her. "That means you'll have to speak."

"I like it... A lot." She blushed and switched to breathy Italian. *"It makes me feel loved. Special. You're so beautiful and elegant, Ms. Demeter, and you're paying attention to me. Me!"*

*"You're a gorgeous, young woman,"* I cooed. *"What older woman wouldn't want to enjoy your delights."*

I ducked my head down and slid my right thumb off her left nipple moments before I engulfed it. I sucked her bud into my mouth. I savored the feel of her between my lips. I latched on her and sucked. She gasped. The sound sent such a delight shooting through me.

I gave this girl pleasure. Delight. It was such an honor to nurse on her. A treat to give this woman the pleasure of my sucking passion. I swirled my tongue around her, awakening her to the pleasures of her flesh. Clothing rustled behind me. Valentina moaned.

Kelly was up to her fun.

"Ooh, those are nice," my cutie squealed. "I love them. So pliant. Gorgeous titties!"

"Thank you," Valentina answered, sounding stunned.

Mirella's gaze lifted from mine to stare past me to her boss and my cutie. The Italian girl let out a soft gasp as she witnessed the sapphic delight behind us. I loved the awe in Mirella's eyes. She would enjoy what was to come.

I sucked hard on her nub. She groaned and shuddered. I nibbled on her. My tongue danced around her nipple, teasing her. She squirmed there, her breast jiggling in my kneading hands. I popped my mouth off and darted up.

I claimed her lips in a kiss.

My hands abandoned her breasts to slide down her silky body. My tongue thrust into her mouth, meeting hers. She groaned, her flesh so hot beneath my touch. She squirmed there. Her hesitant fingers brushed my hips through my dress.

I kissed her harder. Bolder. I swirled my tongue around hers as my hands found her own hips. I gripped her, clutching tight. Her own hands squeezed about my waist as her confidence soared. Her tongue began moving as she savored her first kiss with a woman.

It was so sexy. Young women seemed to exist so that I could have the pleasure of teaching them about sapphic delights. I was a wicked and wanton MILF. I loved it. the desire they had for my mature body. The lust I inspired in them.

Then I was able to satiate.

My hands moved lower to the waistband of her panties. I wasn't wearing any myself. Juices dribbled down my thighs. I loved the feel of them leaking out of me. I groaned, squirming from side to side. I rolled her ugly underwear—which was what they were; underwear and not something sexy like panties—off her hips.

She shuddered against me as I stripped off the last of her. My pussy blazed with fire as I peeled the panties down her thighs and then they dropped past her knees. She shifted, stepping out of them and her pants that I had already pulled down.

My hands found her rump.

I squeezed her ass and pulled her tight against me. I felt her naked breasts on my large tits, separated from mine by only the thin fabric of my dress. My nipples throbbed at the feel of her. I kissed her with more hunger, kneading her rump.

Her hands moved.

This naughty delight shot through me as she grew bolder. She slipped her touch around my waist to my lower back. She hesitated for a moment, trembling in my embrace, and then she shot her hands down and groped my rump through my dress.

I gasped as her fingers dug into my flesh. My pussy clenched. I kissed her with more aggression. We were both moaning now, kneading the other's ass. Our tongues danced. Hers thrust into my mouth. She tasted so sweet.

"Mmm, yes, yes, you got a pussy that needs this," Kelly moaned behind me.

The whir of a vibrator hummed to life. My pussy clenched at that sound. Valentina gasped. Her chair creaked. The feminist shuddered as the naughty lesbian cutie worked her toy up and down that MILF's pussy lips.

I broke the kiss with Mirella and whispered, "How wet is your pussy?"

"Very," she whimpered, trembling against me.

"Go sit that cute rump on the desk," I purred. I licked her lips and then the tip of her nose. "And spread those legs. I'll take care of that."

"With your strap-on?" she asked, quivering.

I winked at her. "Eventually."

She shuddered, her fingers digging into my hands tight, then she broke from me. I followed her, watching her plump breasts jiggle. She sank down on her boss's glass desk, butt-cheeks squeaking against the smooth surface. She spread her thighs, revealing a trimmed, brown bush half-hiding her pussy lips. They blossomed pink and dripped with her nectar.

Behind her, Valentina sat topless on her chair, her big, fake tits jiggling. I glimpsed Kelly through the clear desk kneeling and using the vibrator on the Italian MILF's pussy. Valentina's passionate sounds echoed through the room, reverberating off the walls.

It made my cunt melt.

"You are so beautiful, Ms. Demeter," Mirella moaned, her glossy eyes flicking up and down my body.

I smiled and grabbed the fabric of my dress at my hips and tugged. The stretchy material popped off my breasts. My large and natural tits spilled out, nipples thrusting hard before me. Mirella gasped as she stared at me. Her tongue flicked across her lips. She quivered on the desk, her butt-cheeks shifting on the surface.

*"Gorgeous,"* she breathed in Italian. *"You're gorgeous. Sexy. Oh, Ms. Demeter, you make me feel so hot and wet. What have you done to me? Why are women so sexy?"*

*"Why does the sun rise or the moon set?"* I asked and pushed my dress off my hips to reveal my landing strip of black hair leading to my shaved pussy folds. *"Some things just are."*

She licked her lips as she stared at me. This hunger brimmed in her eyes. Then she threw herself off the desk, knelt before me, and buried her face into my pussy. I gasped at the hunger I'd unleashed in her. I wasn't ready for her to be so bold.

I had unlocked her sapphic desires, and now they overflowed her. She licked and lapped at my pussy with unskilled hunger. It was incredible to feel her passion sweeping out of her. It made me shudder and moan.

"Oh, you delicious thing," I groaned. "Mmm, that's wonderful. But I want to eat you. I wanted to devour you together."

She pulled her mouth away, staring up at me with pussy cream gleaming on her pink lips. "What do they call it in English when two people oral each other."

"Oral each other?" I laughed at that. "A sixty-nine."

Her brow furrowed. "Strange name."

"It'll make sense if you think about it," I said. "Mmm, yes, let's do that. Do you want to be on top or bottom?"

"Bottom!" she moaned, stretching out on her back. *"I want to feel those big boobs rubbing on my stomach. You're so sexy, Ms. Demeter. You make me feel so good. I want to eat your pussy while you eat mine. Then we both can cum."*

I glanced at Valentina, her face contorting in pleasure. Kelly did her thing. She was the perfect personal assistant, ready to seduce any MILF I needed while I handled the barely legal cuties like Mirella squirming on the floor.

I straddled her head and knelt down. Her hands grabbed my thighs, fingers stroking me. I planted my shaved twat right on her face. She licked again, her tongue sweeping through my folds. I gasped at the young thing feasting on me, the pleasure rippling through my body.

Whatever caused this lesbian outbreak, I was thankful.

I lowered myself, my tits swaying before me. They smacked together. I pressed my breasts into her belly. My nipples rubbed across her hot flesh. They throbbed and ached. I groaned at the pleasure shooting through my body.

Her brown-furred muff lay right before my eyes. Her spicy musk filled my nose. I breathed it in as she lapped at me. I savored it, like that heady inhalation you took before sipping a fine wine. It primed you for the delight to come.

I nuzzled my lips into her silky hairs. They spilled over my mouth. Then my lips kissed her hot pussy folds. She gasped into my cunt. She squirmed beneath me, her stomach massaging my nipples. Heat swept through me.

I licked at her again. My tongue darted through her folds. I caressed those wonderful delights. My tongue stroked her. She groaned beneath me. Her fingers squeezed at my rump. They dug into my flesh and held me tight.

I shuddered and savored her tongue probing into my flesh. She swirled her tongue around in me. A hot stimulation ran through my body. I groaned and squirmed atop her. My nipples throbbed against her belly as my tongue lapped at her spicy delight.

"Ms. Demeter!" she groaned into my pussy.

"I know," I purred and licked again.

"You taste so good." She thrust her tongue into my pussy's depths.

"And you taste like ambrosia." I lapped through her folds, caressing her silky petals. Her hair tickled my face. I loved that.

Her stomach flexed beneath my breasts and massaged my nipples. The pleasure rippled through my body. I groaned, my ass clenching as I squirmed. I probed into her pussy's depths, sank into her sheath, and let my tongue marinate in her spicy delight.

"Kelly!" Valentina moaned. "Kelly, you wicked thing. Oh, yes, yes, you are driving me wild. You naughty thing. You are going to make me cum."

"Good," my cutie moaned. The vibrator's buzzing grew louder and softer and then louder again as she worked it in and out of the Italian MILF's pussy. "I want you to drench me."

"Yes, yes, I'll drench you!"

I loved it. I swirled my tongue around inside of Mirella's pussy. She did the same to me, her tongue so lithe in my MILF-pussy. The young thing feasted on me, made my body feel so good. My orgasm built and built. Her hands slid around my hips. She grabbed my rump, clutching on me as she devoured my cream.

Her pussy squeezed around my probing tongue. She moaned into my pussy as she feasted on me. Her thighs twitched around my head. My toes curled from the pleasure she delivered to me. The bliss rippled out through my body.

"Mmm, Ms. Demeter," she cooed. "So good. I could drown in your pussy."

"Make me cum, and you will," I answered.

*"Yes!"* she gasped in Italian. *"Drown me, beautiful!"*

*"Do the same for me, my dear,"* I groaned and then sucked on her clit.

She gasped as I sealed my lips around her bud. She bucked beneath me. Then she found my own clitoris nestled in my thick pussy lips. I groaned as she sucked on it. The cutie nibbled with her lips and then swirled her tongue around me, instinctively knowing what a woman would like.

I responded, delivering her the same treat as the pleasure swirled through my body. I groaned beneath her. I squirmed as the heat swirled through my body. I sucked on her with hunger. I fluttered my tongue around her bud.

She squealed. Trembled. Her stomach massaged my nipples.

"Yes!" howled Valentina. "You sexy cutie. Oh, yes, yes, I want to eat your pussy and fuck your asshole with the vibrator!"

"I love it!" Kelly moaned.

"Ms. Demeter!" groaned Mirella into my clit. "I... I..."

I nipped her clit.

*"I'm cumming, beautiful!"* the girl gasped and bucked beneath me.

Her pussy juices gushed out of her. That spicy flood bathed my face. I gulped down her cream, the warmth spilling down to my stomach. It bled to my pussy. She licked at it frantically as her orgasm swept through her. she brushed my pussy folds. My clit.

Sparks flared.

I climaxed.

My pussy convulsed. Juices squirted out of me and drowned her. She moaned as I bucked atop her, grinding my nipples into her stomach. Pleasure flared from them as rapture swept out of my pussy. The bliss inundated my mind. I drowned in rapture. It swept over my mind. Consumed my thoughts.

I fluttered my tongue around in her folds. I lapped up her pussy cream. I savored every moment of feasting on her. She thrust her tongue into my cunt. She swirled her naughty appendage around in me. The pleasure swelled through my body. I trembled through my bliss.

Loved every minute of it.

My orgasm hit that wonderful peak. I drank her spicy cream as she lapped at my convulsing twat. I hovered in bliss as I heard movement. I sank down into euphoria. My body buzzed with the need to enjoy Mirella more.

"Just bend over my desk," Valentina moaned. "I'm going to ream that asshole out with your vibrator."

"You got it wet enough," Kelly said with perky enthusiasm.

I bet she did.

"Ms. Demeter," mewled Mirella. "Is it time for you to fuck me with the strap-on?"

"Yes, it is," I groaned and rose from her, pulling my pussy from her delicious mouth. And her spicy cunt from my hungry lips. My breasts swayed as I stood up and spotted Kelly bending over the glass desk.

“Have fun, Ms. D.?” she asked me with cunt juices smeared across her features.

“Yes, I did,” I purred and headed over to my purse. I dug out the strap-on. “Mirella, bend over the desk. I'm going to pound you.”

“Yes, Ms. Demeter,” Mirella groaned.

“And plant a kiss right on my lips,” moaned Kelly. “Love tasting Ms. D.'s MILF pussy off another cutie's mouth.”

I smiled at her enthusiasm.

Mirella knelt on the other side of the desk. The two barely legal cuties' mouths came together, lips both coated in MILF pussy cream, and kissed. I shuddered as their tongues danced. It was such a beautiful sight.

My pussy rippled with heat.

I glanced over and made eye contact with Valentina. The Italian MILF had this look of pure delight on her face as she smiled at me. Then she sank down to kneel behind my lover, bringing that vibrator to Kelly's asshole. She pressed it between her butt-cheeks.

Kelly squealed into Mirella's kiss.

I pulled out the fleshy strap-on and drew it up my legs. I worked it from side to side, working it higher and higher, my large breasts bouncing and jiggling. I was so ready to fuck that cutie's pussy. To pound her hard and make her explode. The vinyl harness rolled up my thighs. My back arched, my large breasts jiggling. I pulled it over my hips and adjusted the base to rub on my clit.

Pleasure sparked through me.

I advanced on Mirella beneath over the desk, her tongue swapping pussy juices with Kelly. My assistant moaned into the kiss as Valentina reamed out her asshole. That silvery shaft plunged in and out of her asshole while the MILF plundered that young and tasty cunt.

I smacked the dildo into Mirella's rump. She gasped and broke the kiss with my assistant. The Italian cutie threw a look behind her and beamed at me. Her eyes smoldered with such excitement as she wiggled her ass.

“She's eager for it, huh?” Kelly moaned, pleasure crossing her face.

“I am,” moaned Mirella. “I want that big dildo in me. I want to be fucked by a lesbian! It's so exciting."

"It is," Kelly said. "Mmm, Valentina, that tongue... Ooh, you got that tongue deep in my pussy. Ooh, plunge that vibrator faster in my asshole. Yes, yes, really get it in there. Mmm, you have to go to the show and meet the models afterward. Beata has such a huge pair of tits. You'll love her."

"Yes!" Valentina moaned. "I will. I'll love her if her pussy is half as tasty as yours."

Kelly grinned at me and winked. We had Valentina.

"Ms. Demeter, please, please fuck me," moaned Mirella. She wiggled her peachy romp some more. "I'm going to explode. I need that big toy in me."

"But don't you want to explode?" Kelly asked her.

"On the dildo! Not from frustration!"

I laughed and smacked her ass again. Her butt-cheeks rippled while the dildo massaged my clit. I moved it lower, sliding the tip across her butt-cheek. It dimpled her rump. She groaned at the contact then shuddered as I went lower and lower.

I nuzzled into her brown bush, the base pushing on my nub and pussy lips. I let out a soft groan of delight while she gasped. Her head snapped up. I must be at the entrance to her pussy, her labia already spreading around the tip of the cock.

I thrust into her depths.

"Ms. Demeter!" she howled as I rammed my girl-dick into her cunt. Her pussy lips spread and spread and then engulfed the tip of my cock. "Yes!"

Kelly kissed Mirella then, the pair swabbing tongues as I pushed deeper and deeper into the girl's twat. My dildo vanished into her cunt. This heady rush swept through me. I groaned, my breasts jiggling. My cunt clenched as I pushed deeper into her depths.

A heady rush swept through me. This wonderful passion that burst from my clit. The dildo rubbed against my bud. I loved the steady pressure. My breasts jiggled. Then they bounced when I bottomed out in her.

I loved it. My hands gripped her hips and I drew back. She squealed into her kiss with Kelly. The Italian cutie wiggled her hips, which moved the dildo against my clit. The massage was exquisite. I thrust back into her.

My tits bounced.

"Yes!" I moaned, the heat swirling through my cunt. "Oh, yes, I love fucking young things like you."

"Mmm, they're exciting," moaned Valentina, her words muffled by Kelly's shaved cunt.

"Yes, they are," I panted. "Gifts to MILFs like us."

"MILFs?" The Italian woman thrust the vibrator deep into Kelly's asshole. "What is that?"

"Mother I'd Love to Fuck!" I gasped. "An acronym for a hot, sexy, mature beauty like you. Me."

"Yes! Young women were made for us. I can see it now. Ooh, not for lecherous men, but for refined women."

"So refined," Kelly moaned. "Now jam that vibrator in and out of my asshole harder so I can drown you in pussy juices!"

"Yes, yes, drown her," groaned Mirella. "Oh, Ms. Demeter, your dildo feels so very good in my pussy. Just churning me up. I like being fucked by a MILF!"

Her words propelled my hips. They plowed forward, driving my dildo in and out of her cunt. I buried into her again and again. I reamed her. I loved the feel of the toy's base massaging my clit on every thrust. Sparks burst through me. I savored every moment of it, reveled in every last second of plowing into her snatch.

I buried the dildo into her hard and fast. I rammed into her. I enjoyed the way she moaned as she kissed Kelly. They were both squealing into the other's lips, their orgasm building and building in them at the hands of us naughty MILFs.

My tits bounced and heaved before me. They smacked together while my clit burst with pleasure. Every thrust into her cunt pressed the base of the dildo on my naughty bud. The sparks sizzled through my twat, bringing me closer and closer to my orgasm.

"Oh, yes!" I gasped. "Mirella, you are such a treat to fuck."

Kelly broke their kiss. Her blue eyes met mine. "Churn her pussy up, Ms. D.! She needs to cum hard."

"So hard!" the girl moaned, her head swaying. "And Valentina, you must make Kelly cum. She is such a cute thing. And your pussy tastes so good."

"You're going to be licking it a lot," moaned Valentina.

"I will crawl beneath your desk and eat you out every day!"

I shuddered, loving the words every MILF boss wanted to hear from her sexy assistant. I thrust harder into her, the pleasure flaring. My lusts were out of control. The moans echoed through the office, resounding back and forth.

Kelly's face was twisted. The Italian MILF pumped her vibrator in and out of the girl's asshole while feasting on her cunt. My cutie moaned. I knew that look on her face. She hurtled towards her own orgasm.

I loved it, thrusting away at Mirella's cunt. She gasped. Her head threw back, her moans growing throatier and louder. Her hips wiggled while my crotch smacked into her rump. My tits bounced together, rippling.

Kelly stared at them as she moaned, "I'm going to cum! Valentina, yes, yes!"

The girl's blue eyes squeezed shut. Her cry of passion echoed through the room. I groaned, plowing my dildo into Mirella's cunt as I watched Kelly thrash threw her orgasm. She trembled there, her passion echoing through the room.

I groaned and thrust harder and faster. I buried my dildo deep into Mirella's cunt. I plundered her pussy with my hard strokes. She gasped at the force of my pounding. I loved the sounds she made as she squirmed and wiggled her hips.

"Yes, yes, yes, so good!" she moaned. "Ms. Demeter! *I'm cumming so hard on your dildo!*"

"Italian sounds so sexy!" Kelly moaned, her face still twisting in pleasure.

I thrust into my cumming lover's pussy with the dildo. Her juices gushed out, bathing my shaved twat and thighs. I groaned, my clit bursting with delight. I threw back my head and howled out in pleasure.

My pussy convulsed. Juices gushed down my thighs. They spilled out from my spasming twat while the fires blazed through my body. They roared from my climaxing cunt. The flames consumed my nerves up to my mind.

They blazed across my thoughts.

"Yes, yes, yes!" I howled as my body bucked through my orgasm.

*"Are you cumming, Ms. Demeter?"* Mirella asked me in Italian.

*"So hard, my dear!"* I moaned, the flames burning through my mind.

"Italian is so sexy!" Kelly moaned, bucking on the desk. "Oh, god, that vibrator is making my asshole go numb!"

"We can't have that!" purred Valentina, ripping it out.

I trembled, my mind blazing with my passion. My orgasm consumed me, leaving behind ecstasy. I panted, savoring that rapture filling my body. My breasts heaved as I sucked in deep breaths. I swayed for a moment, dizzy.

Then I pulled out of Mirella.

She turned around and threw herself at me. She kissed me with hunger. Her naked breasts pressed against mine; there was nothing in the way this time. My spicy musk lingered on her lips. I savored the taste, the dildo trapped between us.

"Mmm, what should we do now?" Kelly asked. "Ever been fisted, Valentina."

"What?" gasped the woman in shock. Kelly giggled.

Valentina and I enjoyed our lesbian cuties. Kelly taught Mirella how to fist me by demonstrating it on Valentina. We both gasped and moaned as they plunged their hands in and out of our cunts, stretching them to the limits.

I feasted on Mirella's asshole and she used that naughty vibrator on my pussy. We shared our passion. I reveled in the fun of having an enthusiastic, young woman eager to please me. It was utter heaven.

If only all meetings could go so well.

Later, Valentina and I came to an agreement. Dripping with barely legal pussy juices, she saw the merit of the show, especially its lesbian vibe. She promised to support us and not protest us. I marched out of her office in triumph.

Kelly walked at my side, naked beneath the trench coat. I had missed her stripping naked, too busy making out with Mirella. A pair of red panties peeked out of one pocket. She had such a big grin on her face.

"I could use a late lunch, Ms. D.," she said. "Pussy is great, but it's not filling."

I laughed and pulled her close to me as the driver opened the door. She was a young woman in a black suit that made her look so sexy. I hoped to enjoy her before this trip was done. I nuzzled my nose into Kelly's brushing her piercing.

"We'll find *something* to satiate you," I purred.

"Mmm, sounds perfect," she said and kissed me. I groaned, tasting the mix of pussy juices on her lips. I held her tight, our tongues dancing.

I was glad I brought this cutie with me on my trip to Milan. She made everything so exciting. Her playful attitude and all the mischievous sensuality she oozed titillated me. Being a MILF CEO was hard. Each one of us needed a cute, lesbian assistant to help ease that burden.

And to make you cum on the ride to get lunch. I broke the kiss, eager to enjoy the rest of our time in Milan. I was glad I poached her from her step-mother. Brandy Lorde definitely deserved a raise for introducing me to this exhilarating cutie.

I pulled her into the limo and savored her tongue lapping at my pussy. Oh, yes, Kelly was everything I needed.

To be continued in Mrs. Smart's tale...

# Mrs. Smart's Nubile Surprise

## Lesbian MILF's Date Night 1

## A Lesbian MILF Tale

by

Reed James

# Mrs. Smart's Nubile Surprise

That naughty girl's wish is spreading far and wide. It's reaching across the world and changing women in so many wonderful ways. MILFs are discovering their power to shape young women's sexuality. Barely legal cuties are learning the effect they have on those older hotties.

The world will never be the same.

* * *

## Clarissa Smart – Friday, Day 5 of the Wish

It was date night with my husband.

It was a strange feeling getting dressed up to go out with him. I hadn't yet told him that I was a lesbian. I wasn't really sure how to tell him how that naughty switch got flipped in me the other day when I picked up our new daughter from daycare and found the young babysitter and another mother in the throes of lesbian passion.

A MILF and a barely legal cutie writhing in passion.

It had been shocking to walk in on it. Made my breasts full of milk start lactating. Before I'd known it, Nancy Haverstone and I were making love to the young Charlotte. Just writhing in lesbian passion.

Since then, my desires for women had overwhelmed me. I wanted them, especially the young ones. I was a MILF now. A mother who knew what those nubile things needed: the sensual touch of a mature beauty.

Despite that, I was going out on a date with Thomas. He was behind me right now, knotting up the ties of my dress behind my neck that held the elegant, black affair on my busty figure. It fell down to my ankles but hugged my body, especially at my waist. A silver chain encircled my hips, clinging to my curvaceous form.

"You look beautiful, Clarissa," Thomas said when he stepped back.

"Thanks," I said, gazing at myself in the mirror. It was a little early to be getting ready, but I was a worrier. I might be that rare woman who was ready to leave early instead of rushing around at the last minute and holding up her husband.

We were going to see the local philharmonic symphony play. I loved every part of the elegant affair. First, I got to dress up, and then I was blessed to listen to gorgeous music. I savored symphonies. They could be playing the classics to modern movie scores and even video game music. Just so long as the music was emotional and moving, I didn't mind.

The doorbell rang. The babysitter had arrived.

"I'll get it," I said, a naughty rush surging through me. We were using a new girl for the night. She sounded so young on the phone, only eighteen. Danni... Wasn't that just a cute name? It had my pussy wet and my nipples throbbing.

I sauntered out of our bedroom, my thong already fighting against the juices leaking out of my pussy. My hips swayed, the skirt rustling about my legs. I headed down the stairs, my hand sliding down the banister.

DING-DONG!

Impatient girl. She was eager. I liked them eager.

Since my lesbian awakening, I had had two romps with barely legal cuties. One was a girl at my local coffee shop. We had a wild and frantic encounter in the bathroom, our hands shoved down the other's panties, just frigging each other to our orgasms before she had to get back to work. The other one was at my job. This secretary named Diane. She had been so eager to lick my pussy out in the supply closet.

We'd almost gotten caught.

She'd taken a few other women who I worked within there. I'd seen them emerging with their box of pens clutched in hands and the biggest smiles on their faces. Lesbian passion was spreading. It was a beautiful thing.

DING-DONG.

I opened the front door a moment after, smiling in amusement which turned to groaning lust at the sight of the beauty on my doorstep.

Eighteen and perky. The girl had glasses perched on her dainty nose with set off the vibrancy of her green eyes. Dimples shone in her cheeks when she smiled at me. She'd gathered her long fall of black hair into a ponytail that swished behind her. A pair of jean shorts left her lithe legs bare while a tank top clung to her round breasts. A red bra bled through the white material of her top.

"Danni?" I asked, my voice sugary delight.

"Yeah," she said, bouncing in place. Her tits jiggled, cupped in that red bra. "You must be Mrs. Smart. I'm so glad to be here. You won't be disappointed with my service. I have all my certificates, and I'm CPR certified with infants and children."

"Wonderful," I said, my eyes flicking up and down her. My nipples throbbed, my breasts feeling full of milk even though I'd just pumped. Girls seemed to ramp up how much I lactated. My pussy itched hard. "Come in, come in, let me give you a tour."

I grabbed her arm and gently led her in. She looked around and gushed over the house. "You have such a beautiful home, Mrs. Smart. Did you decorate it yourself?"

"I did," I said, staring out at the living room with the mauve couch and recliner with the gray pillows on them. The furniture's wood was just the right shade of stained brown to go perfectly with them. It held an elegance.

"You have a good eye," the girl said

My gaze slid down to her round breasts pressing out from her top. I licked my lips. "Mmm, I know what I like."

"Excellent!" She glanced at me and smiled, her cheeks picking up a pink hue, her breath quickening.

I slipped my arm in hers and moved her through the living room to the kitchen, my thong drinking in the excitement. She was just perfect. I wanted to babysit her. I wanted to just ravish her so hard. Show her all the delights her body had to offer.

"So where are you and Mr. Smart off to tonight?" she asked. "You look so sophisticated and gorgeous in your dress."

"Aren't you a treasure," I said. "The symphony."

"Really?" The girl let out a longing sigh. "I've always wanted to go. It would be so amazing to hear all that beautiful music."

"You like the symphony?" I asked in surprise. It had been my husband, ironically, who'd introduced me to orchestras on a date early on in our relationship. He'd been trying to show off, and I ended it up loving it while he had only tolerated it. "Not Lady Gaga?"

"Can't I like both?"

"Of course," I said, drawing her into the kitchen. "Now feel free to help yourself to anything in the kitchen, just don't leave a mess."

"I won't," she said. "I'm very considerate. I like cleaning up after myself."

"Mmm, I bet," I groaned, wanting her to clean up the mess she'd made in my thong. I could just smell my sweet musk.

Out of habit, I went to push up my glasses, but I was wearing contacts tonight. I only wore them on special occasions. At work, I liked them because they made me appear sophisticated and knowledgeable.

I opened the fridge and showed off the bottles of milk. "For my daughter, Cherri. They're full of my own breast milk, not formula."

"Ooh, really?" she asked, glancing at my breasts. "That's so wild. I can't imagine what it's like to nurse someone."

"It is simulating," I said, aching to nurse this cutie. My milk was coming in faster and faster. I felt like I'd have to pump myself again. "Now there's more than enough for Cherri. Just make sure you warm it up." I pointed to a bottle warmer on the counter. "Just pop it in, hit the button, and it'll bring it up to the right temperature."

"Fancy."

I led her from the kitchen, loving the feel of her on my arm. She was such a delicious thing. As we headed towards the stairs, I passed my husband coming down them wearing his suit. He looked handsome enough, I supposed. A few days ago, I would have found him dashing and sexy, growing wet for him.

But I was all lesbian now.

"This is Danni," I said to him. "She's a symphony fan."

"Glad someone else is," he said in a jovial way. "We should be going soon, Clarissa."

"We have thirty minutes at least," I said. "I want to give Danni a *thorough* tour and make sure she knows her way around and performs to my desires."

"Yeah, sure," he said and headed to the living room.

As we headed up the stairs, I heard the TV come on. The sounds of a cheering crowd. He'd found a game. He'd much rather stay at home watching that than suffer through the symphony. He did it because he loved me, I guess.

I led Danni up the stairs and then to a door. I cracked it open and put my finger to my lips. She nodded. I opened onto a room lit by an amber nightlight. A crib lay in the center, a mobile dangling above it full of flying Dumbos, the elephants looking so cute with their large ears spread wide as wings. My little baby slept peacefully.

I crept up and smiled. For a moment, all my lusts were forgotten as I gazed at my infant angel. Danni let out a soft sigh beside me. She leaned over the crib and quivered. I smiled, loving the sounds she made. How she stared at my daughter with such joy.

I could gaze at Cherri for hours, I could, but my husband was waiting. I took Danni by the arm and drew her out of the room. On the way out, I motioned to the baby monitor on a little table by the crib. It was white with a stiff antenna thrusting up.

Danni nodded.

Outside the room, I closed the door softly. I took her hand and led her down the hallway. "Now, there are a couple of receivers throughout the house. In the living room, the kitchen, and my bedroom."

"Your bedroom, Mrs. Smart?" the girl asked, her cheeks scarlet now.

"Mmm, yes. We need to make this a *thorough* tour. I have to make sure that you're capable of taking care of my daughter. I need to have all my itches satiated."

She swallowed, her hand gripping mine. Did she know what was about to happen? My tongue flicked across my lips, my pussy on fire. More and more juices soaked my thong. My breasts felt so full. Ripe and aching, my nipples hard.

I opened the door to the master bedroom and pulled her back. Our reflection gleamed in the very mirror I stood before when my husband had tied the straps of my dress. I caught a glimpse of my own flushed face surrounded by my elegant fall of blonde hair.

"Mrs. Smart," the girl whispered, her eyes wide behind her dainty glasses. "I think I know everything... I won't be coming in here. It's your bedroom."

I closed the door behind her and then pulled her close. "I told you," I purred, staring straight into her eyes. "I need to make sure that you know how to satiate all my itches." I let out a throaty purr. "And you're just a sexy thing."

"Mrs. Sma—"

I kissed her dainty lips.

I closed my eyes and loved the feel of the girl's lips against mine. The babysitter stiffened in my arms, her lips rigid, as I kissed them. My mouth, waxy with my lipstick, worked on hers. My hands slid around her waist, pulling her so tight against me. I held her as my tongue flicked across her lips. She let out a whimpering sigh. Her body quivered.

Her lips moved against mine. They were hesitant. Slow. I could feel her body awakening to desires that must be shocking to her. I loved it. I kissed her with more aggression, claiming her lips, savoring her surrender to my passion.

My hands slid down to grab her ass through her tight shorts. I felt her perky butt, my digits squeezing into the denim to grope through the cloth. She moaned into the kiss, her lips moving with more excitement. She relaxed into the lesbian eroticism.

My tongue pushed on her mouth, pressing against those lips. I needed to enter her. I pushed on her, aching to penetrate her and swirl around in her. It would be so hot and naughty. My body trembled, my pussy clenching. This fiery ache swept through me. My nipples throbbed, on fire and brimming with my milk.

Her hands found my hips. She gripped me through my dress, her tongue playing with mine. She kissed me with hunger back. She moaned, swaying in my arms. It was so intoxicating. The babysitter's hands slid around my waist, creeping towards my own rump. I had a decade on her. A woman mature, eager to show this nubile thing all the delights her body had to offer.

She grabbed my rump.

I groaned now as she kneaded me through my dress. The silk caressed over my skin. I shuddered, my body so alive, drinking in all the sensation. Her lips tasted so sweet. I could just kiss her forever. Just stay like this.

But I had to leave to get to the symphony soon.

I broke the kiss. Danni panted, whimpering, "Mrs. Smart? Y-your husband. He's downstairs."

"And?" I grinned at her, my fingers digging into her rump. "This is between us women."

She trembled in my embrace. "I've never... It's not...You know. Never something that turned me on."

"But now?"

Her eyes lit up. "Your so sexy, Mrs. Smart. So elegant and beautiful. I think it's so wonderful you get to go to the symphony in this dress." Her body shivered, her breasts rubbing into mine, separated by our clothing.

My nipples throbbed.

"I would love to wear a dress like this one day, Mrs. Smart."

"Mmm, you will," I purred, my pussy on fire. "God, you are making me so wet. You know that? Mmm, you're so young and nubile. And... Damn, I need to pump my breasts again."

"Pump..." She licked her lips. "You mean... They're full of milk?"

"Would you like to help me?" I asked, pulling away from her I reached behind my neck and undid the ties of my dress. The two triangles covering my tits fell away, revealing my large mounds. They had blossomed up nearly three cup sizes with my pregnancy. They were so large and lush now.

"Where's your pump?" she asked, trembling. She stared at my tits, her eyes tracking their swaying movement. They jiggled.

I cupped my breasts and squeezed them ever so gently. White milk beaded on my fat, dark-pink nipples. My fingers massaged my tits. I wiggled my hips from side to side, my pussy on fire. I shook them at her.

"Who needs a pump when I have a sexy, young cutie like you, Danni?" I purred.

She gasped. "You mean...?"

"Hungry?"

"What about your daughter?"

"She has plenty. I produce enough for her and for any sexy girl who needs a pick-me-up. Breast milk is *very nutritious.* Just what a sexy thing like you needs."

She licked her lips and trembled. Then she let out a groan and took the two steps to me. She ducked her head down, her ponytail swaying down her back. She nuzzled into my left nipple. Her lips kissed at the areola. My nub brushed her smooth cheek before she shifted her head and engulfed it. She latched on.

Suckled.

My pussy clenched as the milk squirted into her mouth. I gasped, my fingers squeezing my tits. Her green eyes squeezed shut. She whimpered in delight and suckled again. Harder. More milk jetted into her mouth. Tingles raced down to my pussy.

Nursing a girl was so exciting. My twat drank it in. I groaned at how sexual it felt. Pure bliss. I swayed there as she suckled. Her cheeks hollowed. She gulped down my milk with hunger. Her green eyes opened, staring up at me.

"I know," I cooed. "Mmm, don't hold back. Drink it all down. Yes, yes, just like that. Ooh, you naughty thing. Drink every drop of my milk. You love it, don't you?"

She nodded, groaning.

"Yeah, you do," I panted. "I can feel it. Just suckle away. Drink down all that yummy milk. Mmm, yes, guzzle it down."

She suckled with such hunger. My moans filled my bedroom. The babysitter worshiped my nipple. Her tongue swirled around it between nurses. Her lips sealed tight, pink and cute. Her flushed cheeks hollowed. Her glasses shifted on her nose.

My pussy soaked my thong. I needed to touch myself. I released my tits to grab my skirt. Her hands took their places. She cupped both my breasts in her warm grip. Her fingers massaged them. She groaned as she kneaded my tits, especially the one she nursed at.

My milk squirted with force into her mouth.

"Yes!" I gasped. "Oh, Danni, you naughty girl, drink my milk. Ooh, that's it. You're making me so wet."

I drew my skirt up my legs, gathering the silky fabric with my hands. It caressed my thighs and hips. My skin blazed while she squeezed my breast like an udder. I groaned again, my cunt clenching. It was so incredible for my milk to get out of my nipple with such force.

Her warm, wet mouth loved my nub. She suckled with hunger, gulping down my treat. I hauled my skirts up over my waist. My sweet musk grew stronger. It filled the air. I wondered if she could smell it with her face pressed into my boob.

"Danni," I panted. "My pussy! Finger my pussy. I need to cum. This is so hot. You're making me feel so good."

Her left hand abandoned my right breast. She shoved it down my body, so obedient. Just the way a barely legal babysitter should be. She shoved her hand down to my thigh. She stroked up it and found my crotch. My thong.

I kept my pussy shaved, only a blonde landing strip. I was freshly groomed down there, extra sensitive. I shuddered as her fingers shoved my thong to the side and brushed over my married pussy lips. Her lithe touch sent a shiver through my body.

"Oh, my god, yes!" I moaned.

Her fingers thrust into my pussy's depths. She pumped them in and out of my cunt. I groaned, clenching my twat down on her wonderful and naughty digits. I shuddered, the pleasure surging through me. It was incredible to feel while she nursed on my tit.

She suckled with hunger, drawing out more and more of my milk. Her fingers felt wonderful in me, bringing me closer and closer to that moment when I would explode in rapture. I threw back my head and let out a throaty sigh of relief.

"Oh, yes, yes," I gasped. "Just like that. Mmm, that's it. That's what I need. You're such a good babysitter."

She moaned around my nipple and squeezed her fingers hard into my tit. She suckled, the milk shooting from my nub. Pleasure shot down to my cunt being plundered by her wonderful digits. I shuddered, shifting on my heels, my blonde hair swaying about my flushed face.

She worked those fingers in and out of my pussy with deep plunges into my juicy flesh. I groaned, the pleasure shivering through me. The heel of her hand ground on my clit. Pleasure sparked through me, meeting the tingles zapping down from my nipple every time she suckled.

It was all so incredible. Such a perfect delight to enjoy. I groaned, my hips swaying from side to side as I enjoyed her nibbling between suckles. Her fingers thrust faster in and out of my cunt. My hands rested on her shoulder, stroking her supple skin.

"Yes, yes, Danni!" I moaned, my body shuddering. "Oh, you delicious girl. Oh, you're such a treasure. I'm going to have such an orgasm. I need this. You're making date night so special."

An idea clicked in my mind.

Her digits pumped away at my cunt and my clit throbbed against the heel of her hand. I came closer and closer to my orgasm. That heady rush of heat that would consume me. I groaned, squeezing my eyes shut and loving her every stroke and touch. She knew just how to caress me to bring me to the edge of my pleasure.

To thrust me over it into rapture.

"Oh, yes, yes!" I groaned. "That's it. Just like that. Oh, I'm going to cum so hard."

She suckled with hunger at my nipple. She squeezed my tit hard. Milk flooded the babysitter's mouth. The jolt of delight shot down to my cunt. I threw back my head, my blonde hair swaying about my face.

And came.

My pussy writhed and convulsed around her digits. The pleasure swept hot through my body. She nursed on my nub as the rapturous heat reached my mind. My thoughts baked in the ecstasy. Stars flashed across my mind.

"You sexy thing!" I moaned. "Oh, yes, yes, that's perfect. That's just what I need. Oh, drink my milk. You're the perfect babysitter!"

She stared up at me with her green eyes, nursing hard as her fingers churned up my pussy. The flood of cream gushed out around her digits and soaked my thighs. More heat sizzled over my mind. It was incredible. I groaned, swaying from the bliss that she gave me. It was awesome. I groaned, my heart pumping bliss through me. I swayed, loving every second of it.

Then my milk ran dry, and she ripped her mouth from that nipple. She thrust up and kissed me on the mouth. I tasted my sweet cream as my orgasm hit that intoxicating peak. My breasts pressed into hers, separated only by her top and bra. My nipples throbbed and ached.

She broke the kiss and purred. "Perfect babysitter, huh?"

"Yes!" I hissed. "You're satisfying *all* my concerns."

"All of them?" she asked, this playful gleam in her eyes. Her glasses made her so adorable.

"Get naked!" I hissed. "I have to make sure you can handle everything."

"Yes, Mrs. Smart," she moaned and grabbed her top. She peeled it off and revealed that red bra I had seen bleeding through her clothing.

I shivered and turned to my dresser. I opened my panty drawer and picked up the toy I had bought at the lingerie store, Secret Delights, today. They were starting to sell sex toys now. That was so exciting. It was a hook vibrator, its body a bright shade of blue. It curved to a hook at the end, around point designed to massage one spot in the pussy.

I turned around to see Danni wiggling out of her jean shorts. She peeled them off revealing a matching pair of red panties. She fell onto the bed and pushed off her panties next, thrusting her dainty legs up in the air.

I licked my lips at her shaved beaver peeking between her thighs. A hot shiver ran through my body. I sauntered to her, pussy cream running down my legs. I was so turned on right now. So eager to just suck her clit and fuck her with the vibrator. I even caught a glimpse of her asshole.

My own tingled.

Her round breasts jiggled in her bra. She sat up and reached behind her as she saw what I held. Delight shone in her green eyes. She wiggled her nose, shifting her glasses. Her bra came undone and she whipped it off to show off her round tits.

They were perky as her. Ripe and gorgeous, her nipples soft pink and so suckable. I licked my lips as I sank on the bed, my large tits swaying before me. Her hot eyes followed their sway as I held up the toy for her approval.

"That looks sexy, Mrs. Smart," she moaned. Then she gasped. "You have a tattoo."

I smiled. The front of my dress had fallen down to dangle before me with my skirt. It showed off my butterfly tattoo on my stomach. "I wasn't always a MILF."

"Mmm, you are so sexy. God, I didn't know older women would turn me on, but when you opened the door, it just..."

"Clicked?"

She nodded, her perky tits jiggling.

I smiled and leaned over her. I brought the vibrator to her pussy while I ducked my head down and kissed at the side of her right boob. She smiled down at me. She brought fingers sticky with my juices to her mouth. One by one, her digits slid past her lips to be sucked clean.

As she did that, I kissed to her nipple and engulfed it. I sucked it. No milk. Well, she wasn't a sexy MILF. Just a cute babysitter. I nursed anyways, loving the moans she made as she popped her digits into her mouth.

I twisted the vibrator's base. It hummed.

She shuddered and whimpered in anticipation.

I pressed the hooked end of the vibrator into her pussy. I stroked it up and down her folds. She gasped and trembled. I was operating blind, but she seemed to love it. Her moans echoed through the room. Her face scrunched up.

"Mrs. Smart!" she moaned.

I loved the sounds she made. I kept sucking on her nipple as I stroked her. It was so exciting watching her squirm as I teased her pussy. I slid it up. She gasped. Had I found her clit? Was I pushing on her bud right now? Her face scrunched up with joy. Her perky tit jiggled from her body's shakes.

"Oh, yes, yes!" she groaned.

I had to see what I was doing.

I gave her nipple a final suckle then I moved down the bed, knees shuffling. A spicy scent rose in my nose. The aroma of her juicy pussy. I loved it. Young and vibrant. My mouth watered to love every bit of my babysitter's flesh.

I settled between her thighs and stared at her pussy. She had a tight slit. The tip of the toy seemed to be pressing on her clit. I smiled, massaging it in circles. My breasts swayed as I played with her. She groaned, her passion echoing through the room.

"Pillow, please," I cooed.

"Huh?" she moaned, blinking. "Oh, yeah." She grabbed my husband's pillow and tossed it down her body to me.

I shoved it underneath her rump, lifting her pussy up in the air. I purred in delight as I bent down. My blonde hair swayed about my face. I breathed in her spicy musk. The heady aroma filled my nostrils. I quivered, reveling in the fragrance. Was there any perfume sweeter than a young woman's pussy?

I pushed the tip of the hooked vibrator into her pussy lips. I loved the way her tight folds parted for it. She gasped, her perky tits jiggling. The buzzing toy vanished into her hole. I pushed it deeper and deeper as I leaned my head down.

As I jammed the vibrator into her cunt, I kissed at her clit. Her bud just peeked out of her tight slit. I sucked on it. She gasped and moaned, her body trembling on the bed. Her stomach flexed. I loved the sounds Danni made as I nursed on her.

"Mrs. Smart, yes!" she moaned. "Oh, my god, I hope I am proving to be the perfect babysitter."

"So far," I moaned, pumping the vibrator in and out of her.

I licked her clit, gathering spicy juices off her petals. The buzzing toy worked in and out of her pussy, teasing her. I twisted it, letting the hooked end massage around inside of her. The way she shuddered made me smile.

She was such a delicious thing to play with. Just perfect for me to do my wicked deeds to. I felt so naughty as I probed my toy into her cunt. I twisted it around in her, teasing her. The wild sounds she made were such naughty delights to hear. My cunt clenched, aching for more.

"Oh, god, Mrs. Smart!" she moaned. "That's incredible. I love this toy. Mmm, I've never felt anything like this. It's true what they say."

"Which is?" I asked, twisting the dildo around as I pumped it in and out of her young pussy.

"That lesbians have the best toys!"

I smiled at that. "I'm just starting my collection. I only went gay on Tuesday."

"It's a great start!" She shuddered. "Oh, my god, I love how it massages around inside of me. This is incredible."

"Mmm, enjoy," I cooed, my hungers growing.

I licked and nuzzled past my toy, caressing her plump vulva and juicy pussy lips. Her spicy cream coated my mouth. I savored her flavor. I licked at her as I went lower. I reached her taint, licking up the juices that had dribbled from her twat.

I nuzzled into her butt-cheeks and found her asshole. I licked her sour butthole. She gasped, her body spasming. Her breast jiggled as I swirled my tongue around her wrinkled backdoor. The earthy flavor soaked my taste buds.

"Mrs. Smart!" she gasped in shock. "That's... Oh, wow, no one's ever tossed my salad."

"Mmm, isn't a rimjob delicious?" I asked and rimmed her asshole.

"Yes!"

I pumped the vibrator in and out of her cunt as I licked her backdoor. My pussy simmered, aching to be touched but not demanding attention. I was having too much fun playing with my babysitter. I caressed her asshole and thrust my toy into her cunt.

I kissed her butthole. Licked it. I sucked at it, savoring the dirty taste spiced with her juices trickling down from her cunt. Her moans echoed through my bedroom. The bed creaked as she squirmed.

"Yes, yes, Mrs. Smart! Oh, god, this is great. I'm going to love being your babysitter."

"You are perfect," I moaned and pressed my tongue against her asshole.

She groaned as I drilled my tongue against her sphincter. Her anal ring parted. She groaned as I thrust my tongue into her asshole. Her body shuddered as I swirled around inside of her. I thrust the dildo in deep.

She trembled on the bed. The cutie filled the air with her passion. I loved every moment of it. her asshole squeezed about my tongue. Her sour, earthy flavor filled my mouth. I loved it. My pussy grew hotter and hotter.

That itch to touch myself grew and grew.

"I'm going to cum, Mrs. Smart!" she moaned. "Oh, god, I'm going to cum with your tongue in my asshole!"

I purred in delight, unwilling to remove my tongue from her asshole.

"Yes, yes, just keep that vibrator humming. Oh, this is incredible."

I swirled my tongue through her anal sheath and twisted the dildo around in her. I turned it in her, not fucking it and out, but rotating that tip. She squealed. My tongue probed as deep as I could reach into her asshole.

"Mrs. Smart!"

Her asshole writhed about my tongue. A spill of spicy pussy cream ran down from her pussy to my lips. Her moans echoed through the room as her orgasm swept through her. My twat clenched in envy. Joy burst through me.

My sexy babysitter cried out in ecstasy.

She thrashed on the bed. I pumped the vibrator in and out of her cunt as I loved her asshole rippling around my tongue. It was so naughty. She bucked, squealing in delight. Her asshole jerked from my mouth, ripping my tongue out of her.

"Mmm, listen to your moans, Danni," I purred, my body on fire.

"This is incredible, Mrs. Smart!" she gasped, bucking on the bed. "Oh, yes, yes, this is just amazing. You're driving me wild!"

I licked my lips, so glad I could do that to her. I loved how she moaned. How she trembled on the bed. It creaked and groaned as she whimpered in delight. Her pleasure surged through her. It was incredible to witness.

"Yes, yes, yes, yes!" she groaned. "Oh, that's good. That's amazing! I love it. I fucking love it, Mrs. Smart!"

I grinned and ripped the vibrator out of her pussy. I ducked my head in and licked at her twat, lapping up the spicy cream as she shuddered through her orgasm. Her whimpers were so beautiful to hear as she quaked through her pleasure.

Then she collapsed into pants. Her breasts rose and fell. She groaned, eyes fluttering.

I smiled at her, watching the cutie panting. She licked her lips and then adjusted her glasses. Her gaze shot to me and a wicked smile crossed her lips. She flicked her tongue across them and purred in a hungry tone, "My turn, Mrs. Smart. I need to use that vibrator on you. Prove I know how to handle it."

"Yes, you do," I groaned, my cunt clenching. "I want to make sure that you are able to expertly execute every naughty thing I need.

My idea was so exciting. I brimmed with it. This would be the best date night ever.

She cupped my lips and kissed me. She had to taste her sour musk and didn't care. Her tongue thrust into my mouth. I groaned, savoring the deep, soulful kiss. Her tongue penetrated past my lips this time. She danced it around inside of my mouth. She caressed me with it, the heat sweeping over my body.

It would be incredible. I was so eager for this. I groaned, kissing her with hunger. Our tongues danced together. It was such a delight to enjoy. To share with her this passion. My hips wiggled from side to side, my cunt on fire.

I broke the kiss with her, panting. She licked her lips, her eyes glossy with her pleasure. She wiggled her hips from side to side, her eyes sparkling with this wild heat that had my cunt dripping juices down my thighs.

"Now turn around, Mrs. Smart," Danni said with such confidence in her voice. She sounded so sure of herself. Like she knew just what she had to do to me.

I loved it. A young woman coming into her sexual mastery was a delight to experience. I turned around, my dress whisking over my rump. My pussy clenched, my juices dribbling down my right thigh. My thong was shoved to the left still, absorbing the cream and stopping the flow down that leg. My large breasts swayed before me, the right aching, needing to be suckled from.

She grabbed my skirt and dragged it up my thighs again. I shuddered at the silken caress. A heady shudder ran through my body. I groaned, my heart pounding so fast. Every inch of cloth sliding up my skin brought me closer and closer to unveiling my beauty to her hungry delight.

"Oh, my," she groaned as she pulled my skirt over my rump.

She snagged my thong and hauled it out of my crack and hooked it over to the left side of my rump, stretched out of the way. I felt so wonderfully exposed to her. My married pussy on display, dripping with my juices.

"Mmm, Mrs. Smart," she groaned. Her hot breath washed over my pussy. I heard her inhale, drawing in a deep one. She let out a groaning sigh, stirring more air over my cuntlips. "You smell divine."

"Ready to devour your first cunt?" I asked her.

"Yes!" she moaned.

She kissed right on the middle of my pussy. I groaned as her lips smooched against my labia. Pleasure tingled through me. I shuddered at that young thing taking that full plunge into lesbian delights. To the ultimate sapphic pleasure.

She kissed up and down my slit, brushing my pussy lips and my clit. I groaned, my twat clenching. My breasts swayed back and forth as I trembled. My fingers dug into the fabric of the sheets. I groaned, my blonde hair rustling.

"Oh, Danni. That's good. Ooh, yes, yes, definitely the perfect babysitter."

"But I haven't done this yet," she cooed and then flicked her tongue through my pussy folds.

I gasped at the wicked heat of her tongue fluttering up and down my twat. She licked me, teased me. She pleasured every bit of me. I loved every second of it. My hips wiggled back and forth. I groaned, my heart pounding with the pleasure she stirred in me. That wonderful bliss that would burst out of my cunt and flood her mouth.

She brushed my clit. I gasped, my entire body shaking from the delight of her hot tongue sliding over my bud. Then she flicked up to the entrance to my pussy. She pushed her tongue into my sheath and wiggled it around in me.

"Yes, yes, yes, Danni!" I groaned, my back arching. "That's so good. Ooh, you naughty delight. That's just perfect."

She let out a throaty moan like she agreed. Her tongue swirled around in my pussy folds. She drove me wild. I shuddered, clenching around her, my fingers squeezing at the sheets. Her lips worked on my labia as her tongue probed into my cunt.

The vibrator buzzed to life.

"Yes, yes, use it on me!" I moaned as I heard that buzzing toy behind me.

Her tongue fluttered up and down my pussy folds now, licking and lapping at me as she pushed the vibrator, wet from her cunt, in between my butt-cheeks. I gasped as the hooked end massaged down my crack to my asshole.

"You wicked girl," I moaned. "Do it! Jam that into my asshole!"

She pressed the tip against my sphincter. I gasped at the intrusion pushing on my anal ring. Lubed by her pussy juices, it slipped that round, hooked end past my asshole. I groaned as the delicious buzzing entered my bowels.

She pushed it into me. The naughty babysitter lapped at my cunt while sodomizing my asshole with the vibrator. The widening shaft stretched my aching sphincter wider and wider. It almost went numb from the humming. The buzzing tip massaged into the depths of my bowels.

"You wicked thing!" I gasped, my body trembling. "Oh, Danni, you know how to use that delight!"

"You taught me so well," she moaned as she pushed it deeper.

Her tongue fluttered against my clit, drumming against my bud as the vibrator sank deeper into my asshole. It reached to the depths in me. I groaned, my eyes squeezing shut as the pleasure rippled through my bowels. I savored the heat of that toy buzzing away inside of me.

The hooked end concentrated that vibrating delight on one spot. I shuddered, squeezing my asshole around the toy. Then she pulled it back. She pumped it away inside of me, the velvety friction melting down to my pussy being so thoroughly licked by her tongue.

I shuddered, my breasts swaying beneath me as she pumped that vibrator in and out of my asshole. I groaned. Then she turned it. Twisted it. The buzzing hook swirled around inside of me, caressing other areas of my bowels and filling my body with such delight.

"Yes, yes, yes!" I moaned. "Oh, my god, that's it! That's incredible. Oh, what are you doing to me?"

"Driving you wild," she cooed, her eyes bright and mischievous."

"Yes, you are!" I panted, my heart pounding in my neck. "Oh, yes, yes, you're going to have me cumming hard, aren't you?"

"Uh-huh," she cooed, pumping the dildo in and out of my bowels. "You're going to explode."

She thrust her tongue into my married depths. She swirled her tongue around inside of me and jammed that buzzing toy in and out of my asshole. I groaned, savoring the heat. I squeezed my eyes shut, whimpering. Moaning.

My bowels clenched about the hooked vibrator. I savored the pleasure it gave me. The heat of it churned up my asshole. I groaned, my hips wiggling from side to side. I loved how she stirred me up. It was incredible to enjoy. It was outstanding for me to experience. I loved every moment of it. The heat swept through my body. I bit my lip, the rapture surging through my body.

"Yes, yes, yes!" I panted. "Oh, my god, that's good. That's so good. Don't stop. I'm getting closer and closer."

My pussy squeezed about the probing tongue. It stroked around inside of me. She stirred me up. The heat from my asshole melting around the vibrator mixed with the delight she churned in my cunt. I gasped, my body shaking. My orgasm swelled so fast. My toes curled.

Then she kissed my clit. She sucked on my bud. Her lips nibbled on it. I gasped, sparks of heat shooting through me. My body bucked. My tits rocked forward. I threw back my head, my asshole drinking in all the vibrations. They fed the growing bliss.

She nipped my clit with her teeth. A sharp flare of pain that transformed into ecstasy.

I exploded.

"Danni!" I howled as my pussy convulsed.

Juices gushed out to bathe her face. The cutie licked up the folds. My babysitter lapped at the cream flowing out of my mature pussy. She devoured me while jamming the vibrator deep into my asshole. My bowels spasmed around it, worshiping that buzzing toy.

The waves of bliss swept out of my writhing pussy and flooded my body. Every bit of me trembled with the euphoria of my orgasm. Then the bliss reached my mind. The tide surged over my thoughts. ecstasy drowned me.

"Yes, yes, yes!"I gasped, quivering there.

I trembled through my orgasm, savoring her tongue licking and lapping up my cream. Danni loved it. The naughty girl twisted the dildo around in my spasming asshole as my climax screamed towards its peak.

I hit it. I hovered at perfection.

"Oh, Danni, you sweet delight."

"Mmm, Mrs. Smart," she purred and licked at my snatch, flicking her tongue up and down to gather up my cream.

Panting as I came down from my orgasm, I turned around and faced the sexy cutie, the vibrator slipping out of my asshole. She had pussy cream dripping down her face. The idea I had earlier brimmed inside of me. This wicked and naughty delight I wanted to share with her.

"Would you like to go to the symphony tonight?" I purred, staring into her green eyes.

For a moment, she sat there stunned like she couldn't believe what I had just said. Then her face broke into such facets of joy. She clasped her hands together. Her pussy-stained mouth burst open wide in a squeal of, "Yes!"

She threw her arms around my neck and peppered me with sweet-tasting kisses. I loved her enthusiasm, my breasts swaying and jiggling as I enjoyed her enthusiasm. It was so genuine. She was so thrilled to be my date for the evening.

We had to act fast. I knew just the gown for her to wear. I

pulled out a dark-red sheath dress that no longer fit me thanks to my increased bust size. But she was roughly my height and size. Her tits were a little smaller than mine had been, but it turned out to be close enough.

She looked gorgeous with the dress clinging to her round tits, the stretchy material clinging to her nubile curves. Her glasses added that right level of cuteness and her ponytail was just adorable. No time to do more with her hair.

I had to fix my own dress. She tied it back up, the triangles once more covering my breasts. My right one still ached. She would have to nurse from me again, but that would be just a delight for us to enjoy on our date.

As she touched up her lipstick with a borrowed stick from me, I went to my panty drawer and snagged a few of the other delights that I'd bought today at the lingerie store. I closed my glittering purse, all silver sequins that matched my belly chain, and grinned.

I offered her my arm. "Shall we?"

She giggled and then gasped, "What about your husband?"

"It's game night," I said and took her arm.

After checking in on my sleeping baby—who was a perfect cherub right now so I didn't feel guilty about having a night of fun—we headed downstairs. The crowd was cheering. My husband sat on the edge of his seat watching the silly men throw their ball back and forth. I sauntered up before him, blocking his view. He blinked and looked up.

"Finally ready and..." He blinked. "Uh, why's the babysitter dressed up?"

"Turns out that Danni *loves* the symphony," I said. "So we're going out on a date instead. Plenty of breast milk in the fridge. Pay attention to the baby monitor. And don't wait up."

He gaped at me.

I turned and kissed Danni on the lips right before him, my hand groping her tit. He had to know I was a lesbian sooner or later. My sexy, nubile date groaned, kissing me back, her lips tasting so sweet and delicious.

"C-Clarissa?" choked my husband. "What's going on?"

I broke the kiss. "Enjoy the game. Love you." I led Danni to the door. “And, honey, if you could sleep in the guest room because I'm sure Danni and are going to want privacy when we get back.”

“I... well... I...” He just stared at me in disbelief.

Danni giggled, clinging to me as we headed out for date night. A sexy MILF and her nubile babysitter. Tonight would be exciting.

To be continued...

# Mrs. Smart's Lesbian Dining Affair

## Lesbian MILF's Date Night 2

## A Lesbian MILF Tale

by

Reed James

## Mrs. Smart's Lesbian Dining Affair

### Clarissa Smart – Friday, Day 5 of the Wish

"This is so exciting, Mrs. Smart," my babysitter, Danni, said as she slid into the passenger seat of my car.

She looked so elegant in the borrowed, dark-red dress that clung to her body. The strapless sheath gown gripped her eighteen-year-old flesh with all the curves that she had. She looked stunning in it, her breasts round and plump, filling out the stretchy material. Her black hair still fell down her back in a simple ponytail. She adjusted the dainty glasses on her adorable nose, her green eyes shining bright.

"I can't believe it," she continued gushing as I started up the car. "This is amazing. I'm so beautiful, and you're so elegant. And we're going to the symphony."

"But first, dinner," I said, smiling at her. "This *is* a date."

"Oh, my god!" she squealed, trembling. "I still can't believe this is happening."

It was a little surprising to me, too. My husband was inside, probably still sitting stunned on the couch. Well, he had to learn I'd become a lesbian in the last few days. Gone all-in on Team Sapphic. Women were just wonderful. Especially young women like Danni that I could teach all about girl-on-girl passion.

I was a sexy MILF. Older. Wiser. I knew how to do such naughty things to her young and nubile body. When she had walked into my house tonight to babysit my infant daughter while my husband and I went out on date night, I had been overcome with lust.

I had seduced her. While my husband waited, I had nursed the naughty girl, letting her drink my breast milk, while she fingered me. Then I had stripped her naked and used a hooked vibrator on her cunt. She screamed her head off and returned the favor.

My asshole still tingled from that toy plumbing my anal depths.

When I heard that she loved the symphony, too, the idea popped into my head. My husband hated it. He was doing it for me. So why not let him stay behind, watch the game and our child, and I would go out and have a great time with a sexy thing who'd appreciate it.

And who made me wet.

Now I had that cutie beside me as we drove out to the restaurant, Enchanted by the Sea. She squirmed and fidgeted. My right breast ached. She'd drained my left of all the milk, but I hoped to nurse her more tonight.

I loved having her mouth on my nipple. It had been so exciting. So stimulating. The pleasure shot straight to my cunt. It wreathed my twat. The bliss flowed through me. It swept through my body. I groaned, having loved every moment of it. My hips wiggled back and forth on the seat as I drove in my elegant heels and my tight, black dress.

She licked her lips, a naughty gleam sparkling in her eyes. Then her hand shot out and rested on my leg. I shuddered as she stroked up and down my hot flesh. She pushed beneath my skirt, her digits sliding higher and higher.

"Mmm, what are you up to, you naughty thing?" I asked, her touch shivering up my flesh. She went higher and higher, caressing me, making me feel so wicked.

"Why do you think I'm up to anything, Mrs. Smart?" she asked with such innocence, her hand sliding higher.

"Because you're a naughty little girl."

Danni giggled and thrust her hand boldly higher. She shoved

up between my thighs and rubbed at my landing strip of blonde hair on my pubic mound. She traced the silk down to my pussy. I shuddered at her touch. She reached the tops of my folds.

I *had been* wearing a thong. After our wild rump, I'd removed it. I was glad. I shuddered as her fingers rubbed up and down my pussy lips. She brushed my clit, sparks bursting through me. Both my nipples throbbed, especially my right. She danced her digits across my bud then slid down.

"You wicked thing," I moaned, slowing to a stop as I drove us towards the waterfront and the elegant restaurant.

My right hand drifted from the steering wheel and landed on her thigh right above her knee. I stroked up and down her hot flesh. I caressed her, loving the smoothness of her skin. I pushed beneath her dress. I couldn't wear this gown any longer—my tits had grown two cup sizes with my pregnancy—but it fit her delicious C-cup titties. My hand crept up her thigh, stroking her higher while hers rubbed at my pussy.

"Mmm, shouldn't you be focused on driving, Mrs. Smart?" asked the girl, her thighs spreading wider.

"You think I can't drive my car and your pussy?" I asked, my hand thrusting boldly up to find her young, shaved vulva. Her juices soaked my fingers.

Already, the mix of our musk—my sweet and her spicy—filled the car.

"Is that what you call this?" she moaned as my digits stroked up and down her tight slit. Unlike me, she didn't have thick labia protruding out of her vulva. I had to push into her twat to feel those silky folds and brush her small clit.

"I'm revving your engine," I purred, gripping the steering wheel tight in my right hand as we fought through Friday evening traffic. "Getting you nice and primed to charge ahead at full speed."

"Is that something you do in a race?" she moaned, her fingers thrusting into my pussy.

"No idea," I moaned as those wonderful digits penetrated into my cunt. I shuddered, my breasts jiggling. "But it sounds fun."

I jammed two of my digits into her pussy, my ring and middle fingers. Her hot cunt engulfed them. She squeezed about them, gasping in delight. Her body shifted beside me, her breasts jiggling in her tight dress. She whimpered and moaned, twat squeezing about my digits.

She made the drive through the terrible traffic bearable. I shuddered as her fingers worked in and out of my cunt. Not fast. Just a slow thrust, teasing me. Little flutters of delight washed out of my body.

I worked my fingers in and out of her. Deep and hard thrusts into her juicy snatch then slow pullbacks, her cunt clinging to my digits. She gasped, her glasses slipping down her face. I smiled, glancing at her as we spent more time stopping and waiting for lights to change than driving.

Our pants and moans filled the car. The windows started to fog. I had to reach for the heating controls with my left hand, my right far, far too busy to stop enjoying her pussy clinging to my fingers. The wonderful perfume of our cunts filling my nose.

I breathed in the heady rush, my mouth salivating for more than dinner.

"Oh, I can't believe I'm eating at Enchanted by the Sea," she moaned. "Ooh, what's good there?"

"Their fish," I panted. "You never know what they'll have on the menu. It's all fresh-caught, local fish. So whatever they got that morning. They know how to make it delicious. Trust me, whether it's the sea bream or the cod or delicious tuna, you'll savor it."

"Yes, yes, yes!" she moaned, pumping her fingers fast in and out of my cunt.

I squeezed my snatch down around her digits, loving the friction. I could just relax into my orgasm, but we were almost there. I wiggled my digits into her as I spotted the restaurant ahead. Cars were pulling into the valet.

I shuddered and pulled my fingers out. "Mmm, we'll have plenty of time to make each other cum in the restaurant, Danni. My husband always gets the booths that are secluded. It makes you feel like you're dining by yourself. We can have some fun."

Maybe a cute waitress would join us. This lesbianism was spreading. There could be another young thing that needed a MILF to teach her all about her budding awakening into sapphic lust. My cunt squeezed tight about Danni's fingers.

I shivered as she pulled her digits out of my pussy. As we pulled up to the valet, she smeared her juices on her lips. She leaned over and kissed me just as the young man opened her door for her. His greeting trailed off.

I kissed her with hunger, savoring the taste of her sweet pussy, my fingers soaked by her spicy delight. I shuddered, our lips working together, waxy with our lipstick. It made her mouth buttery soft on mine.

I loved it.

Then I broke the kiss, threw open the door and stepped out while a panting Danni was helped out by the valet. He had a big grin on his face, a young kid with blonde hair. He moved around and handed me a ticket I thrust into my purse.

"Enjoy you're evening, ladies," he said, no doubt loving the thrill of seeing us kiss.

I winked at him, amused. I took my date by the arm and pulled her close. Yes, she was wasted on babysitting. My husband could do that just fine. This girl needed to be taken to fancy restaurants and elegant symphonies. She needed her naughty appetites for older women fed.

And I needed to feast on her young flesh.

We strode up to the doors. I grabbed it for her, my heart racing. The maître d looked up from his ledger at us. He was an older man, thin, with a weaselly mustache on his upper lip. His eyes flicked over us, but his expression never changed from his welcoming smile.

"Good evening, ladies," he said.

"We have a reservation under smart," I said, my arm hooked around Danni's.

He slid his finger down his list. "Ah, yes, Mr. and Mrs...." He trailed off and looked at us.

"That's Mrs. and Mrs. Smart," I said, turning to my date. I kissed her hard on the mouth. She moaned as we put on another show. She shuddered, her lips working with hunger against mine. She kissed me with such delight.

Her tongue danced in my mouth for a moment while the maître d cleared his throat.

"My mistake, madams," he said. "We have your booth ready. The, uh, usual spot." He stared at me like he remembered me being with my husband last time. I broke the kiss with Danni and smiled back at him, not showing any shame at all.

I was out on a date with my young lover. What was wrong with that?

A young woman appeared in black slacks and a white blouse, a black tie dangling down the front of her body. The blouse wasn't flattering, not showing off her figure at all. The slacks, however, hugged her cute rump, but it was a shame the blouse wasn't more flattering.

"This is Ashley," he said. "She'll take care of you tonight."

"Mmm, I hope so," I groaned. "I have some interesting dietary needs."

"Me, too," Danni said, her arm nudging into my right breast.

"We'll accommodate you, right, Ashley?" the maître d said.

"Of course," Ashley said brightly. Her fiery hair added the only color to her uniform. "This way, madams."

She whirled around her, fiery hair sweeping behind her. She wore it back with a black headband. It fell with full volume down the back of her blouse and had a nice bounce to it. I smiled as I sauntered behind her, Danni clinging to my arm. That waitress had no visible panty line.

"What naughty and depraved thoughts are going through your mind, Mrs. Smart?" my date whispered. "Dietary needs?"

"Isn't feasting on pussy a need I have?" I asked.

She giggled. "Mmm, and I need breast milk. I haven't forgotten about your right boob."

"Nor have I," I groaned, my nipple throbbing and aching.

Ashley led us to our booth. As I'd hoped, it was nice and secluded, screened by growing plants and the wall. We slipped in, this privacy sweeping over us. It was an intimate spot, us sitting side by side, for couples on a date.

"Here is the wine list," Ashley said. "I'd recommend our house red. It's a delicious bottle of a 2015 Catena Zapata Nicolas from Argentina. You won't be disappointed with it."

I glanced at the list and then said, "The Chateau de Meursault

Clos Du Chardonnay."

"Of course," she said and then glanced at my friend. "And you *look* twenty-one." Ashley winked. "I'll be right back."

"Oh, my god, Mrs. Smart," my babysitter squealed. She looked around at the opulent surroundings. "The fanciest restaurant I've ever eaten at is Olive Garden."

"You poor, poor thing," I told her, rubbing my arm into hers. "Mmm, you keep babysitting for me on date night, and I'm sure you'll have wonderful experiences."

"And your husband...?"

"Gets to watch the game. Just sit there, drink a beer, and make sure that our daughter is taken care of. He's a good father. He won't neglect her."

"This is all so strange," she said. "I mean, he just let us go."

"Why wouldn't he? I'm gay now." I looked at her. "And you're just such a scrumptious thing. Mmm, I'm going to do such—"

Ashley appeared, setting down a basket of breadsticks that looked warm and fresh. Then she set down a pair of wine glasses and uncorked the bottle. She poured out the wine in each. I smiled, loving a good Chardonnay.

"I'll be back when you're ready to order," the waitress said. "The sea berm is excellent today, freshly caught, and we have an excellent white cod with a plum sauce that will melt in your mouth."

"That sounds so promising," I said, grabbing a breadstick while my babysitter grabbed her wine and took a sip. She smiled and took a deeper one.

Ashley flashed a friendly smile, her cheeks tinged with a touch of pink. From the exertion of working, or was she feeling that attraction? That awakening to lesbian delights that only a sexy MILF like me could give her.

I brought the breadstick beneath the table. Danni glance at me, her tongue flicking across her lips to gather up the residue of wine on them. She set down her glass and then gasp as I rubbed the warm shaft of bread on her thigh.

"Mrs. Smart, you're such a wicked woman," she groaned, her thighs spreading. "I'm eighteen and the naughty things you want to do to me."

"I know," I said, sliding the tip of the bred up her inner thigh. "I'm going to do so many kinky things to you. Mmm, you're my date. My little plaything."

"Yes!" She shifted, the breadstick climbing higher. "I am so glad that Mrs. Gardner recommended me for the job."

"Mmm, I just hope she enjoys you as much as me the next time she needs you to babysit." Linda Gardner was a gorgeous friend of mine.

"Oh, yes!" Danni moaned. "She's a sexy MILF."

I nuzzled the breadstick into her vulva now. I had to operate on touch. I felt it pressing into her pussy. She gasped as I worked the breadstick into her cunt, soaking it in her juices. It was rigid enough and thick enough to make a delicious dildo.

She snagged another one off the plate. I smiled as she grabbed my long skirt and hauled it up and over my thighs. The silken fabric caressed my thighs. My pussy, still simmering from her fingers in the cars, was ready for this.

The restaurant buzzed with conversation. The clatter of utensils on plates. A waitress with blonde hair walked by us with a platter, oblivious to the wicked fun we were getting up to. My pussy clenched, anticipating that warm breadstick filling me.

My naughty Danni wasted no time jamming it up beneath my skirt.

"Yes," I groaned as that freshly-baked warmth slid up my thigh and then nuzzled into my pussy. I worked the breadstick in and out of her pussy faster.

She groaned as she found the entrance to my twat with skill. I shuddered as she pressed the improvised dildo into my cunt. The warmth of it was incredible, and the texture was both smooth and rough. Just the right amount to stimulate my pussy.

I leaned back, groaning, my hand pumping away at her snatch. She jammed her breadstick deep into my cunt and then pulled it back. My twat clung to it, my toes curling in my shoes. It was amazing to feel. This wild heat that swept through me.

Danni stared at my tit. She let out a hungry moan of, "Mrs. Smart!" then she ducked her head down.

My breasts were covered by triangular strips of cloth that rose up to thin strips knotted behind my neck. It was no effort for her to yank the silk to the side and expose my naked breast and fat nipple. Milk beaded the dark-pink nub.

Her head shot down. She latched on and suckled.

My pussy clenched down on the breadstick marinating in my sauce. I thrust mine deep into her pussy. Milk squirted into her mouth. She gulped it down with hunger. I shuddered, my right nipple throbbing in her mouth.

The pleasure flowed down to my pussy, fueling my orgasm building and building. It was coming fast. The fingering in the car and then doing this in public had me turned on. The blonde waitress swept by again, not realizing my babysitter nursed at my tit.

"Mmm, Danni, yes," I groaned, my milk flowing into her hungry mouth. She gulped down the cream and suckled with noisy hunger. "You wicked thing. Ooh, yes, yes."

She winked a green eye up at me.

We pumped our breadsticks out of the other's twat. We fucked each other while the naughty thing nursed. She drank my breast milk with greedy hunger, her appetizer for the main course. My twat squeezed down on the breadstick reaming my cunt with hard thrusts.

My pleasure built and built faster and faster. It was incredible to enjoy. I squirmed in my seat, my cunt juices soaking the bread thrusting into my depths. I shuddered, clenching around it. Her mouth suckled harder.

"Oh, yes!" I groaned, jamming the breadstick deep into her pussy.

"Okay, have you had a chance to..." Ashley's voice trailed off as the waitress appeared at our table. She let out a gasp.

Danni popped her mouth off my nipple and licked her lips. "Mmm, told you I had dietary needs."

"Yes, yes, I have to nurse my young lover," I moaned, pumping that breadstick in and out of Danni's twat while she kept using the makeshift dildo on my cunt.

"It's delicious," Danni moaned to the blushing waitress. "Want a taste? Nothing like nursing from a MILF. It's something every girl should try."

"W-what?" stammered the sexy Ashley. She shivered.

"Mmm, you know you want to," Danni groaned, her left hand pleasuring my pussy with the breadstick, her right grabbing the waitress's tie. She tugged on it, pulling the cute redhead to lean over the small table. "Just give her a quick suckle."

"Yes," I moaned, jamming my breadstick deep and hard into Danni's cunt. My back arched, thrusting out my exposed, right boob to Ashley.

"I shouldn't," she whimpered. "You shouldn't be doing this here, either. This is... I mean... We're in public."

"Yes!" I groaned, on the verge of my orgasm.

"Just a little suckle," Danni cooed. "Mmm, you don't want to be rude. She's in pain. She needs her milk drained."

"Well..." The redheaded waitress licked her lips. Her fiery locks spilled around her face. Her mouth neared my nipple. Danni gave a final tug.

I gasped as the waitress's lips nudged into my nipple. They opened wide. She latched on and suckled. I groaned at that, my cunt squeezing about the breadstick plunging into my depths. I shuddered, savoring every last thrust of that naughty, improvised dildo while my milk streamed into the young waitress's mouth.

She suckled with hunger, drinking down my mother's milk with delight. Her green eyes squeezed shut. I groaned, my orgasm swelling so fast now. It was so hot. The restaurant bustled while I pumped my breadstick in and out of my date's pussy.

That naughty babysitter reamed mine.

"Oh, god, yes," I moaned.

"I know, Mrs. Smart!" gasped Danni. "I'm going to cum. She's just suckling. This is so hot. What is happening to the world?"

"Something beautiful," I gasped, another stream of milk jetting into the waitress's mouth.

I burst in rapture.

My pussy convulsed around the breadstick thrusting deep into my body. I clenched my jaw to keep from screaming out. My nipple throbbed in the girl's sucking mouth. She nursed with hunger on me. She suckled and swallowed all that wonderful milk that gushed out of me.

It was insane. It was amazing. I loved every second of it. She suckled down every drop of it that she could. My pussy convulsed around the breadstick. I groaned, my body trembling through the rapture. It was such an intense delight.

"Mrs. Smart!" gasped Danni. Her thighs clamped around my hand thrusting the dildo into her young cunt. "Yes!"

"Oh, that's good," I groaned, my orgasms screaming to the peak as Ashley suckled more and more of my breast milk.

I hit that wonderful peak, Danni squealing in delight beside me. Then I descended into the buzzing warmth of my afterglow. Ashley kept suckling. She nursed with hunger on my nub. I squeezed my eyes shut and panted, my nipple aching as the milk squirted into the girl's mouth.

I let out a hungry sigh, savoring this delight. Danni gasped out loud, her body bucking, her tits jiggling in her dress at the corner of my vision. Ashley's warm lips worked on my nub. She gulped down my milk.

"Oh, that was good," I groaned.

Ashley ripped her mouth from my nipple, her green eyes glazed over with passion. She blinked and licked her lips. She looked around and gasped. Her cheeks flamed bright. I smiled at her, loving how flustered she looked as I pulled my breadstick out from Danni's pussy.

I held up the gleaming end. There was no doubt what had caused that sheen on its surface. I took a bite of the spicy-flavored bread. I groaned, the buttery taste mixing with the pussy cream. I shivered, my pussy clenching on the piece marinating in me.

When I swallowed, I held it out to the waitress. "Care to try it? Sauce ala Danni."

The waitress looked around and then leaned over. Her ruby lips opened wide. She took a large bite of it and groaned. Her entire body shuddered. She let out a whimper as she swallowed it, her body swaying.

"Oh, my, that was..." She swallowed. "I've never..."

"Enjoy pussy sauce?" Danni asked, ripping the dildo out of my cunt. She held it out. "Try Sauce ala MILF."

The waitress leaned over. I trembled as the girl tore into the tip of the breadstick soaked in my pussy cream. Her eyes squeezed shut as she chewed. She groaned in delight, feasting on it while my lover thrust it into her mouth and took a large bite.

I took a bite of it, too, reveling in the wicked flavor of my own cunt cream. The waitress's face shone with ecstatic delight. She looked so wicked and delicious. This dinner date was going off to such a wicked and wonderful delight.

Danni swallowed hers. "Now, if you want to try more of the MILF's yummy sauce, you can always crawl beneath the table and sample it straight from the source."

I glanced at my lover and she winked at me. She was a naughty thing. She had grown so bold.

The barely legal waitress licked her lips. She looked around, her cheeks on fire. She trembled there, caught by indecision. She looked so cute and adorable. Her hair tumbled around her face. She shivered, her breasts rising and falling.

Her knees buckled. My smile grew as she sank down and crawled beneath the table. A wicked thrill shot through me as I felt her hair on my thighs. She said something, but it was lost to the noise of the restaurant. Her head moved between my thighs.

"Oh, she's going for it," I moaned.

"Good," my lover moaned and took another big bite of her breadstick. She chewed it, delight in her eyes.

The waitress came closer and closer to my married twat. Her hair stroked my thighs. My skirt rustled. I felt her breath washing up my legs to my twat. My snatch was getting so much love tonight. I could get used to being a lesbian MILF.

Then the waitress nuzzled into my pussy. She kissed right on my cuntlips. She smooched around, murmuring. The blonde waitress swept by again, having no clue her coworker was on her knees making out with my cunt or that my boob was still out.

Danni cupped my exposed, right breast and leaned over. She nuzzled my blonde hair aside to whisper in my ear, "How is it?"

"She's kissing all over my cunt," I moaned. "She's getting to know it and..." My words trailed off as a shiver ran through me. "Ooh, she just licked me for the first time. She's getting her first real taste of pussy."

"I know how delicious that is," moaned Danni. She licked my ear, sending another shiver through my flesh. "Just enjoy, Mrs. Smart. I want you to cum on her face. Just drown her in your passion."

"What are you going to do?" I moaned, her hand kneading my tit.

"Why, I think you still have breast milk left in your tit." She let out a purring moan. "Mmm, all that yummy breast milk."

She darted her head down as the blonde waitress strode back to the kitchen. I shuddered, my lover latching on. We could get caught, but I didn't care. I had one cute, young thing licking at my pussy and the other suckling at my nipple.

My breast milk jetted into Danni's mouth. She moaned and swallowed it down. She suckled with hunger. I shuddered, the bliss sweeping through my body. It was incredible to feel. I squeezed my eyes shut, my heart hammering in my chest.

It was incredible. Such a delight to experience. Ashley's tongue grew bolder and bolder. She licked with more and more confidence as she explored all my married folds. She loved my pussy, savoring the taste of a woman matured.

A mother's passion.

My nipple throbbed in Danni's hungry mouth. Her lips sealed tight about my nub, forming a seal. Her cheeks hollowed. She suckled with hunger. I gasped, the milk squirting out of my nub and bathing her mouth. It was incredible to enjoy. I shuddered, savoring every nurse.

Danni moaned around it, her passion buzzing around my nipple. My nub felt connected straight to my cunt being so wonderfully explored by Ashley's tongue. The waitress licked my folds and brushed my clit.

Then she thrust her tongue into my depths.

"Yes!" I gasped, my body shuddering at the delightful plunge of her tongue into me.

She stirred it around in me. I groaned, squeezing my eyes shut as the heat washed through me. This wonderful stirring of bliss through my flesh. I squirmed in place, loving every moment of it. The pleasure swept through my body. My toes curled as the passion swelled and swelled. It built in me.

"Yes!" I gasped. "Oh, yes, that's good. That's so good. Ashley!"

Danni popped her mouth off my nipple. Milk coated her lips. "What's she doing?"

"She's got her tongue jammed so deep into my cunt. She's wiggling around, just getting soaked in my juices."

"Good," Danni purred and then leaned down.

She latched onto my nipple again. She suckled hard. My mother's milk flowed into her mouth. I gasped, arching my back in the booth. My pussy clenched around Ashley's probing tongue. She stirred it around in me. It was incredible.

I groaned, loving every moment of her tongue probing in me. She swirled it around, stirring up all that wonderful passion in my snatch. It was incredible. I loved every moment of it. I whimpered and panted, my heart beating faster and faster.

Ashley's nose rubbed into my clit. Sparks burst as the naughty girl plundered my cunt. She moaned as she feasted on me, stimulating my labia with her passion. My body squirmed. My blonde hair rustled about my face.

Danni's hand massaged my tit now. She worked it like an udder, squeezing it. I groaned as my milk jetted out of my nipple and splashed against the back of her throat. I trembled, the bliss building and building in me. It was incredible.

I whimpered and moaned. The heat was amazing. It was incredible. This was what I needed. It was just delicious. A true delight that would have me exploding. I groaned, my heart pounding in my chest. My eyes squeezed shut.

"Oh, yes, yes!" I gasped. "Mmm, that's it. That's delicious. I'm going to cum. You two cuties are driving me wild."

Danni suckled hard. She squeezed my tit, working out more and more of my breast milk. I gasped, my pussy clenching around Ashley's probing tongue. Then she flicked it out and brushed my clit. I gasped, my entire body bucking from the surge of bliss that shot through me.

"Oh, god," I groaned. "That's it. Attack my clit. I'm going to cum."

Ashley swirled her tongue around my clit. She caressed me.

Teased me. I shuddered, this heat building and building in me. It was hurtling towards me. I squeezed my eyes shut, the sounds of the restaurant—the people talking, the clink of cutlery, the sounds of footsteps—washed over me.

I would cum right here. Right now. I would just howl out my pleasure. It was building so fast. That naughty, young waitress sucked on my clit. She nursed on it. The pleasure was incredible. My toes curled in my heels.

"I'm going to cum!" I gasped. "Yes!"

I exploded.

"This is the—"

Danni's head ripped and she kissed me before I could howl out. She shoveled my sweet breast milk into my mouth as I bucked through my orgasm. My pussy convulsed. Juices gushed out of me. Ashley lapped them up as I trembled through my ecstasy.

I kissed Danni with hunger. My tongue danced with hers. We passed my sweet breast milk back and forth. That warm delight spilled over our lips and ran down our chin. I groaned into the kiss, the pleasure washing out of me.

Wave after wave of delight swept through my body.

It was incredible. Intense. Stars danced before my eyes. I flowed through the wonderful rapture. It was amazing. I whimpered into the kiss, the milk spilling down my throat. It left this cantaloupe aftertaste behind.

Just delicious.

I panted, breaking the kiss. "Oh, god, that was good."

"Mmm, I bet it was," Danni panted.

Ashley licked my pussy one more time and then she crawled out from beneath the table. I shuddered as my date covered my breast. I panted, my entire body buzzing from that intense orgasm. The waitress stood up and grabbed a napkin.

She wiped at her sticky lips. When she finished, she said, "Um, are you ready... to order?"

"The sea bream," I groaned. "She'll have the cod with the plum sauce."

Danni nodded.

"Okay," panted the waitress. "It'll be up soon."

Soon... We had time to kill. "Do you have a break coming up?"

The waitress hesitated. "I could take it right now."

I grabbed my wine and took a long sip. "Do it. Meet us in the restroom. I'm not done with you."

She nodded.

Danni quivered.

The pair of us headed to the restrooms. The restaurant had remodeled a few years ago. Now they had a collection of gender-neutral restrooms, all single use, instead of a men's and a women's room. Very progressive and inclusive. And perfect for my fun. I pulled Danni into one.

"What are we doing?" she asked as I sat my purse on the counter beside a glass bowl holding decorative soaps shaped like seashells. I opened it and pulled out one of the toys I'd packed.

A thick, fleshy dildo attached to a stretchy, vinyl harness. I held it up to Danni. The girl gasped in delight. She gave me a wicked grin as she took it from me. Then she popped the tip into her mouth and sucked on it.

"You wicked thing," I groaned, gathering the skirt of my dress. I pulled it up my thighs. "I wanted you to put that on me, not suck it."

She winked at me, still nursing it.

I laughed at how sexy she looked. Her ruby lips slid up and down the fleshy shaft. She bobbed her head, her black ponytail swaying behind her. I groaned, pulling the dress up to my waist where a silver chain wrapped about my curvy hips.

I exposed my shaved pussy.

Danni popped the toy out of her mouth and fell to her knees. She leaned in, breathing in heavily a few inches from my pussy. Then she licked it. I gasped at the flicking contact across my bud. Sparks flared.

"Naughty babysitter," I moaned.

She giggled and held the strap-on for me to step into.

I did and shuddered as she worked the vinyl harness up my thighs. She tugged it here, pulled on it there. She brought it higher and higher up my body. I shuddered, this wicked heat billowing through me. It was such a kinky delight to experience her drawing the strap-on up my thighs. I groaned, my pussy on fire as she brought it higher and higher.

Past my knees, the harness caressed my thighs. She grinned up at me, the fleshy shaft bobbing before her face. Her glasses gleamed in the artificial light. She flicked her tongue over her lips. I groaned as she thrust the stretchy harness over my ass and waist. The dildo's base rubbed into my pussy lips.

"The girl at Secret Delights said this needs to be right on my clit for it to feel amazing for me," I moaned as Danni adjusted it.

"How's that?" she asked, smoothing the vinyl straps.

"Perfect," I groaned. The doorknob rattled.

"It's me," I heard a whisper.

Smiling, I opened the door and found Ashley standing there. She gasped at the strap-on thrusting from my crotch. Her eyes bulged at the gleaming tip. Then her gaze shot up to me. She quivered in her uniform, her tie swaying.

I grabbed it and pulled her in, the door closing behind her. I locked it with my free hand as I kissed her. The dildo pressed into the crotch her pants. She whimpered, her lips tasting of my sweet pussy. I loved it. My tongue danced with hers.

Then I broke it. "Drop your pants and panties, bend over the counter, and prepare to get fucked."

"Yes!" Ashley moaned.

"Ooh," Danni moaned, hopping onto the counter and spreading her legs. "Yes, yes, bend over right here. You haven't tried my sauce straight from the source yet."

"I haven't," Ashley moaned, her hands attacking the fly of her slacks as she headed to Danni.

My naughty babysitter's skirt rode up enough to show off her hairless pussy. That delicious twat beckoned to be eaten. I licked my lips, this wild heat blazing through me. I wiggled my hips from side to side, the dildo bobbing before me. It massaged my clit.

Delight tingled through me.

Ashley shoved down her slacks. She wore a purple thong beneath. It vanished into her butt-crack. I smiled in delight as I stared at that cute rump. My MILF lusts rose through me. My tongue flicked across my lips, heat swelling through me.

Then she hooked her thong next, throwing a look over her shoulder. She smiled, her cheeks blushed as bright as her hair, and thrust the skimpy panties off. It peeled out of her butt-crack and pulled away from her pussy. She bent over, showing off a trimmed, red bush framing her juicy pussy slit.

Her panties fell down to her ankles with her pants. She stayed bent over and nuzzled between my babysitter's thighs. Danni grinned in delight and then gasped as the naughty waitress began her feast. It was so hot to watch.

Danni grabbed her dress and yanked it down. Her breasts popped out. They jiggled there, round and perky and perfect. I shuddered at the sight of those eighteen-year-old titties. They were just so appealing.

My tongue flicked across my lips.

"Ooh, she's just going to town on my pussy, Mrs. Smart." Danni's green eyes sparkled behind her glasses. "Just feasting on my cunt. Mmm, she must have made you cum hard. She's not shy at all."

"It's just so good," moaned Ashley.

"Yes, it is," I purred, advancing on her, my pussy cream dripping down my thighs. The scent of hot cunt filled the air. My sweet, Danni's spicy, and a tangy musk from the waitress. I breathed in the heady mix.

What a delicious bouquet.

I pressed my fake dick against her pussy, nuzzling through the trimmed curls. The base massaged my clit. Little waves of delight washed through me already. I shuddered, savoring it as I worked the rubbery tip up and down her folds.

I found the entrance to her twat and pressed in. Slowly. I took my time, groaning at the pressure rubbing on my clit. My bud pulsed and sparked. Delight rippled through me as I went deeper and deeper into the girl's twat.

She groaned into Danni's pussy. Ashley wiggled her cute rump, feasting away on Danni's twat. The redhead's moans grew louder the more of the dildo I pushed into her cunt. It was so exciting to do this to her.

A heady rush.

I groaned as I bottomed out in her. My breasts jiggled. My smile grew while my pussy clenched. This heat was such a wicked thing to enjoy. I then drew back my hips, pulling the dildo out of her pussy. It emerged gleaming in her juices.

"Oh, yes, yes, just like that," Danni moaned. She threw back her head, hair dancing. She's doing such *naughty* things to my pussy, Mrs. Smart."

"Good," I panted and reached behind me. As I thrust my dildo back into Ashley's pussy, I untied the knot holding up the top of my dress.

It came undone.

The two triangles fell away from my breasts. The dress draped over the girl's rump. My large tits appeared, both large and ripe. They quivered as I buried into the girl while Danni stared at them with such hunger. Her hands grabbed her own perky titties, squeezing them.

She moaned in wanton passion. I grinned at her and grabbed Ashley's hips. I held her tight, brushing the tails of her blouse, and thrust harder into her pussy. My clit burst in delight, loving every moment of it. The pleasure swept through me.

"Oh, yes, yes!" I gasped, pumping away at the barely legal pussy. My dildo slammed into her over and over again. "You naughty waitress. You're going to make my date cum."

"Yes, Mrs. Smart!" Ashley moaned.

"Big time!" Danni gasped. "Ooh, that's right. Just do that to me." Her fingers dug into her tits. "Mrs. Smart, this is the best date ever!"

"I know!" I groaned as I pumped away.

I fucked into Ashley hard and fast. I drilled into her with my big dildo. I buried into her again and again, my crotch smacking into her rump. The pressure on my clit flared with every thrust. My pussy clenched, drinking in the pleasure. It swelled through me with every thrust.

I pumped my way to an orgasm. This was so different. I gasped and groaned, burying that dildo over and over into Ashley's cunt. She moaned into Danni's twat. The redhead wiggled her hips as she feasted. The dildo shifted around my clit, stroking it. I loved it.

My breasts heaved. They bounced and smacked together. The bathroom echoed with the sounds of our passion. Danni threw back her head, her glasses shifting on her nose. Her tits jiggled in her hand as she kneaded them.

"Oh, yes, yes, just like that!" she groaned. "Oh, Ashley. You naughty slut. Yes, get that tongue in me." A shudder ran through Danni. "I'm going to cum. I'm going to cum so hard on your mouth!"

"Do it!" I moaned, my own orgasm building faster and faster.

Ashley moaned. And then she squealed. Something hot splashed my thighs when I buried into her. Juices ran down my leg. I groaned, the cream on the dildo emerging from her twat covered in froth now. I gasped, slamming back into her as the girl climaxed on my dildo.

She groaned into Danni's pussy. I fucked Ashley hard. My clit throbbed and ached as the trembling waitress took my dildo over and over again. More cream gushed out of her pussy, splashing my vulva and running hot down my thighs.

"Oh, fuck, yes!" Danni howled, throwing back her head. "Lick up all my cream!"

"Yes, yes, feast on my sexy babysitter!" I moaned and thrust forward.

My clit burst with pleasure. I came.

My pussy convulsed. I trembled there, gripping Ashley's hips as my orgasm swept through me. My tits heaved. They smacked together. The pleasure blazed through me. Cream gushed down my thighs while I whimpered.

"Oh, my god!" Ashley moaned, her voice muffled. "So good."

"It is!" Danni moaned, squirming, her face twisting in rapture.

The pleasure soared me to the heights of ecstasy. I quivered there, my tits swaying together. My pussy sent out a final wave of delight. I gasped, my blonde hair dancing about my shoulders. I savored it. I loved being a lesbian MILF.

"This is amazing!" I groaned.

Panting, coming down from my orgasmic high, I pulled out of Ashley's pussy. My dildo dripped in rapture. The girl slumped to her knees, panting, whimpering. She had such a climax on me. Danni hopped off the counter, her tits bouncing.

She grinned at me and pulled down the strap-on off of me. My skirt fell down my thighs again. As I tied my dress back behind my neck, covering my tits, Danni sucked on the dildo. She nursed on it, cleaning off the waitress's pussy juices.

"Mmm, that's so good," she moaned when she finished. "Shall we?"

I grinned at her.

Danni and I left Ashley panting and happy in the restroom. I loved using my strap-on. Such a great purchase. I was thrilled with it. Danni and I returned to our table where our wine awaited us. We sipped it.

Soon, the blonde waitress brought us our dinner since Ashley was still on her break. It was delicious. The sea bream melted in my mouth, and I stole a few bites of Danni's cod in the plum sauce. What a wonderful treat to enjoy.

We didn't have time for dessert. The symphony was starting soon. Ashley took the bill, back from her break. I gave her a generous tip on my husband's credit card. She'd earned every penny of it, the naughty delight.

I stood up and offered my arm to Danni. "Ready to enjoy beautiful music and decadent pleasure?"

"Yes, I am," she cooed, beaming at me.

I was so glad that I took Danni out on date night. She was so much fun. Being a lesbian MILF was just a treat. I was eager for how this night would end. My pussy simmering, we left the restaurant behind to have more sapphic fun.

To be continued...

# Mrs. Smart's Sapphic Symphony

## Lesbian MILF's Date Night 3

## A Lesbian MILF Tale

by

Reed James

# Mrs. Smart's Sapphic Symphony

## Clarissa Smart – Friday, Day 5 of the Wish

Date night was going great.

I just wasn't on it with my husband. but instead, the sexy babysitter we'd hired for the night.

Danni was a radiant and adorable cutie sitting in the passenger seat of my car, a huge smile on her lips. Glasses perched on her adorable nose, her green eyes flashing in the passing headlights and streetlamps. She wore a borrowed sheath dress of mine. Dark-red and clinging to her nubile and young body like a glove.

It didn't fit me any longer.

I had a baby recently and my tits grew two cup sizes. I wore an elegant, black dress, my large breasts covered by two triangles that had thin straps that were tied behind my neck. A silver chain clad my curving waist. My body buzzed with excitement from dinner.

And that sexy waitress we'd enjoyed, Ashley, had been a true joy to fuck with my strap-on in the bathroom while she ate out my date's pussy.

Becoming a lesbian MILF was the greatest thing in the world. There was nothing like teaching nubile, young girls the delights of sapphic passion. I didn't know what was happening to the world, why women and cuties were making the plunge onto the other side, but I was loving it.

"Oh, god, this is going to be great, Mrs. Smart," Danni said, her body shuddering in the seat. "What are they playing tonight?"

"It's a collection of baroque pieces," I said. "It's going to be stirring. You'll love them. There's nothing like hearing a symphony play live."

The girl groaned in eager anticipation.

It was ironic that I only liked symphonies because my husband, while we were dating, took me to one to show off. We dressed up all fancily and we're pretending to be adults. I had fallen in love with the music. The majesty of it. Since then, he had to tolerate it. When I found out that Danni loved the symphony after she'd shown up at our house to babysit, I had an idea.

Why not take her instead of my husband? He could watch the game and our daughter, and I could have a passionate evening with a young woman. And since I'd become a lesbian MILF a few days ago, it seemed perfect.

It wasn't like there would be any passion between my husband and me.

I squirmed in the driver seat; we were approaching the philharmonic. I shivered, my pussy growing so wet. I had no panties on, my juices soaking my thighs. There was a definite musk in the air. A mix of my sweet and her spicy delight that tickled my nose.

It was just a wonderful bouquet to enjoy.

"There it is!" Danni squealed. The eighteen-year-old girl bounced in her seat, her ponytail of black hair swishing behind her as she leaned forward. Her seatbelt pressed between her round tits, her nipples poking hard at the dark-red material. She pushed up her glasses as she moaned, "Oh, my god, Mrs. Smart. This is like a dream. Or a fairy tale."

"Oh, no," I gasped in mock shock, putting a hand on her thigh. "I'll have to get you back to my place before midnight."

She giggled. "And what are you going to do there?"

I winked at her.

My pussy simmering, I pulled us off to the side before we got to the valet parking. She glanced at me, brow furrowing. "What? Are we going to do some making out before we get up there?"

"Can I have your phone?" I asked.

She blinked and then handed it over. I took it and went to the website. The salesgirl at Secret Delights had shown me how to do this. It was so weird having to use a website to install an app and not the Google Play store. I had to give it all sorts of permissions, but then it was downloading it and installing it.

"What are you doing?" Danni asked.

"Putting a naughty app on your phone," I said and then opened my purse. I dug around in it to find the exact toys. I pulled out a pair of egg vibrators. They were blue and smooth. I had to juggle them and operate her phone to mine. But in a moment, I had them paired, one each to our devices through Bluetooth.

I handed her the egg paired to my phone and her phone back. She blinked and then she looked at her phone. The app showed a simple bar that let her control the settings of the egg vibrator. How hard it hummed.

"You have control of this one," I said, holding it up. Then I began hiking my long skirt. I drew it up and up my legs. I reached beneath and pressed the egg vibrator into my pussy lips. I groaned as it slipped inside. My back arched as it vanished into my twat. I could feel it in me. I gripped.

"And you have this one?" she gasped and then shoved hers beneath her skirt, her legs spreading wide. She shuddered and let out a whimpering moan. Then she pulled her hands back out. "Done."

"Good," I said and pulled my hand out from beneath my thighs. I approached the front of the music hall, my pussy clenching around the egg. I had such a naughty smile on my face.

Just as we pulled up at the valet, my toy buzzed inside of me.

I gasped, "Danni!"

"Ooh, it worked!" she said, grinning at me. "This is going to make the music even more intense, isn't it?"

"That's the plan," I said, shuddering as the egg buzzed away. Was that the lowest setting? It was just the slightest hum to get me squirming.

I grabbed my phone as the valet opened Danni's door to help her out. As she stepped out with the young man's help, I activated her toy. The young girl gasped. She stumbled for a moment, clutching onto the valet's white sleeve.

"You okay?" he asked her.

"Yes, yes, just a shocking itch," she said. "I'm fine."

I smiled, savoring that slight hum in my pussy.

The valet helped me out. I thanked him and sauntered around the car to my date, the egg vibrator shifting in my pussy. I shuddered, my cheeks warm with the delight rising through me. My inner thighs grew stickier with the juices leaking out of me.

"Mrs. Smart," Danni groaned, "oh, my god, that feels so naughty. I can't believe we're doing this."

"I know," I said, taking her arm.

We sauntered towards the doors, following in a few others, the men dressed in tuxedos, the women all elegant on their arms. I shuddered, my pussy gripping that naughty toy. It massaged my inner walls. We were both feeling such naughty pleasure.

And no one around us had any idea.

I gripped my phone in my left hand, my breasts rising and falling. I handed over the tickets when we got inside and an usher led us to our seats. It was almost showtime, the main stage in darkness. I noticed that they had the balcony's blocked off with velvety ropes.

"This is amazing, Mrs. Smart," gushed Danni. She looked around at the grand hall. I must have felt like this the first time I saw the place. I would have had that same of awe on my face as I gazed around at all the majesty.

"I know," I told her, smiling at her enthusiasm. "Mmm, we're going to have a great time, aren't we?"

She nodded, a shiver running through her body. She licked her lips, her head casting back and forth. We reached our row and moved through the seats. We were near the edge. We passed a few people then I took my seat beside a gorgeous woman in a blue dress. She was older than me by a few years, mid-thirties. Her brown hair fell in curls about her lovely face. Her neckline had a swoop cut to it, showing off a delicious amount of cleavage. Dark stockings covered her legs.

When she shifted, her skirt's hem moved. She wore thigh-highs. How delightful.

I smiled hungrily at her as I sat down. She glanced at me and smiled back. She shifted in her chair. I wondered if she was feeling it. That lesbian switch flicking inside of her. Sometimes, I met women where it had already happened to them. Other times, I could see it blossoming in their eyes. That moment of sapphic awakening.

"Oh, my god," whispered Danni as we sat by each other. She clutched a program in her hand she'd gotten from the usher, staring at the music that would be played tonight. Her phone was in her other hand.

She tapped that.

I gasped as the vibrator buzzed louder inside of me. I crossed my legs tightly, squeezing my cunt around that naughty toy. I closed my eyes and enjoyed the humming sensation. My heart pounded faster, the heat pumping through my veins.

Danni had such a big grin on her face. She arched an eyebrow in a daring manner. I licked my lips and then casually turned on my phone and tapped the screen. Her eyes widened. She arched her back and then let out a happy sigh.

"Thanks," she moaned. "Mmm, that's good."

I nodded. "Dim your phone's screen. We don't want to distract others."

"No, no," she moaned, doing just that. I did the same, lowering the brightness so I could barely see the screen. "Ooh, Mrs. Smart, I could just simmer like this for hours."

I leaned over and kissed her on the mouth. I didn't care who saw us. The woman on my left shifted, her skirt rustling. My tongue played with my lover's while the egg vibrator buzzed away with happy delight in my pussy.

It was incredible. It buzzed through me while my tongue danced with hers. Then the house lights fell. A ripple of applause washed through the symphony hall. I shuddered, kissing my date for one more second then breaking it.

The conductor stood on the stage, the orchestra spread out behind him. They were all dressed so elegantly. A woman on the left edge with a violin had a long slit up her dress's side, showing off her gorgeous leg to the audience.

Danni quivered beside me as the conductor gave his spiel, introducing the theme of the night. Danni had such rapt attention on her face, staring forward, waiting for the music to start. She was such a gorgeous creature.

I casually tapped my screen.

She bucked and gasped beside me. She leaned forward and then rocked back. I knew my vibrator, only on the second setting, wasn't easy for me to ignore. So what must the third setting be like for Danni?

I knew I would find out soon.

Danni squeezed her eyes shut, her lips parted as she sighed. Plump, ruby lips that gleamed. They demanded that I lean over and kiss her again. She licked them and then her eyes opened. She glanced at me.

I winked at her.

She turned her phone on as the conductor tapped his podium. He faced the symphony. He raised his arms. The orchestra was all ready to play. Then the first of the woodwinds and the strings played. Clarinets and violins with an oboe in there.

My vibrator buzzed faster.

My thighs squeezed tight. As the beautiful music swept over me, pleasures rushed through my body. My pussy gripped the humming toy, drinking in the pleasure. My breasts rose faster and faster. My date had such a huge smile on her lips.

She tapped her phone again.

I shuddered as my vibrator kicked up to level four. I hadn't even gotten used to the third setting. I clenched my jaw against the moan wanting to burst from me. It was churning up my pussy now. Pleasure radiated out through my body. I shifted, crossing and recrossing my thighs, my skirt rustling.

That little brat smirked while the symphony grew louder. More strings came in. A timpani played a beat in the back. Wind chimes rang. My breasts rose and fell as the brass section came in, adding power to the swelling song.

"You little slut," I groaned beneath my breath.

Danni just smirked there.

I would get her back. I squeezed my eyes shut for a moment,

my body drinking in the bliss that swept through me, adapting to it. God, I could just surrender into this and cum already. It was so wonderful.

The music washed around me. The aural delight mixed with the rapture buzzing away in my cunt. Classical music and vibrators went so well together. I groaned, gripping my phone. My pussy melted around the toy. The scent of my sweet musk grew.

I opened my eyes and glanced at Danni. She was caught up in the music, staring with starry eyes at the front. Her glasses slipped down her nose. She absently pushed them up as she watched. I casually turned on my phone. Glancing down, trying not to move my head or make it obvious, I tapped my screen twice.

She joined me at level five.

Her entire body bucked. She clapped a hand over her mouth and squirmed in the seat. Her round breasts jiggled so wonderfully in her sheath dress. They bounced around as the egg vibrator went to town on her. She squeezed her eyes shut. Squeaks breached her mouth.

I smiled and savored the buzzing in my own pussy. The music and her trembling filled me with such joy. My body was alive. The orchestra's power and passion spilled over me. I drank it in along with the naughty egg stimulating my cunt.

"Mrs. Smart," she breathed as she relaxed. She shot me a grin.

I winked at her.

At the middle setting, the buzzing could bring me to an orgasm if I surrendered to it. My pleasure built and built in me as the symphony played through the song. They reached the end of the piece and went into something light and airy, springtime personified.

That time of heady romance and sweet kisses.

I grabbed Danni's hand. She squeezed mine, shuddering beside me as we both experienced the naughty humming of our toys blazing away in our pussies. My breasts rose and fell, nipples poking at the fabric. Juices soaked my thighs.

Her spicy musk filled my nose, mixed with my sweet aroma. Her hand twitched in my hand. She whimpered as the music swelled again. Her breasts rose and fell. It was so majestic. Just absolutely perfect.

My body felt so alive when the second song ended.

The third began with a whisper that built and built. The intensity of it swelled my orgasm. As the orchestra rose towards their crescendo, so did my pleasure. I shuddered, wanting to make this even naughtier.

I grabbed my phone and nudged hers up to level six.

Danni bucked in her seat while the woman beside me glanced at us. I could feel her eyes watching us. She knew we were doing *something*. She licked her lips, her nipples poking at the front of her dress. She crossed her legs, her nylons whisking.

As my egg kicked up another level, the naughty toys sending rapture through me, I leaned over and whispered, "We have vibrators in our pussies and are controlling them with our phones."

The woman's eyes widened.

"Mmm, isn't my date just a cutie. Eighteen. Oh, just the perfect thing for a married MILF to enjoy. We're going to make each other cum so hard. Nothing like a young woman to make a mature beauty like us cum."

The woman glanced at the man on her right then back at me in shock. I smiled at her, noting her wedding ring. I leaned back and let the vibrations ripple through me. I was going to have such an amazing orgasm.

The music filled the hall as my vibrator churned away inside of my cunt. I couldn't take much more of this. I gripped Danni's hand. She squeezed tight. I glanced at her, seeing the pleasure crossing her face. Her green eyes met mine.

We both hit our phones at nearly the same moment.

Level seven.

It was intense. That little egg in me buzzed, churning me up. My pussy drank in the rapture. I couldn't fight it now. I let out the softest sight as the music surged around us. The strings and woodwinds, the percussion drumming and the brass singing. It was all so wonderful. It filled the air with majesty.

Passion.

My body fed on it. I gripped my lover's hand as I climbed towards my release. My pussy clenched about the buzzing egg. I squirmed in my seat. I squeezed my jaws shut while stars danced before my eyes. I was so close. I hovered on the edge.

"You're not going to..." the woman beside me whispered.

"I am," I breathed. "Oh, lord, I am."

Right there in the middle of the symphony, the orchestra's passion ringing out through the air, I climaxed.

My pussy convulsed and writhed around the egg vibrator buzzing away in me. Waves of rapture swept through my body. I let out a groan, my words drowned out by the majesty of the orchestra playing their hearts out.

They serenaded my lover and me. They celebrated our pleasure. Danni gripped my hand, her breasts jiggling as she squirmed through her orgasm. I could tell she felt that same ecstasy I did. That her climax gripped her flesh.

I squeezed my thighs tight. My pussy clenched around my egg vibrator. More waves of bliss washed through my body. That euphoria spilled through my mind, caressing my brain with rapture. I felt the MILF to my left watching with stunned awe. My large breasts strained at my dress, wanting to escape.

I wanted to cry out. The orchestra's passion hit their peak and died into silence. For a moment, I whimpered and then applause thundered around us. Everyone was clapping at that majestic performance.

"Yes, yes, yes!" I moaned, my pussy gripping that buzzing egg.

"It's majestic!" gasped Danni, her body bucking through her orgasm.

"I can't... You two..." moaned the woman to my left.

I shuddered and then I turned off Danni's toy.

A moment later, my vibrator shut off, too. Without the buzzing, my orgasm hit that climax. As the applause died down, so did my pleasure. I panted, my eyes fluttering. My breasts rose and fell with my gulps of air.

"I can't believe you did that," the woman whispered.

I glanced over at her. "Did it make you wet?"

She blushed and looked away as the symphony began its next performance. On my other side, Danni slumped back into her seat, staring up front with lidded eyes. Her tits swelled the front of her dress. She pushed up her glasses.

"Magnificent," she purred, glancing at me.

I leaned over, my body buzzing from the rapture, and kissed her on the mouth. I savored the feel of her against me. Her lips were magnificent. They felt so soft and kissable against me. She closed her eyes and whimpered, her mouth working against mine.

Then the next song started up. I broke the kiss and leaned back, buzzing on my orgasmic high and enjoying the music. The MILF squirmed. She kept glancing at me, her hands rubbing at her stockings. The poor woman needed satisfaction.

I had to help her.

I leaned over to the woman and shivered, "I'm Clarissa. Clarissa Smart. I think you need to cum."

"W-what?" the woman whispered back, a playful song starting up, the flutes almost laughing like maidens.

"You need an orgasm. Come with us. We're going to get you off. You ever have a barely legal cutie and a fellow MILF eat out your pussy?"

"N-no." She glanced at her husband.

"Just tell him you have to powder your nose." I smiled. "We're women. We're infamous for going to the bathroom in flocks."

She swallowed, her cheeks blushing bright. She seemed shocked that she was even doing this. She leaned over and whispered something to her husband. My pussy clenched on the vibrator buried in my twat.

My date leaned over, "Are we playing with a MILF now?"

"I thought you'd like that," I said and stood up, the egg shifting around in my twat.

Danni grinned and rose. "You're the best, Mrs. Smart."

I winked at her.

The three of us filed past the few people on the end and reached the aisle. We swept up it, passing all these elegantly dressed people who had no idea that we were going to have a lesbian threesome. Two MILFs and one young thing.

Perfection.

I could feel the other MILF's eyes on my rump as I walked, following me, confused about what was going on. This heady rush shot through me. My heart pounded in my chest. It was incredible to experience, my twat on fire.

We climbed the stairs, my hips swaying. I fanned my face, the blazing heat threatening to consume me. My breasts jiggled while that naughty vibrator, even off, sent delight spilling through my twat. We stepped out of the hall into the quiet mezzanine, the music muted.

"I can't believe I'm doing this," the woman said. "You two aren't really going to...?"

"Share your pussy and eat you out?" I asked, giving her a big grin. "Yes, we are."

"You don't even know my name," the brunette groaned, her stocking thighs whisking together. She looked around, frightened. "What if my husband finds out."

"My husband knows I'm on a date with Danni. He took it mostly well."

Danni giggled. "He did look stunned. You are a wicked wife, Mrs. Smart."

"And you're a naughty cutie," I purred and pulled her to me. I kissed her right there in front of the other MILF. I felt her watching us, trembling. Her body squirmed. Those wonderful nylons rubbed together, making that beautiful sound.

Danni broke the kiss and then she went to the MILF and threw her arms around the woman's neck. "I'm Danni. Eighteen and just so eager to do naughty things to you."

"Shannon," she groaned.

"Last name?" My lover quivered. "I have to address you properly. It's hotter for me."

"M-Murphy."

"Well, Mrs. Murphy, I'm going to eat your pussy out and make you explode. How does that sound?"

"Oh, god," she whimpered, her entire body trembling.

"I know," Danni said. "You're going to be saying that a lot." Then she kissed the MILF.

I shuddered, watching my babysitter making out with Shannon. My pussy clenched, juices running down my thighs. Their lips moved together. Their tongues danced. The MILF and the young cutie moaned as their bodies melted together, dresses rustling.

Danni broke the kiss. "Mmm, see, that's better than kissing your husband."

"Oh, my, it was," she groaned, fanning her face. "What are you doing to me?"

"So many, many things," the girl cooed. "You're going to love it!"

I winked at Shannon. "This way."

I led them to the roped-off area to the balcony. No one was around. I unhooked it and grinned at them. Danni giggled and Shannon looked worried, her large breasts rising and falling as she looked around. But she let herself get dragged to the stairs by Danni. Once they were passed, I rehooked the rope and hurried up after them.

God, that egg vibrator felt incredible just massaging my flesh as I rushed up the stairs.

It led up to the private boxes. We went into the nearest one, four seats that overlooked the audience and the symphony. The music surged over us. I shuddered as Danni kissed the MILF again, the girl's hands squeezing the woman's boobs through her dress.

I watched the pair, my smile growing. I knew this would be such a wild night. Danni hooked her fingers into the front of Shannon's dress and tugged. She pulled the fabric down and exposed those big and lush breasts. They spilled out, soft and gorgeous, cupped by the stretch material of her dress. Diamonds glinted about her neck as she shuddered.

"Mmm, boobies!" Danni cooed and ducked her head down. She engulfed a dark-red nipple and sucked.

Shannon moaned.

The married woman swayed there. Pleasure crossed her face. A smile grew as if she were surprised by the delight she received. That expression of opening a present and finding out that it was just what you needed. I smiled.

Danni cupped the woman's left tit and jiggled it as if in invitation to me. My naughty date kept sucking on the woman's nub. I shuddered and swept in. I leaned over and nuzzled into that nipple. My mouth latched on.

I suckled with hunger.

I nursed on her nub. I loved the feel of her in my mouth. My tongue darted around her areola and stroked her nub. It was such a wonderful experience to feel that fat nub in my mouth. Her nipples were so much larger than Danni's.

It was fun sucking on them even without breast milk.

"Oh, my god," Shannon moaned, her voice mixing with the delicious strings filling the music hall with majesty. "That's... Oh, that's so good. I didn't know..."

"How good a woman's mouth felt on your nipple?" Danni asked. She nipped her nub and then sucked on it.

"Yes!" Shannon moaned.

I popped my mouth off her nipple and straightened. I stared into her hazel eyes, leaning in to kiss her. Before our lips met, I purred, "Wait until we're eating your pussy."

Her mouth tasted so sweet, her lipstick waxy smooth. I tasted a bit of Danni on her, loving that. The naughty girl kept nursing while her hand shot up. She reached behind my back and untied the knot holding up the front of my dress.

As I made out with my fellow MILF, our tongues just starting to play, the triangles covering my large breasts fell away. The air kissed my nipples. I groaned in delight, rubbing my right boob into her left, our nipples brushing as our lips worked together.

It was so exciting.

"Ooh, two nipples," Danni squealed.

The girl sucked both our nubs into her mouth. Shannon groaned. I moaned. It was so exciting to feel my nipple and hers together in Danni's mouth. The girl's tongue caressed over them. She teased us. The pleasure rippled through my body. I groaned, my cunt on fire. I squeezed my thighs tight, the bliss tingling around my flesh.

Shannon broke our kiss and moaned. "She really likes nipples."

"Mmm, she suckled dry all my breast milk," I moaned. "Such a naughty babysitter."

"She's your babysitter?" gasped Shannon.

I winked at her. "Now she's my naughty date. So much more fun than going out with my husband. He *hates* the symphony."

"So do I," groaned Shannon. "Or I used to. This is... I mean... You two are making me so wet."

"Maybe we should do something about that," I said, my nipple throbbing beside hers in Danni's hunger mouth.

She suckled hard. A bit of my milk squirted into her mouth. Then she popped her lips off of our nubs and moaned, "Let's eat her out, Mrs. Smart. Let's make Mrs. Murphy cum so hard, she'll always remember the symphony with delight."

"Mmm, that music *is* getting romantic," I moaned, a harp strumming with the woodwinds. "Feel that passion, Shannon?"

"Yes!" she gasped. "I feel it."

"Embrace it!"

I sank down to my knees before her, Danni joining me. She grabbed the front of her dark-red dress and shoved it down. Her breasts popped out, round and perky, They swayed together as she nodded her head in satisfaction.

"Feeling left out?" asked as I pushed up Shannon's skirt.

"You two have your boobs out," she said. "Why not me? My tits are top-notch."

"Yes, they are," I groaned, my pussy on fire. I was having such a magical time with Danni.

I rolled Shannon's skirt up and over her waist. She wore a pair of black panties, lacy and ruffled. Her musk bled through the fabric, a wonderful, tart aroma. My nose breathed it in. I groaned, my mouth watering. My pussy clenched, a wicked heat surging through me.

I glanced at my naughty date. She reached up with me, and our fingers hooked the waistband of the MILF's panties. Shannon's big boobs swayed heavily over us as we drew down her naughty delights. A brown bush appeared, curls trimmed. The tart aroma swelled. Dewdrops appeared on her curls. I could just make out her thick pussy lip in the dim light of the balcony.

As we revealed her pussy, the orchestra's melody reached a passionate crescendo, two lovers coming together in ecstasy. I licked my lips, aching for the three of us to find that same release. The panties rolled down Shannon's thighs. They slid down the MILF's legs to pile around her feet.

She stepped out of them, trembling. "I need this. Please, Clarissa and Danni..." Shannon parted her legs, her wonderful musk spilling over my nose. I breathed it in, that heady aroma spilling over my nose. "Eat me out."

"Yes!" Danni exclaimed and dove in.

"You little brat!" I gasped as she beat me to the MILF pussy.

I nuzzled in as Danni licked, having to push her face over to make room between the MILF's thighs. My tongue licked and lapped at the MILF's pussy, sliding through her tart folds while her silky curls rubbed on my nose and right cheek. My left cheek rubbed against Danni's smooth features. I felt her jaw moving as she licked.

Our tongues passed each other.

"Oh, my god," Shannon moaned.

"Mmm, told her," Danni murmured and fluttered her tongue up and down the MILF's slit.

I joined her.

We licked and lapped at Shannon's married twat. Her tart cream spilled over my chin. My pussy gripped the vibrator buried inside of me as I devoured this wonderful twat. Shannon's hips wiggled from side to side, her passion singing through the air. It was incredible to hear, blending in with the passion of the performance.

That fiery heat from the orchestra fed my tongue dancing and licking over her pussy. Mine slipped past Danni's all the time. We brushed, almost kissing each other over and over as we shared this tart and mature pussy.

Danni's tongue buried into Shannon's cunt. She bucked, her tits heaving over our head. She grabbed them, squeezing them as she moaned. Her juices ran over my tongue as her pussy grew hotter and hotter.

I brushed her clit with my tongue.

I played with it.

"Oh, my god!" gasped Shannon. "You two. I've never... This is... Oh, my god!"

Such joy burst through me at the delight we were churning in her. The wonderful bliss that we stirred in her cunt. My tongue danced over her hot clit. I caressed her bud. Licked at that naughty pearl. I savored every moment of teasing her. Juices spilled down my chin.

My pussy clenched. The heat dribbled down my thighs. My tongue swirled around her clit. Then Danni's was joining mine licking at that naughty pearl. I let her enjoy the MILF's clit while I went for her pussy hole. I thrust my tongue into Shannon's depths

She gasped.

The music sang ecstasy. It thrummed in the cellos deep, melodic rumble and in the trumpets breathy declaration. The sigh of flutes and the whimpers of the plucked harp shivering through the music hall.

Shannon's cunt clenched around my tongue. I massaged her pussy walls. I swirled around in her, watching her squeezing her tits. She gripped them, held them tight. Her passion spilled across her face. She whimpered, her body shuddering from the pleasure I gave her.

It was so exciting. I fluttered my tongue around in her delicious cunt. I massaged her while Danni sucked on her clit. Pleasure spilled across her face. She threw back her head, her brown hair swaying about her face.

"Yes!" she cried out as the orchestra burst with rapturous harmony.

Her pussy went wild around my tongue. Tart juices squirted out.

I moaned, licking and lapping up the flood. Danni groaned beside me, her tongue fluttering, too. We gathered up that cream, licked it out of Shannon and sharing in the MILF's pleasure together. It was such a heady thrill.

Then the music died. Thunderous applause celebrated Shannon's first lesbian orgasm. She whimpered and moaned through it. I bet her husband was clapping, oblivious to his wife's sapphic pleasure.

"Oh, my god!" moaned Shannon. She stumbled back and caught herself on a seat. She panted. "That was amazing."

"Yep," Danni said, turned, and kissed me. With passion. We shared the MILF's tart flavor while Shannon moaned over us.

She looked down, breathing heavily. I could feel it. She wanted to do naughty things to us. I shuddered, broke my kiss with Danni, and stood up. I grabbed my phone out of my discarded purse and then hiked my skirt. I pulled it higher and higher, Shannon's eyes staring at my legs. She licked her pink lips with hunger. They gleamed with her saliva.

She shuddered and groaned when I unveiled my shaved pussy, the landing strip of blonde hair leading to my folds.

"Oh, my god," moaned Shannon as she sank to her knees before me.

"Pull out her vibrator and shove it in your own pussy," Danni said, gripping her own phone.

"Just reach in me," I purred and turned on Danni's to three.

She gasped behind me.

Shannon pressed her fingers into my pussy. I groaned as they sank into my hot flesh. She found the egg vibrator. She grabbed it and tugged it out. I shuddered, squeezing my cuntal muscles to push it out. I groaned, strained.

It popped out into Shannon's hand, gleaming with my cream. With eager delight, she shoved it up between her thighs and into her married pussy. She shuddered as she sank it in and then gasped. Danni giggled behind me.

"Oh, my god, yes!" moaned Shannon, the pleasure rippling through her.

She buried her face between my thighs. I gasped as her lips kissed at my pussy. Then she licked at me. Her tongue fluttered through my folds, stroking me with such wild hunger. My moans joined the serenading clarinets filling the music hall with passion.

I pushed Danni's vibrator up to four. The sexy girl moaned behind me. Then she grabbed my right butt-cheek and parted it from my left. She exposed my butthole. The naughty minx dove in and kissed my asshole. I shuddered, her tongue sliding around my sphincter as Shannon's fluttered through my pussy folds.

"Yes!" I moaned out to the growing passion of the symphony's finale. A stirring piece that had me shivering.

Danni swirled her tongue around my asshole. She caressed it, teasing me. Her tongue slathered over my sphincter. She worshiped it with passion. I groaned and turned the intensity up on her vibrator. She moaned.

Shannon groaned.

I stared down at the MILF past my heaving tits. Her hips wiggled, her exposed rump curvy and bubbly. She thrust her tongue into my pussy. She swirled it around in me and feasted on me with such hunger.

At the same time, Danni pressed her tongue against my asshole. She swirled and danced around it, teasing me. The heat swept through my body. I groaned, my heart pounding in my chest. I threw back my head, my fingers flexing and relaxing. It was such a wonderful treat to enjoy. I savored every lick and lap.

"Oh, yes, you two are amazing!"

Their tongues danced through my holes. They stirred up my velvety bowels and my juicy pussy. The MILF and the cutie both played with me. Both had me adding my passionate voice to the beauty of the symphony.

It was like they played just for us, their passion building with mine. I groaned, my breasts swaying and jiggling. My hips wiggled from side to side, the heat surging through my body. I bit my lip, groaning in delight at the passion that was swelling larger and larger in me.

The amazing orgasm I would have. It was incredible. A true joy to experience. I whimpered, my fingers flexing and relaxing. My heart pounded in my chest as the pleasure swept through my body. It was incredible to experience.

I squeezed my eyes shut. My heart pounded faster and faster. The blood roared hot through my veins as their tongues danced through my holes. I turned up the buzzing on Danni's toy. She squealed into my asshole.

"Mrs. Smart!"

"Oh, Danni!" Shannon moaned into my pussy. "Oh, that's good. I'm going to cum."

"Yes, yes, yes!" I gasped. "Let's all cum!"

Danni sealed her lips around my asshole and sucked. I gasped at the naughty pressure on my asshole. My cunt clenched about Shannon's tongue darting into my folds. Her large breasts rubbed into my thighs as she feasted on me. She gripped my hips, devouring me.

My own big boobs heaved. I groaned, my orgasm building and building. The music sang around us. Wonderful string and bold brasses filled the audience hall. Cymbals crashed and shivered. The timpani thundered with the same fiery passion that pumped through my veins.

"Oh, my god!" I moaned and turned Danni's vibrator to max.

She sucked so hard on my asshole as she squealed. Her left hand squeezed on my butt-cheek. Then she jammed her tongue deep into my bowels. She wiggled it around, adding that naughty stimulation that flowed to my pussy.

Shannon's lisp found my clit. She sucked hard on it. "Yes!" I gasped. "Oh, god, yes!"

My hips wiggled from side to side, grinding my pussy lips on Shannon's mouth. She nursed on my bud while Danni's tongue swirled through my asshole. Sparks flared through my pussy. My blonde hair swayed about my face.

Shannon sucked so hard on my clit. Then she moaned. Her fingernails bit into my thighs. She was cumming. I could feel it in how she moaned around my bud. My pearl burst with sparks. They showered through me.

"Mrs. Smart!" howled Danni into my asshole. "Yes, yes, yes!"

I joined them in rapture.

My pussy convulsed. My asshole spasmed. Juices gushed out to bathe Shannon's face. I drenched her in my pussy cream as I howled out my orgasm. The orchestra blared, hitting the peak of their song as I trembled through my ecstasy.

Rapture bathed my mind. It washed out of my cunt over and over again. I drank it in. I whimpered out in pure delight. Stars danced before my eyes. These two women were something amazing to experience. They were outstanding. I savored every last minute of that pleasure. I quivered through the bliss, my heart pounding out with such rapture. It was incredible.

"Yes, yes, yes!" I moaned. "Oh, my god, that's amazing. That's fantastic."

I hit the peak of my pleasure. I floated there, the two women licking at my holes. Danni rimmed me while Shannon devoured my cunt. We were all moaning, gasping, crying out with the orchestra. I hung there.

The music ended.

My orgasm died to rapture.

The thunderous applause for the symphony's climax, and my own, surged around me. I shuddered as Danni's tongue pulled out of my asshole and Shannon took a last lick at my pussy. I hit that wondrous high. I clicked on my phone, turning off the vibrator buzzing away in Danni's pussy.

"Oh, my god, that was amazing," Shannon said. "That egg vibrator... Ooh, that's good."

"Keep it," I purred. "It's yours. Use it on a lover."

"I will," she promised.

"Mmm, that was great," groaned my lover. "The best concert I ever went to."

I could only nod. It was over. So was our fun with Shannon Murphy. We straightened our dresses. I tied mine back behind me, buzzing from that wonderful climax. Danni's breasts vanished, covered up by her dress. What a shame.

Danni gave her number to Shannon and kissed her on the lips, the pair sharing the taste of my pussy and asshole. Then the three of us swept down the stairs like we belonged up here. Shannon broke off to find her husband while Danni and I merged with the flow.

I was glad we sat beside the other MILF and showed her how much fun dates with a naughty, young woman could be.

"What a wonderful evening," Danni said as she snuggled up against me on the walk out of the music hall. "I came so much."

"Mmm, yes," I said. "I should get you to babysit next date night."

"You mean get your husband to babysit while we have a wild time?" the wicked thing said, her eyes sparkling.

"Yes."

"You're one naughty MILF."

We giggled together as the valet fetched the car.

On the drive back to my house, I felt so wonderfully relaxed. It was a beautiful evening. Twenty minutes later, I pulled my car in the driveway, knowing this evening wasn't over yet. I parked in the garage and stumbled out into the house.

I found my husband in boxers and a t-shirt in the kitchen getting a beer. He looked up, blinked. Danni was clinging to me, her hands wandering my body. She giggled as my husband swallowed. I smiled at him.

"We had a wonderful evening, Thomas," I groaned. "How was Cherri."

"She's sleeping," he said. "She's been good. I fed her. Laid her down for a nap."

"Wonderful," I said. "Mmm, we are off to bed. I haven't worn this minx out yet."

"So you're... gay, huh? One of those women who just went..."

"Yeah. Sorry." I smiled at him then led Danni past. I was a lesbian MILF now. I had a cutie to play with. I would ravish her until we fell into a sapphic haze.

Best date night ever. I was so glad my husband and I started them.

* * *

The lesbian wish continues to spread. The world is taking notice of all those straight women plunging into sapphic delights.

The girl who made her wish is enjoying all those MILFs she craved. She's having the time of her life not realizing how far it's spread. From preacher's wives to new mothers to nubile babysitters and beyond. Models in Europe and CEO of lingerie companies. Housewives, businesswomen, teachers, nurses, and more are taking the plunge and loving it.

To be continued in the Little Lezzie Delights' tale...

# Sydney Prowls the Mall for Hot MILFs

## Prowling for Lesbian MILFs 1

## A Lesbian MILF Tale

by

Reed James

# Sydney Prowls the Mall for Hot MILFs

Lesbianism is spreading faster and faster thanks to the young girl and her wish.

One wicked MILF has started a business with her friends: Little Lezzie Delights. The perfect service for other naughty MILFs, hot wives, and kinky businesswomen eager to enjoy those nubile and young girls with their tight bods and tighter slits.

* * *

## Sydney Miller – Friday, Day 5 of the Wish

The business cards were in.

Excitement rippled through me as Samantha opened up the box. She was an ebony-skinned cutie, barely legal like me. She pulled out the express order from Vistaprint and opened up the first smaller box that she found inside.

"Mine," she said and grinned as she produced her first business card for our new job at Little Lezzie Delights. I was so glad that Mrs. Wright and Mrs. Greene had seduced me into lesbian sex. It had been hot as they lusted after me while they watched me sunbathe.

And then they called me over to have sex with them. Wild,

nasty, delicious, sapphic sex with the two older women. They had loved what I did with them so much, that they had decided every older woman needed a barely legal cutie to pleasure them.

So why not make money at it?

I was an eighteen-year-old lesbian whore eager to go out there and find new clients.

"And these are yours, Tiffany," Samantha said, sliding the second of the small, white cardboard boxes held in the larger order.

Tiffany, a brunette with an eyebrow piercing, grinned as she took hers. She opened the box and pulled out her business card. "Fucking hell, this is going to be so much fun. We're going to get wild. Find some sexy MILFs."

"On the prowl for that MILF poontang!" Samantha said as she grabbed the last box and handed it to me. "Right, Sydney?"

"That's right," I said, taking the box from her. My hand shook as I ripped it open and saw the five hundred business cards. That was a lot more than I had imagined it would be. It was just so cheap to order so many of them. I pulled one out and shivered.

**Sydney Miller**
**Naughty Escort**
**Little Lezzie Delights**
**Every MILF deserves a little delight!**
**$20 and I'll lick you. $100 and you lick me**
**(253) 555-4891**

I shivered, rubbing the image of the lipstick kiss that was on each of the glossy cards. It was like I had personally kissed it. I shivered, licking my lips. I then grabbed a handful of them and shoved them into my jean skirt pocket.

"Let's prowl for some older pussy," groaned Tiffany. "I have the perfect neighborhood to go door to door in. Find me some housewives in need of getting their twats waxed by my tongue." She thrust hers out and wiggled it between a V she made with two of her fingers.

I burst into giggles as Samantha said, "Naw, boo, you got to hit the gym. Find those women getting their asses tight on the StairMaster. I'll bounce a quarter off their booties."

"The mall," I said. "That's where I'm going. Find them

shopping. Ask if they want to try me on for size." I licked my lips. I could almost taste it. I *loved* going down on a MILF.

"Then let's go," said Samantha, thrusting her cards into her purse. "Let's find some MILF pussy and have fun."

Tiffany and I nodded. We rushed out of Samantha's house and onto the street. She lived near me. I was just a few houses up the street. I darted across the cul-de-sac while she hopped into her own car. I reached my driveway, so ready to get wild. I opened the door to the sedan my parents had bought me. I slid in, started the engine, and backed out.

I drove fast to the mall. I wanted to get there and get prowling for MILF delights as soon as possible. I licked my lips, just so eager for it. I would do such naughty things to them. And they would do even naughtier things to me. There was a reason we only charged $20 for us to lick them. That was the gateway.

Once they had their first orgasm on our lips, they'd want more lezzie sex with us. Then they'd shell out the money to go down on us. We had other prices for other services. If they wanted to lick our assholes, that was $150, and to fuck us with a strap-on was $200, or $250 for anal.

We were hot and sexy. All of us with tight, young bodies. And mine was going to get wild.

I parked at the mall and climbed out of my sedan. I smiled as I spotted a woman heading to her SUV with a few bags. She was older, a delightful MILF. She glanced at me and smiled. I flicked out a card to her. She took it and blinked.

Then she gasped as she read it.

I kept walking, feeling her eyes on me as I did. I could *feel* her sudden awakening to lesbian delights. It was such a strange thing, this passion. It was spreading. You were starting to hear about it on the news. More women going lesbian. Actresses. Politicians. Wives of the powerful. There were all sorts of salacious rumors hitting the gossip sites.

I didn't know what had flicked that lezzie switch in us women, but I loved it.

I passed another MILF and slipped her the card and kept going. I knew the calls would start coming in. I couldn't wait. It would be so hot to start setting up dates with hot MILFs and make my lady pimps some moolah.

I entered the mall, my pussy dripping with juices. I had no bush to contain my cream. Nor any panties. Beneath my jean skirt, my thighs were getting sticky as I stared out at the people moving through the mall. So many older women. I gripped a handful of cards and started handing them out. To women with their husbands and boyfriends. To ladies shopping with friends. If they were in their thirties or more, I gave them a card.

I felt their eyes trailing after me as they gasped. Burst into nervous giggles. Let out little moans of longing. I swayed my hips, letting them get a good look at how great my eighteen-year-old ass looked in my jean skirt while my short, brown hair danced about my face.

I spotted one MILF that caught my gaze. She was with her husband and heading into a clothing store. I was ready to close a sale. To get a MILF to hire me right in the mall. And this blonde older woman was just the sort of hottie I was looking for. Her husband being with her just made this naughtier.

That *proved* she needed a hot, young lesbian to love her. there was no way she was getting what she needed from a man. Oh, no. Her body deserved to be worshiped. I could tell just from the distance as I rushed towards the clothing store.

I gave a red-haired lady a card on the way. Her gasp made my pussy clench.

I slipped into the mall, my breasts rising and falling in my tight belly shirt. I wore no bra, my lush mounds jiggling unconstrained. My nipples poked against the tight material. My gaze swept around the store. It wasn't the trendiest clothing store. The place that more mature women would shop to find casual wear. I'd never be caught shopping for clothes here.

Luckily, I was here shopping for MILFs.

I spotted her browsing at some tops. Her husband was staring bored at his phone, her other shopping bags on the floor beside him. She pulled out one top and held it up to her. It was a fairly plain blouse with ruffled sleeves and just a little bit of a scoop neckline.

I stepped up beside her as she held it up to her torso. Then she glanced at me and smiled. "What do you think?"

"It's a little boring," I said, sliding through the rack like I would buy any of these. They were all so staid and...

Well, this top was daring. A nice purple with a V-neckline.

"Boring, huh?" said the woman. She glanced down at the peasant blouse she wore that fit loosely on her, almost hiding those large breasts of hers. But they were too big to be entirely concealed by her clothing.

"Just calling it like I see it," I said. "A woman should dress to show off her body."

"I'm not twenty any longer," the MILF said with a sigh of regret. She glanced at me, seeing the tight clothing. "I used to dress like that."

"Why can't you dress like that now?" I asked, wiggling my hips. I loved the feel of the denim of my skirt clinging to my rump.

"Well, I'm married," she said, glancing at her husband.

"And?" I glanced at her. "Don't you want to feel like a sexy woman? I mean, you got those big boobs. You should be showing them off."

She flicked her eyes up and down my body. Her cheeks spotted with color. I loved the way her hips moved in her mom jeans. They did nothing for her body. She looked like she was in great shape. Ooh, I wanted to do such wicked things to her.

She put that boring blouse away and flicked through the racks, searching for something riskier. She pulled out a red blouse that would fit tight in her bust and stomach with a deeper neckline. It had short sleeves.

"How about this?" she asked.

"Come on, you can go even more risque. Show off those tits." I pulled the purple one off the rack. "How about this one."

"Oh, my," she said. "She held it up to her. I could see just how plunging that neckline would be on her. "This is rather daring."

"Don't you deserve to be daring?" I asked her, a simmer to my voice. "I mean, you have that body. Show it off. Be proud that you're a woman. Don't worry about what your husband will think."

She glanced at him. He was a tall man, heavyset with dark hair and glasses. He scrolled on his phone and yawned. He hadn't paid a bit of attention to her at all. I could see that she yearned for his attention.

But she had mine.

"I mean, he'd rather play on his phone than see what a hottie you'd be in that blouse, Mrs..."

"Audrey. Audrey Carter."

"I'm Sydney," I said and then I found a blouse that wasn't too staid for me to try on. I held it up. "What do you think."

"It would be cute on you," she said. "You need something to go with it."

"Just like you need for that sexy purple blouse," I said. "Mmm, a flirty skirt, I think. Not a pair of baggy jeans."

"They're not that baggy, Sydney," Mrs. Carter protested. She looked down. "I mean..."

"They're mom jeans, Mrs. Carter."

"I *am* a mom."

I shivered. A true MILF. My pussy clenched. Heat washed through me. This woman was old enough to be my mother. That was what made her so damned sexy. My pussy clenched, the heat rushing through me. I fanned my face, my cunt on fire.

"Come on," I said. "I want to find a skirt that makes your ass come alive. I bet you have a great booty."

"Booty?" she asked, a smile playing on her lips.

I turned and wiggled my rump at her. "Yeah, a booty. With some nice jiggle to it. You got some curves to you, Mrs. Carter. Let's find something that shows it off. Something that makes you look just perfect in it."

"Sure," she said, following me as I moved towards the skirts.

There were some ugly ones. To my horror, Mrs. Carter went for them. They were long, falling well past her knees, and they were so loose, they wouldn't make that ass of her look good. She held her blouse and the boring bottom to her, arching an eyebrow.

I shook my head. "Nun's don't even wear skirts that long."

She arched an eyebrow back at me. "Are you saying I dress like a nun?"

"Worse, Mrs. Carter. Worse." I grinned at her. Then I snagged a pleated, white skirt off the rack and shoved it at her. "Try this."

"That's short," she said as she held it against her waist. It fell not even to her mid-thigh.

"Why hide those killer legs I know you got." I found an even shorter skirt to go with my blouse. I held it to me. "What do you think."

"That if you're not careful, you'll be flashing your panties if you bend over," said Mrs. Carter. "That's way too short. Why would they sell it?"

"Because it's fun to bend over and flash a hottie," I said. I turned over and dropped my skirt. "Whoopsie."

I bent over, my ass thrust out at Mrs. Carter. My jean skirt rose up and up. It came just to the limits of my ass-cheeks, an inch or so from showing off some real naughty flesh at the MILF. Did she want to see what sort of panties I was wearing?

She would be so shocked to see a naked twat instead.

"See," I said. "I come close to flashing some poon in these ones, but not close enough."

"I wouldn't do that where my husband can see," Mrs. Carter said. "He's liable to pass out from the rush of blood to his cock."

I giggled. "I just want to get the blood flowing." I wiggled my rump by flexing my legs one after the other. Then I straighten up. "It's healthy, you know, to have the heart pumping."

"You must be doing a favor to every guy who sees you in that," Mrs. Carter said, her cheeks scarlet, her thighs rubbing together.

"Mmm, but what about you, Mrs. Carter?" I slid up to her. "Are you one of those naughty older women that secretly cruise around the mall looking for cute, young things to enjoy behind your hubbies back?"

She gasped, "Of course not. I don't need to find a young man."

"I wasn't talking about a boy," I said and winked at her.

"You are a wicked girl, Sydney."

"I know." I shivered, my pussy on fire. "Let's see if we can find a skirt even shorter for you to wear."

"No," she groaned as I headed over to some tight miniskirts they had on here. These were promising.

I pulled off a black one. I thrust it at her. "Look at that. Mmm, that would just hug your ass and barely cover anything."

"I can't wear this," she said, sounding scandalized.

"Sure you can," I said. "Let's go to the changing room and see just how sexy you are in those. Mmm, I but you have an ass that will have every young hottie on their knees just begging to worship that booty."

"You are a bad, bad influence," she groaned as I hooked her arm and pulled her to the changing room. "I'm the older woman here. I shouldn't be letting you drag me into doing this."

"Mmm, I'm not dragging you into doing anything. I'm giving you the excuse to do what you really want to do," I purred. "That's all."

She licked her lips then said, "Honey, we're going to try some clothes on."

"Sure," he grunted, staring at his phone.

"I doubt even you in this miniskirt would get him away from his phone," I said. "He's watching porn or something."

"Porn?" the MILF gasped.

"Yeah, probably some hot lezzie stuff. Guys love it. Some hot MILF getting seduced by a barely legal thing. 'Oh, Mrs. Miller, I do not understand how to masturbate, can you show me?'" I said in a breathy voice. "You know, that sort of thing."

"In the mall?" she said, her cheeks red. Then she gave me a sharp look. "You're not going to ask me to teach you to masturbate?"

"I already know," I promised her. "For years."

She stared at me with a look that was halfway between relief and disappointment. I could tell she was getting closer and closer to crossing that line into an adulterous, sapphic passion with me. I couldn't wait to have this MILF—or even better, her oblivious husband—pay me to do wicked and naughty things with her.

We reached the changing rooms. They had two, but I led her into the nearest one. It wasn't uncommon. I shared changing rooms with my friends all the time. Of course, I hadn't done it since I'd gone lezzie.

So this was exciting.

Mrs. Carter closed the door and hung her clothes on a hook. She glanced at me, blushing as she untucked her blouse from her jeans and started pulling it up and over her body. I licked my lips, eager for the show. She had a flat stomach, her skin pale. She needed to do nude tanning like me. I was golden-brown all over, tits included.

She wore a beige bra. Nothing sexy other than they held those ample tits. My pussy melted. More juices ran down my thighs. I squirmed and bit my lip as she pulled her blouse over her head, covering her face for a moment. Her blonde hair popped out and fell around her shoulders.

"Yeah, you're going to look hot in that blouse," I said and pulled off my own top. I pulled it up and over my round breasts. They spilled out perky and jiggling. She froze as she reached for her fly.

"Forget something?" she asked, her voice strangled.

"I'm young," I said, squeezing my tits. "And they're perky enough. I don't need the support. And I just hate wearing bras."

"When you have tits my size," she said, "they're necessary."

"I bet," I said, sighing in envy. "I'd love to have tits that big."

"They used to be your size. Two children..." She shrugged and reached for her blouse.

"You should take your bra off, too. See how your top fits when your tits are naked. I think they'll look great in them."

"I think you just want to see my breasts," the MILF said. "I can see that gleam in your eyes. I have children. I know when a girl is being naughty."

"Guilty," I said and popped the fly of my jean shorts. The zipper rasped down.

I turned around and wiggled them off. I bent over, my tanned tits jiggling. Mrs. Carter sucked in a breath as my cute ass was unveiled. I bent over more, shoving my rump out in her direction, letting her see that perfect, firm delight.

"You shouldn't tease a woman like that," muttered Mrs. Carter.

"Oh?" I asked and turned around. "Did my booty get you wet?"

"Of course not," she said. "I'm not into girls."

"Pity," I said. "I have this new business, and I thought you would be a perfect customer for it. But if you don't like girls..." I grabbed my jean skirt and fished out a business card. I flicked it over to her. "Oh, well."

She took it, her mom jeans unbuttoned but still clinging to her hips. She flipped my card over. I watched her eyes widen as she read the front. Then her gaze flicked to my naked and perfect body quivering right before her. She bit her lower lip, the shock of what she read spilling across her features.

"You really..." She flipped the card over to look at the back then back around again. "I mean..."

"Yep," I said.

"You're a prostitute," croaked from Mrs. Carter's beautiful lips. Her cheeks were blazing red. God, she was so sexy and delicious. "I can't believe it."

"I'm a hot, young thing that gives a MILF what she needs," I said, sliding my hands up my body. I cupped my breasts. "For a price. Mmm, I'm just a naughty and kinky cutie ready to do whatever wicked things my customers want."

She bit her lower lip again, holding it tight as she studied my card. Her breasts rose and fell in her beige bra while her hips wiggled in such a naughty way. They slipped down to reveal a pair of boring panties with a paisley flower print all over them. She really, really needed to dress to impress the young things. She was lucky she met me.

I could see the desire in her eyes. She wanted me. Her husband was out waiting on her while she was getting wetter and wetter. She wanted to do such wicked and naughty things with me. I could see it in her blue eyes.

"Why is it more to make *you* cum?" she asked, her voice strangled.

I winked at her. "I can eat you out. Finger you. Fuck you with a dildo. I can suck on those titties. For an extra $20, I'll even rim that delicious asshole." I flicked my tongue over my lips while my hands squeezed about my tits. "Interested in buying my services?"

She shuddered. A croak rose from her throat. "Yes." She swallowed. "I want you too... too... suck on my tits and finger me."

"Done."

I shoved my hands behind her and unhooked her bra. She shuddered as I popped the fastener with skilled ease. Then I slid the straps off her shoulders. The cups fell away from her large breasts. I groaned at the sight of them. They were so large and plump. Just such sexy and delicious things to stare at.

My hands cupped them. I held her breasts. I squeezed and kneaded them. My fingers dug into her boobs. I shook them and then smacked them together, loving how they rippled. They were such wonderful titties to play with. I grinned as I leaned down, so eager to suckle on her dusky-pink nipples.

Shame I only had one pair of lips.

I latched my mouth onto a nipple and nursed. The MILF groaned, her body shaking. Her gasp echoed through the changing room. Her fat nub felt so wonderful between my lips as I suckled. My cheeks hollowed while my fingers kneaded her tits.

"Sydney," she moaned, her voice throaty. "Oh, my god, you wicked thing."

I winked at her as I nursed. My right hand abandoned her left tit to fulfill the other part of her request. I pressed my hand down and down her belly to find the waistband of her panties. I slid my fingertips just into the waistband, feeling the elastic. She groaned, her jeans rustling. They must be falling down her legs.

Suckling hard, my fingers pushed deeper into her panties.

I slid through her brown bush, feeling her getting warmer and wetter. She gasped when I brushed her pussy lips. Then I cupped her twat. I rubbed at her delicious flesh while she whimpered and moaned. Her voice echoed around us as my fingers stroked up and down her cuntlips.

"Oh, my god," she moaned. "I can't believe I'm doing this."

I just winked up at her blue eyes staring down at me as my fingers slid up and down her slit. Then I found her entrance and thrust two of them into her depths. Her cunt squeezed about my digits as they slid into her.

"This isn't me," she panted. "I'm not gay, but... but... Oh, god, I want to be. You have me so turned on."

I popped my mouth off her nipple and purred, "I know just what you mean. I'm soaking wet right now. My cream is just running down my thighs, Mrs. Carter."

She licked her lips, her twat clenching down on my digits. "Oh, god, you're in me. You're fingering me. My husband's right out there."

"Uh-huh," I said and latched onto her nipple again.

I nursed on her. I suckled with passion, her pussy clenching about my pumping digits every time I did it. My cheeks hollowed as I loved that wonderful nub in her mouth. It was such a naughty delight to nurse on her. To worship her with all my hunger.

She groaned, her breasts jiggling as my left hand still kneaded her right. She threw back her head, her tits rising and falling as I loved her nub and fingered her twat. I pumped my digits in and out of her hot, married sheath. Her juices dribbled down the back of my hand.

She groaned as I nursed. The suckling sounds echoed through the changing room. She made such husky pants and wanton moans as I worked my digits in and out of her snatch. My own cunt was getting wetter and wetter.

I wanted to make her explode. To cum hard. My left hand clutched to her right boob. I kneaded her tit as I suckled on her nub. My lips popped off with wet plops, her nipple quivering. I flicked it with my tongue then nipped it with my teeth.

"Sydney!" she gasped, her cunt tightening down on my fingers. "Oh, my god, Sydney. That's so good."

"It's about to get better," I purred and then swirled my tongue around her nub.

My digits thrust deep into her pussy. Then I curled them along the top of her pussy wall, moving so slowly. I stroked her silky flesh, searching for that oh-so-wonderful spot. Her panties' waistband dug into the back of my hand as I worked, my fingers sliding against her delicious flesh.

Her cunt clenched down on me. She gasped and bucked.

Bingo!

I massaged her G-spot. Her snatch grew hotter around my fingers. I nursed with passion on her nipple while her moans grew louder. Her hands shot out and grabbed my perky tits. She squeezed and kneaded them as I massaged that wicked bundle of nerves in her twat.

"What is that?" she moaned. "Oh, my god, Sydney. What is

that? What the fuck are you doing to me? That's... that's... I'm going to explode."

I rubbed harder at her G-spot, my fingers moving in fast circles against her silky flesh. The tangy musk of her pussy rose through the air, overpowering my own tart delight. I loved the aroma as I suckled on her nub.

"Sydney!" she gasped.

Her pussy spasmed.

The MILF squeezed my perky tits as her orgasm burst through her. The gasps and moans she released echoed through the air. They resounded around me. They were so delicious to hear. I smiled, savoring her passion echoing around me. My cunt clenched, the heat washing over me. Things were about to get even wilder.

"Yes, yes, yes!" the MILF groaned as her pussy convulsed around my digits. Her juices gushed out. "You... this... Sydney!"

I kept sucking as she trembled through her orgasm. My fingers massaged her G-spot, giving her that wonderful delight. Her pussy spasmed around my digits. Her silky sheath sucked at them. I loved it. She bucked and then gasped.

I ripped my fingers out and popped my lips off her nipple. I shoved those digits into my mouth, reveling in her tangy passion. She panted, standing there with her jeans around her ankles, her boring panties rumpled. I nursed on my fingers as she fluttered her eyes and then focused on me.

"You..." she panted, those big and lush breasts jiggling as they rose and fell. "What was that, Sydney?"

I slid my fingers from my mouth. "Your G-spot."

"That's real?" she gasped.

I winked at her.

She shuddered, her tits swaying from side to side. They smacked each other. The way their flesh rippled was so impressive to see. I smiled at the sight of her breasts jiggling together. They were so lush to witness. Such a fantastic delight.

Then I noticed the brown hair peeking out of the waistband of her panties. I gasped and yanked them down off her hips in a flash. She had a thick bush that adorned her pussy, her hairs gleaming with cum.

"You're not a natural blonde?" I looked at her hair. "That's a dye-job. That's incredible. I didn't even notice!"

"Thanks," she said, smiling. "I like feeling pretty as a blonde."

"Then you need to dress like one," I groaned as her panties fell down her thighs. She stepped out of them and her jeans. "You are fucking hot, Mrs. Carter."

"So are you," she moaned. "So it's a $100 to lick your pussy?"

"You understand now, don't you? Why it's more."

"Because it's what I really want to do," she whimpered and fell to her knees before me. She grabbed my hips and breathed in as she stared at my shaved pussy. "Oh, my god, you smell so good. When did pussy become what I crave? What did you do to me?"

"I was just hot and sexy," I told her, wiggling my hips, loving her grip on them.

"Yes, you are," she moaned and leaned her head in.

Her dyed-blonde locks rustled about her face as she came closer and closer to nuzzling into me. This wicked delight surged through me. My body trembled at the heat that was building and building in me. I would have such a huge orgasm. Just an explosion of bliss that would burst out of me.

Then her lips kissed at my vulva. She smooched at my pussy, working her mouth up and down it. That was incredible to feel. Her hair caressed my inner thighs with their silky locks. My body trembled, the heat rushing through me.

"Mrs. Carter," I groaned. Then her tongue flicked through my folds. "Oh, yes, Mrs. Carter!"

"You taste so good," she moaned before she licked me again.

I savored that wonderful tongue fluttering up my slit. A shiver ran through me. My toes curled in my shoes. Her tongue fluttered up and down my slit. She did such wicked and naughty things to me. My entire body shook as she loved me. The heady rush of heat shot through my body.

I threw back my head and moaned out in delight at the feel of her tongue parting my folds. The pleasure built and built in my twat as her tongue licked and lapped at me. She brushed my clit. Sparks flared through me.

It was incredible to enjoy.

"Mrs. Carter," I moaned in delight, my body trembling. My breasts swayed before me. "Oh, yes, yes, you love it."

"This is worth a $100," she moaned. Her tongue thrust into my pussy. She swirled it around in me.

My twat clenched about her tongue. She danced it in circles in me, sending such heat rushing through me. It was incredible to feel. Such a wicked experience. I closed my eyes and savored every moment of her tongue dancing through my folds. She teased me. Pleased me. She would make me explode on her mouth.

I wanted to drown the MILF in her first taste of pussy. I ached for it to just gush out of me. That would be incredible. I would flood her with all that cream. It would squirt out of me and bathe her mouth. She would drown in it.

God, that would be so hot.

"Yes, yes, yes!" I moaned.

"Mmm, you taste so good, Sydney," she purred. "I love it. I love your young pussy!"

The MILF feasted on me. She thrust that tongue deep into my cunt, her hands gripping my hips. My breasts swayed as I trembled there. My back arched, the locks of my short hair caressing my cheeks. My nipples throbbed as she devoured me.

I grabbed my nipples and squeezed them. I twisted them, loving the pleasure that burst through my body. It rushed down to my cunt. My snatch grew even more sensitive. My clit throbbed as her nose rubbed into it.

I climbed towards my orgasm. She feasted on me with such enthusiasm. She licked at me with all that wonderful passion. It was her first time, but she was learning how to devour me. How to make me shudder and gasp. I would have such a huge climax on this sexy MILFs mouth.

"Mrs. Carter," I moaned, my hips undulating. I ground my shaved, barely legal twat on her hungry mouth. The pleasure rushed through my body. "Oh, yes, yes, this is amazing."

"So is your twat!" she moaned, her hands sliding around my hips. She grabbed my ass and pulled my twat tight against her hungry mouth.

Her tongue thrust so deep into me. That wicked MILF licked

around in me. She fluttered her nimble appendage through my folds and made me cry out in rapture. I would have such a huge orgasm on her naughty mouth. My hips undulated back and forth, savoring every wicked and wanton moment of her tongue fluttering through my folds.

She swirled it around. She danced it about in me. I groaned, my eyes fluttering from the wonderful delights she shared with me. I whimpered, biting my lower lip. I was so ready for that orgasm to burst through me.

I ached to drown her.

"Yes, yes, yes!" I groaned. "You're going to love this. You're going to savor every bit of this pleasure rushing through your body, aren't you?"

She whimpered and then swirled her tongue around inside of me.

"Good!" I groaned. "I'm almost there. Mmm, just keep licking me. Ooh, like that. Yes, yes, just like that. I'm going to have such a huge orgasm. Just a mighty explosion of rapture."

"Yes!"

She fluttered her tongue to my clit. I gasped as the sexy MILF sucked on my bub. My body bucked. My pussy clenched. The heat built in my cunt. I wiggled my hips from left to right, savoring the wonderful delight as it swelled in me. I would have such a huge orgasm. A mighty climax on her amazing mouth.

Her fingers squeezed at my rump. Her plump lips nibbled at my clit. My bud burst with delight that this amazing and naughty beauty gave me. I groaned, so thrilled to get to enjoy her. To savor her passion rushing through my body.

Her tongue darted around my clit.

"Yes!" I hissed as the sparks flared. "Mrs. Carter!"

I came.

My pussy convulsed in celebration. The waves of delight washed out of my cunt. She groaned as my juices gushed out. I bathed her mouth with my passion. My pleasure rushed out of me while the bliss surged through my veins.

"Mrs. Carter!" I gasped, tits heaving as my mind drowned in ecstasy. "Oh, Mrs. Carter. That's hot, young cunt cream! Mmm, you love it, don't you?"

"Yes!" she moaned between licks.

Her tongue flew up and down my pussy slit. She lapped and licked at me with such enthusiasm. It was amazing. The pleasure shuddered through me. My hips wiggled in her grasp, my cunt getting juicier and juicier by the minute. I would have such a huge explosion of bliss. Just a mighty burst of rapture that would gush through me.

"Oh, my god, that's amazing," I moaned, my breasts heaving. "Oh, Mrs. Carter, yes! Yes!"

I quivered through the bliss. I savored it as she thrust her tongue into my snatch and fluttered it around in me. She stirred up my cunt. Her tongue danced through my folds. She gave me such bliss. Such a wonderful delight. I hit the peak of my orgasm.

"I bet you want more," I moaned as I came down from my heights. "I have a vibrator in my purse."

"How much?" she asked.

"$50," I moaned.

"And another $40 to have you rim me while you do it?" the MILF asked as she stood up. She turned around and pressed her hands on the wall, wiggling her rump at me. Her butt-cheeks jiggled.

"Mrs. Carter, you dirty MILF," I moaned. "Mmm, yes. That brings you up to..." I did some quick math. "$210."

"No getting those boots now," she moaned. "But this is better. Do it!"

I snagged my purse, pulled out the silver vibrator Mrs. Wright had provided, and fell to my knees. I pressed my face boldly between her butt-cheeks. Not an ounce of hesitation. I smooched down her crack, her silky flesh rubbing on my face. She whimpered, her breathing quickened. I reached her asshole.

Kissed it.

"Sydney," she moaned. "Oh, Sydney, I can't believe you're going to rim my asshole. I just... I want it."

"You'll get it," I cooed and swirled my tongue around her sour hole.

As I savored the texture of her sphincter, I turned on the

vibrator. I held it in both hands. It hummed away. I used her thigh to guide me up to her pussy, sliding the buzzing toy higher and higher. At the same time, my tongue lathed against her sphincter, caressing her back door. She moaned, her butt-cheeks clenching on my face.

The buzzing toy reached her pussy. She moaned louder as I slid it around, searching for her hole. I pushed upward. She gasped when I found it, the humming shaft sinking into her married twat. I swirled my tongue around her asshole and worked that naughty vibrator in and out of her snatch.

My left hand shot between my thighs. I cupped my bare pussy, rubbing myself. The sour flavor of her asshole soaked my tongue. Her juices ran down the buzzing shaft to coat my finger gripping the rubber base. My other digits caressed up and down my slit, teasing me, sending pleasure through my body.

"Ooh, that feels so naughty," she moaned. "Having you rim my asshole and pump that vibrator in and out of my twat.

"I'm glad you're enjoying it," I cooed. I sealed my lips around her asshole and sucked.

"Oh, my god, Sydney!" she gasped. "That's so nasty. Ooh, yes, yes, suck on my butthole."

I did. I nursed on her dirty backdoor. I thrust my fingers into my cunt and ground the heel of my hand against my clit as I did that. The sucking sounds echoed around me. My twat clenched down on my probing digits, the pleasure rippling through me. My bud sparked.

I jammed the vibrator deep into her cunt. Her silky bush rubbed on my knuckles as I stirred it around in her. She moaned, her butt-cheeks clenching and relaxing about my face. She was just such a sexy thing. I would have her cumming so hard.

I fingered myself faster. I ground my heel against my clit with more pressure. The ache built in me as I sucked and rimmed her asshole. I plunged the dildo to the hilt in her cunt over and over again. The sour flavor of her bowels spread through my mouth.

I loved it.

I wanted to taste it more. I pressed my tongue against her asshole. I felt that naughty ring parting for me. She groaned as I wiggled my tongue inside. I swirled through her bowels, caressing her velvety flesh.

"Oh, my god," she moaned. "Oh, that's so nasty. Ooh, what are you doing to me, Sydney?"

"Loving you!" I moaned, thrusting the buzzing toy deep into her cunt and then pulling it back. "Giving your married flesh the pleasure it deserves."

"Yes!" she moaned, her asscheeks clenching on me. "That you certainly are doing. Oh, yes, yes, you're going to make me explode."

I was so thrilled to do that to her. To deliver her that wonderful bliss. I sucked hard on her asshole. Her gasps were wicked to hear. She moaned, her butt-cheeks gripping my face. Her sour bowels warmed my tongue as it danced in her.

I frigged myself hard now. I drove my fingers into my cunt, building and building myself to my own orgasm as I pleasured the hot, married MILF. Her husband was out there waiting on us. He had no idea his wife was paying me to please her.

That added thrill built my orgasms faster and faster. My clit throbbed against the heal of my hand. I massaged it, sending such pleasure rushing through my body. I would have such a huge one. Just explode in delight.

"Oh, my god," she moaned. "That's it, Sydney. You're going to make me just burst, aren't you?"

"Uh-huh," I groaned between plunges of my tongue into her asshole. "Cum!"

"Getting there!"

More of her juices soaked my hand gripping the vibrator's base. The toy hummed happily away as I worked it in and out of her. My tongue fucked deep into her asshole. I wiggled it about in her velvety depths. I loved how she moaned. Gasped. The way she trembled from what I did to her.

I thrust a third finger into my cunt. My own orgasm built and built faster and faster. I reamed myself and massaged my clit. I groaned into her snatch, my body trembling. My breasts swayed as I pleasured the MILF.

She was paying me $210. I bet her husband was the breadwinner. He gave her money to buy things, and she spent it on me. Me!

This heady rush shot through me. I jammed my fingers deep into my cunt. My clit throbbed. I fucked my tongue in and out of her asshole as my body trembled. I hurtled towards my orgasm. There was no stopping my wild climax.

I was getting paid to worship this ass. This cunt. This gorgeous, married MILF. I was the luckiest girl alive.

I exploded.

My pussy convulsed around my fingers. I moaned into the MILF's asshole as the waves of pleasure washed through my body. My cunt sucked at my digits. My juices gushed out while the rapture drowned my thoughts.

"Oh my god, yes!" moaned the MILF, her butt-cheeks clenching about my face. "That's it. That's so good. Sydney!"

Juices gushed down the vibrator to my hand. I made the MILF cum. That intensified my orgasm. New waves of euphoria washed through my body. They swept through my thoughts and drowned me in ecstasy. I groaned, my thought beset by the swirls of bliss.

"Yes, yes, yes!" I groaned into her asshole as my orgasm hit that wonderful peak.

"Mmm, Sydney!" she moaned.

I kissed at her asshole. I smooched it while I stirred the vibrator through her twat. Her moans echoed through the room, growing softer and softer. They were such an amazing delight to listen to. I shuddered in delight to give her this bliss.

"Oh, god, I want more, but my husband's waiting," she whimpered.

I pulled my face from her butt-cheeks and the vibrator from her cunt. I turned it off and panted, understanding. My pussy quivered around my fingers, my orgasm dying down to that wonderful, buzzing bliss.

"That'll be $210," I said as we panted in the changing room. It smelled so wonderfully of sex.

She groaned and then she counted out the money, her wedding ring flashing. Her large tits jiggling in her blouse. Her face was flushed, her blonde hair swaying about it. I loved her dye. Maybe I should try it.

Blondes have more fun, or so "they" said. Whoever "they" were.

"Thank you so much," I moaned. "And if you ever need it again, just call that number. That's my cell. We can set up a date."

She nodded and slipped my card into her purse.

I dressed with a hum, pulling on my tight top and jean skirt. Then I sauntered out of the changing room. Her husband was sitting looking bored and defeated to how long it took. He glanced at me, his eyes flicking across her body.

"She's almost ready," I said. "Sorry, we were showing off in there."

He shrugged as I headed up to the clerk with my new outfit. I paid for the blouse and skirt—it turned out there were a few pieces of clothing here worth checking out—with the money his wife paid me. I couldn't help but grin at that.

She emerged, looking breathy and flushed. "Sorry, honey."

He shrugged. "Find something nice?"

"Oh, yes. Just a big surprise. A taste of being young." She licked her lips and glanced at me.

I winked back at her. I loved how oblivious her husband was to the wicked things I had done to his wife. I could still taste her sour musk, the dirty flavor of her ass lingering on my lips. The clerk bagged up my order. She was an older woman with glasses.

I left her my card. As I walked away, she gasped. I bet she was figuring out what had gone inside that changing room and why I had that roll of twenties. I took out the cut for Mrs. Wright and Mrs. Greene, my MILF-pimps needed their moolah, and slipped the rest into my pocket. There were better clothing stores to shop at.

My phone buzzed before I got too far. I pulled it out and saw a text message. "I need your services. When can we meet?"

I smiled. I was going to enjoy being a barely legal lesbian prostitute. I would give all the MILFs the pleasures they craved and get paid to do it. I hummed in delight as I texted back the woman to work out the details.

Prowling for lesbian MILFs at the mall was a great idea. I hoped my friends were having as much success as I had found.

To be continued...

# Tiffany's Door to Door Lezzie Sale

## Prowling for Lesbian MILFs 2

## A Lesbian MILF Tale

by

Reed James

## Tiffany's Door to Door Lezzie Sale

### Tiffany Tate – Friday, Day 5 of the Wish

I had a pep to my step. "Tiffany," I told myself as I left Samantha's house to go on the prowl for some lesbian MILFs, "you're going to kick some ass!"

I would give all the lesbian MILFs the delights that they deserved. I would eat out their pussies. Fuck them with my dildos. I would make them cum and cum and cum. It would be glorious. I couldn't wait for the first one to pay me to make her explode in orgasmic delight.

Yep, cum.

I was a barely legal lesbian prostitute.

It was so hot. A few days ago, these lesbian MILFs named Mrs. Wright and Mrs. Greene had seduced me into all the sapphic delights I could enjoy. They gave me and a few other girls a chance to be lesbian prostitutes and seduce every hot and sexy woman we could with our nubile bodies. It was so wild.

Today, our business cards had arrived. Sydney was off to the mall to troll for lesbian booty while Samantha was hitting the gym to seduce those hot wives getting their asses tight. I had a different plan. I wanted those women at home. Those bored housewives who needed a pick me up in their day. Something to get their blood pumping.

Mmm, just thinking about it had my pussy getting all juicy.

I slid into my car and flipped down my sun visor. I popped up the cover over the built-in mirror and stared at my reflection. I had a cute and wild face enhanced by the silver eyebrow piercing. It glinted as I moved, a twinkle of naughty delight. I pursed my lips and fluttered my eyes. I was eighteen and sexy as fuck.

I squeezed my thighs together beneath the yoga pants I wore. They hugged my thighs and ass; just cupped them like a lover's soft and feminine hands. My clit ached. I had a fat one. Just perfect for some hot MILF to suck on.

"Yes!" I purred to myself. "Tiffany, you are going to lick all their cunts. Let's go!"

I flipped up the visor and squirmed in eager delight. My breasts jiggled in the crop top I wore, leaving my midriff bare. I backed out of Samantha's driveway, her car following mine. Up the street, Sydney was getting into her own car at her house.

I tore down the road, driving fast. I wanted to get to the neighborhood I had scouted out for today. We had to build up a clientele of MILFs to pay us to have sex with them. Honestly, I'd do it for free—I now loved sexy, older women—but it was so hot getting paid for it.

It made me feel so wet.

The itch tingled through my pussy lips. That heat suffused every knock and cranny of my twat. I wiggled in my seat, rubbing my ass against the cushion. The music thudded, the beat pulsing through the car matching the rhythm of my heart. My blood howled through my veins.

"Yes!" I whooped.

I breathed in, catching a whiff of my tangy musk. That wonderful scent of my hot, young twat. I couldn't wait for a MILF to bury her face into my snatch and lick through me. Just flutter her tongue up and down. She would make me explode. It would be incredible. I couldn't wait for that exhilarating delight to whip through me.

I gripped the steering wheel. I held it tight. My fingers slid over the vinyl, feeling its sleek surface. My body felt so alive as the excitement pumped through me. That tingling, anticipatory rush of heat flowed out of my cunt.

"Yes, yes, yes!" I groaned as I turned onto the street. It was a quiet neighborhood. One of those suburban paradises that still existed in parts of America. All the houses were well-maintained. Two-story with wood siding painted grays or browns or blues. Lawns mowed. Bushes trimmed. Trees large and graceful.

I pulled my car to the curb and parked. I slid out, my stack of business cards in hand. I slung my purse over my shoulder, heavy with all the delights I had stored in it, and stepped out. I breathed in the air, smelled the lilac drifting from the purple flowers to my right.

"Let's do this," I said. "Mmm, you're perfect for this, Tiffany. Perfect!"

I marched up to the door. It was painted a red-brown color. A rich huge portal, the latex paint giving it a shiny look. I stepped onto the welcome mat and hoped for a loving one. I pressed the glowing, orange button.

The doorbell chimed.

The notes rang through the house. A nervous squirm writhed through my guts. That sort of sickly twist anticipation brought. It warred with the excitement rising out of my pussy. I waited, the sounds of the world muting as I listened for footsteps.

All I heard was a crow cawing in the background and wind rustling through a dogwood tree. I pressed the doorbell again. My stomach tightened with each one of the gongs that echoed through her house. I rubbed my sweaty palm on my left thigh.

"Well, fuck," I muttered, glancing at the window to the right. I peered through a haze of lacy curtains at the impression of an empty living room.

Sighing, I slipped my business card into the seam of the door above the knob. I hoped the woman of the house found it and was intrigued. It was a naughty card. Something that my friends and I had ordered from a company called Vistaprint.

**Tiffany Tate**
**Naughty Escort**
**Little Lezzie Delights**
**Every MILF deserves a little delight!**

**$20 and I'll lick you. $100 and you lick me**
**(253) 555-3491**

I whirled around and headed down the street to the sidewalk. My steps felt heavy. I couldn't believe I'd whiffed on the first door. I wanted to scream out my frustration. I reached the sidewalk and paused there, looking down it.

This was supposed to be a perfect street.

"It was just one house," I told myself. "There are plenty on here that are going to have sexy MILFs who want to pay to love my body." I squeezed my tits through my crop top. Nipples throbbed, firing tingles down to my cunt. "Mmm, they're going to be all over you."

I marched down the sidewalk, my sandals smacking on the pavement. I focused on the next house. It had a car in the driveway. A champagne-hued SUV. That was promising. I passed a property divider of rose bushes, their flowers open to a riot of reds, purples, and pinks. A brick path led up to the white-painted door with a gold knocker.

And a glowing doorbell button.

I jammed it. The chimes played. My entire body tensed. Every muscle tightened. I wanted this so bad. My cunt clenched, the juicy heat rushing out of it. The crotch of my yoga pants, the stretchy cloth clinging to my shaved vulva, must be growing with a damp spot.

Good thing I wore black.

Footsteps echoed through the house. I let out a relieved sigh as came closer and closer. They sounded dainty. A woman's. Hope blossomed in me. I put on a sultry smile and my left hand on my hip, ready to seduce.

The door opened and a woman in sweatpants and a t-shirt appeared. Even without her makeup on, she was a gorgeous, older woman. In her earlier thirties, her black hair pulled back into a simple ponytail. Her brow furrowed at the sight of me.

"Hello?" she asked with uncertainty.

"Hi," I said brightly. "I'm Tiffany Tate, and I'm here to offer you the ultimate relaxation that you deserve."

"Relaxation?" She took my proffered business card, her plump lips pursing together. God, they were so kissable. I could just lean in and kisses her.

She gasped, her left hand covering her mouth as she read it. The diamond on her engagement band gleamed, drawing the eye. The fiery brilliance in the gemstone flared as it caught the sunlight. Her brown eyes flicked up to me, rich and soulful.

"This... Is this...?" Cheeks blossomed crimson.

"It's not a joke, ma'am," I said in a naughty purr. "I will do *anything* to relax you. I'm here to please. However, you want. You are a sexy woman. But do you ever feel that appreciation? Does your husband make you cum any longer? Don't you yearn for something different? Something soft and feminine that will melt your bones?"

Her eyes flicked up and down my figure. They widened. Her blush deepened while she shuddered. "You're serious."

"I'm *very* serious." I winked at her. "That's my cell phone. If you ever want to set up a date, give me a call. I'll run on over and lick that married twat of yours until you drown me in cunt cream. I'm eager to please."

"This is... I..." She grabbed her door and started closing it. "This is insane. You can't just walk up to someone's house and offer them *this.*"

"If you ever change your mind, call me." I licked my lips slowly, wetting them. My tongue glided over the waxy smoothness from the coating of lipstick. "You won't regret it. There is nothing like getting your pussy eaten out by a cute, young thing."

She gave a slow nod as the door creaked closed. The sight of her dwindled, her eyes staring down at the card. I could tell she was shocked. But would she call? Would the ache for a cute and nubile girl she could pay to make her cum grow in her?

Well, I was trolling for lesbian MILFs. Chumming the waters with my hot bod. I wanted those sexy, older women to circle me, getting more and more ravenous until the surged in and pounced on me. I wanted them to feast on me.

"God, I hope one of them takes me up right away," I moaned to myself. My pussy blazed with that aching need.

My clit throbbed as I walked back to the sidewalk and heading to the next house. This one had all sorts of flowers growing around the edge of the foundation. Some sort of bushy things with purple or blue petals and small leaves. They filled the air with a sweet perfume that almost overwhelmed my tangy musk.

My yoga pants clung to my pussy now, the stretchy fabric soaking up more and more of my juices.

The housewife opened the door almost the moment after I rang the bell. She must have seen me coming. She had a polite smile on her lips, her brown hair tumbling down around her oval face. She was cute, late thirties, her breasts stretching out the t-shirt she wore.

"Hi, I'm Tiffany from Little Lezzie Delights, and I'm here to offer you the chance to have your mind melted in sapphic pleasure." I thrust my card at her. "For just $20, I will fall to my knees and eat that pussy of yours. Just devour your cunt until you gush juices on me."

The woman's jaw dropped. She absently took the card.

"That's right. You're going to love every second of it." Then I swept my hands up to cup my breasts, my right hand pressing the business cards into my tit. My purse swung as I groped myself, my nipples tingling against the cloth of my crop top. "Mmm, for $100, you can love my body. How does that sound?"

"Crazy," the woman croaked and then slammed the door in my face, the brass knocker rattling.

"But..." I let out a sigh then said louder, "I will make you cum harder than any man. You'll love it. Just give me a call. For $40, I'll lick your asshole. And for $150, you can fuck me with a strap-on. You'll like that."

But the woman didn't answer.

"Damn," I muttered and turned around.

My sandals scraped across the cement as I slouched back to the sidewalk. I was halfway down the cul-de-sac. About a quarter of the houses done. This was not how I pictured this going. Eating a MILF right there as she stood in her front door, her silky bush rubbing across my lips and her yummy juices soaking my lips and tongue, were what I had imagined.

"Fuck, fuck, fuck," I moaned, my clit throbbing and aching. It was in such need of being played with. It had to be stroked and rubbed and loved. A clit *needed* love. People had to understand that.

But they didn't always.

I came up to house number five. No one answered. I pressed the card into the door jamb. Was Sydney doing better at the mall? How was Samantha making out at the gym? Was this a mistake? I needed to get me some MILF pussy.

What I wouldn't give to dive into some sweet cunt or tart twat. To lick up all those juices from the folds of a spicy pussy while the MILF's thick bush rubbed across my face. It would be amazing. I would drink down the cum.

I drifted up to the sixth house in a haze of foggy lust, the sodden fabric of my yoga pants rubbing on my poor, aroused clit. The tingles rippled through me. I just wanted to masturbate now. That was how bad I needed to cum.

"Please," I whispered to the sky. I didn't know if I was praying to god, the universe, or the flying purple people eater. I just wanted a hot MILF. "Please, give me some pussy."

I pushed the rectangular doorbell button.

DING-DONG-DING-DONG! echoed through the house.

I heard footsteps. I perked up and put on a big smile. This was it. Make the sale, get that cunt, and make her cum. The door opened to a woman in a sleeveless sundress, the skirt flowing light and airy around her thighs. She had red hair that swayed about her gorgeous face. In her thirties, sexy, nearly old enough to be my mother.

Just what I wanted in a woman.

"Who is it, Alanna?" another woman called. Beyond the redhead, sitting on her couch with a glass of white wine in hand, was a woman in jeans. Another MILF with large breasts swelling out the baby doll t-shirt she wore. Black hair as glossy as a waterfall spilled down past her shoulders. She sipped her wine as she stared at the door.

"I'm not sure," said Alanna. She stared at me. "Hi? Can I help you?"

"I'm here to help you both," I said, handing her my card. "I'm Tiffany Tate, and I am your cute, little lesbian here to make you both cum."

"Did she say cum?" asked the woman on the couch.

"She did, Natasha," croaked Alanna. The redhead stared down at the card. Her lips moved as she read it silently. "Is this a joke?"

"No joke," I said.

Natasha stood up and sipped her wine as she drifted closer. Her eyes held an interested gleam in them as she stared at me. I winked back at her and thrust out my hand with a card to her. She took it and arched an eyebrow.

"I am here to do whatever kinky or naughty things you two want," I said. "For a price, of course."

"Of course," Natasha said, amusement thick in her voice. Her brown eyes sparkled as she flicked her gaze up from the card to me. Her body trembled.

The scent of my tangy pussy swelled in my nose.

"You aren't really..." Alanna trailed off. "I mean, this is illegal."

"And? You never sped?"

"Speeding isn't the same thing."

"Sure it is. It's you saying that you know what to do better than the rules. What's so wrong with us working out a deal for me to do things to you. How's it any different paying me to clean your house."

"Yeah, she just wants to clean your pussy with her tongue," Natasha said and then sipped at her wine.

"This isn't funny," muttered Alanna.

"It's certainly not funny," Natasha said. "It's interesting. Mmm, you really will do things for us?"

"Yes," I said and, thinking quickly. An idea sparked in my thoughts. It tingled across my mind. "We have a group rate. A discount. I can lick both your pussies at the same time for $30."

"Ooh, how can you lick us both out?" Natasha asked.

"Natasha!" Alanna gasped. "You're married."

"And my husband doesn't offer to lick my pussy out ever. Let alone do us both at the same time. Why don't you need this?"

"Because I'm married," Alanna protested. "I don't need a girl to eat me out."

"Eat *us* out. A group discount."

"For $75, I can use a double-headed dildo to fuck both your pussies, and if you want to both eat my twat out at the same time, that's $150."

"I don't want to eat out your pussy," Alanna protested, her cheeks blushing ruddy with her embarrassment.

"But don't you want *her* to eat your pussy out?" Natasha asked. "I know I do. I haven't had anyone go down on me in a year or longer. And I've never had a woman do it."

I licked my lips. "I'll make it something special."

"What, you're not saying you *want* her to eat us out," Alanna gasped.

"I think that's what she's saying." I grinned, shifting my heavy purse, the strap digging into my shoulder. "Now, if you both want to put on strap-ons and fuck me together, one in my pussy and the other in my asshole, that's $200. Isn't that's more than reasonable? Wouldn't you say that's a fair price for you two hot MILFs to enjoy my body?"

"Hot?" Alanna asked.

"Mmm, she thinks we're MILFs."

"You are MILFs." I quivered there. "I would love to fuck you both."

"We are so doing this," said Natasha. "We're at least going to pay her $30 to eat our pussies at the same time. You can pay for me. You owe me for lunch the other day."

"I thought I'd buy you lunch," muttered Alanna as Natasha pulled me inside.

"Well, we're buying her lunch instead." Natasha grinned at me, her black hair contrasting with the blushing delight of her cheeks. "Mmm, how hungry are you?"

"Ravenous," I said as I sauntered into the living room. Then I sat down my purse with a thud on the glass coffee table. The items inside shifted. I turned to face them and pulled off my crop top.

It peeled over my round breasts. They spilled out with a quiver to them. My nipples thrust out hard. They throbbed with the pulsing beat of my heart. My cunt was on fire, melting heat that rippled out through my body.

Both women stared at me, Alanna's jaw-dropping while Natasha licked her ruby lips. The corners of her mouth curled up in a smile that screamed her hunger. I squeezed my breasts, loving their attention on me.

"I love that tattoo..." She glanced down at the card again. "Tiffany... That's sexy."

I ran a finger around the rainbow I had tattooed over my left nipple. The arc of it followed the circle of my areola. "Thanks. Now you two MILFs need to get naked so I can eat you out."

"Yes!" Natasha said. She grabbed her hem and pulled it up her body revealing a pair of large breasts straining against the soft-blue bra she wore. A trim of white lace added a delicate and sensual feel to it.

I peeled down my yoga pants next, shuddering as the soaked cloth peeled away from my pussy lips. I shuddered as they came apart, my juices making a sticky mess. The tangy aroma of my hot twat swelled in the air.

"Shaved. Nice," said Natasha.

"Eager to eat my bald beaver?"

The woman nodded.

"Natasha!" gasped Alanna, wrenching her gaze from my naked form to glance at her friend unhooking her bra. "What are you doing?"

"Getting naked so she can eat our pussies," said Natasha, her large tits spilling out as her bra cups fell away.

I smacked my lips at those big and lush and sexy breasts. A heat rushed through my body from my pussy. My cunt clenched. A trickle of juices tickled my thighs, the cream running down in hot rivulets from my pussy.

That naughty Natasha then unsnapped her jeans, her tits swaying before her. They smacked together, both rippling from the impact. The way they quivered had my mouth watering. My fingers dug into my tits as she shoved own her jeans. She wore a pair of high-cut panties in the same style as her bra. Light blue and trimmed in lace. Stray strands of midnight hairs peeked out the sides.

"This is insane," Alanna moaned. "You have to put your clothes back on. Both of you!"

"Nonsense," said Natasha and grabbed the hem of her friend's dress. She drew it up and up the woman's body.

"Natasha!" gasped Alanna. She fought against her friend for a moment, but Natasha kept tugging upward. She grappled at it, pinning her arms to the side. "This isn't right. We're married women."

"And?" I asked. "Does that mean you can't have your pussy licked by me? That you can't experience the best orgasm of your life."

"The best, Alanna," Natasha purred. "Weren't you just complaining about the lack of sex in your marriage ten minutes ago?"

"I wasn't suggesting I hire an eighteen-year-old girl to eat my pussy."

"Our pussies." Natasha tugged harder. "I need this, Alanna. Please."

Alanna glanced at my naked body. I winked at her. She shivered and then her arms relaxed. She didn't fight as Natasha peeled the sundress up and over Alanna's head. A pair of red panties hid her naughty bits while a gray bra cupped her tits. They were about my size, looking so delicious cupped by her brassier.

"Get naked," moaned Natasha as she dropped the dress. Then she shoved down her panties, revealing her black bush dripping in juices. "God, I'm so wet. You're turning me on, Tiffany."

"Good," I moaned. "How about you, Alanna?"

The red-haired MILF blushed as bright as her locks. She squirmed in place and muttered something that sounded like, "I'm getting wet, too." Then she reached behind her and unhooked her bra. She slipped the straps down her shoulders. I bit my lip.

God, she had great tits. I couldn't wait to enjoy them. I would squeeze them and love them and then she would explode. It would be just so awesome. I couldn't wait to lick from pussy to pussy. From furred muff to yummy snatch.

"Get those panties off," Natasha ordered.

"I can't believe I'm doing this," moaned Alanna. "I'm not into girls."

"Until you were," Natasha said. "Right? She appeared, and suddenly girls are turning you on."

"Yes!" hissed Alanna as she thrust down her panties. She peeled them down her thighs, her bush as bright as her hair. Her breasts swayed before her. They jiggled and then slapped together. They rippled apart as she straightened up and gave me a direct look.

I grinned at her, my pussy so wet. The cream was just running down my thighs.

"Now, how do we do this?" Natasha asked as I advanced on them.

I grabbed Alanna. The MILF licked her lips, her breath coming fast. The fresh scent of soap and a hint of eucalyptus oil wreathed her. I gripped her hands, skin like satin, and pulled her to the couch. Her eyes were locked on my perky tits. I loved the attention. I turned her and pushed her down on the couch. She sat there, legs closed.

"Spread those legs," I said, "and sit your rump right at the edge of the couch cushion."

She swallowed and then pried her thighs apart. I breathed in deeply. A new scent touched my nose. A sweet musk that had my mouth salivating. I ran my tongue across the roof of my mouth, my saliva soaking it.

"Now, Natasha, straddle her. Get that pussy right against hers. Then I can lick from one MILF cunt to the other."

"Yes," moaned the raven-haired woman. Her mature form sauntered to me, her large tits swaying from side to side. A tart musk tickled my nose. I breathed in deeply.

Groaned in delight.

"Wait, why is she straddling me," Alanna gasped as her friend sank down on the couch. Those large tits pressed into Alanna's face, muffling her next words. "This isn't what I thought. We're not..."

"Oh, we will be," cooed Natasha. "We're going to be lovers after today, Alanna. Can't you feel it?"

"I can," I moaned and then opened my purse. I pulled out a naughty toy, a U-shaped dildo that could fuck two pussies at once. It was for fucking your asshole and twat at the same time, but it would work great on the pair of them.

Just in case they wanted more than my tongue.

I fell to my knees before my altar. Two MILFs cunts pressed tight. Red pubic hair led to black. Their dew gleamed on their silky strands. I breathed in their scents. The perfume of their passion sent heady tingles through my body. Natasha's curvy rump jiggled as she shifted, her cheeks almost clapping.

It was perfection.

I dove my head down for Alanna's cunt. I went for her first, wanting to lick and lap at her. I wanted to make her squeal in rapture. She would cum so hard. It would be amazing to do to her. My mouth hungered for that wonderful moment.

Her silky hairs caressed my face. My lips and cheeks came alive, loving the caress of those strands on my features. A moment later, my lips found her pussy. I kissed at her twat. My tongue flicked out to caress her. She moaned as I stroked her.

That wonderful sound of passion echoed through the air. I savored the wonderful delight. The heat of her twat melted across my tongue. It was amazing to taste. My tongue dragged up her pussy folds, drinking in her sweet delight.

"Oh, my god!" she moaned, her voice muffled by a large set of tits.

"Mmm, is she licking you?" Natasha asked. "I can feel her nose rubbing through my bush and... Yes!"

My tongue flicked to Natasha's pussy. Her silky hairs had a finer texture to them. Not as wiry. Her pussy's tart flavor contrasted with Alanna's sweet cream. I groaned as the two delights mixed on my taste buds, setting different parts of my mouth alight with rapture.

I reached her taint and darted back down to lick from Alanna's again. I dragged from sweet to tart cunt, feasting on the two MILFs. They both squirmed and moaned. Their passion echoed through the living room as I went to work.

"Oh, my god," groaned Alanna. "I can't believe this is happening."

"Believe it," moaned her friend. "Mmm, and don't be shy. Play with my tits. They're around your face. Lick them. Kiss them."

"Yes!" I groaned then licked from pussy to pussy again.

"Oh, god," whimpered Alanna.

My tongue danced over their pussy lips. I caressed their folds and brushed their hard clits. They both jumped and moaned as I did that. I loved it. My tongue caressed over their naughty delights. I savored the taste of them. The mix of sweet and tart.

Natasha's ass clenched before me every time I brushed her pussy lips. Especially if I grazed her clit. I loved how she moaned. How they both groaned. Alanna's were muffled by those large tits. Their passion coated my lips, a sweet and tart delight.

Like cherries.

I fluttered my tongue again, stroking up and down from Alanna to Natasha and back to Alanna. As I did that, brushing their clits in the process, I heard a wet sound. Like suckling. Natasha moaned, her ass clenching tight.

"See," Natasha moaned. "Mmm, yes, yes, suckle on my nipple. Ooh, yes, yes, just like that."

This excitement washed through me as I heard the nipple suckling and Natasha's moans of delight. That was such a naughty thing to hear coming from the two women. The sound echoed from them both as my tongue fluttered up and down their snatches.

I caressed them. Lapped at them. I devoured them with hunger. My tongue flicked up and down their pussies. Their juices soaked my taste buds. Alanna suckled harder, making more sounds. Wet smacks. Juicy plops. They echoed through the air as I feasted on them.

"Mmm, your pussies are getting hot," I moaned, my cunt dripping. "How would you two like me to use a dildo on your cunts? It's shaped like a U. I can fuck you both at the same time."

"Do it!" Natasha moaned. "I don't care what the cost is."

I grabbed the U-shaped dildo, holding the base of the pink toy. I pressed it against both their pussies, my cunt on fire. I smacked sticky lips, loving the feel of their cream cooling on my face. I pushed the toy into their twats, sliding through their hairs to find their married pussies.

I thrust the ends of the toy into them.

Both moaned, Alanna's mixed with suckling. Natasha's back arched. Her butt-cheeks clenched as their cunts swallowed inch after inch of the dildo's shafts. I pushed the wicked toy deeper into their cunts until only the curved part connecting the two halves was left out.

Then I grinned and drew back.

I fucked the toy in and out of their pussies, the shaft emerging gleaming in cunt cream every time. The scent of their horny twats filled the air. I could get high just from the aroma of MILF pussy. I loved the aroma, savoring it as I fucked them.

"Oh, my god, yes!" Natasha moaned. "Mmm, Tiffany, you're amazing. And Alanna... Keep sucking my nipple. You two are going to make me cum."

"Perfect," I said, ramming the dildo in and out of their cunts. I fucked them hard with my naughty toy. "I want you two cumming. I want you both exploding. You deserve it."

I leaned in and lapped at the bottom of Alanna's pussy, giving her some extra stimulation as I reamed the sex toy out of their cunts. I held the curved bottom of the toy as I thrust it in and out of their cunts. Sweet pussy cream coated my tongue with my naughty fluttering.

I pumped harder and faster. Natasha's moans swelled in volume. Her ass clenched tight together. Alanna suckled with hunger. She nursed with passion on her friend's nub. The sounds echoed through the living room.

I shoved the toy deep into both women.

"Oh, my god, fuck!" gasped Natasha. "Fuck, fuck, fuck!"

Gushing out around the sex toy came a flood of MILF juices. The tart cream soaked my fingers. I shot my tongue up to lick at her snatch as I kept fucking both women. Her ass jiggled from her bucks. Her black hair danced down her pale back, silky shadows playing over bright skin.

"Yes, yes, yes!" she moaned. "This is amazing. Tiffany!"

A wet smack preceded Alanna howling. "Oh, my god! I'm cumming!"

I ripped the dildo from their pussies and feasted on the cream gushing out of their married twats. Alanna's bathed my face. She soaked my cheeks and chin. Natasha's joined her, the tart passion flavoring that sweet delight. I lapped them up. I drank them as they shuddered through their orgasms.

"I have to eat your pussy!" moaned Alanna. "Tiffany! Tiffany! I have to eat your cunt."

"Yes!" gasped Natasha. "Oh, my god, yes, yes, yes! That's what I need. Let's eat your cunt!"

I smiled and stood up. I sank down on the recliner, no doubt the throne Alanna's husband ruled from. I felt so naughty planting my naked rump on it. My legs spread wide, throwing one each over the armrests. A hot shiver ran through me. I was so ready for this. So eager for them to feast on me and make me cum.

That would be so hot.

The two women fell to their knees between my thighs. Alanna had this eager gleam in her green eyes while Natasha flicked her pink tongue over her ruby lips. I squirmed, the woven texture of the chair rubbing across my rump.

Then they dived into the feast.

The two MILFs pressed their cheeks tight together and licked at my cunt. They flicked their tongues up and down my pussy folds. It was incredible to feel. To experience. I squirmed there, my eyes closed. I loved every moment of them licking and lapping at me.

"Yes!" I gasped, my pussy already simmering from pleasuring them. It wouldn't be long. "Eat me!"

Their two tongues caressed up and down my folds. I felt each MILF stroking me. One went up as the other went down, passing each other. Red locks spilled across midnight tresses. Two sets of eyes stared up at me with feverish light.

I squeezed my tits, my legs draped over their shoulders, and enjoyed their ministrations. They licked and lapped and gave me just what I needed. They feasted on me with aplomb. I loved every moment of it.

"Oh, my god!" I groaned, squirming. "The only thing better than one MILF eating my cunt is two!"

"You taste so good!" moaned Alanna, her eyes glassy, almost like a window fogged up by heavy breathing. "Mmm, just delicious."

"Right?" Natasha asked. Then her tongue shoved into my pussy's depths.

I gasped, my body bucking. My breasts jiggled as the heat swept through me. It was incredible to feel that wonderful passion sweeping through my body. She swirled her tongue through my twat while Alanna went for my clit.

She fluttered against it. I gasped at the burst of pleasure. I groaned, my heart pounding in my chest to the rhythm of Alanna's licking. I squeezed my eyes shut, loving every moment of this bliss. The two MILFs devoured me.

"Oh, my god, yes!" I moaned. "I'm going to cum so hard. You two are going to make me explode!"

"Good," moaned Alanna.

"Shower us in cream!" moaned Natasha.

Their tongues both thrust into my pussy. I gasped at the feel of two MILF tongues wiggling around inside of me. That was insane. It was amazing. I loved it. My body twitched from the delight, the pleasure racing through me. I hurtled towards my orgasm. I was moments from completely exploding in delight.

Their tongues were driving me wild. Their noses rubbed into my clit as they feasted on me. My toes curled. The pressure swelled in my cunt as they fucked their tongues in and out of my depths. They were devouring me.

"Yes, yes, yes!" I gasped. "Oh, fuck! Oh, that's good. Yes!"

I came.

My pussy convulsed around their tongues. The juices gushed out into their hungry mouths. They licked it up. My back arched into the recliner. The springs groaned beneath the fabric. I whimpered, my tits heaving. The tangy aroma of my snatch filled the air.

"You two are amazing!" I moaned.

"So good!" Alanna gasped between licks.

"You're so tasty!" groaned Natasha.

The waves of delight inundated my mind. I squirmed there as they lapped up my cream, stimulating my sensitive flesh. They brushed my clit, adding small ripples of ecstasy to wash through me. It was amazing to experience. The best bliss in the world.

"Yes!" I gasped as I hit that peak. I hovered there for a wonderful moment and then I panted into gasping moans. "You two are amazing."

"So are you," groaned Alanna, lifting her head from my twat, my pussy juices smeared over her gorgeous lips.

"So..." Natasha said as I came down from my orgasm. My cunt

cream gleamed on her lips. "We can fuck you with strap-ons?"

"Yes, you can!" I moaned and launched into action.

I pulled out the two strap-ons I had bought out of the large purse, its woven-straw sides creaking. I tossed a simulated flesh dildo with a black harness to Natasha and a slick red aluminum dildo with canvas straps to Alanna.. Then I snagged a bottle of lube.

"Alanna, you're getting my ass," I said, tossing her the bottle. "Get that nice and covered then come join me in your bed."

"What?" Alanna gasped.

I winked at her and then darted naked to the stairs. My tits heaved before me. The women gasped. I heard them scrambling. I reached the second floor. I passed a child's room, school was in session, and then burst into the master bedroom. The dark-stained posts and headboard contrasted with the ivory cream of the comforter. I threw myself on it, lying on my side, so ready to be fucked by the two MILFs.

I didn't have to wait long.

The cacophony of their footsteps pounding up the stairs preceded them. Then they burst in, Natasha leading the way with the fleshy dildo thrusting out before her. It bobbed as she moved, her tits heaving with her steps. She slid onto the bed as I lifted my thigh, flashing my twat.

"You sexy minx!" she moaned and then kissed me. Her tangy-flavored lips sealed about my mouth. Her tongue thrust past my lips. I shuddered at the feel of her. It was such a wonderful delight to have her sliding up against me.

Then her breasts caressed into mine. They were so soft and wonderful to feel against my skin as they dragged up to slide over my tits. Our nipples caressed. Sparks flared. I shot my hand down and grabbed her cock, guiding it to my pussy.

As I pressed it into my excited twat, Alanna crawled onto the bed. The red, metallic shaft gleamed in the lube. That slick wetness had my asshole tingling. I was so ready to be double-fucked by these two sexy MILFs.

Natasha thrust her toy into my cunt.

I squealed into her lips.

"My, oh, my," whimpered Alanna as she moved behind me.

"This is really happening. I can't believe it. I'm so wet. Ooh, this is going to make me cum hard, isn't it?"

I broke the kiss to moan, "Yes!"

I savored that big dildo thrusting in and out of my cunt. Natasha fucked me hard, her hands grabbing my rump. Fingernails bit into my flesh as she pulled apart my ass-cheeks. I gasped at the hot flares of delight. Alanna moved into position. She guided her toy into my crevice. The cool, smooth tip slid down to my asshole.

She pressed against it and moaned. Her round breasts hugged into my back as she drilled that dildo into my tight asshole. Natasha fucked my cunt with her veiny shaft, stimulating me. I groaned, savoring it. My anal ring stretched and stretched to engulf Alanna's fake-dick.

"Oh, my god," gasped Alanna. "I can feel it rubbing on my clit. Ooh, this is hot."

"I know!" panted Natasha. Her tits jiggled against mine, full of their pillowy softness. "Sodomize her!"

"She is!" I groaned as that dildo popped into my asshole.

"Yes!" Alanna gasped in triumph and slid her dildo into my bowels.

I shuddered between the two MILFs. I reveled in how great this felt. It was amazing to experience the two shafts double-stuffing my body. My holes welcomed the dildos. My bowels drank in the lubed, metallic cock plundering my anal depths while my pussy clenched down on the rubbery dick ramming into my silky sheath.

I trembled between them. Alanna's wiry brush rubbed into my ass-cheeks. I had ever inch of her dildo in me. At the same moment, Natasha's silky pubic hairs caressed the folds of my pussy. The pleasure shot through me.

It was incredible.

I shuddered between them. I loved the feel of their silky hairs caressing me. That wonderful heat swept over my body as they both fucked me. Two sets of breasts rubbed into me. One against my supple back, the other into my perky tits. They pounded me.

"Oh, my god, yes!" Alanna moaned as she fucked my asshole on her marital bed. "Oh, that's amazing. That's awesome."

"Uh-huh!" I said, loving that dildo ramming into my bowels

while the rubbery cock fucked my pussy. "You two MILFs are stirring me up."

"My clit is loving it!" groaned Natasha. "Oh, yes, yes, you naughty cutie!"

I licked at her face, cleaning up my juices off of her. Alanna panted in my ear, hugging me tight as she sodomized me. She fucked me harder and harder. They both rammed their dildos into my holes. My naughty sheaths clenched down on their toys, drinking in the friction.

I trembled between them, my orgasm building so fast. It was incredible to be double-fucked by them. They pounded me hard and fast. They rammed those two shafts into me. The sexy MILF fucked me hard.

The mattress creaked beneath us. I loved it. I fluttered my tongue over Natasha's lips. She sucked it into her mouth. My pussy clenched on her dildo slamming hard into me. Her silky bush caressed my cunt lips. My clit. Sparks burst through me.

My orgasm swelled so fast. I whimpered as Natasha sucked on my tongue. It was so naughty to feel the MILF doing that. My body trembled, toes curling. I squirmed on my side, the comforter rubbing on my arm and hip.

"Oh, my god!" Alanna moaned. "I'm going to cum from ass-fucking you with a strap-on. I love it. I love being a lesbian!"

Natasha slid her lips off my tongue. "Me, too!"

"Yes!" I howled and exploded in rapture. "I'm cumming!"

My pussy and asshole writhed around their dildos plunging into them. They slammed hard into me. They fucked me with passion. I gasped and moaned, my holes convulsing harder and harder. Waves of delight washed through my body.

"Oh, yes, yes!" Alanna moaned and slammed her dildo into my asshole, her nipples rubbing into my squirming back. "Tiffany! I'm cumming!"

We trembled together. My nipples slid over Natasha's soft breasts. Stars burst across my vision. She slammed her dildo to the depths of my convulsing twat. Her head threw back, her tits pressed tight into my boobs.

"Fuck, yes!" the black-haired MILF moaned. "Oh, Tiffany!

You're worth every penny!"

"So worth it!" Alanna howled.

The three of us bucked through our orgasm together. The waves of pleasure carried me to that wonderful pinnacle of ecstasy. Our bodies quivered there, the pleasure blazing through my mind. The heat sizzled. I savored every second of it.

Then it died down.

I groaned as the two MILFs suddenly leaned over me and kissed each other. I shuddered at that. They were having there fun. I squirmed between them, my body buzzing from the orgasmic bliss that we just shared. I savored being between them as they kissed each other.

Soon they broke apart. They were clearly wanting to play with each other. They had to pay with a credit card, but that was no biggie thanks to the Square app. I slapped a little card reader into the bottom of my phone and swiped them. In moments, I had the money depositing into my Stripe account.

I walked out with $425 between the pair of them, leaving them to sixty-nine with each other in lesbian bliss.

After dressing and gathering my things, I hummed as I stepped out of Alanna's house. They both promised to hand out my cards to friends. More married MILFs that needed a young, lezzie cutie like me to please them. I marched out into the afternoon sunlight, the warmth spilling over my face.

Kissing me like a lover.

I was halfway to the seventh house when my cell phone rang. It wasn't a number I recognized. I took in a deep breath and cooed, "Tiffany speaking."

"You're the girl who... who gave me the card," the breathy voice said. "Are you still in the neighborhood? I could use, um..."

"My tongue licking at your married twat?" I asked, turning around.

"Yes!" she moaned. "I'm at 1403. Third house on the right side of the street."

I smiled. That was the woman who slammed the door in my face. "I'll be there in thirty seconds. I want you naked and ready for me to devour you."

"Yes!" she moaned.

I smiled. I loved my new job. There was nothing like showing sexy MILFs the wicked things they needed to experience. My clit throbbed against my yoga pants, pulsing with the delight that would come. I shifted my purse's straps digging into my shoulder and jogged down the street.

Time to get paid to have fun. It was the best. I was so glad I had been seduced into lesbian delights by those hot MILFs. Now I wanted to pass that treat on to all the older beauties I could.

To be continued...

# Samantha's Hot MILF Workout

## Prowling for Lesbian MILFs 3

## A Lesbian MILF Tale

by

Reed James

## Samantha's Hot MILF Workout

### Samantha Reid – Friday, Day 5 of the Wish

Tiffany and Sydney rushed out of my house with their new business cards. We were all working for the wickedest new company in the world: Little Lezzie Delights.

We were barely legal dyke prostitutes.

That sent a naughty shudder through my body. I rubbed at my white shirt, my dark hands standing out. I wanted to get to the gym and find a bunch of White wives getting their asses tight. Nothing like a MILF to get a cute, young thing like me wet and horny and rearing to go.

I would make so much money at the gym. Sydney was off to the mall to prowl for sexy MILFs to seduce into lesbian sex while Tiffany thought going door-to-door like a sapphic saleswoman was the key to getting all that mature pussy the three of us craved. There was nothing like being eighteen and feasting on older women's twats.

I slipped into my car as Tiffany pulled out of the driveway to race off. Up the cul-de-sac, Sydney had reached her house and was hopping into her sedan. I was so glad that a pair of MILFs named Mrs. Wright and Mrs. Greene had come a knocking at my place looking for barely legal pussy to enjoy.

She had seduced me right there beneath my now ex-boyfriend's nose. He thought it was hot watching a MILF do lezzie things to me. Little did he realize those two older hotties had flipped this switch in me.

I didn't want guys at all now.

As I sat in my car, I wrote on my business cards. I had my own idea. This wicked plan to get wild in the locker room. I just wanted all the pussy I could lick and lap and devour. I closed my eyes and squeezed my thighs together. Wearing a pair of athletic shorts left my dark-brown legs bare. I shuddered as I wrote.

Once I had a good thirty of my new business cards containing my notes, I was ready to get wild. I backed out of the driveway and headed to Curves, the all-women's gym. Just the name made my cunt drip with excitement.

Curves...

What a hot name for a gym for women. I pictured all those curves as I drove. MILFs with big breasts heaving over me as I ate their pussies. Plump booties jiggling as I pounded them with a strap-on. Sleek thighs. Hourglass hips. Mature beauties that need a cute, young thing like me to make them cum.

"I'm coming for you," I moaned to myself. "Especially you White MILFs. I'm going to give you a taste of brown sugar."

I shuddered, my thighs squeezing tight as I waited at a traffic light. My clit throbbed and ached. With my pussy shaved, the tight fabric of my jogging shorts molded to my snatch. The black shorts would flash anyone a cameltoe that would melt their snatches. It rode into my butt-crack, outlining my asscheeks. My slender body quivered. I wanted to cup my small breasts, little mounds topped by hard nipples.

The light changed, and I was off. My thighs squeezed so tight together. I was so ready for the pleasure that would come. The gym would be such a rocking place. My sweaty palms slid across the steering wheel. Over the pine air freshener dangling from my rearview mirror, my sweet musk filled the air.

God, it was a lovely scent.

I breathed it in the entire way to the gym. It took ten minutes, and I had to wait *forever* to make the left turn into the parking lot. I squirmed their, my destination in sight as I waited for a break in traffic. Cars drove by, the five lane street busy. I bounced in my seat, so eager to get there.

In the parking lot, a blonde with short hair marched out of her car and headed inside. I smiled at the sight of her. She was the type of woman I was here to play with. She looked older. A MILF. A hot wife who needed to learn that lesbianism was far, far better than what her husband offered.

The break in traffic appeared. I turned quickly, tires squealing from the sudden acceleration. Burned rubber stung my nose. Shocks squeaked as I passed over a small lip at the transition from street to parking lot. I found a parking spot and hopped out of the car. I rushed to the door and...

Turned around and ran back to my car to get my gym bag.

"Keep your shit together, Samantha," I told myself. "Don't be a fucking moron. Need to be on top of things."

I snagged my gym bag. It had a couple of neat treats inside of it. I slung it over my shoulder and headed for the door. I hummed in delight, my business cards held in my hand. The edges bit into my palm as I held a stack of thirty of them.

I opened the door and surveyed the sight.

A woman named Kelly was sitting at a receptionist's desk. She was young, like me. Not the clientele I was after, though she was cute with a brown ponytail and a sports bra that cupped her round tits. She looked up at me and smiled.

"Welcome to Curves. Membership card?" she asked, eyebrows narrowing. "It's Samantha, right?"

"Yep," I said. My mom had bought me a membership. I should come more often.

Kelly typed in the system and smiled. "Enjoy your workout. Wipe down your station after using it."

I nodded. I wasn't here to exercise.

There were about twenty or so women at various exercise machines. Three were on the StairMasters, their asses swaying in their yoga pants or jogging shorts, clinging to those curvy booties. I groaned at the sight of them. A few others were on the treadmill. Some worked at the various resistance machines, the ones that had weights attached to various bars that you pushed our pulled on. They let you work on specific body parts like your legs or your arms. Others were working up a sweat on the ellipticals and exercise bikes.

It was a paradise of older women for me to enjoy.

I shifted my bag on my shoulder and headed for the women on the StairMasters. They were pumping their legs as they stimulated climbing upstairs. The nearest one, a Hispanic beauty with big tits, had a gleam of sweat across her golden-brown face. Her breasts heaved in her tank top.

"Hi," I said. "I'm Samantha. I'm here to help you relax."

"What?" she panted as I slipped a card into her left hand that had a wedding ring glinting on it.

"Just read the card," I said and licked my lips at her.

As she glanced down and furrowed her brow as she read the card, I moved onto the next woman on the StairMaster. It was the woman with the short, blond hair I spotted coming into the club. She was just working up that wonderful gleam on her face as I slipped her the card.

"Looking good," I said. "But if you want to really feel awesome, I'll be waiting in the locker room."

"What?" she asked in confusion. Then she stared down at the card. "Wait, what?"

I just kept going. I slipped my card to the other two women on the StairMasters, loving the shake of their breasts and the passion on their faces. Then I was off the exercise bikes. I slipped a card to a brunette with huge breasts. She was young but had a wedding ring on. That made her sexy enough for me.

"You're going to love it," I told her and then moved onto the next hot MILF who needed to be loved.

It was so hot to hand out the cards to them. As I did, the ones who'd gotten it earlier were watching me. I spotted that Hispanic woman standing by the StairMaster as she studied my card. She was reading it, seeing the naughty things it said. My pussy clenched as I knew my business card by heart.

**Samantha Reid**
**Naughty Escort**
**Little Lezzie Delights**

**Every MILF deserves a little delight!**
**$20 and I'll lick you. $100 and you lick me**
**(253) 555-9431**

It made me so wet knowing that she was realizing just what I was selling. My body. Her pleasure. It had me dripping as I came upon a Black woman on a resistance machine. She was thrusting her legs forward, her ebony thighs flexing in such delicious ways.

"You're going to want to enjoy my services," I purred to the older woman.

"Huh?" she said, her brow furrowing in concentration as she pushed again.

I just winked at her and then was moving over to an Asian woman as she worked her arms before her, opening and closing them like they were the shell of a clam. She had a great body, her face round and her tits small in her sports bra. But she was a MILF. I slipped the card into her fingers and blew her a kiss.

She stopped and read the card as I walked away. I heard her gasp in shock. That sent such a wicked thrill through my body as I handed my card to another MILF on a different machine. It was so hot. My pussy was on fire as I came over to the free weight station. A woman was pumping a pair of five-pound irons, curling first her right arm and then her left. She had big tits and her black hair tied back in a ponytail.

She was the last woman in the gym that hadn't gotten a card. "You're going to want to come and enjoy my services."

She blinked as I boldly shoved the card into her cleavage. She froze. Her eyes met mine. They brimmed in shock. I smiled at her and turned. I sauntered towards the locker room, my ass swaying in my tight shorts.

I felt so many MILFs watching me. Many of them were no longer exercising as they studied their cards and then glanced at me. One turned it over and read the note I wrote on the back.

**"I'll be in the locker room waiting to eat your pussy."**

I hoped they would come and hire me. I would do such wicked things with them. I sauntered by the blonde with the short hair and winked at her. She swallowed, her nipples poking at her sports bra. Then I fluttered my tongue at the brunette. She rubbed a hand at her wedding ring.

I vanished into the locker room, my pussy on fire. I threw my gym back down and then peeled off my shirt. I exposed my flat stomach. Dangling from my bellybutton was a charm, a short length of gold chain with a heart at the end. My small breasts quivered. I shoved my shirt into my gym bag and kicked off my shoes. I peeled off my socks, standing on the bare tile. There was a faint musk of sweat in the locker room. That feminine aroma of hard work. I licked my lips and shoved down my shorts.

"Ooh, I am so juicy. Going to get me some MILF pussy."

I stepped out of my shorts as the first of the MILFs entered. It was the Hispanic woman. She stared at me as I stripped naked. She held my card in her hand. She was turning it over and over again as she stared at my body. A moment later, the Asian woman entered. She trembled, her small breasts rising and falling in her sports bra.

"Just $20, and you'll get eaten," I said. Then I pulled a fleshy dildo and a clit rocket out of my bag. I sauntered back to the shower area. It was open, a place where women could wash off. No privacy at all. Just an open area.

A small drip fell from one shower head. The floor had a sheen of water over it. I knelt down on it, my breasts jiggling. A third MILF had joined the other two, standing behind them. They were all watching me, holding the cards.

I winked at them and then turned on the clit rocket. I set the fleshy dildo beside me and pressed the small, buzzing vibrator against my nipple. It was the size of a bullet and buzzed away with wicked intensity. My nub burst with pleasure.

"Oh, my god, yes," I moaned to the watching MILFs as I ran the toy around my nipple. A fourth one had joined, the black-haired woman whom I had tucked the card into her cleavage. She'd fished it out, staring at me. "Ooh, the things I'll do to you sexy women. Get naked and join me."

I ran the vibrator over my nipple. The areola drank it in. I shuddered in delight, my hips wiggling from side to side. This wicked tingle race down to my cunt and fed the growing heat in me. This fire would blaze through me in orgasmic fury.

I pushed the vibrator harder into my nub.

I watched them squirm. Their faces flushed. The Black woman appeared. I winked at the sexy older sistah as I rubbed the bullet vibrator against my dark-brown nipple. The humming massaged it. My body trembled. Pussy cream ran down my thighs.

That wonderful, sweet musk filled my nose. It was growing stronger and stronger as the MILFs watched. The brunette squeezed at her tits through her sports bra as she watched, her eyes so wide as she stared at me. There were ten or so of them watching me know.

"Mmm, yes, yes, you know you want me to eat you out," I purred. "$20. That's worth it to get off on a sexy, young lesbian's mouth. I know you wall want to drown me in your cunt cream. You all want to drown me in your delicious juices."

"Oh, my god," one woman moaned, her passion rising out of the crowd.

Then the brunette peeled off her top. Her large breasts spilled out. They held a pillowy softness to them. They swayed together. The hot wife grabbed her naked tits as she stared at me rubbing the clit rocket on my nipple.

Then she broke away from the others. She shoved down her yoga pants as she did. She pushed them over her thighs and then hopped forward on one foot and then the other. Those big tits of hers heaved before her. They smacked together. I bit my lip, my cunt clenching as I loved the sight of her. She was down to a pair of panties, her wedding ring flashing. She paused to shoved those off.

She was shaved and had a pierced clit.

I gasped at the sight of the gold ring flashing amid her thick pussy lips. She stepped out of her panties and left them on the floor. She rushed over as the other MILFs moved closer. They were squeezing tits and wiggling hips, getting turned on.

"God, I want my pussy devoured, Samantha," she said. "If that's even your real name."

"Oh, it is," I said and realized we could have come up with naughty names. Like Sapphic Samantha or something. Oh, well. I licked my lips. "Just yank my head forward and make me eat your cunt."

"I haven't had a woman ever eat me out," she moaned as she stepped up beside me. "Why are you so fucking sexy?"

"Because you're a naughty, White bitch that wants a hot Black girl to devour her cunt," I said. "Got some lezzie jungle fever burning in you."

"Yes," she moaned and then grabbed my thick, black hair. She yanked my head forward to those thick and juicy pussy lips. The tangy aroma of her pussy filled my nose moments before she buried my face into her snatch.

Her hard clit ring rubbed on my upper lip. Her tangy juices bled into my mouth. They soaked my taste buds with that delicious flavor. My tongue flicked out, parting through her thick folds. She moaned. Tits swayed over my head.

I batted her clit ring.

"Mmm, yes," she moaned. "I need this. I need a good cum."

"Yes, you do," I moaned, sliding the clit rocket from my nipple and down my body.

I slid my left hand around her waist and grabbed her plump booty. I squeezed her curvy ass and fluttered my tongue up and down her folds, brushing her clit ring. She moaned, her lush breasts swaying above my head. They smacked into each other, rippling from the impact.

Her tangy cream soaked my mouth. Her thick juices coated my tongue as I slid through her fold. I reveled in it. I loved the feel of her thick cuntlips rubbing on my cheeks. Her scent filled my nose. I couldn't smell anything else.

I shoved the clit rocket between my thighs. I rubbed it up and down my shaved slit. Pleasure rippled through me. I moaned into her twat, my tongue dancing up and down her folds. I loved her clit ring. I played with it as I rubbed my cunt with the buzzing bullet.

I caught movement around us. The other women were moving in. I spotted the Hispanic woman's naked tits. They were big and soft, that wonderful shade of golden-brown. She squeezed her nipples as she watched what I was doing. The Asian woman kneaded her conical tits while a thick bush formed a shadowy tangle of silk between her pale-olive thighs. The blonde peeled off her top, her round boobs popping into view.

I loved it. They were watching me give my service. They whispered to each other, an almost hum of feminine excitement around the brunette moaning as she ground her pussy and clit ring against my hungry mouth.

"Oh, my god, I need this," the MILF moaned. "I haven't had anyone eat my pussy in two months."

"You poor thing," I groaned and then thrust my tongue into her pussy.

"God, yes!" Her pussy squeezed about me. The tangy flavor increased. Her cream poured down my tongue into my mouth.

I loved it. Her clit ring rubbed on my upper lip as I tongue-fucked her twat. My left hand gripped her ass. Her muscles played beneath my fingers as she squirmed from side to side. My pussy clenched. I rubbed the vibrator up and down it.

A shiver of heat ran through me. I loved the feel of playing with my pussy. I slid that buzzing toy up to my clit and then back down. The buzzing bliss burst from it. An explosion of sparks that showered my cunt in such wicked heat.

"She's so sexy," one of the watching women purred.

"Mmm, I'm going to have her eat me out," another said.

"I want that tongue in my pussy!"

"She has that dildo."

"I can't believe she's doing this. That I want her to do it to me!"

"I know. I'm not even into girls."

"Me either."

It was so hot hearing their voices drift around me. It had me fucking my tongue deep into the brunette's pussy. Her MILF titties heaved while her tangy juices grew stronger and stronger. I pressed the clit rocket hard into my bud. My body shook and cunt clenched.

My orgasm built from the attention.

Then I flicked my tongue up to the MILF's pierced clit. I fluttered against that gold ring, twisting it up and down. She groaned as I did that. Her hands squeezed her tits. Then I sucked her bud and its naughty jewelry into my mouth and nursed.

"Oh, fuck! I'm going to cum!" The MILF's fingers dug into her tits. "You naughty, little slut. You're going to make me cum."

Breathy moans came from the watching MILFs. I felt their excitement billowing through the air. Like a warm surf washing over my body. I savored it. I groaned around the clit in my mouth and suckled hard, wanting to make the MILF explode in rapture.

My tongue batted that clit ring as I nursed. I suckled with hunger. Juices ran down my chin. I wiggled my hips from side to side, my cunt on fire from the buzzing vibrator pressing on my bud. I moaned around her clit, giving this White MILF all the pleasure I could.

"Yes, yes, I'm going to cum! Oh, my god, that's amazing. You're amazing, Samantha!" Her head threw back. Her tits heaved forward. "Yes!"

Her pussy juices gushed out. That wonderful spray of cunt cream bathed my face. I abandoned her clit to drink down her tangy delight. Juices ran over my chin and down my throat. My hand clenched at her ass. I held her tight as she bucked against me.

"Oh, my god, that's great!" she moaned. "You're amazing. You all have to have her do things to you! Oh, my god!"

"She does so many naughty things," a watching woman moaned as I drank that cunt cream down.

"Ooh, I have to try that," another cooed.

"I want to do that one."

I rubbed my clit rocket against my bud. I squealed into the pussy grinding on my mouth. My orgasm burst through me as I lapped up that delicious cream. The brunette MILF gasped and stumbled back from me.

I quivered there, my small titties jiggling, as all the sexy, older women were around me, naked, squeezing their tits. They stared down at me with such wild lust in their eyes. I groaned, my body quivering. My clit throbbed and ached as I rubbed the vibrator against it.

"Who's next?" I moaned, my orgasm blazing through me. It burned out of my cunt.

"Me!" the blonde moaned. She stepped up before me, turned around, and thrust her ass out at me. "I've always wanted someone to rim my asshole. I never had the courage to ask my husband or my old boyfriends. Please, please, do it! I'll pay that $40."

"Yum!" I moaned, staring at that plump, White ass before me. Her blonde bush peeked out beneath her thighs, but I had eyes for only that booty.

With a moan, my pussy still convulsing through my orgasm, I thrust my head forward. I slid my face between her pale butt-cheeks. The sour aroma of her asshole filled my nose. My wet cheeks and lips smooched down lower and lower, the dirty flavor growing. The silky feel of her rump on my face sent a naughty thrill burning through me as I came again.

Then I found her asshole. I kissed it.

"Yes!" the blonde MILF moaned, her butt-cheeks clenching about my face. "Oh, my god, that feels so good. That's wild."

"She's really willing to do anything," another woman moaned.

"I am going for it next!"

"Not if I don't get her first!"

I loved it. Their words swirled around me as I feasted on the White woman's booty. My tongue danced around her asshole. I swirled about it, savoring the sour flavor. That wonderful, puckered texture soaked my tongue. A hot shiver ran through me as I rimmed her.

She moaned, her back arching. Her short, blonde hair swayed just above her shoulders. Her butt-cheeks gripped my face as I swirled my tongue over that asshole. I kept shuddering, my body convulsing through my second orgasm. My clit throbbed as I kept rubbing the clit rocket on it. Juices soaked the bullet vibrator.

I didn't care. I was just happy to lick and lap and feast on her booty. To rim this sexy MILF. It was so wild. I fluttered my tongue up and down her naughty hole. I caressed her puckered sphincter, drinking in the heat while my body burned with climactic delight.

"Oh, this is amazing," moaned the blonde. "You have to try her mouth on your asshole."

"God, that's hot," whimpered a MILF.

"Her tongue was amazing," the brunette moaned. "I'm leaving the $20 on your gym bag, Samantha."

"I can't wait for my turn."

"Oh, damn, I have to pick up my kids. I'll call you, Samantha! I want you to eat my pussy out soon!"

I loved it. I kept rimming the woman's sphincter, my clit throbbing against the vibrator. My bud grew more and more sensitive as the orgasmic delight burned through me. Pussy cream flooded down my thighs. I shuddered, moaning into the hot asshole.

I sucked on the Blonde's sphincter. I loved the feel of it on my lips. It was wild to enjoy. I swirled my tongue around her sphincter. The wicked texture rubbed over my mouth. My tongue fluttered dance around it, the earthy flavor soaking my taste buds.

"Yes, yes, yes!" moaned the sexy White woman. "Oh, my god. That's it. You're so amazing, Samantha."

I was.

My clit throbbed more. It started to hurt from the vibration. As my tongue danced around the MILF's asshole, I ripped the rocket from my bud. My orgasm hit that wonderful peak. I groaned as I came down, the heat dwindling.

What a great cum.

I thrust my tongue against the White woman's asshole. I forced more on her, wanting to give her so much pleasure. The other women whimpered and moaned around us. I caught whiffs of tart and tangy and spicy and sweet cunts over the sour musk of the blonde's asshole. Wonderful hints of perfume, those delicious twats that I wanted to devour.

But I had a booty to please. I would make the blonde cum. I thrust my tongue into her asshole and brought the fingers of my left hand to her pussy lips. I rubbed up and down her cunt as my tongue pushed on her asshole.

Her sphincter widened and swallowed my tongue.

I sank into her velvety sheath. She moaned louder. Her bowels clenched on my probing tongue. The earthy flavor swelled. I groaned at how nasty this was. It made me shiver. My cunt clenched. I was so ready to make her cum from this.

"Yes, yes, yes!" the blonde moaned. "It's even better than I thought. Thank you, Samantha. I love it. Oh, I could cum from just this, but... If you use the vibrator on me, I'll pay for that, too."

I turned the clit rocket back on by squeezing the vinyl casing. It buzzed to life. I shoved it up her thigh, my tongue dancing around in her bowels. I pressed the toy into her silky bush. I slid through her folds, caressing her.

She gasped. Her butt-cheeks clenched and asshole tightened. Her supple back arched as she moaned out in delight. I rubbed the rocket up and down her pussy folds and fucked my tongue in and out of her asshole.

"Yes, yes, yes!" she moaned. "Oh, my god, that's it. That's what I need. Samantha! Samantha!"

A wicked thrill ran through me to give this sexy MILF what she craved. I danced my tongue around in her asshole, teasing her. I shoved the clit rocket into her pussy. My fingers sank the toy into her hot cunt. Her flesh squeezed about my digits holding the toy humming away in her.

Her moans echoed through the locker room. Her passion rose over the watching women's murmurs. I loved it. My cunt clenched, aching for more pleasure. My clit throbbed again, calming down from one orgasm and craving another.

Craving the vibrator.

But it was buried the blonde's twat.

I twisted it around in her as I feasted on her booty. I swirled that naughty toy about in her cunt. I loved how she gasped and moaned. Her passion echoed around us. Her juices ran down my hand gripping the buzzing toy.

"Samantha!" she groaned. "I'm getting there. Oh, yes, yes, you're going to make me cum."

"Good," I moaned and slid the clit rocket out of her pussy. I dragged it up her folds, searching for its namesake.

She gasped. Bucked. I found it.

I rubbed the clit rocket there and tongue-fucked her sour bowels. Her silky butt-cheeks squeezed and relaxed about my face. Her hair danced. Her entire body swayed. I loved it. I feasted on her asshole and teased her clit.

"She's about to pop," a woman whispered.

"I want to pop," another panted.

"Mmm, I want to eat that young thing's pussy!"

"God, yes. When did girls get so hot?"

"No, fucking idea. But she makes me think about my step-daughter."

"That's hot."

It was.

I pushed the clit rocket against her bud. My tongue danced

through her asshole. She clenched her butt-cheeks tight about me. Her moans grew louder. Her hands suddenly thrust over her head, fingers reaching for the ceiling.

"Samantha!" she howled.

Hot pussy juices gushed out of her cunt and bathed my hand. Her asshole writhed around my tongue. This thrill ran through me, racing out of my twat dripping for her. I moaned into her asshole. I sucked on her sphincter as she bucked through her pleasure.

"Worth it!" she gasped. "This is so worth the cost! You all have to try this sexy cutie."

"Oh, I am!" a woman moaned. "I'm eating that pussy next."

"Ooh, and she can fuck me with the dildo while you do that!" another MILF moaned.

I wanted that so much. I kept sucking at the blonde's asshole, my pussy clenching. She bucked through her orgasm. Her whimpers and moans were incredible. Her passion soaked my hand. Then she groaned and stumbled forward.

"I can't take any more!" she panted as she grabbed a row of lockers for support. She pressed her naked body into it and then turned around. She slumped to the ground, her sweaty skin squeaking against the metal surface. "Oh, that was amazing. You're amazing, Samantha."

"So use that dildo on me," moaned the Asian MILF. She sank down before me and spread her thighs. Her black bush dripped with her cream. It was so thick I couldn't see her pussy lips.

"Gladly," I said, clicking off the bullet vibrator. I grabbed the fleshy dildo and then flicked my tongue over the tip. I sucked on it as I crawled between her thighs. The tart scent of her pussy filled my nose.

"I want that pussy," another woman moaned. I threw a look over my shoulder to see the Black MILF falling to her knees. "I need it. Damn, that looks so yummy. You're shaved, Samantha."

I pulled the dildo from my mouth and moaned, "Mmm, sistah, get to lickin'."

"Yes!" gasped the Black MILF. She grabbed my rump and lowered her head.

"Fuck me!" the Asian MILF moaned. She shuddered on the

floor, staring at me with such heat in her almond-shaped eyes. Her small breasts quivered, jiggling about as much as my little titties did.

"Yes, ma'am," I groaned and leaned in. I pressed the dildo into the silky curls of her bush. Those midnight strands swallowed the tip. Then I hit resistance.

"Yes," she groaned, squirming. She lay on her back and grabbed her titties. She kneaded those small mounds as I rubbed the toy up and down her slit, searching for the entrance to her pussy.

I found it. Thrust.

She gasped as the fleshy dildo vanished into her flesh. I loved the feel of sliding it into her. The thick, beige shaft reamed into her. I could feel the resistance of her expanding pussy as she stretched to take it. Her moans echoed.

Then the Black MILF smooched my pussy. I gasped as she planted her lips right on my slit. It sent a wave of heat through me. She kissed all over it, lips hot on my plump vulva. She brushed my clit. Sparks flared.

I moaned in delight and fucked the dildo in and out of the Asian MILF's cunt. I loved having my pussy kissed by the Black MILF. She peppered my twat with those hot smooches. My body trembled, my ass clenching.

"Ooh, that's good," I moaned.

"Girl, your pussy tastes delicious," the MILF eating me moaned. "Damn, I love it."

She licked me.

I gasped, toes curling, as her tongue slid from just below my clit and up to the top of my slit. I wiggled my hips from side to side, savoring the heat of it. My eyes squeezed closed. I jammed the dildo deep into the Asian MILF's pussy.

"Yes, yes, yes, Samantha," she moaned. "Ooh, that's so thick. Bigger than my husband's."

I bet. Those Asian men were supposed to have small cocks.

I plunged it in and out of her cunt while the Black MILF fluttered her tongue up and down my slit. She had no real skill, but her enthusiasm was amazing. The older woman was discovering just how much she loved the taste of pussy.

That was so hot.

It had my pussy melting in delight. I groaned, my cunt clenching from the thrill that raced through my body. I wiggled my hips, grinding my cunt onto her mouth. The pleasure swelled through me. It was perfect. Just the wonderful rapture that I needed. I would have such a huge orgasm on her naughty tongue.

I leaned my head in and nuzzled my lips into the Asian MILF's silky pubic hair. Her wiry strands caressed over my face. They felt so wonderful against my features. I closed my eyes, loving every second of this.

I found the top of her pussy. Her clit. I sucked on it as I reamed her pussy with the dildo.

"Samantha!" she gasped, her fingers twisting her nipples. "Yes, yes, that's it. This is amazing. Fuck me. Fuck me harder."

"Of course," I moaned and thrust the dildo hard into her. Fast.

I loved how she bucked on the ground. My tongue danced over her clit. I caressed her with hunger as I fucked her. At the same time, the other MILF feasted upon my cunt. She feasted on me with hunger. She devoured me with wild swipes of her tongue.

"God, that looks so much fun," a watching MILF moaned. "How is her pussy?"

"Delicious," groaned the sexy woman eating me out. She thrust her tongue into my pussy and swirled it around for a moment. "Mmm, just so sweet."

"I am," I moaned into the Asian beauty's twat.

I fucked the dildo faster and faster in and out of her pussy. I shifted my grip to the base, holding it by the rubbery grip, and slammed it into her snatch. She gasped, her back arching. I nursed on her clit, her silky hairs tickling my nose and cheeks. Her tart cream melted through my taste buds.

The other MILF thrust her tongue into the depths of my pussy. She fluttered around inside of me, teasing me. My cunt drank in the sensations. My orgasm built and built. I would have such a delicious cum on her tongue. It would be amazing.

"I can't wait for my turn!"

"What are you going to do to her?"

"Have her sit on my face! I want to eat that pussy!"

"God, I want to eat that asshole!"

"Nasty. I love it!"

So did I.

Their conversations swept around me as I nursed on that delicious clit. I sucked on the Asian MILF's bud as I fucked her cunt. My own pussy clenched on the other sexy woman's tongue. She had it wiggling around in me, stirring me up. Her chin rubbed on my clit.

Sparks flared.

My orgasm swelled faster and faster. All the attention around us had me shivering and shaking. I would have such a huge cum. I couldn't wait for it. Just a big burst of pleasure that would erupt through me. I wiggled my hips, grinding my cunt against her mouth.

Then her fingers rubbed at my shaved pubic mound. They slid down and down to the top of my pussy. They traveled over my clitoral hood to find my bud peeking out. I gasped about the Asian MILF's pearl as the pleasure shot through me.

I fucked her harder. Faster. She gasped, her body trembling. Her moans echoed through the air, mixing with my own groans. I was so close to cumming. Those naughty digits rubbing on my clit in fast circles mixed with the delight of the MILF's probing tongue.

"Oh, my god, yes!" the Asian MILF moaned. "Don't stop sucking, Samantha! Keep ramming that dildo into me. I'm going to cum.!"

"Cum!" a watching woman shouted.

I sucked with all my might, hovering on the edge of my own orgasm. I jammed the dildo deep into the sexy MILF's cunt. Her fingers twisted her nipples. Her stomach flexed, her body shuddering. Then she gasped.

"Yes!"

Hot juices gushed out of her pussy. I groaned and licked around the dildo, gathering her tart cream. That was so hot. That sent me over the edge. I cried out in my own climactic release. My cunt spasmed around the other MILF's tongue.

I gushed juices into her mouth.

"Oh, my god, yes!" I moaned.

"So good!" she gasped between frantic licks at my convulsing twat.

Her tongue flicked up and down my pussy. She sent such wonderful heat flowing through me. It was such a rush to experience. I loved every second of that bliss shooting through my body. I whimpered as I lapped up the Asian MILF's passion.

"Samantha!" she groaned as she hit that peak of delight. "Oh, my god, that's great. You're amazing. That was the best orgasm I've had in so long."

"God, I bet," a woman moaned.

"Yes!" I gasped, my head throwing back. "I'm here to please you all. Lesbianism is amazing. You all have to embrace it. You all have to enjoy this wicked pleasure. You're all going to love it. I promise you."

The sexy MILFs around me quivered, tits swaying. Most had big and soft boobs. Their bodies all delicious curves. Juices dripped from their bushes. My orgasm hit that wonderful peak as I gazed out at all of them.

I ripped the dildo out of the Asian beauty's cunt. "Who's next?"

"Sit on my face!" the black-haired woman said. She stretched out on her back, her big boobs spreading out into two lush mounds.

"I want to eat that asshole out," a redheaded MILF said, her green eyes sparkling.

"Mmm, and you need to eat my cunt," groaned the woman who'd just devoured me.

"Only fair!" I panted, my body on fire.

I sank my cunt down on the black-haired MILF's face. I grabbed the White woman's big titties. I squeezed them. Kneaded them. I loved how they felt in my hands. My fingers dug into them. I licked my lips, so hungry for this fun to begin.

Her hands grabbed my thighs. She yanked me the last few inches to her mouth.

I planted my shaved cunt right on her face, my ebony fingers digging into her ivory tits. Her tongue thrust right into my pussy. I groaned at that. It was so incredible. I ground my pussy from side to side on her mouth.

"Mmm, that booty!" moaned the redheaded woman. "They still call it that, right?"

"Oh, yes, eat my booty out!" I groaned.

Silky hair caressed over my rump. Then her hands parted my butt-cheeks. Her head dipped in and her tongue swirled around my asshole. I groaned as her tongue danced over my sphincter while the black-haired MILF's churned up my cunt.

The older sistah stepped up before me. The wiry curls of her black bush dripped with her excitement. I smacked my lips at the sight of her. This hungry heat washed through me. I was so ready to feast on her. Just devour her cunt and make her explode.

It would be intense. Amazing.

I would devour her to a huge orgasm. She would be crying out in rapture on my mouth. She grabbed my weave and boldly yanked my head forward into her snatch. Her silky hairs spread over my mouth and lips.

Her spicy pussy juices soaked my mouth.

"That's it," she moaned, her large, ebony tits swaying above me. "Get that tongue in me, girl. Yes, yes, that's it. Ooh, yes, that's what I need."

I feasted on her as the two White MILFs devoured me. They licked and lapped at my holes. One's tongue danced over my asshole while the other's fluttered around in my pussy. Two different heats stirred through me. They were wild. Amazing. I loved them.

I thrust my tongue into the Black woman's cunt. I feasted on her. I licked and lapped at her with hunger. My hands grabbed her thighs as my tongue wiggled into the depths of her spicy cunt. She groaned, her big boobs swaying above me.

I wiggled my hips, grinding my twat on the sexy, black-haired woman beneath me. She feasted on me, moaning with her delight into my hungry mouth. That redhead beauty danced her tongue around my asshole.

Then she pressed on my sphincter.

I groaned.

My anal ring widened.

Her tongue popped into my bowels. It was so naughty to feel two tongues dancing around in my holes. They both stirred different pleasures up in me. Different delights for me to enjoy. I drank them in, my body quivering.

I would have such a huge orgasm. I would just detonate. It would be incredible. Amazing. The delight I craved. What I enjoyed. I was so ready for it. I would have such a huge explosion of bliss. A mighty detonation of delight.

"Yes, yes, yes, girl!" moaned the woman I devoured. "Mmm, you're just little, lezzie slut, aren't you?"

"That's what it says on her card!" shouted a watching MILF. Laughter burst around us.

"Mmm, I'm such a slut for sexy, older women!" I fluttered my tongue through her pussy.

My orgasm built faster and faster as I feasted on her. I ground my cunt on the black-haired MILF. The redhead fucked her tongue in and out of my asshole. My cunt clenched about the other's tongue, drinking in both of those wonderful delights.

I swirled my tongue around my fellow sistah's pussy. I ate that older beauty with hunger. Her spicy cream ran down my throat. Her silky pubic hairs tickled my face. She felt incredible grinding on me. Her tits swayed as I feasted on her.

The redhead sucked on my asshole.

"Fuck!" I moaned, my pussy growing hotter around the other MILF's tongue. "Yes, yes, make me cum!"

"Make me explode, you nasty, little dyke!" gasped the Black MILF I feasted on.

I winked at her and flicked my tongue to her clit. I latched on and sucked.

"Yes, yes, yes," she groaned, her back arching. Her tits swayed together. "That's what I need. I made you cum, now it's time to return the favor, whore!"

"I am a whore!" I howled, trembling on the verge of my orgasm. "A lezzie whore who loves sexy MILFs!"

I sucked as hard as I could on her clit, my asshole and pussy melting beneath the older women's tongues. I wiggled my hips from side to side, my body trembling. I was moments away from that wonderful explosion.

I nibbled on the MILF's clit. My lips worked on it. She gasped. Her face scrunched up. She licked lips still gleaming with my cunt cream on them. Her fingers dug into my hair. She pulled my head tight against her pussy.

Cried out in orgasmic rapture. "Yes!"

Her spicy pussy juices gushed into my mouth. I drank it down. I loved the taste of her cream spilling over my chin. My tits jiggled. My body trembled. Tongues thrust into both my holes, churning me up.

I exploded.

"Oh, my god, I love MILFs!" I howled.

The waves of rapture washed out of my spasming pussy. Juices gushed into the black-haired MILF's mouth. The redhead tongued my asshole. My body bucked. I drank down her spicy cream as the waves of rapture washed into my mind.

They were intense. Delicious. They drowned me in euphoria. I savored it. Women were gasping, moaning, groaning around me. They all wanted me. They wall wanted to pay me to do naughty things to them. They hungered for my body.

I loved this. My orgasm hit that amazing peak. I drank down spicy cream as I reveled in sapphic delights.

After that, it was a blur of sex. I licked cunts. Fucked assholes with the dildos, had my own pussy pounded with the strap-on. I fisted one sexy woman, her tits heaving as her pussy juices gushed down my arm.

It was wild. Heady. Amazing. The orgy spilled around me as the waiting MILFs enjoyed each other. The locker room rang with sapphic delight. I even spotted that receptionist girl getting her ass tossed by the blonde MILF whose butthole I'd eaten.

Finally, I had to stop. There was such a thing as too much fun. But I had a blast. So many orgasms.

I didn't get to please all the MILFs. Some had to leave, but they all had my card. I left the others satiated as I sauntered out of the gym, my bag slung over my shoulder. It was full of money that they had thrown in.

I tossed it onto my passenger seat and slid in, my tits quivering beneath my t-shirt. I counted it out, smiling in delight at how much money I had made for Little Lezzie Delight. Mrs. Wright and Mrs. Greene would enjoy their cut. I wondered what they would do with their share?

I blinked when I finished: $1560.

"Damn, I'm good," I said as I smiled at those crisp twenties, tens, fives, and even a wad of ones I had found in them. I fanned out the money I made. So much. I would have pleasured all those sexy, older women for free, but getting paid was even better.

I wondered how my friends did today. I was about to call them when my phone rang. I snagged it up and didn't recognize the number. "Little Lezzie Delights, Samantha speaking? How do you want me to make you cum?"

"Oh, my god," a woman moaned. "My kids are over at the neighbors. My husband won't be home for two hours. Can you get over here and fuck me with that dildo and suck on my tits. I need to cum."

"What's your address, boo," I said. "I'm on the way."

I loved this job. I was so glad that the MILFs of the world had gone crazy with love for lesbian cuties like me.

* * *

Lesbian passion was spreading fast all thanks to that very special girl's wish.

No one else knew what she'd done. All these barely legal cuties and sexy older beauties didn't know whom to thank for the sapphic passion they now enjoyed. But she was having all the fun she could enjoy.

So she didn't need their thanks. Not when she was enjoying two or three sexy MILFs every day; all her wishes had come true. She was in sapphic heaven.

To be continued in Officer Beverley's Tale...

# Officer Beverley Searches the Young Wife

## Lesbian MILF's Naughty Search 1

## A Lesbian MILF Tale

by

Reed James

## Officer Beverley Searches the Young Wife

Lesbianism is spreading, thanks to the girl's wish, even to those women who live lives free of sin. And for those who don't, well, they are going wild.

* * *

### Officer Shanisa Beverley – Friday, Day 5 of the Wish

"Angel, Angel, Angel," I purred as I caressed the heart tattooed on the flight attendant's pubic mound. "Does your airline know you have such a naughty tattoo?"

"No," she moaned as she sat on the steel table in the exam room. Her shaved pussy lips were parted before me, her pink depths on display. Her blue pencil skirt was bunched up around her waist, her lilac thong dangling off her right foot. "It's against the rules for us to have *visible* tattoos, Officer Beverley."

A smile spread on my lips as I stroked my finger over her mound. The White girl's skin felt delicious, her pale hue contrasting with my ebony digit. I looked up at her. She had her flight attendant uniform on, her light-blue blouse open and her lilac bra shoved up and over her small breasts. Her pink nipples gleamed with saliva from my exam. She had a red scarf tied about her neck, a feminine and silky delight. Blonde hair spilled about her youthful face bursting with naughty excitement.

"Mmm, now let's see if you have any contraband in here," I said, my fingers sliding down to her pink pussy lips. I stroked down her folds, her juices coating my digit. The White girl gasped and shuddered.

"Yes, yes, make sure I'm not smuggling anything, Officer Beverley," she moaned.

I smiled. I loved being a TSA officer now that I had become a lesbian MILF. It was so exciting to search pretty, young White girls. To delve into their pussies and assholes and make sure they weren't up to anything bad. Ever since yesterday when that naughty Kelly triggered the alarms with the metallic vibrator she had shoved up her cunt.

It had been hot searching her while her boss, Ms. Demeter, had watched. The young Blonde had been such a naughty thing. She had turned me on. Opened my eyes to women. It was spreading. Lesbianism. I was hearing more and more women turning to each other. It was wonderful being opened to the delights of a young girl like Angel.

Twenty and fresh, the tangy aroma of her pussy filling my nose. She shuddered, her small breasts jiggling as I stroked her. I had to search them all that came through my security checkpoint. I had to show all these cute, young things the delight of an older woman.

Sexy, young White girls had to cum hard on my mouth and fingers and toys.

"Officer Beverley," moaned Angel. She threw her head back, her tits arching out. She leaned back on her hands as she whimpered. I stroked my digit up the left side of her pussy, loving the feel of her flesh.

"Mmm, you've been so bad, haven't you?" I cooed, lifting up my finger. "Look at how wet you are."

"So bad," she moaned. "That's why you had to suck on my titties."

"How else could I find out if you were a naughty, little slut?" I asked. My finger slid up the other side of her folds for her clit. "I had to see if you would get wet."

"So wet!" she moaned. "I drenched my panties. "I'll have to fish out a spare pair from my carry-on."

"Poor you," I cooed and then I leaned in and rubbed my cheek against her pussy lips. Her hot juices coated my skin. The tangy scent of her pussy intensified even more. My cunt was on fire in my pants.

My hands slid down and unfastened them. I had already taken off my equipment belt. Now I slid a hand into my fly while I turned my head. I kissed at her spread open pussy lips. My tongue fluttered through her folds. I licked up her slit. I savored the taste of her, that tangy delight.

She moaned while my hand pressed into my panties. My fingers slid through the curls of my bush to find my own hot pussy. I was just as wet as she was. I was so naughty, too. Such a wicked MILF. I shuddered as I stroked myself and thrust my tongue into Angel's pussy.

"Officer Beverley!" the sexy flight attendant moaned. Her pale tits quivered. I loved that lovely shade of light-beige. She whimpered as she squeezed her thighs about my face. "Oh, yes, yes, Officer Beverley."

I thrust my tongue into her pussy. I swirled around inside of her. I danced it in slow circles. She shuddered, her breasts jiggling. She held my head to her pussy as I "searched" her. My digits caressed her clit while my left hand frigged my own pussy.

I thrust two fingers—middle and ring—into my cunt. My snatch clenched down on my digits. The heel of my hand ground on my clit, my pubic hair tickling my palm. I thrust in and out of my twat, moaning as I did, the pleasure flowing through me.

I swirled my tongue around inside of her pussy. I devoured her with hunger. I pumped in and out of her, loving every second of this delight. My tongue danced and swirled around in her snatch. I loved the feeling of her cunt clenching about me. My tongue caressed inside her, loving the taste of her.

She groaned, her pussy clenching about me. She squeezed her snatch about me as her body shook. She humped against my face, her small tits quivering. Her blonde hair danced around her face, her cheeks flushing red.

"Officer Beverley!" Angel moaned. "Oh, yes, yes, search my cunt! Ooh, you naughty MILF! God, yes!"

My finger rubbed at her clit, her bud throbbing beneath my stroking touch. I rubbed it in faster circles as my tongue caressed her inner walls. I stroked her, loving the feel of her pussy clenching down on me. She groaned, her passion echoing through the room.

My lips nibbled on her pussy lips in between thrusts of my tongue into her depths. I loved her snatch as I frigged my own with my left hand. My fingers stirred up my snatch, sending rippling pleasure through my body.

I loved being a lesbian MILF. I savored eating White girl pussy. I feasted on her with hunger. My tongue stroked up her folds. Her tangy juices dripped down my chin. Her face contorted. She leaned her head back. Her breasts jiggled.

"Oh, yes, yes!" she moaned. "Oh, my god, that's good. Just like that. Ooh, you're going to make me melt. Don't stop. Just lick me. Just devour me."

I did. I thrust my tongue into her depths. I fluttered up and down her. I licked and lapped at her with hunger. She shuddered, her cunt clenching about my tongue. I swirled it around in her as her face contorted.

My own orgasm built with her growing moans that echoed through the search room. I thrust my tongue into her snatch while my clit throbbed beneath my palm. I ground hard on it, my cunt clenching about my two digits. The heat swelled inside of me.

"Oh, yes, that's it!" she moaned. "Oh, my god. That's... that's... Fuck!"

Hot, tangy pussy cream gushed into my mouth.

"Officer Beverley!"

The White girl came hard. The tails of her scarf fluttered as she bucked. Her little titties jiggled. I lapped up the flood of her cream, gulping down those delicious, young juices. I jammed my fingers deep into my cunt and ground my clit hard into the heel of my hand.

I detonated and joined her.

The pleasure rushed through me. I groaned into her snatch, licking up her passion as my rapture flooded my body. My cunt convulsed around my digits and soaked my fingers. I trembled as the heat rushed through my body. Wave after wave of delight that slammed through me.

"Yes, yes, yes!" I moaned, my body trembling. My cunt rippled and writhed around my digits. "That's it. That's so good. You're not smuggling anything."

"Good! Good!" she moaned, bucking through her pleasure. "Oh, Officer Beverley!"

My orgasm hit that wonderful peak as I licked at her pussy. I fluttered my tongue up and down her, making sure I lapped up every drop of her I could. I shivered, my pussy clenching a final time on my digits. Then I pulled them out of my pants.

"Mmm, you are free to go," I moaned as I held up my digits.

The White girl slid her ruby lips over my dark fingers. She sucked hard on them. I smiled as she did, her tongue dancing around my digits. I savored it for a moment, then I pulled my fingers out of her mouth. I stood up, a shiver racing through me.

I zipped up as she panted, her blue eyes glossy from the orgasm I gave her. I put on my utility belt and smiled as she slowly fixed her bra. She looked dazed from the pleasure I gave her. I smiled, knowing she would have memories of this.

"I've never had such a good time going through TSA," moaned Angel.

I winked at her. "And if I see you trying to smuggle those cute tits through my checkpoint again, I'm going to have to search them."

"Yes, Officer Beverley."

My uniform straightened, I pulled on a fresh pair of the blue gloves we had to wear. The heavy-duty ones that law enforcement used. I slipped out of the search room and stared at the bustling TSA line. People were putting on their shoes and belts to my right, cleared through the sensors. Someone was getting their bag checked. My co-worker Carl was swabbing through the contents with a treated piece of cloth on a stick for the bomb residue test.

I moved up to my position. As the only female agent on this gate, I had to do the in-depth searches of all the female passengers. That was done in privacy, of course. We didn't want them to be embarrassed. My pussy clenched as I licked my lips.

They tasted of tangy pussy.

I had my eyes peeled for the next cute young thing that needed to have a lesbian MILF awaken her to the pleasures of her body. Preferably a White girl, but I would take an Asian or Hispanic or even a fellow African-American. She just had to be adorable. Young and sensual.

My eyes flicked over the passengers with a practiced eye, not just sussing out if they were smuggling contraband into the airport. There were a lot of passengers moving through, and many of them were just a little too old for what I craved. It was always a risk getting it on with a woman on the job, so I had to be selective.

Find the right delight to enjoy.

A bag beeped. Someone had left their laptop in it. I had to do the search while a mousy looking guy squirmed. I took out his laptop and ran it through the machine again and then lectured him on wasting everyone's time.

As he scooped up his things protectively and scurried off, I looked up to see her. The perfect girl that needed me. She was so innocent. So delicious. My pussy melted at the sight of her. A hot wave of delight washed through my body.

She had a youthful face that was gorgeous despite its lack of makeup. She wore a dress like she was a schoolmarm. It was long sleeves and a long skirt. It was baggy and dark, not at all hip or trendy. She was a slender thing with such an innocence about her. She looked ultra-religious, which only made my pussy wetter.

She had a black hairband holding back her long fall of brown hair. Eighteen and gorgeous. My heart pounded in my chest as she put her carry-on bag, purse, and her shoes into the tray. She looked nervous as she stared at the body scanner. She stepped in when motioned, holding up her hands.

My pussy melted. This was the girl. She was the one I had to search. Her bag emerged from the x-ray machine. I grabbed the tray off the conveyor belt and set it on a table to the side. As she headed through the scanner, she glanced at the conveyor belt for her stuff then blinked.

"Is there a problem, officer?" she asked in such a quiet, timid voice. "That's my stuff. There's nothing in there. I wouldn't..."

"Of course you wouldn't," I said. I unclipped a vinyl belt that ran between two pylons. "Come with me."

Her face paled. God, she was adorable.

"Ruth?" a young man asked. He wore black slacks and a white shirt. He was tall with dark-brown hair. He looked as young as she was. "Is there something wrong?"

"She's being searched for contraband," I said, grabbing Ruth's arm and gently pulling her back. "And you are?"

"Jebediah Marsden," he said. "I'm her husband."

Husband? At eighteen. They looked so young, but they must be part of some super ultra-conservative sect. I mean, Jebediah? Who named their kids that? It wasn't the 1800s any longer. He had a look of concern while his wife trembled.

God, a barely legal wife who probably knew next to nothing about sex. She *needed* an older MILF to teach her. This innocent, young White girl had to cum and cum and cum. Had she even had an orgasm? Her husband looked too scared to even know what to do with a girl.

An idea popped into my head. "Grab her things," I told the husband. "And yours and then follow. I have to do a search of your wife."

"I mean..." He swallowed. "We have a flight to catch."

"And if you followed airline suggestions, you're here early enough that you won't be delayed." I paused. "Assuming I don't find something."

"You won't!" he said, his voice cracking.

"Jebediah?" Ruth whimpered, staring back at her husband as I led her to the door.

"It'll be okay, Ruth," he said, gathering his stuff as he followed after. "You'll see."

"That's right," I said. "You're in good hands, Ruth. I'm Officer Beverley, and I'm going to do a *thorough* exam of your body. It'll be intimate."

"Oh, Lord," she breathed. "That's... I mean... Really?"

"Really," I told her and opened the door to the search room. I guided her inside. I wasn't rough with her. The poor thing looked about to faint. I didn't want to scare her.

I wanted to make her cum.

Her husband followed, carrying their things. He looked as scared as she did. That made this so exciting. I closed the door, the air in here still thick with the scent of Angel's tangy pussy. I breathed it in, hoping Ruth did, too.

I had a naughty plan. I peeled off my rubber gloves as I stopped before the young wife. The annoying things off, I shot my hand to her blouse and said, "I just have to strip you naked."

She whimpered.

"Now, now, I'm a woman," I said, my fingers sliding down her blouse. "And your husband *has* seen you naked before."

"Not in such a well-lit room," she said, her eyes looking away.

"Oh, girl, what are you two kids even doing?" I asked her, shaking my head. "Your sexy body deserves to be shown off."

"S-sexy?" she asked as I opened her blouse. She had a white bra cupping her small breasts. They looked like such perky things. She pulled off her blouse, untucking it from her long skirt. She had a slender body. No fat on her.

"Yes, you are a sexy, young woman," I told her, sliding my dark hands over her pale flesh. "I'm sorry that your husband hasn't been appreciating you."

"I don't—" the husband started to say until I glared at him.

"You need to stand there and be quiet, sir," I said. "I'm searching your wife for contraband."

"There's none," he said. "Please. We wouldn't have that. We're good people."

I slid my hands around Ruth's torso and found the clasp of her bra. I undid it with a twist. I shuddered as I peeled off her bra. I slid the straps down her arms. I pulled away to expose those small breasts of hers. They came free with a naughty jiggle to them. Her nipples thrust out pink from them.

Just so cute.

"See," said her husband. "Nothing. Can my wife cover up?"

I frowned at him. "You are acting very suspicious." I glanced at his bag. "Is that yours? Do I have your permission to search it?"

"Y-yes," he said, swallowing. "But you won't find anything."

"Are you sure about that?" I demanded. "Because if I do, I'll have you arrested."

"Arrested," the wife gasped. "You can't do that. We're not doing anything wrong."

"Then you have nothing to hide. Open up your bag, sir." I glanced at Ruth. She had her hands over her breasts. Her fingers were squeezing at them. She was kneading her breasts. Was she getting turned on? "And you, hands at your side."

She bit her lip and did. Her nipples were hard now. I smiled and grabbed one for a moment. I twisted it as her husband was distracted unzipping is luggage. Ruth whimpered as I tweaked her nipple. Her body shuddered.

"Now that's interesting," I purred. My hands slid from her breast. I leaned in. "Are you getting wet, Ruth? Is your naughty pussy getting turned on? I'm going to have to search it. Will I have to deal with juices dripping out of you."

She blushed so prettily. She whimpered.

"I'll take that as a yes," I said, reaching her skirt. I felt around it and found a zipper on the side keeping the waistband tight about her torso. I unzipped it and her skirt fell to the floor. She wore a pair of plain, white, boring panties. Her pale-beige skin looked so sexy in contrast.

A dark spot soaked the front.

I pressed my hand into her panties as her husband turned the bag. He looked back at me and then froze as I rubbed my fingers through his wife's bush to find the hot and dripping-wet folds of her young pussy.

"Just searching your wife," I purred. "Mmm, and she's getting wet. Her pussy's hot. That's not good."

"Not good?" he asked, freezing.

"Not good at all," I said. "A woman whose pussy gets this wet is a woman who likes to eat cunt." I glanced at Ruth. "Do you like to eat cunt?"

"N-no," she gasped as I stroked up and down her folds, my own cunt on fire. "Of course nooooot!"

Her last word stretched out into a moan as I thrust my fingers into her young, married depths. She was tight and hot. Her juicy flesh squeezed about me. The White girl gasped and trembled, her brown hair dancing about her flushed face. She whimpered, her snatch squeezing about my digits. Her tongue danced across her lips.

I pumped them in and out of her, loving the feel of her juicy flesh engulfing my digits. She felt so delightful. And with her young husband watching me corrupt her into lesbian passion, it had my own cunt molten. My panties were doing a valiant job of containing my cream, but I was getting wetter by the second.

"Officer Beverley," moaned Ruth. "What are you doing to me?"

"Searching you for contraband," I said. "This pussy is drenched. I know what that means. You're a lesbian."

She shook her head, her eyes wide. Her pussy clenched on my digits. "No, no. I'm not. That's a sin. I'm married to a man. I can't be a lesbian."

"Yeah," her husband said, watching. He trembled there at the table, his hands gripping his open carry-on bag. "We're m-married."

"Hmm," I said. "Are you *sure* you don't love my fingers sliding in and out of your pussy." I leaned in closer. "That you don't want me to do this?"

I ducked my head down and sucked a pink nipple into my lips. The White girl gasped as I nursed, her fingers clenching down on my digits. I loved the feel of her silky twat around my digits. I pumped them in and out of her snatch. I buried them deep into her cunt.

The religious girl gasped and whimpered. Her husband let out strangled groans while I nursed on that nipple. I sucked hard. Ruth shuddered. Her pussy gripped my fingers thrusting in and out of her. I plowed into her hard and fast.

I frigged her. I buried to the hilt in her. I caressed her with powerful plunges of my fingers. I wiggled my digits around in her. She bucked and whimpered louder and louder. I love diddling her. Hearing the sound she made.

I ripped my mouth off my nipple. "So, you didn't love that, lesbian?"

"I'm not a lesbian," she whimpered. She glanced at her husband who watched dumbfounded. "I'm not. I don't know why I'm so wet and... and..."

"Then why do you love me sucking on your nipple?" I purred. I slid my thumb through her bush and found the folds of her pussy. Her hard clit.

She gasped and bucked, her pussy clamping down on my digits. She whimpered, her eyes widen as I rubbed that naughty spot. She quivered there, her panties' waistband shifting around my wrist as she moved.

"Ooh, my. You like that, don't you?" I purred. "You like my fingers being buried in your naughty pussy. Mmm, you're a lezzie, little White girl, aren't you?"

"I'm not," she pleaded, her hands rubbing at her stomach. Her face contorted. Her pussy grew hotter and hotter around my fingers. "It's just... You're... You're making... I... I... Lord!"

To my utter delight, she came.

Her pussy convulsed around my digits. Her small breasts jiggled. Joy burst across her face. She threw back her head and howled out in rapture. Her moans echoed through the screening room. Her husband's jaw dropped.

"That's the sound of a lesbian cumming hard on my fingers," I groaned to him, thrusting my digits in and out of her snatch. I pumped them fast and hard. I buried them into her again and again. "Your wife is gay."

"N-no," he groaned.

"Lord! Lord!" Ruth squeaked, her small titties jiggling. Her juices soaked my hands. Her pussy writhed around my digits. Her flesh convulsed, sucking at me. "Oh, Lord, that's good. What have you done to me, Officer Beverley?"

"I made you cum," I purred. "Only a lesbian would get off like that. And so fast... Such a slut."

"No, no, I'm not a lesbian," she pleaded, her face flushed, her brown eyes glossy. She panted, her small titties rising and falling. "Please, I'm not."

"Hmm," I said and pulled my fingers out of her panties. Her cream dripped from my digits. They were coated in them. The White girl gasped as she stared at them. "Yeah, that's all you. You soaked me." I glanced at her husband. "Look at how wet your wife is. I mean, that's impressive."

The cream ran down my wrist. I smeared my juices over her pale breast, my ebony fingers running over her delightful boob. I left her gleaming, this sweet musk filling the air. She had such a wonderful scent.

I breathed it in. "Mmm, that's the scent of a hot, lesbian pussy that came hard during my search. I was just doing my job, and you came on me. That's something a depraved lesbian would do."

She whimpered.

"M-my wife isn't a lesbian," the husband insisted. "We're happily married. You just... You did something to her. You molested her."

"I performed a cavity search for contraband," I said. "But if you think your wife isn't a lesbian, we can find out. There's a simple test."

"There is?" Ruth asked, clutching at it.

"Sure," I said. "It's the MILF pussy test." I unsnapped my utility belt. I sat it down on the table. It clinked with my gear. "A cute, young lesbian can't resist an older woman's mature pussy. So, Ruth, if you're not a lesbian, you won't feel the need to fall to your knees and eat my cunt."

A look of fear flashed across her face. She swallowed as she stared at me opening the fly of my black slacks. The zipper rasped down. I shoved them off my hips, the tails of my white blouse draping over my dark skin. She bit her lip.

"What's wrong?" I asked as I shoved my pants down to my ankles. "Don't tell me you're tempted by my pussy, Ruth."

"Of course she's not," her husband said. He just watched, his cheeks as flushed as his wife's. "You're not a sinful woman, Ruth. You're a good woman. A proper wife."

"T-that's right," she squeaked, her hands rubbing up her stomach to her breasts while she stared at me.

"Well, let's find out," I said and shoved down the red panties I wore. My black bush came into view, the hairs so inky compared to my ebony skin. I slid the panties down my sleek thighs. They fell down my calves to join my pants. I spread my legs apart and ran my fingers through my bush. "Well, Ruth. That's a wet, MILF pussy right there. Just dripping. It's in need of a sexy, young lesbian to eat it out. A budding dyke in need of eating her first cunt. Interested?"

Ruth whimpered. Her tongue flicked over her pink lips.

"Ruth?" groaned her husband. Worry flashed across his face. "You're staring at her."

"It's just..." Ruth squeezed her tits. Her hips wiggled from side to side. Her breath quickened. "I mean... That's..."

"You know you want to press your lips through my bush to eat me out. Mmm, yes you do, you pretty, White dyke." I shuddered and begun unbuttoning my blouse. "You want to devour my mature cunt. To eat your first twat. Just fall to your knees and do it. Show your husband what makes you wet. It's not him. He doesn't make you cum. You'd never felt that good in your life, had you?"

Ruth whimpered, almost a strangled groan. She shook her head, standing transfixed. Then she let out a moan of hunger. She fell to her knees before me. She grabbed my hips and buried her face into my pussy.

I gasped as she nuzzled right into my twat. Her lips kissed at my cunt. Her husband gasped as she feasted on me. She licked with hunger. I stared down at her as I opened my blouse, exposing my large breast constrained in a red bra. My black curls spilled over her pale face. Her nose nuzzled into my bush.

Her tongue lapped at me with such hunger. I slid my blouse off my arms and savored her licking and lapping. She was incredible. She stared up at me with this feverish heat in her eyes as she devoured my cunt.

"Mmm, you love the taste of my pussy, don't you?" I asked as her hands slid around my hips to grab my rump.

The White girl moaned into my cunt.

"Yes, you do, Ruth," I purred. "Mmm, just feasting on me. You got that tongue deep into my pussy. Oh, yes, you do. Oh, lick and lap. Just devour me."

Ruth did while her husband watched. He sat down on the table, his jaw dropped as his good, Christian wife devoured my cunt like a lezzie whore. The girl's tongue was so nimble. She lapped everywhere stroking my pussy lips and my clit.

Sparks burst every time she brushed that bud. The pleasure rushed through my body. My cunt clenched as I savored her naughty tongue licking me. She danced it through my folds. She teased me with her passion.

"Yes, yes, yes!" I moaned, my hips undulating. I ground my twat on her hungry mouth. "Mmm, that's it. You like it."

Ruth moaned.

"Say it," I hissed. "Let your husband *hear you* say it."

"I... I... I love the taste of your pussy, Officer Beverley!" the once-innocent White girl said. She thrust her tongue into my pussy's depths.

"Yes!" I groaned as her tongue danced around in me.

I unhooked my bra. I freed my large tits. They swayed before me. I felt Ruth's eyes on them as she devoured me. She licked and lapped with such hunger. She was such a pussy-licking delight. She swabbed that tongue through my folds.

"Oh, yes, yes!" I moaned. "Oh, that's so naughty. That's so wicked of you to do. Mmm, yes, yes, keep licking me like that."

She did. She thrust her tongue into my cunt. She swirled it around in me. It was this amazing delight to experience. I groaned as her tongue did such naughty things to me. I clenched down on her. I squeezed my twat about her.

This was amazing. A delight. I groaned, my face scrunching up as she ate me towards my orgasm. Her husband could only watch in strangled silence. He looked so stunned that his innocent bride could be devouring my cunt with such hunger.

"You taste so good, Officer Beverley," moaned Ruth, her fingers digging into my rump. "Oh, yes, yes, so good. Sweet. And your hairs... They feel so good tickling my face. I love this. I *am* a lesbian!"

"Yes, you are," I moaned, loving this girl's plunge into sapphic delight. That switch had gotten flipped in her, too. "Ooh, you're going to make me cum. I'll drown you in my MILF juices. Suck on my clit."

"What's your clit?" she asked.

"That bud in my pussy folds. Then I rubbed that felt so good. That's your clit."

"I never knew I had a place like that," she groaned. Then her tongue slid through my folds. She brushed it.

"That's it! That's my clit!" I moaned, my tits heaving as she latched her mouth on it.

She sucked hard. I shuddered at the feeling of her naughty mouth nursing on my clit. My cunt clenched; the heat rushed through my body. My breasts swayed from side to side as my orgasm swelled fast. She nursed on me, her fingers digging into my rump.

The delicious White girl's mouth felt wonderful on me. She was such a sexy thing. I loved it. My pussy ached. My body shook as my orgasm hurtled towards that moment of explosion. I couldn't take much more.

She sucked.

I came.

"Drink my MILF juices!" I gasped as my pussy convulsed.

I was old enough to be this girl's mother. It was so hot to flood her mouth with my pussy juices. To drown her in cream. She groaned as she drank down that wonderful flood. She gulped it down. I groaned as she licked it up. Her tongue lapped through my folds. She stroked through me. My body bucked.

"Yes, yes, yes!" I gasped, my head swaying from side to side. Stars burst across my vision. "Oh, that's good. That's amazing. Yes! Your wife is a pussy-licking slut! She loves my MILF cunt."

"Love it!" she moaned between licks.

I drenched her face as my orgasm carried me higher and higher. I hit this wonderful pinnacle of rapture. I floated there. I hung there, drifting at the very heights of ecstasy. It was so amazing to hover atop all that euphoria.

Then I stepped back, pulling my pussy away from the girl. Ruth panted, my pussy cream smeared over her lips. She had this wild look in her eyes. I could tell she needed more. She needed to cum and cum. I had to do such wicked things to her.

She popped up to her feet before I could stop her. She cupped my face. The cute, young White girl kissed me hard. My sweet pussy cream adorned her lips. My large breasts pressed into her small pale ones. Her lips were so hot on mine.

I thrust my tongue into her mouth. She moaned, sucking on it. Then her tongue thrust into my mouth. They dueled each other. Her fingernails bit into my flesh as she kissed me with hunger. Her lips nibbled on mine. She was so hot.

My nipples throbbed against her firm tits. Her husband groaned in the background as he witnessed our wild kiss. I grabbed Ruth's ass through her panties. I squeezed and kneaded her. I pulled her tight against me.

She was so wonderful to kiss.

This young delight set my blood on fire. I was so glad that I got to awaken her to lesbian delights. It was every MILF's job to turn on a cute, young thing like her. I savored kissing her, sharing our passion.

She broke the kiss, her eyes wild.

"You need to cum again, don't you?" I asked. "You need to howl your head off?"

"Please, please, you've done something to me," she moaned. "I never looked at a woman before. Not like this. I liked men. I did, and now... Now... Now all I want is women. You made me feel so good."

"Because I made you cum?"

"Yes, yes, you made me cum. I never felt like that with my husband. It was nice after the first few times, but this..."

"It was rapture."

"Yes!" Her eyes sparkled with such delight. "Yes, it was. It was such wild ecstasy. I know it's a sin, but..."

"But you want to drop your panties, bend over that table, and let me go to town on you."

She nodded.

I shivered. "I have something for you. Something that will make you explode in rapture."

"Yes!" she moaned and spun away from me. She darted to the table. She glanced at her husband. "I'm sorry, Jebediah, I am, but... I'm a lesbian. You married a lesbian and... and... I need her to do things to me. To make me cum."

He just let out a strangled, "Okay." He swallowed. "I mean... I... This..."

He had no idea what to do. That made this so exciting to me. My pussy clenched. I watched as Ruth shoved down her panties. She peeled those white delights off her ivory rump. She had a shapely round rear. As she bent over to step out of her panties and her brown bush appeared framed by her thighs, I salivated. She was so sexy.

"That ass," I groaned. "Mmm-hmm, for a White girl, you got yourself an ass, Ruth."

"Does it make you wet?" she asked as she bent over the table. "Your, uh. Your hoo-ha?"

"Don't be shy about saying pussy," I said, bending down to unlace my shoes. I slipped out of them fast. "Not after the way you devoured my cunt."

"That's so naughty," she said. "I did... I ate your... your cunt!" She squeaked. "Cunt! I like eating cunt!"

Hearing her say those words, reveling in their naughty meeting, was such an intoxicating experience. A shiver of heat ran through me. My cunt clenched. I stepped out my bunched-up pants and panties, so glad I had educated this sweet young thing about the delights her body had to offer.

After my pants were off, my eyes locked on Ruth's delicious ass, I felt around in the pockets and found the contraband I had taken out of Kelly's pussy yesterday. That silver vibrator. A smooth shaft of gleaming metal with a rubber grip at the bottom.

I sauntered up to the girl and glanced at her husband. "I have to search her last hole," I said, pressing the vibrator into her pussy. "Just be patient."

"Yes, yes, be patient, Jebediah," moaned Ruth. "She has to search my naughty cunt again. I'm such a bad, bad lesbian. I'm so sorry for being a wicked dyke, but I love it and... Oh, yes, that's so thick."

I smirked as I pressed the vibrator into her pussy. The shaft sank into her depths. Her cute butt-cheeks clenched as the toy went deeper and deeper in her twat. Her labia clung to the shaft, gripping it with their delicious pinkness. I plunged it to the hilt in her and then twisted it.

She shuddered. The table creaked beneath her. The girl's moans echoed. Her ivory rump clenched tight before me, hiding that cute, brown asshole I was about to rim. I licked my lips and then pressed my face into her crack.

I licked her asshole.

"Oh, Officer Beverley," she gasped. "What are you doing?"

"Searching your pretty, little ass," I moaned to the White girl. "Mmm, just need to get my probe nice and lubed. Luckily, you're such a dyke-whore that your cunt has more than enough."

"I am a dyke-whore!" Ruth moaned. Her transformation was so startling and delicious. It made me so wet. "Oh, honey, look at me. I'm such a wicked and naughty lesbian. I can't help it. I want Office Beverley to search my ass."

Having her stunned husband watching was the best. He had no idea his woman was a slut. He had married some repressed girl who didn't even know she had a clit or could have an orgasm. She did now. She would never be able to bottle it up again.

She would be looking for pussy from whatever hot MILFs she could find.

I licked at her asshole, loving the taste. Her pale cheeks squeezed about my face. The sour flavor of her asshole soaked my tongue. It was such a naughty delight to enjoy. I swirled my tongue around it, loving every moment of her moans and gasps.

I poked my tongue against her anal ring. Her back arched. She groaned as my tongue penetrated into her anal depths. I danced around in her bowels, soaking her while her pussy drenched the vibrator. I shuddered, so ready to play with her.

I pulled my mouth away from her asshole and the vibrator from her cunt. The silvery shaft emerged drenched in her juices. Her sweet musk, a fresher flavor than my own twat, filled my nose. She whimpered, squirming on the table.

"Please, please, search my asshole," she moaned. "Just ram that probe in me. Make sure I don't have any contraband."

I glanced at her young husband, the cuckold, just watching as I enjoyed his wife. He stood by and let me turn her into a lesbian. This was so hot. It made my pussy drip with such excitement to do this to the girl.

I pressed the tip of the vibrator against her asshole. I rubbed the end into her hot flesh. She gasped as I drilled it into her bowels. Her body twitched as her anal ring spread open to engulf the shaft. I watched her naughty hole swallow the toy. I pressed into her bowels, loving as she groaned.

"Oh, oh," she whimpered. "You're pressing that into me, Office Beverley. That's so naughty. That feels so wicked. So thick. Oh, Lord!"

Her butt-cheeks clenched. The white girl moaned as more and more of the vibrator vanished into her asshole. Her sweet cream filled my nose. I nuzzled into her brown bush, her wet curls caressing my face. Then I kissed her right on her pussy.

My tongue fluttered around her folds. I licked and lapped at her, caressing her with my tongue. She shuddered as I tongued her. I sank the vibrator to almost the hilt in her, just the round base poking out of her asshole.

It was time. I twisted the rubbery base.

The vibrator hummed to life.

She bucked and gasped out, "Oh, Lord! That's... It's... It's buzzing in me. What is that?"

"A vibrator," I purred. "Enjoy." I thrust my tongue into her young pussy. I savored the White girl's sweet cream.

I pumped the vibrating toy in and out of her asshole. Her cunt clenched down on my probing tongue. My left hand squeezed her rump, her pale skin contrasting with my dark flesh. Her juices dripped down my chin as I feasted on her.

I fucked her asshole with the vibrator. I plunged it into her bowels' depths before pulling it back out. The table creaked as she shuddered on it. Her moans echoed through the screening room. Her husband watched, stunned.

"Mmm, yes, you love that, you little dyke," I moaned.

"I do!" Her pussy clenched around my licking tongue. "So much. Oh, Jebediah, I'm so sorry for being a dirty lesbian. I love it. The vibrator is melting my butt. And her tongue is licking through my pussy. She feels so amazing."

My tongue danced around in her pussy. I stroked her flesh and feasted on her juices. They tasted so wonderful. So sweet. My dark fingers dug into her ivory rump while my other hand slammed the vibrator into her bowels.

I churned up her anal sheath. Her passion echoed through the air. It was so exciting to hear. I loved every moment of it. I fluttered my tongue around in her. I licked and lapped at her. I caressed her with my hungry tongue.

She moaned, her pussy clenching around my tongue fucking into her depths. I slammed the vibrator deep into her bowels. Her butt-cheeks clenched and relaxed. She squirmed. Her husband rubbed his hands on his jeans, his eyes locked on our lesbian sight.

I loved it. I was cuckolding him with his sexy, young bride.

I kissed down and sucked right on her clit. She had a fat one, bigger than mine. I sealed my lips around it and nursed. She gasped. The table groaned beneath her body. Her whimpers grew throatier and throatier.

"Officer Beverley! You're going to make me cum! Yes, yes! I want it. I'm such a naughty lesbian. I love what you're doing to my clit and my butthole and... and... Hallelujah!"

Her pussy cream gushed out of her cunt.

Her sweet delight bathed my face. I shoved the vibrator deep into her cunt and drank down her young passion. I savored her awakened delight. I gulped down the cream gushing out of her, my lips sealed about her pussy hole. Her bush rubbed against my face.

Her body bucked. The table groaned as she thrashed through her second orgasm ever. She flooded my mouth with all that delicious cream. I drank it all down as her moans echoed through the search room.

"Officer Beverley!" she moaned.

"Mmm, yes, yes, Ruth!" I purred.

She collapsed. Panting. Her orgasm passed. I licked at her pussy, gathering up more of the sweet cream. Her husband groaned. I loved him watching. He saw what his wife was now. A naughty, young lesbian.

"I was wrong," I said as I stood up and pulled my vibrator out of Ruth's asshole. "You're not smuggling in *any* contraband. You're free to go."

"I'm not sorry," the religious wife said. "Oh, Lord, that was amazing. I'm a lesbian. I had no idea, but now it's all so clear to me."

"Yes, you are," I said. I turned off the vibrator and then licked the toy. I savored the sour flavor of her bowels clinging to it.

Ruth turned around and then she joined me. Her tongue licked up that naughty shaft. She dragged up and up it, tasting her own asshole. Her husband just watched, still looking stunned like he couldn't believe this had happened. His wife reached the tip of the vibrator.

Then she kissed me. Our lips melted together, tasting of her sweet pussy and her sour bowels. Her tongue thrust boldly into my mouth. Her hands cupped my breasts. She gave them both a hard squeeze, her fingers so wonderful on my tits.

"We have to get to our flight," she moaned, breaking our kiss. "We're visiting Jebediah's family."

"Have a wonderful trip," I said. I leaned in. "I bet his mother is a hot MILF. Find out."

"I will," she whispered back. She gave my boobs a final squeeze then broke away from me.

She dressed while her husband just stood there stunned. Ruth went from that lesbian slut to a prim and proper young wife like she'd stepped out of pilgrim times. She smoothed the front of her dress, her face flushed so beautifully.

It was the only makeup she needed.

"Shall we, husband?" she asked. "We have a flight to catch."

"I... um... yeah," he said as she took his hand and led him away. I smiled and dressed. What a wonderful search that was.

I sauntered back out to my post. My supervisor, a tall White woman named Helen Reynolds glanced at me. She frowned. I gave her a nod, a serious look on my face, as I took my position. I didn't look at Ruth and her husband. I was here to do a job.

Find more hot, young things to seduce. With only a half-hour left on my shift, I *might* get to squeeze in one more search. I just had to hope the right cutie came through the line that needed a sexy MILF like me to awaken her.

I loved being a TSA security officer. It was such a rewarding job to screen those nubile passengers. I put my all into it. Just ask Ruth.

I glanced up and smiled at a redheaded cutie in a tank top. Perfect.

To be continued...

# Officer Beverley Searches the Nubile Cutie

## Lesbian MILF's Naughty Search 2

## A Lesbian MILF Tale

by

Reed James

# Officer Beverley Searches the Nubile Cutie

## Officer Shanisa Beverley – Saturday, Day 6 of the Wish

"I don't get why I have to do this," a young girl snapped.

The outburst drew my attention to a girl of eighteen or nineteen. Slender, in a belly shirt that clung to her small breasts and left her flat midriff bare. A pair of tight jean shorts left her long legs bare down to her shoes and socks. Red hair spilled down around her face.

A bratty White girl.

My pussy clenched. She was just the sort of girl who needed some "extra" screening from me at the TSA line. A hot shiver ran through me as she threw her purse down into the container, her red hair swaying.

"I mean, this is so dumb," she continued on her tirade, glancing at an older woman with dark-brown hair. "God, do I look like a terrorist?" She glanced at another TSA officer, a stout guy named Mitch. "Do I?"

"Everyone has to go through the screening, miss," he said. "That's the law. Now stop making a scene."

"Dumb law," she said. "Why do I have to take off my shoes? Huh? Want to stare at my feet? I know you want to see my naked body with that dumb thing."

"Honey," the dark-haired woman said. She was my age, early forties, and looking so sexy. A MILF. I didn't see much familial resemblance, though. A step-mother probably. That would be exciting. She wore a pair of jeans and a loose t-shirt, something more practical for traveling than the booty shorts and a belly shirt the step-daughter wore. "Don't be like this."

"Don't be like what?" the girl demanded. "Huh, *Mom?* Tell me. You suck Dad's cock, so that must make you an expert on how I'm supposed to obey."

I arched an eyebrow at that. The MILF didn't protest. She just wilted and muttered something. Like an apology. I folded my arms as I stood by the X-ray machine. This girl definitely needed extra screening. This was getting me so wet. This redheaded tart needed to learn all about consequences.

MILFs needed to receive respect from young girls. Respect and orgasms.

That switch that had been flipped in me two days ago had me simmering. Ever since Kelly and her MILF boss had come through TSA, I had been craving young pussy. Barely legal twat. I went from loving the D to loving the V like someone had found a toggle switch inside my head and changed my default setting. And I wasn't the only one.

Even Ruth Marsden, the ultra-conservative, newlywed wife had succumbed to depraved, lesbian passion. She had devoured my pussy yesterday when I pulled her and her young husband out of line. Right in front of the man she loved, she had become a lezzie whore. It had been so exciting to teach her about sapphic delights.

That was the responsibility of a MILF like me.

"You better not paw through my shit," the girl shouted as she put her stuff on the conveyor belt. It moved towards the X-Ray machine while she stepped up to the body scanner. She marched in and huffed as she lifted up her arms over her head and stand with her feet spread apart. "Oh, yeah, you're getting an eyeful, aren't you, perv."

"Just doing my job," said Vic as he monitored the body scanner display.

"Yeah, so enthusiastically," sneered the girl. "You normally got to pay to see me naked. I don't give this away for free."

Pay?

The device whirled around her, seeing through her clothing. Nothing came up on the scan. She was waved through but I grabbed her tray as it came through and said, "This your bag?"

"What of it?" she asked. "You want to steal my lipstick?"

"Honey," the older woman said as she stood in the body scanner. It whirled. "You can't speak like that."

My supervisor, Helen Reynolds, was passing by. She paused at the commotion, raising an eyebrow. I waved her off as I set the tray down at a screening station. I then headed to where the girl glowered at me. I opened the vinyl barrier, a strap that ran between two pylons, and motioned to the girl.

"I have to search your bag," I said.

"Fuck that," she muttered and marched through. She went to grab her bag.

I grabbed her wrist and twisted it behind her back. She gasped in shock as I did that, rising up on her tiptoes. She let out a squeal of pain like I had just broken her arm or something. Which I hadn't. I grabbed my handcuffs and slapped the restraint onto her wrist. It ratcheted as I tightened it around her just enough so she couldn't get out. Then I grabbed her other hand and pulled it back.

"W-what are you doing?" the brat whimpered. "You're hurting me. Help, help. Mommy!"

Mommy?

"I-is that necessary," the brunette MILF asked. She had such a cowed voice, hugging herself.

"You're her mother?" I asked and smacked the cuff onto the girl's other wrist. The redhead trembled while my pussy melted. My ebony fingers gripped her pale flesh, contrasting with that light-beige skin White girls had.

"Step-mother," the woman answered. "I'm Rita. Rita Kemp. I know Evette can be a brat—"

"Brat!" shrieked the girl. "I'm not a brat. Now let me go. These cuffs are hurting. Don't you know who I am? I have 10,000 *subscribers* on Twitch. My OnlyFans page has 3000 more. I have 300,000 followers on my Instagram. They're going to hear how you treated me! So let go of me, bitch!"

"Bitch?" I asked, a smile spreading on my lips. I had no idea what Twitch or OnlyFans was, but I had heard of Instagram. I very much doubted that this girl had all those followers on Instagram. "Do you know who I am, Miss Evette?" I hauled her towards one of the screening rooms.

Her step-mother followed.

"The woman with the ratty hair arresting me for nothing!" The girl glared at me. "Nothing! Some of my followers are powerful men. They have influence, too. They're *all* going to hear about it. If I could grab my phone, you'd be so dead."

I snorted and threw open the door to the screening room. I shoved her in and let her mother scurry in after with their stuff, holding the trays stacked in her arms. She looked so frightened. Her face so pale. I had to do something about that.

I closed the door and then locked it.

"Now let me go!" the girl screeched. "Mom, make her let me go! She's being so mean to me."

"I-is this really necessary?" Mrs. Kemp asked, her voice soft. This poor MILF was utterly cowed by this brat. I had to do something about it. This wasn't right at all. Mrs. Kemp needed to learn to take charge of a young woman.

Luckily for her, I was here to do just that.

I pressed the girl down over the table. She gasped as I pinned her down with a hand planted on the small of her back. She squirmed there, her fingers flexing while her hands pulled at the cuffs. The metal rattled while she squirmed and shrieked.

"Let me go!"

I winced against the ear-piercing sound. She was a brat. A stuck-up White girl that had to learn her place. I would teach her. Show her how she needed to act around a pair of MILFs. She needed to be appreciative. On her knees. She needed to be doing such naughty shit to us.

I glanced over at the bag I had placed in the corner. The one full of all those delights I picked up at Secret Delights. The lingerie store was now carrying all manner of sex toys for their female customers to enjoy. And there had been a lot of MILFs buying toys to use on their young lovers. It had been so hot realizing just how far this lesbianism had spread.

I slid my hand up the brat's inner thigh. Evette gasped as my ebony hand caressed up her pale flesh. She threw a look over her shoulder, her red hair flying. My hand went higher and higher until I cupped her pussy right through the crotch of her booty shorts. The denim felt warm beneath my touch, the fabric rough as I rubbed at the seam.

"You nasty dyke!" gasped the girl. "Why do you think you can cop a feel? Huh?"

The step-mother just watched, swallowing.

"You stop right now! Ooh, I'm going scorched earth all over your skank ass! Let me go! Right now! Stop that! Stop rubbing me."

"I'm searching you," I said, my fingers digging into her pussy. "You wanted to make a scene. These are the consequences."

"That's not searching," the girl groaned. She squirmed more, but I kept her pinned down. "You're rubbing my cootch. You think you get to do that without paying? Do you know how many guys pay me to only *see* my cootch? Huh. I have *3000* OnlyFans subscribers."

"And I don't care," I said. "In here, I'm the queen-bitch, and you, little Miss White Girl, are just a brat who needs to learn her place. You ain't nothing compared to me. You should be on your knees worshiping a sexy MILF like me. Or your mother."

"You are a dyke!" the girl hissed. "I'm not going to get on my knees and worship that skanky cunt you got. Not eating no rancid pussy. Fucking let me go."

"She really, really doesn't know when to shut up, does she, Mrs. Kemp?" I asked.

The step-mother stared at me like she had fallen on the train tracks and the engine was screaming down at her. I rolled my eyes. No wonder this girl was such a brat with such a pushover for a step-mother. How could the girl learn any proper behavior?

I shoved my hand around the girl's waist and found the fastener of her jean shorts. I popped it open. The girl gasped and spewed out her objections while her zipper rasped down. She squirmed more, struggling to sit up.

I held her down with ease.

"What the fuck are you doing?" the girl demanded as I pulled down her shorts. It was hard doing it one-handed. I had to keep tugging on either side to work the tight denim over her curving rump. "You don't get to see my booty without paying. $5 a month for that. You payin' up, dyke."

"You really, really do not get that I give one fig about the pathetic losers who jerk off to your lily ass on the internet. You're in *my* screening room." I exposed more and more of the girl's ass. She had a red thong that vanished between her butt-cheeks. "You're being punished for causing a scene. You want to be arrested."

"For what?" demanded the girl. "Using my Third Amendment right to say what the fuck I want."

"It's the first, you blithering dumbass," I said, her jean shorts falling down her thighs. Her thong cupped her pussy. She clearly was shaved.

"Blithering dumbass?" snorted the girl. "Is that the best insult you got? Or are you that stupid? Is that why you go to the blind hairdresser to get that nasty do done."

I ground my teeth. She did *not* just insult my hair. It took a great deal of self-control not to really hurt the girl. But I was here to educate her. So I grabbed her thong next and yanked it down her ass with a snarl.

Too hard.

The thong ripped free of her body. The torn cloth dangled from my hand. It swayed there. I blinked in shock as I stared at it. Then I glanced down at her juicy pussy between her thighs. She clenched her butt-cheeks together as she gasped in shock.

"You did *not* just rip off my thong, bitch?" demanded the girl.

"You're being searched," I said. "I can destroy property to find any contraband."

"What, do you think I got a weapon shoved up my snatch?" the girl demanded. "You're just a nasty dyke who wants to rub my cunt. Well, there it is. Rub it. Huh, just dig those fingers in there like you want. Fucking Black bitch!"

I did want to rub that tight pussy. The White girl's shaved twat peeked between her thighs. She had a dainty slit creasing her plump vulva, not a hint of her inner pussy lips peeking out. Her juices gleamed on her flesh. A spicy musk drifted up into my nose.

"Yeah, you want to finger my cunt," the girl said. "Just jam those fingers in me and molest me. Well, why aren't you doing it? Huh? Just jam them in and finger my cooze, bitch!"

"Evette, honey," the mother said. "I'm sure that the officer..."

"Officer Beverley," I said, my fingers twitching to do just that.

"I'm sure Officer Beverley isn't going to, um, finger you. She's just doing her job."

"You are such an idiot, Mom!" Evette let out a frustrated snarl. "And you're so fucking useless, too. Do something. She's got me handcuffed and is going to finger my cunt until I cum. I can tell. She wants to get her digits into my young pussy. She's that nasty of a dyke. She wants it bad."

I did.

But instead, I drew back my hand. "You think you get away with calling me a Black bitch, you spoiled brat? I don't take no lip from a prima donna White girl that thinks her cunt's worth any fucking thing."

SMACK!

My hand cracked down on her left butt-cheek. The stinging sound echoed through the screening room. The girl gasped. Her face widened in shock as she stared at me over her shoulder. Her pouty lips pressed together. A bright, red handprint blossomed across her pale ass. She had skin so light she was practically snow.

Which made spanking her such a delicious treat.

"You... you..." spluttered the girl. "You spanked me."

"You're being disciplined," I said. "There are consequences to making a scene and insulting a TSA officer doing her job."

"But you don't get to spank—"

SMACK!

"Fuck! Fuck! You bitch!" she gasped, her right butt-cheek now blossoming with a bright handprint. "Ooh, you think you're getting away with it. That—"

SMACK!

The stinging sound was so satisfying. My pussy clenched as the girl bucked. A bead of her pussy cream ran down her inner thigh.

That spicy musk permeated the air. I breathed it in, reveling in the wonderful aroma. My mouth watered.

I glanced at the step-mom. She watched with awe now. She had her hands clasped to her big boobs stretching out her t-shirt. She had pulled the fabric tight over her breasts, showing off just how delicious they were. She rubbed her thighs together, too, watching with shocked eyes.

"You want to give her a spank, Mrs. Kemp?" I asked. "She's a brat. I bet you've wanted to spank her ass so many times."

"Well..." the woman said.

"Mom!" shrieked the girl. "You have to stop her. Please, please, she's spanking me. My butt hurts. She can't do this to me."

I rubbed my dark hand over Evette's blushing ass. I gave her rump a squeeze. She gasped and bucked, my right hand still keeping her pinned down on the table. The handcuff chain rattled while the metal table she was bent over creaked.

"Tell me you don't want to spank this delectable rump," I purred. "This girl's derrière is just begging to be spanked by a hot MILF. Don't you think?"

"I mean..." Mrs. Kemp bit her lip. Her wedding ring flashed as she took a few steps closer. "She can be... difficult."

"Difficult?" gasped the girl. "Mom, she's *spanking* me. I'm eighteen! I'm too old to be spanked. You have to stop her."

SMACK!

The girl bucked again while the step-mother shivered. She took another step closer, her eyes locked on her step-daughter's glowing rump. I rubbed my hand over the girl's ass, sliding from Evette's right cheek to her left, my fingers dipping into her crack in the process.

"You know you want to give her a spank," I purred. "She needs to learn to respect such a gorgeous MILF like you. You're her step-mother. She should be on her knees worshiping you, not treating you like a doormat. Aren't you tired of it?"

"Well..." The sexy MILF stopped beside me, her wedding ring flashing. I smiled, so excited by this. Spanking a girl the same age as my kid was a thrill. "I mean... she has been... difficult. Out of control. She never listens to me. She just runs off to my husband

and sobs to him. Or to that horrid woman who birthed her and got her into doing titty streams. That what she calls them. Titty streams where she spends all day pretending to play video games."

"I don't pretend!" the girl gasped.

"While a bunch of horny guys gives her money as she giggles and dresses in the least amount of clothing she can." Mrs. Kemp shook her head, her anger growing. Her cheeks flushed. "Then she takes pictures of herself or even videos of herself masturbating and sells them to her fans."

"It's what every hot girl is doing!" Evette hissed. "There's nothing wrong with it, Mom! Fuck, you could even make the moolah. Lot of guys are pervs for old women with flabby tits."

SMACK!

"The fuck!" Evette gasped, her butt-cheeks clenching.

"Your mother is not old," I growled. "She's a ripe and mature MILF. A sexy woman with big tits and a lush body. You show her some respect."

SMACK!

"Fuck that!" the girl moaned. "Let me go. I have rights!"

I glanced at the step-mother. I arched an eyebrow at her. "Go on. You know you want to. She's been a brat. Don't you deserve to be rewarded for putting up with her? You've raised her, haven't you?"

"Not like that whore of a mother she has," muttered Mrs. Kemp. "I'm the one who's been there for her. I won't spoil her, so Evette thinks she can walk all over me."

"I'm sorry, Mom," Evette hissed, not sounding sorry. "Just get this bitch to stop—"

SLAP!

I blinked at Mrs. Kemp's half-hearted swat on her step-daughter's rump. It was enough to get the flesh jiggling, but not much else. My brow knitted, and I shook my head. Even the girl seemed stunned by how feeble it was.

"Oh, come on!" I said. "Put some effort into it."

SMACK!

As Evette gasped in pain, I said, "Really spank her. She's a brat. A naughty, nubile slut that needs her MILF of a step-mother to step up and give her what she needs. Discipline. Order. Domination. Be in charge of the little skank. Make her obedient."

Mrs. Kemp swallowed, raising up her left hand. Her wedding ring sparkled.

"You can do this," I cooed. "I believe in you."

She nodded.

CRACK!

The sound echoed through the screening room. Evette's reddened butt-cheek rippled from the impact. The girl gasped, her back arching. The table creaked. More pussy cream ran down her thighs, the spicy scent of her musk filling the air.

"Fuck, fuck, fuck, Mom!" she hissed. "That hurt. Why did you —"

CRACK!

"Because I'm tired of you being a little brat!" Mrs. Kemp hissed, her frustration finally boiling out of her.

CRACK!

"I'm tired of hearing you whine!"

CRACK!

"Complain about every little thing like it was the end of the fucking world!"

CRACK!

"You need to grow up! You're not a little girl any longer! You're an adult!"

CRACK!

"Mom! Mom!" the girl gasped, her butt-cheeks bright red now. She squirmed, my hand still pinning her to the table. She clenched her asscheeks tight, her pussy weeping juices. Rivulets ran down her cunt.

"What do you say?" I asked her, stroking her left butt-cheek. Her step-mother's hand caressed her right, both of us rubbing the nubile cutie's hot flesh. "Huh? What do you say to your step-mother that's sacrificed so much putting up with you?"

"I'm sorry," the girl muttered. Tears gleamed on her eyelashes. Her spicy musk filled my nose.

"You don't sound sorry," I said and raised my hand up.

SMACK!

"Ouch, fuck!" the girl gasped. "I am. I am, Mom! I'm sorry for being a brat. Okay?"

"And what do you say to Officer Beverley?" Mrs. Kemp asked.

"I'm sorry for calling you a bitch!" moaned the girl. "Okay, I'm sorry for being a brat and making a scene. Please, please, don't spank me any longer. My ass fucking hurts."

"Mmm, wasn't that sweet of her?" I asked the step-mother. I grabbed her hand rubbing at her daughter's asscheek. I moved it lower. "Now, we have to give her a reward. Positive reinforcement. She's done something good, so..."

I thrust the step-mother's hand over Evette's pussy. The White MILF gasped as my dark fingers pressed her digits into her step-daughter's twat. She dipped into the folds, spreading apart that tight, virgin-looking twat. Though I knew Evette was no virgin.

She'd lost her cherry ages ago.

I pushed the step-mother's fingers into that tight, young twat. I groaned, my own digits sinking in with hers. I felt that hot flesh. The step-mother and her daughter both moaned. Shock crossed the MILF's face.

"There you are," I said. "Mmm, finger her twat."

"Yes, yes," the girl moaned. "Oh, Mom, finger my cooze. Ooh, that's nice. That's real nice. I'll be a good girl. Yes, yes, I'll be a good girl for my sexy mommy!"

A shiver ran through me at those taboo words. It had happened. That lezzie switch had been flipped in both of them. Mother and step-daughter were uniting as Mrs. Kemp slid her fingers in and out of her daughter's snatch, her wedding ring flashing on one of those digits.

I shuddered and began stripping off my uniform. I took off my equipment belt. Then I undid my white blouse with my nametag and the TSA's logo on it. I shrugged out of that as the MILF kept fingering her step-daughter. Evette moaned, her fingers twitching. The redheaded White girl whimpered in delight.

This was so hot. My pussy was on fire.

I dropped my blouse and then undid the purple bra I wore today. I freed my large breasts. They spilled out, lush and lovely. I squeezed my darker flesh as I watched the White mother fingering her step-daughter's cunt faster. It was such a hot sight.

"I can't believe I'm doing this," Mrs. Kemp moaned. "Ooh, Evette, your pussy feels so wet and warm around my fingers."

"Your fingers feel amazing, Mom." The White girl squirmed. "Holy shit, that's good. Ooh, when did you get so sexy, Mommy."

"Mommy..." The step-mother shuddered. "Yes, yes, I am your mommy. And you have a hot pussy. You keep being a good girl, and Mommy will finger your twat."

That almost made me cum right there as I unlaced my flats. They were comfortable shoes with Dr. Scholls inserts in them. I peeled off my black pants next, rolling them down my thighs. I shuddered, so eager to fuck the MILF with my naughty toy. Slacks off, I peeled off my purple panties next. My sweet musk filled the air now. I was dripping wet.

I bet Mrs. Kemp was, too. Her ass looked good in those mom jeans of her. They weren't the most flattering cut, but with her slightly bent over and fingering her step-daughter's cunt, a wild wave of heat washed through me. My fingers flexed, the heat building in me.

I opened the bag and pulled out the strap-on dildo I'd bought. It was a thick shaft of black vinyl attached to a matching harness. Little bumps covered the smooth cylinder to add an extra bit of delight to my lover's twat.

The girl at Secret Delights had demonstrated how well it worked when she fucked me hard with it. I had cum and cum and cum.

I slipped the harness up my thighs as the girl kept moaning, her step-mother still fingering her. Mrs. Kemp's right hand fumbled at the fastener of her jeans. She popped open the fly and shoved her hand inside.

As I adjusted the straps, the dildo pressing right on my clit, I said, "I have you covered, Mrs. Kemp. Why don't you drop those pants and panties then fall to your knees and eat your step-daughter out? I'll make you cum."

"Holy shit!" Evette said. She looked over at me. "Where did you get that, Officer Beverley?"

"I like to be ready to deal with problematic young women," I said. "And their sexy step-mothers. Mmm, MILFs got to look out for each other."

"Yes!" moaned the girl. "You are one sexy Black MILF. Ooh, look at those big titties of yours. Those are so fucking hot."

"They are," moaned Mrs. Kemp. She pulled the fingers of her left hand out of her daughter's cunt. They dripped with the girls' juices. Cream even ran down the back of the MILF's hand. She flexed her fingers, the droplets flying from her digits and dripping across the floor. It was so hot to see.

My pussy melted. My cunt was on fire. I was dripping wet, just so eager to get wild with her. I licked my lips as Mrs. Kemp shoved down her jeans and her gray panties in a single go. The round curve of her rump came into view. A peachy and delectable ass that had my mouth drooling.

I licked my lips, my heart pounding so fast. She peeled them off. She had never put her shoes back on, so she was down to a pair of white ankle socks and her t-shirt. She popped that off, her large breasts dancing in a green sports bra. That followed, her large and lush tits coming into view.

"Shit, Mommy," moaned the naughty Evette. Her butt-cheeks clenched and her fingers twitched. The handcuff chain rattled as she groaned, "That's a lush pair of big titties. I love them."

"Thanks," the step-mother said, smiling. "So they're not saggy, huh?"

"No! They're hot. Fuck, MILFs are so fucking hot."

"Mmm, and you're sexy, Evette," Mrs. Kemp moaned. She fell to her knees, her big, ivory tits heaving. White women had such delicious breasts. They were so sexy. My cunt clenched.

Grabbing both of her step-daughter's reddened butt-cheeks, her wedding ring glinting, Mrs. Kemp buried her face into her daughter's shaved twat and licked. The taboo sight sent a ripple of heat through me. I groaned at the sight while Evette whimpered in delight.

"Oh, my," Mrs. Kemp purred. "I had no idea pussy teased so good. Mmm, young, delicious pussy. My step-daughter's pussy."

"Mommy!" groaned Evette. She squirmed as her mother licked her. "Oh, yes, yes, Mommy. That's it. Eat my pussy. I'll be a good girl if you lick my pussy all the time."

A hot shiver of delight ran through my body. I fanned my face, this wonderful heat rushing from my pussy. I moved behind Mrs. Kemp. I fell to my knees, my dildo bobbing. The base rubbed against my clit. The pleasure of that contact sent such delight through my body. I groaned, loving it. My pussy clenched.

I lined up my dildo at the MILF's cunt. I pressed it right into the White woman's married twat, her dark-brown curls spilling over the tip of the dildo. It was such a hot delight to witness. A wave of heat washed over me. I groaned at the wicked sight of the dildo pushing into her. This wonderful heat rushed through my body.

I groaned, my twat clenching. Sparks flared from the pressure on my clit. More and more of the dildo vanished into her pussy. She groaned into her step-daughter's cunt, licking and lapping at her as she swallowed the thick, black shaft.

"Oh, yes, yes," I groaned, my large tits jiggling. My ebony hands grabbed the White woman's pale hips. I held on tight. "Ooh, you like that, Mrs. Kemp. My girl-dick in you."

"Yes," she moaned into her step-daughter's twat. "Oh, that's so big. Bigger than my husband. Yes! You're sexy, Officer Beverley."

"What about me?" moaned Evette. "Aren't I sexy, Mommy?"

"Yes, you are, you little brat," the MILF said fondly. "And you taste divine."

Mrs. Kemp's head moved. Her step-daughter squealed.

I shuddered, my pussy clenching. I slid my hands up the MILF's pale flesh to grab her large tits. I gripped them and drew back. She moaned again. I loved the sounds she made as she devoured the brat's pussy. I slammed back into her cunt, my crotch smacking her plump ass.

Her butt-cheeks rippled. I loved that jiggle. I squeezed and kneaded her tits. I pumped away at her pussy, my clit drinking in the pressure on her base. Every time I thrust in, rapture flared. Then I had the anticipation as I drew back for that next burst of ecstasy.

The girl squirmed as her step-mother ate her out. The girl's fingers flexed, the handcuff jingle. The table creaked. Her moans echoed through the room, mixing with her mother's muffled groans. I fucked the married MILF hard. I slammed into her cunt while kneading her tits.

I massaged them. My hands dug into them. I loved every moment of it. I squeezed into them. I jiggled them as I fucked her hard and fast. I buried to the hilt in her over and over again. It was a powerful delight to pound a woman with a strap-on. A wonderful thrill to ram my fake-cock into her pussy.

My clit loved it. My bud throbbed. Pulsed. My pussy drank in the pleasure bursting from my naughty pearl. My fingers dug into the MILF's tits as I slammed harder and harder into her pussy. My own boobs heaved before me.

"Fuck!" I moaned, loving fucking the White MILF hard. "Ooh, you like that, don't you, Mrs. Kemp? You like my girl-dick fucking your cunt!"

"Yes!" she moaned, her fingers kneading her daughter's rump. "I love it. Oh, yes, yes, fuck me. Pound me. Ram that dildo into me."

"Make my mommy cum!" the step-daughter moaned. "Oh, shit, she's melting my cooze. I'm going to cum so hard. Just squirt my cream on her face. Fuck, Mommy, you know how to eat pussy."

"It just feels right," groaned the MILF. "Ooh, honey, your pussy is so yummy. Cum for Mommy."

"Fucking explode!"

"Yes!" I panted, my orgasm building and building with every stroke into the MILF's cunt.

I pounded her harder and faster. My pussy clenched, juices soaking my bush. The dildo's base massaged my naughty clit. That bud loved it. My hands gripped Mrs. Kemp's big tits. I kneaded those soft mounds, my own bouncing before me.

The MILF's ass jiggled. That plump booty rippled from the impact. The scent of pussy filled the air. My sweet, Evette's spicy, and a tart musk that must belong to the married twat that I pounded hard. I loved it.

"Yes, yes, yes!" the girl gasped. "Oh, fuck, Mommy, I'm cumming!"

Her passion resounded through the screening room. The sound echoed off the cinder block walls. It reverberated through the room. I loved it. I slammed into the step-mother's cunt hard. The MILF licked up her daughter's juices.

"Oh, Mommy, you're loving my cream, aren't you?"

"So much," the married MILF moaned, her wedding ring flashing as she kneaded her cumming step-daughter's rump. "It's so good and... and... Officer Beverley!"

A flood of hot cream gushed out of her pussy and bathed my thighs. I shuddered as I drove into the married MILF's cumming pussy. My dildo reamed her. I shuddered, drawing back and thrusting in again. My clit burst with pleasure.

I exploded.

"Yes, yes, yes!" I howled as my orgasm swept through me. The heat burned across my thoughts. A wildfire. "Oh, my god, that's so good. Ooh, yes, yes, that's amazing."

My tits heaved. My pussy clenched. The cream ran down my thighs. Waves of ecstasy washed through me. All three of us were cumming. The girl's handcuffs rattled as she squirmed on the table. Her step-mother moaned into her cunt, licking out those juices.

I rode the orgasmic rush to its limits. I shuddered as I hit those heights of ecstasy. I floated there, my mind bubbling with the rapture of my climactic bliss. The heat melted through me. I shuddered and descended into a whimpering mess.

"That's so good," I moaned, so dizzy from the ecstasy that had just consumed me. "Oh, yes, yes, that's amazing."

"Mmm, yes," Mrs. Kemp moaned.

"It was," I purred. Then I smacked the White woman on the rump. "Want to fuck your daughter with the strap-on?"

"Oh, say yes, Mommy!" moaned Evette. "Please, please, say yes. I want you to fuck me with that dildo. Ooh, fresh from your pussy. That will be hot."

"Yes, it will," I said. "So?"

"Of course," the wicked mommy said. "I want to do it. I want to ram that dildo into my naughty daughter's cunt. She needs it."

"That's right," I groaned, this heady heat rushing through me.

I pulled the dildo out of Mrs. Kemp's pussy. The dick emerged gleaming, the bumps coated in that lovely, MILF cream. I shuddered and worked at the harness, my body buzzing from the rapture we just shared.

The heat rushed out of my pussy. I fanned my face as I peeled the strap-on down my thighs. My heart thundered, the beat pumping delight through my veins. I worked off the harness, a shiver racing through me. This was so intense. Such a wild thrill to get to experience.

I stepped out of the harness, my cunt on fire. The cream ran down my thighs, this hot passion dripping out of me. I shuddered, my cunt blazing. I felt dizzy with euphoria. This was such a wicked thing to experience.

I dildo off, I paused to lick it.

"Does she taste good?" Evette asked. The girl squirmed, still handcuffed, her belly shirt and ankle socks all she was wearing. Her reddened ass clenched. "Huh?"

"Delicious," I moaned and then handed the strap-on to Mrs. Kemp.

She took it and then surprised me by kissing me on the mouth. Our large breasts pressed together. Her nipples hard on mine, our tits pillowing tight. I loved it. Her lips tasted of that spicy excitement. The wonderful taste of her step-daughter's yummy cunt. It was such a delicious thing to experience.

I was so glad I got to. The heat rushed through me. My nipples throbbed against hers. My tongue danced with the MILFs. We kissed each other with hunger. It was such a hot thing to experience. I was so happy to enjoy it.

I broke the kiss and pulled back. She shuddered, blinking her eyes. She shook her head, her dark-brown hair dancing around her face. She bit her lower lip. "I think I like being a lesbian mommy."

"Mmm, so do I," I said. "Now put on the strap-on and fuck that step-daughter hard. Make her explode."

"Yes!" hissed the brat. "I need it. Oh, Mommy, I need it so much."

"Yes, you do," I said, sauntering to the table. As the step-mother donned my strap-on, I sat down beside the girl. "Mmm, and you know what I need?"

Evette glanced at me, her fiery locks spilling over her ivory face. The White girl watched me sliding back along the table. Then I threw my leg over her head and shifted over so that I was sitting before her, my black bush inches from her face.

"You need that MILF twat eaten, don't you?" she asked, hunger in her eyes.

"Yes," I groaned. I grabbed a fistful of her red hair and pressed her face right into the wiry curls of my pubic hair. "So what are you waiting on? Get to licking."

"Yes, Officer Beverley," she cooed.

The girl lapped.

I shuddered, whimpering as her tongue slid up through my folds. She stroked my pussy lips and then brushed my clit. Sparks flared. I loved it. She swirled her tongue around it, the naughty minx, and then fluttered her tongue back down to my pussy folds.

As she licked me, I watched her step-mother's heaving tits. Mrs. Kemp worked on the strap-on. She adjusted the dildo and her eyes widened. A hot shiver ran through her as she pushed the base against her pussy lips and clit.

"Oh, my," she said. "Mmm, no wonder you were having so much fun fucking me with it. That's very naughty."

"Isn't it?" I asked while her step-daughter's tongue did a naughty dance over my pussy lips, brushing my clit again. I shuddered, my big tits aching.

"Ooh, this is going to be fun," Mrs. Kemp said, her hands stroking up and down that big, black shaft, her pussy cream lubing the way.

"God, that's hot," I moaned.

"It would be hotter if it was in my pussy," moaned Evette into my cunt.

Mrs. Kemp stepped up and smacked the dildo against her step-daughter's welt rump. The White girl hissed into my pussy, her asscheeks clenching tight together. "You behave. I can always fuck Officer Beverley instead of you."

"I'll be good, Mommy," the girl moaned. She kissed my pussy. "See, I'm licking Officer Beverley's pussy. So, please, fuck me, Mommy! Fuck me so hard. Just pound that dildo into me and make me cum."

"How can you say no to that?" I asked.

"No naughty step-mother could," Mrs. Kemp said, winking a

brown eye at me.

I shivered and smiled, knowing it to be true.

The MILF moved her dildo down. The girl gasped into my pussy. Mrs. Kemp thrust into step-daughter's twat. Both White women groaned. I shuddered, loving it. The girl fluttered her tongue up and down my pussy. She devoured me with hunger.

I groaned, squirming against the wall. This wonderful heat rushed through me. I smiled as the girl licked and lapped at me. She fluttered her tongue around in my pussy. She stirred me up. It was amazing to feel.

"Oh, yes, you little brat," I panted, my large tits rising and falling. "Mmm, get that tongue in me. I want you to make me cum. Oh, yes, just make me explode!"

The girl whimpered and thrust her tongue deep into my cunt. She swirled it around in me, stirring me up. Her green eyes stared up at me, glossy with her hunger. She moaned into my cunt while her step-mother fucked her pussy.

Mrs. Kemp rammed that dildo hard into her step-daughter's twat. The busty MILF's tits heaved with her every stroke. She gripped her daughter's hips, holding on tight as she plowed into the girl's juicy cunt.

"God, you're fucking my cooze hard, Mommy," the girl moaned. "Just pounding it. Mmm, that's good."

"Yes, yes, it is," the step-mother moaned. "Ooh, you are so much fun to fuck."

"Good, 'cause I love it! Ram that dick into me, Mommy! Fuck me hard. Yes, yes, just plow that girl-cock into my snatch. I'm going to fucking cum while drowning in Officer Beverley's MILF juices."

"Yes, you are," I groaned.

She thrust her tongue back into my pussy. She stirred me around, my orgasm building fast. It was so hot to have dominated this naughty brat. To have shown her how she needed to love sexy MILFs like her step-mother and me.

Her tongue fluttered around in me. Danced. She stirred me up as she moaned into my cunt. Her mother fucked her hard. Fast. The White woman groaned as she fucked her step-daughter's cunt hard with the dildo. Pleasure crossed the MILF's face.

"Oh, yes," Mrs. Kemp moaned.

"Mmm," the girl cooed. She licked her tongue up to my clit.

She sucked on it hard. She nursed on my bud. My cunt spasmed. The pleasure built and built me towards my orgasm. I couldn't take much more of this. I squirmed, my body on fire. My bud burst with sparks.

"Oh, god," I groaned.

She nursed harder and harder. She groaned around my clit, her step-mother fucking her hard. My entire body shuddered. My cunt clenched. I couldn't take much more of her nursing. She suckled hard on my clit.

"That's it," I whimpered. "I'm so close, you little slut."

"Make her cum!" the MILF moaned.

Mrs. Kemp fucked her step-daughter harder and harder. The girl's handcuffs jiggled. She squealed around my clit as she sucked so hard. She nursed on it. the pleasure swelled through my pussy. I came closer and closer to that wonderful eruption.

"Oh, my god, yes!" I moaned. "Oh, that's it. That's so good. Fuck, fuck, fuck!"

My pussy cream gushed into Evette's mouth. She lapped up the flood as the pleasure rushed through my body. My eyes squeezed shut. I grabbed my big boobs. I held onto them tight. My fingers dug into them. This wonderful heat roared through me.

Then the girl squealed, "Mommy!"

She moaned into my pussy as she bucked on the table. Mrs. Kemp gasped in delight, her big tits heaving. She buried the dildo hard into her step-daughter's cunt. The White woman threw back her head and howled out her rapture.

"I'm cumming!" the MILF moaned.

"Yes, yes, yes," squealed the girl between licks.

All three of us were climaxing together. Sharing our lesbian passion with the other. It was so wonderful. Stars burst across my eyes. My breasts jiggled in my squeezing grip. I surged towards that rapturous heights.

I hung there, reveling in my orgasm.

"So good," moaned Mrs. Kemp. "Oh, I have to buy one of these."

"Yes!" the step-daughter moaned. "Oh, Mommy, yes!"

"Mmm," I moaned, my pleasure dying down. I panted there, sucking in a deep breath.

All of us were gasping for air as we came down from our orgasmic highs. The girl nuzzled into my bush, kissing at my pussy. No one said anything for a few minutes and then I groaned and slid off the table. Mrs. Kemp pulled the strap-on out of her step-daughter's pussy.

"This has been fun, Officer Beverley, but are we free to go?" The MILF undid the straps of my dildo. "We have a flight to catch."

"Yeah," I said, smiling. "I think she's learned her lesson.

Evette gave a wicked giggle.

I thrust the key into the cuffs and undid the lock. They ratcheted off, leaving red impressions around the girl's wrists. She groaned and sat up, her nipples poking at her belly shirt. I never did get to see those cute titties, but I had enjoyed the rest of her.

She grabbed both of my boobs and buried her face between them. Her fiery locks spilled over my ebony skin while her ivory features looked up at me from in between the valley of my dark tits. Her green eyes sparkled.

She groaned, "Such gorgeous boobies, Officer Beverley. Mmm, you are so hot. I'm sorry for being a brat."

"No, you're not," I said. "You're glad because it let you have all this fun. Let you know what you are."

"A little lezzie slut that needs busty MILFs to spank me," she moaned. A grin spread on her lips. "I'm going to make sure Mom has so many reasons to spank me."

"Wicked girl," I groaned. "Your poor mother."

Evette pulled her face from my tits and looked over at her dressing step-mother. "I'll make sure to take care of her all the time. She'll get to cum from my licking and lapping and tongue fluttering."

I winked at her.

I joined in the dressing. Unsurprising, with her thong ripped, all Evette had to do was pull on her booty shorts, drawing them up and over her reddened rump. The denim hugged those bubbly cheeks like a second skin, the seam digging into her crack.

God, I wanted to eat that White girl's ass out. Just go to town on her and make her explode. She would scream her head off once I was done with eating out her booty.

Mrs. Kemp finished next, drawing on her t-shirt over her breasts constrained in a green sports bra. She patted her hair then pulled wet wipes out of her purse and attacked her mouth and face. She handed one to me and then to her daughter.

The girl just licked her lips and said, "I'm good smelling like MILF pussy."

I smiled as I wiped at my hands.

I finished dressing last. Then I opened the door and the pair headed out holding their trays. My supervisor glanced over at them as I let them out to where the other passengers were donning shoes and putting away electronic devices.

"It's all settled," I said. "No need to go any farther with her. She won't cause any more distractions in the line. She understands."

Helen's eyes narrowed. Then she nodded. "If that's what you think is best, Shanisa. Get back to your post."

"Yes, ma'am," I said and headed to my position. I was eager to find another cute, young thing to search. I loved being the only woman working at my TSA checkpoint. It made things so incredibly wicked.

To be continued...

# Officer Beverley Searches the Naughty Hotties

## Lesbian MILF's Naughty Search 3

## A Lesbian MILF Tale

by

Reed James

## Officer Beverley Searches the Naughty Hotties

### Officer Shanisa Beverley – Saturday, Day 6 of the Wish

The line going through security moved slowly but steadily. I stood at my post, aching for the next cute young thing to search. Hopefully a sexy White girl with blonde or red hair. Those were the hottest to me. Pale skin contrasting with my ebony flesh. A vanilla treat for me to enjoy.

It had been an hour since I had enjoyed Mrs. Kemp and her bratty step-daughter. That had been one hot and taboo threesome. The step-mother and I had spanked her daughter then enjoyed her. I fucked the mother with my strap-on and then she fucked her step-daughter while the girl, Evette, ate me out. It had been hot.

One delicious romp.

Now I was aching for more. I had to find just the right girl. The perfect pretty young thing to educate on lesbian matters. That was my job as a hot MILF. My nipples throbbed in my bra and my pussy was soaking the purple panties I wore beneath my uniform. The heat rippled through my body. My hips had a slow wiggle to them, a sensual roll as I thought of all the naughty things I would do.

I stood my post, scanning faces.

My supervisor appeared. Helen Reynolds moved from screening checkpoint to screening checkpoint making sure that things were running smoothly. She paused, studying the line. Her eyes flicked to me. I gave her a smile.

She was a MILF, like me. Just into her forties but in great shape. She wore the same white blouse and black slacks as me and the rest of the agents, blue gloves adorning her hands. Her blonde hair fell about her face. She was a busty woman.

Then she moved on, and I turned back to my post.

"Look at him," a girl said. "God, he's staring at your ass, Lori."

The words drifted out of the cacophony. I glanced to my right and spotted a pair of young women, eighteen or nineteen, putting their carry-on bags and other belongings onto the trays to run through the x-ray machines. I smiled at the pair of White girls.

"If you weren't dressed like my mother, he'd really be drooling," continued the girl. "Lori, we have got to do something about how you dress."

Lori said something, but it was too soft to hear. She pushed up the dainty glasses she wore, giving her youthful face a cuteness to it. Something adorable. She was blonde, which had my mouth salivating, and wore a one-piece dress that was dark and had long sleeves and a longer skirt. It didn't show off her body well. High-necked. It was out of place on such a young girl.

"It's the 2020s, not the 1920s," the friend continued. She was dressed more like young women typically did these days. A pair of hip-hugging, low-riding jeans that showed off her red thong. Her crop top clung to her round breasts. Whatever her real hair color was, she had hers dyed purple and cut short. A nose ring glinted as she talked.

A girl with a piercing was a girl down to getting her pussy devoured by a MILF with little prompting. She didn't need much education. I bet she'd eaten cunt before, but her friend Lori definitely needed it.

"I like how I dress, Hannah," Lori said.

The purple-haired girl definitely didn't look like a Hannah.

She just shrugged. "How can you like it? You dress like a spinster. Your nineteen. You're never going to get a boy if you keep dressing like that."

"When do you want to keep a boy?" asked Lori. They were

putting their trays on the conveyor belt now and heading for the scanners.

"Variety is the spice of life," said Hannah. "Mmm, you should try at least one of them. It's no biggie. It's a lot of fun after you get broken in. Just find some guy to get your cherry popped, then hook up with a Chad or Tyrone and get railed. You'll thank me."

No, she didn't need a guy to do that. She needed a woman. A MILF. I licked my lips, ready to pull them aside. What was my excuse to search them? I glanced at the x-ray machine and watched as their carry-ons went through. I could see inside them on the computer screen. Things looked weird sometimes. You had a strange sense of depth and...

Hannah had packed a metallic vibrator. It appeared plain as day on the x-ray. I smiled. That was perfect. I could use that to get them into the screening room. The girls were passing through the body scanner, Hannah with a flirty wink to the technician staring at the monitor like she was getting off on being seen beneath her clothing.

I grabbed the carry-on bag as it came out of the scanner and set it on the table. The girls came up and I asked, "Whose is this?"

"Mine," Lori said, her face paling.

I blinked in shock. *She* had packed a big, fat vibrator. Did Hannah realize Lori had found another way to pop her cherry? It sent this wicked surge through me. This was even better than I thought. The heat rushed through my veins.

"I need you both to come with me," I said. "Grab the rest of your stuff."

"What did you pack?" Hannah whispered in awe to Lori. "I'm impressed."

"Just normal stuff," whimpered the blonde girl, her face going as pale as milk.

I opened the door to the screening room. The scent of hot pussy still lingered in the air from my romp with the MILF and her bratty step-daughter. I loved it. My pussy melted as I set down the carry-on bag, a purple hard-shell. The girls set their things on the table, Lori looking frightened.

"Do I have your permission to look inside of here?" I asked even as I unzipped it.

"Yes," squeaked the girl. "But I don't understand. There's nothing in there. I followed all the rules on your website!"

I unfolded it. There were her toiletries, the liquid stuff in small bottles and then in plastic bags. She had a paperback novel, *Above the Storm*, tucked into her neatly folded clothing. I dug around in her clothing, disturbing a few pairs of folded panties, and found the vibrator.

I pulled it out. Long and a metallic red. It was similar to my own vibrator I had confiscated from this naughty girl named Kelly. She had smuggled it in her pussy and had started me down this route of searching sexy, young women.

"What are you doing with this?" I demanded as sternly as I could.

Lori's blue eyes bulged behind her glasses. Her jaw dropped. Then she shrieked, "Hannah!"

"I thought you'd like to have some fun while I'm out hooking up with boys," Hannah said. "If you're going to be hanging out in the hotel room, you might as well get off a few times. I didn't think it was against the rules."

I thrust the vibrator at Hannah. "So you put this in her bag?"

She squirmed. "Well, I mean, I guess, technically." Her cheeks paled. "I mean, it's a vibrator. It's not a weapon or anything. That shouldn't be a big deal to take on a plane. I bet a lot of women do it."

I gave her a direct look. "Depends on how you planned on it being used. Show me how you intended Lori to use this."

Hannah gave me a strange look. Then she licked her lips and flicked her gaze up and down my body. A shiver ran through her, hazel eyes dilating, a flush spreading across her round face. She nodded and unsnapped her jeans.

"Hannah!" Lori gasped. "What are you doing?"

"Why, showing how I wanted you to use this," said Hannah, a smile spreading on her lips. "Officer Beverley here needs to see it in action so she'll know we're not intending to use it as a weapon or anything. I mean..." Hannah hefted the vibrator. "With those D-sized batteries in it, it's got a heft to it."

She sat the vibrator down on the table and then shoved down

her tight jeans. She worked at the denim, her hips wiggling back and forth as she squirmed. Her breasts bounced in her tight crop top while her purple locks danced about her face. She groaned, sliding the jeans lower and lower down her hips.

With a moan, she worked them down her thighs. She bent over, her breasts jiggling in her top. She stepped out of her jeans, Lori watching on in shock. She had her hands clapped over her mouth, trembling as she watched her friend. Hannah hooked the string waistband of her thong with her fingers.

Hannah shoved the red garment down.

It peeled away from the shaved folds of her pussy, her juices already flowing. Sticky lines of cream connected panties and vulva for a moment before they snapped. A wonderful, tart aroma filled the air. I breathed in the White girl's scent, reveling in it. I licked my lips, hungering for that barely legal cunt.

"H-Hannah," groaned Lori. She trembled there, looking so cute.

She was just adorable. I wanted to do such naughty things to her. A shiver ran through me. My cunt clenched tight, my panties absorbing my juices. The heat rushed through my body. I fanned my face as Hannah sat down on the table, her legs spread wide.

Her pussy lips peeled apart as she did that, showing off her pink, inner depths. They gleamed with her arousal. She bit her lip and smiled at me, her hips wiggling back and forth. She fanned her face, looking so goddamn sexy. I licked my chops, just so hungry to do wicked things to the girl. Naughty and terribly kinky things.

It would be fantastic.

"I was hoping she'd use it like this," Hannah said, twisting the base of her vibrator.

It hummed to life, the shaft blurring into fuzzy red. She then brought it to her pussy lips and rubbed it up and down. She gasped, her back arching as she masturbated right before us. She slid the toy up and down her snatch, massaging her flesh. She brushed her clit.

"Mmm, yes, yes, Lori," Hannah moaned. "This was what I wanted you to do with it. Circle your clit." The purple-haired girl did, her body bucking and shuddering. She let out a long, slow whimper as she did. "Yes, yes, just like that. Ooh, it's great. You'll cum so hard. Then you would do this."

She thrust the vibrator into her pussy, her snatch swallowing up the toy with ease.

"Yes!"

My pussy was on fire as I watched Hannah pumped the toy in and out of her snatch. The heat grew and grew in me as my mouth watered. I flexed my fingers. It was so deliciously wicked to witness this. Lori groaned, her eyes so wide. She stared at that toy vanishing into her friend's twat over and over again.

My hips swayed back and forth. I bit my lip and groaned. That was so hot. This White girl and her shaved twat were such a delicious sight to witness. My passions were swelling inside of me. I wanted to do such naughty things to this girl.

"That's not what I meant," I said. "I wanted you to show me how *Lori* would have used it."

Hannah stared at me with lidded eyes. She shuddered, the vibrator humming away in her snatch. It was like it took her mind a moment to process what I was saying as she quivered through the delight created by that naughty toy.

"Right," Hannah said. She stood up, the vibrator staying buried in her snatch, the whirring motor of the toy half-muffled by her twat. "Mmm, Lori, Let's get that dress off of you."

"W-what?" Lori gasped.

"We have to prove to her that we're not terrorists," said Hannah. "Just horny college girls."

"I'm not horny," Lori whimpered even as Hannah attacked the buttons of the blonde's dress.

"Riiiiight," Hannah moaned. "That's why you're letting me strip you naked before that hot MILF. Mmm, she's sexy, right. That ebony skin... Those motherly features staring at you like you're her naughty daughter that she needs to 'discipline.' Fuck, it has my pussy melting around the vibrator."

Oh, yes, Hannah knew what was up and loved playing along with me. As she opened her friend's blouse, I casually took off my equipment belt and set it down on the table.

A plain white cotton bra hid Lori's round, plump breasts. It was such a shame. She just stood there trembling as her flirty friend pulled the dress off her shoulders and then down her torso. In moments, the garment fluttered down Lori's long, pale thighs. She wore matching panties to her bra, white and boring. Hannah hooked those with her fingers.

Tugged.

"Wait, Hannah!" gasped the girl, her eyes bulging. "You can't. That's not right. You can't do that."

"Relax, relax," purred Hannah as she dragged the panties down her friend's thighs, falling down to her knees to do it. "Things are going to be okay."

"But..."

"Shhh. Just relax. You're going to love this." Then Hannah ducked her head in and kissed at her friend's blonde bush covering the girl's pubic mound.

Lori squeaked and jumped. She almost fell with her panties bunched around her ankles. They stretched as her feet shifted. Then her left foot popped out. Hannah grabbed her friend's hips, steadying the girl before guiding her to sit down at the table.

Lori squeaked, probably from the cold metal on her rump. Hannah grinned and pulled the vibrator, still buzzing away, out of her pussy. The scent of tart musk swelled again. Then she nudged it against her friend's bush. She nuzzled it through the blonde curls.

Touched the virgin's pussy.

Lori gasped. Her legs kicked out, panties swinging from her right ankle. My hands began unbuttoning my white blouse that had the TSA's logo on it. I bit my lip, working as fast as I could as I stared at the lesbian sight before me.

"Hannah!" squeaked Lori.

"Mmm, I know," Hannah cooed as she ran the vibrator up and down her friend's pussy. "We just have to show her how you were going to use it."

"I never was going to use it."

"Well, I wanted to use it on you," said Hannah. "So, this is good enough."

Lori gasped as the vibrator pressed into her pussy. I guess she didn't have her hymen any longer. The girl whimpered as the toy sank into her. She sucked in deep breaths, almost hyperventilating. I slipped my blouse off, my purple bra holding my large tits.

I freed them.

Lori's blue eyes fell on my breasts. She stared at them, her flushed face twitching. The vibrator hummed as Hannah pumped it in and out of the blonde's pussy. It was so hot. I squeezed my tits for Lori to appreciate, seeing her falling into these lesbian delights.

"Ooh, that's nice," purred Hannah. "Right? You love it. And you smell so good. Spicy. I like—"

The door to the screening room unlocked. I gasped as it opened. My stomach lurched as Helen Reynolds stepped into the room. My supervisor's blue eyes hardened as she surveyed the sight of Lori in her bra, Hannah in only a crop top, and me in just my pants. The vibrator hummed away as the door boomed close behind my boss. She planted her hands on her hips.

I was so busted. I didn't know what to say. What to do. My mind went blank, my hands full of my heavy tits. Hannah gasped, jamming the vibrator deep into Lori's cunt. She squealed and covered her bra-clad breasts like they were naked, her glasses slipping on her face.

"So you *are* molesting girls in here, Officer Beverley," Helen said, using my last name and not my first name, Shanisa, like she normally would.

"I'm, uh..." I struggled to think. There was no excuse for this. No way to get out of the certainty that I was about to be fired.

"I want in," moaned Helen. She shuddered. "You're so bold, Officer Beverley. You're enjoying all those cute, young things that prance through here. I've been wishing I had the courage to do it. God, the last few days, they've been turning me on. Even my own step-daughter..." She peeled off her blue gloves, her large breasts straining the front of them. Then she marched up, grabbed Hannah by the shoulders, and pulled the college girl in for a hot kiss.

Lori squeaked as Hannah was pulled from her, leaving the vibrator buried into the girl's pussy, the toy buzzing away. The MILF and the naughty hottie kissed, my supervisor's hands grabbing Hannah's tight rump, gripping and massaging it.

My cunt clenched. The heat rushed through my body. It was this exciting tingle that flowed through my flesh. I unsnapped my slacks and shoved them down as I watched my boss kissing Hannah and groping that rump. The vibrator hummed away in Lori's pussy, the girl still clutching at her bra-covered tits, her eyes wide. A spicy scent came from here.

That delicious pussy.

I bent down, unlacing my shoes and seeing up between Hannah's legs at her shaved twat. It was incredible to see a MILF kissing a barely legal thing. I loved every second of it as I pulled off my shoes. I breathed in and savored the wonderful aromas of young cunts.

Lori just watched, the vibrator humming away in her body. Her hands were kneading her tits, squeezing them. Rubbing them. I shuddered and then peeled off my panties. Naked, I advanced on Lori while my supervisor continued her make-out session with Hannah.

I grabbed the red vibrator and pulled it out of the girl's pussy. "You're supposed to be playing with this."

She snapped her gaze to me. "O-Officer Beverley?"

"The vibrator," I said, waving it in the air before her. "You're supposed to be playing with it. Jamming it into your pussy. Stirring it around in you. Not just sitting there while it buzzes away inside you."

She blushed, her blue eyes sparkling behind her glasses.

"Mmm, you're just such an adorable little thing," I said, turning the vibrator off. I held it up before her. "Look at all your juices soaking this toy."

"That's all from me?" she whispered, cream running down the shaft.

I licked up the spicy cream, shuddering at the delicious flavor of the girl's barely legal twat. I shuddered, my cunt squeezing tight. The rapture rushed through my body. It was such a delight to taste her mixed with a metallic tang. My hips wiggled back and forth, the heat rushing through my flesh. It was exciting. Outstanding. I was so eager for the fun to begin.

I kissed Lori.

She gasped as my spicy-coated lips planted on her mouth. She froze as I kissed her. I savored every moment of kissing her. My tongue darted past her lips. I stirred around in her mouth. I danced my tongue in hot circles through her mouth. It was such a wonderful delight to enjoy.

The heat built and built in me. This wild rush of passion. I groaned, kissing her with hunger. The pleasure rushed through my body. It was exciting to experience. Clothing rustled beside us as I kissed that sexy girl.

Lori whimpered as my tongue invaded her mouth. She started moving her lips. I loved it. She tasted so sweet. I played with her tongue, coaxing her into more motion. She groaned, her head tilting to the side.

I savored her kissing me back.

"Ooh, these are killer tits," Hannah moaned. "Big and soft MILF boobies."

My supervisor groaned, clearly loving the attention her big boobs were getting. I shuddered, wanting to play with Lori's tits. But she still had her bra on. I broke the kiss, noticing that Hannah was naked and my supervisor was down to her pants. The purple-haired girl had her face buried between my fellow MILF's tits, rubbing her face back and forth.

I grinned at the sight. It was so hot.

Then I turned to Lori. "Take off your bra."

"Y-yes, Officer Beverley," she stammered and reached behind her. She fumbled at the clasp of her bra. Her blue eyes were so wide as they stared at my boobs.

She slipped her bra off, unveiling her perky round tits topped by pink nipples. Her areolas were small rings encircling those nubs. I groaned, my left hand shot out and groped her right breast. My dark fingers kneaded her pale flesh. She gasped and grabbed both of my boobs with her ivory fingers. She kneaded them.

It was so exciting. I clutched at the vibrator I gripped in my right hand, my heart thundering through my chest. This was all so exciting. My cunt blazed with a wild heat. My hips wiggled back and forth, my desire stewing inside of me. I wanted to get wild with her. I needed to cum.

"You need to learn how to use this," I said, and then stepped back, pulling my tits from her hands. Her fingers curled like they were still holding my boobs. I pressed the vibrator into her hand. "You were just letting it buzz away. I'll teach you. You're going to make me cum with it."

"Yes," Hannah moaned to my supervisor. "Ooh, I wish there was another vibrator here for me to make you cum, Officer Reynolds."

"My black bag in the corner," I said and then sat my ass down on the cool, metallic table. "Now, Lori, you have to use that vibrator on me. Make me cum." I leaned back, my large tits jiggling.

As Hannah darted for the bag that held my collection of toys, Lori slipped off the table. Hannah's chortle of delight echoed around us as the nervous Lori held the vibrator in both her hands. Her breasts rose and fell with her rapid breathing.

"Mmm you can do this," I said. "Start by turning it on."

Hannah shouted in triumph and held up the silver vibrator I'd confiscated from the naughty Kelly's pussy. As she did that, Lori twisted the base of the one in her hand. She squeaked as it hummed to life. She flicked her gaze to my pussy hidden by my black bush.

"Just start by rubbing it up and down my pussy slit," I purred. "That's the best way. Get yourself nice and ready for that buzzing shaft to penetrate you."

"Mmm, that's right," Helen said as she sat down next to me. "You listen to Officer Beverley. She knows what she's talking about." The blonde MILF leaned back, her large tits jiggling. They were as large and soft as mine, only a pale-beige instead of my rich ebony. "Now, Hannah, show me if you know how to use a vibrator."

"Oh, I know," purred Hannah. The silver vibrator purred to life. She stepped up to my boss. I smiled, seeing that Hannah had her left nipple pierced and had the only shaved pussy in the screening room.

Lori pressed the metallic-red dildo into my curls. I gasped as the buzzing tip massaged my pussy lips. The pleasure rushed through my body. I groaned, my breasts swaying. The tingling delight swept through me, and I knew I would have such a huge climax. Just a mighty explosion of rapture that would burst out of me.

It would be incredible.

"That's it," I told the cute blonde girl. Her glasses slipped on her nose as she stared down at the tip of the toy sliding through my bush. My pussy drank in the massaging hum. My cunt clenched. "Mmm, up and down. Get me nice and wet."

My sweet musk filled the air between us, mixing with her spicy musk. I groaned while beside me, Helen whimpered. Hannah worked her dildo on the blonde MILF's pussy with such enthusiasm. It was hot to watch. Had my blood boiling.

I groaned, my cunt clenching as the heat washed out through my body. The vibrator slid up and down my pussy. Lori guided it. The toy brushed my clit. I gasped, my legs buckling from the sudden burst of bliss.

"Mmm, that's my clit right there," I moaned. "Slide it up a bit more... Yes!"

"Wow," Lori said. "That felt nice when Hannah rubbed me there."

"Real nice," I groaned. "Ooh, yes, yes, you're going to make me cum, aren't you?"

"Uh-huh," Lori said. She blushed. "I'm really going to make you cum. This is... I've never felt like this in my life. I mean, I never really had much interest in sex. Boys, I guess, made me feel something, but now..."

"You're going to be a naughty, lezzie slut like me!" Hannah moaned and jammed the vibrator into Helen's cunt. "How do you like that, Officer Reynolds?"

"Oh, that's good," my supervisor moaned, her hair, a more golden shade than Lori's, swaying down her back. "Fuck that vibrator in and out of me, slut."

Hannah grinned and pumped away.

"Should I do that to you?" Lori asked, her voice tight. Nervous.

"Do you think my pussy is nice and warmed up for that?" I asked her.

"Y-yes," she said. Then she swallowed. "I mean, your pussy must need it so badly."

"So badly," I purred and winked at her.

I shuddered as the White girl slid the tip of the toy down my pussy folds. She found the entrance. Thrust. My cunt lips swallowed the buzzing shaft. I groaned, my face twisting in delight as she pressed the toy deeper and deeper into me.

"Oh, fuck, yes," I moaned, my cunt clenching down on that buzzing delight. "Ooh, ooh, that's delicious. That's wonderful. Mmm, aren't you just such a naughty thing, Lori?"

"I guess," she said as she slid it deeper. "So I just pump it in and out of you?"

I nodded, the pleasure rushing through my body. I groaned, my cunt clenching down on the vibrating toy. It felt amazing in my pussy. This wonderful heat built in my depths. I smiled, loving every second of it.

She pistoned the vibrator in and out of my pussy. That buzzing shaft massaged my inner delights. I gasped, my big boobs heaving. I leaned back and reveled in the bliss. It felt incredible having this naughty girl doing such wicked things to me.

"Oh, my," she said, her free hand groping her tits. She squeezed from her right boob to her left, gripping them hard for a moment before moving on to the other. "Your pussy is just swallowing it. It's so amazing."

"Uh-huh," I moaned.

"You're so gorgeous, Officer Beverley," the girl added, her voice throaty. "I mean, you have those big boobs and... and..."

"Suck on them!" I hissed. "Get your lips around my nipple. Do it, girl!"

"Y-yes, Ma'am!"

She darted her head down and latched her mouth onto my right nipple. She sucked hard on my nub as she reamed my pussy. She pumped the vibrator in and out of my cunt. She fucked me hard with it. I groaned, loving every minute of it thrusting in my cunt. It was such a hot delight to experience. The rapture rushed through my body.

My pussy clenched down on her vibrator. I gripped it, the humming swelling my orgasm so fast. I whimpered, hurtling towards my climax. Lori moaned around my nipple. The White girl suckled hard, her blue eyes squeezed shut behind her glasses.

"Yes, yes, yes!" Hannah moaned. "Oh, Officer Reynolds."

The purple-haired girl rammed her dildo in and out of the blonde MILF's pussy. At the same time, Helen suckled hungrily at

Hannah's pierced nipple. It shuddered, loving the sight. We were getting wild.

"Oh, yes, Lori!" I moaned. "You're going to make me cum. Keep fucking me with that vibrator."

"Hell, yeah, do it!" groaned Hannah. "Ooh, yes, yes, that's it. That's amazing. You're going to make her explode. Just make her cum hard. That's it. Yes! Let's make our MILFs climax, Lori!"

Lori squealed around my nipple; plunged the vibrator faster into my cunt.

My pussy clenched down on that buzzing toy. I gasped and whimpered. My eyes squeezed shut. I bucked. Her hot lips nibbled on my nub as she jammed the vibrator to the depths of my cunt. Her hand gripping the base brushed my clit.

Sparks flared.

I detonated.

"Fuck, yes!" I moaned, my pussy convulsing around that toy. "Oh, that's it. That's amazing. Yes, yes, yes!"

My pussy juices gushed out and bathed Lori's hand. Waves of bliss rushed out of my pussy. They inundated my mind. Stars burst across my vision. The pleasure burned in my thoughts. It was amazing. Rapturous. The delight swelled through me.

My cunt convulsed. The pleasure surged through me. I shuddered through my orgasm. My body bucked. Stars danced before my eyes. They shone so bright. I whimpered, my pussy spasming around the toy.

"Oh, that's good," I moaned. "That's amazing. Oh, fuck, that's wonderful."

My orgasm hit this amazing peak of ecstasy. Lori kept jamming the vibrator into my cunt while she nursed on my nipple. My pussy spasmed around that naughty toy while the bliss drowned my mind. Euphoria smothered my thoughts.

"Ooh, Officer Reynolds," groaned Hannah. "You're cumming hard, aren't you?"

A wet plop echoed as my boss ripped her mouth off Hannah's pierced nipple. "Yes, I am! Mmm, that's good. That's fucking good. You sexy girl."

"Yes, so good," I moaned, my pussy writhing around that

vibrator. "Take it out. Ooh, I came. I came hard."

Lori popped her mouth off my nipple and pulled the vibrator out of my cunt. She stared at me and then whimpered. She shoved the vibrator between her thighs. She rubbed the shaft right against her pussy lips, holding it there.

I watched in awe as the once-virginal girl bucked. Her round breasts heaved. She squealed out in obvious orgasmic delight as she held the shaft against her pussy, the vibrator's length massaging her entire slit at once.

"Yes, yes, yes!" Lori gasped.

"Holy shit, Lori," Hannah said, watching in awe. "You're just exploding. Look at you. That's hot."

"Yes, it is," I purred in delight.

"Oh, my gosh!" Lori moaned. "This is incredible. I love it. I love it so much! Yes!"

Her head threw back. Her perky tits bounced before me. I groaned, loving it. I wanted more. I wanted to do such wild things. I stared at the girl and then grinned at her. I knew just the sort of naughty things I had to do to Lori.

"On your hands and knees," I purred. "Mmm, I got to eat that pussy. I just want to dive into it."

"And you can eat my pussy while she does it," Helen said. My supervisor slid off the table and saunter by us. "Just do whatever she does to your cunt on mine."

"Yes, Officer Reynolds," moaned the girl. "I will. I'll do a good job, too."

"I know you will," I said, giving her ass a squeeze. "Give me that vibrator."

The girl did. I took it, holding it with a tight grip. I would do such naughty things to her. I would make her explode. It would be incredible. Lori fell to her hands and knees. She presented that tight, cute rump at me, her blonde bush, dripping with juices, peeking out between her thighs. She wiggled her hips. She looked so sexy. Just such an adorable delight to devour.

I fell to my knees and grabbed her pale rump with my left hand. I hungered to eat her spicy pussy. At the same time, my supervisor sank down to the floor before the girl. She spread her legs wide and grabbed the back of Lori's head.

"Oh, wow," moaned Lori as she allowed her head to be pushed down to Helen's twat. "That smells so good, Officer Reynolds. I think... I think I really am a lesbian."

"I know I am," groaned Hannah. "I'm convinced. You fucking MILFs make one great case for going lez. Now... I saw something naughty in here. Where is it..."

The purple-haired girl dug around in my bag. I heard the clink of my toys. What was she grabbing? I wanted to find out, but I also wanted to devour that sweet pussy right before my eyes. Just bury my face into some hot, young cunt.

God, it would be incredible.

"Ah-hah!" gasped Hannah. "Here it is."

"What?" Helen asked. "How many sex toys did you bring to work, Officer Beverley?"

"A few," I said.

"God, she's got it all in here," said Hannah. "Anal beads. Ben wa balls. Dildos. Clit rockets. Strap-ons. And a U-shaped dildo. Ooh, yes." Hannah grabbed that one. It was a strapless dildo. She shoved one end up into her pussy, the shorter, thicker end covered in several rings so her cunt could grip it. The other end thrust out from her, a sleek curve of pink plastic. "I'm going to fuck you hard, Officer Beverley."

"Good," I moaned and then buried my face into Lori's pussy.

Her blonde curls spilled over my lips and nose, her spicy musk filling my nose. I would have such an amazing time devouring her. I licked her. She shuddered as my tongue fluttered up and down her slit. I caressed her twat, feasting on her snatch with hunger.

I kissed at her twat. I smooched up and down her slit between licks, her curls tickling me. Hannah padded around as I did it. I kissed and nibbled and loved the girl's twat. She groaned and gasped as I smooched on her. I fluttered my tongue up and down her folds, licking and lapping at her.

"Ooh, that's hot," moaned Hannah as she strode by. "Look at you, just going to town on that muff. Mmm, make my friend cum hard."

"That's the plan," I moaned and slid the vibrating shaft across

Lori's butt-cheeks.

"Naughty Officer MILF!" gasped Hannah. "You're going to do *that* to Lori."

"Do what to me?" Lori asked, her voice muffled by Helen's hot pussy. "Wait, why are you putting the vibrator into my butt-crack, Officer Beverley?"

"You'll figure it out," purred Hannah.

I shivered and moved the dildo down Lori's crack, staring right at her puckered asshole. I thrust my tongue into the folds of her pussy just as I reached it. I caressed her inner sheath with hunger while massaging her backdoor with the wet, vibrating tip.

Then I pushed against it.

Lori gasped. Her butt-cheeks clenched. "You can't put it in there, Officer Beverley!"

"Sure she can," Hannah said. "Anal's hot. Enjoy."

"Oh, oh, oh my!" gasped Lori. "That's... You're... Oh, my!"

Her anal ring widened to engulf the metallic vibrator. The red toy slid into her bowels. I fluttered my tongue inside of her clenching cunt as her bowels swallowed the buzzing shaft. It was so hot to watch. Such a delight.

She groaned, her voice muffled by hot pussy. She ate out Helen while I fucked the girl's bowels. Her spicy juices dribbled down my chin and soaked across my taste buds. It was such a hot thing to taste. To do to her.

Then the end of Hannah's U-shaped dildo pressed into my cunt. I groaned as she slid it up and down my slit, massaging me. It felt narrower than I thought it was, almost like a cone. She pushed it in, my pussy lips spreading around it. I groaned and then whimpered as she pulled it away.

She slid it up and up my taint. She was going to fuck me in the ass.

I groaned into Lori's pussy and jammed the vibrator deep into her bowels. The girl squealed as I plundered her anal depths with the buzzing toy. My tongue lapped up her spicy juices, feasting on her as the conical tip of the dildo nuzzled up to my asshole.

Hannah pressed it against my anal ring.

"Yes," I moaned as it widened to swallow the dildo. "Ooh,

that's nice."

"I bet," purred Hannah.

She somehow twisted the toy, drilling it into my bowels. How did she do that? My anal ring widened wider and wider. I groaned, my asshole stretching to my limits. Then it popped all the way in me. I blinked, feeling a slender rod sticking onto my asshole and Hannah's hand on the end, pushing a red base into my butt-crack.

"A butt plug?" I groaned. "Ooh, you are wicked."

"I couldn't resist," moaned Hannah, pulling her hand away and leaving the butt plug buried to the hilt in me.

Then she pressed her end of the U-shaped dildo against my pussy lips. It felt much more phallic. Thick. She thrust in hard. My pussy clenched, my bowels gripping hard about the conical butt plug. I groaned into Lois's pussy, rubbing my cheeks into her pubic hair.

"Fuck her," moaned Helen as Hannah's crotch smacked into my rump. "Mmm, fuck her hard. Just pound her with that dildo."

"Oh, I plan on it," purred Hannah, her hands gripping my hips.

She pounded me with her U-shaped dildo. She thrust that wonderful toy in and out of my cunt. I groaned, clenching my twat around the fake cock. I moaned into Lori's cunt, my tongue dancing through her young folds.

I pumped the vibrator in and out of Lori's asshole. I fucked it in deep and then pulled it back out. She groaned, her butt-cheeks clenching. From the way my supervisor moaned, the girl was doing a wonderful job at eating the MILF's cunt.

My breasts swayed beneath me from the force of Hannah's strokes. She plowed that dildo into my pussy. The friction stirred me up. It mixed with the fullness in my asshole. The butt plug added that extra zest, feeding my orgasm.

"Oh, yes, yes, Lori!" moaned Helen. "Ooh, that's it. You're doing good. Mmm, you're going to make me cum."

"I want that," Lori moaned. "I want you to cum. Your pussy tastes so good. Just shower my mouth in all your juices."

"Yes, yes, yes!" I moaned, plunging the dildo into her asshole. "Make her cum."

SMACK!

"Yes, yes, do it, Lori!" gasped Hannah, her spank stinging on my rump. "Ooh, make that MILF cum."

"You, too, Hannah," Lori moaned. "Officer Beverley deserves it for how good she's making me feel. My butt is melting. That vibrator is incredible."

"I knew you'd love it!"

Hannah thrust harder and faster into me. My orgasm swelled, my hot cunt gripping her shaft. I held tight to her, the pleasure rippling through my body with her every thrust. The heat swelled faster and faster. My body was on fire.

I wiggled my hips. I stirred my cunt around that dildo, adding that extra bit of stimulation. My asshole savored the butt plug filling up my bowels. Every time she buried the strap-on into me, the force of her strokes pushed the naughty anal toy a little bit further inside me.

I was on fire. My breasts heaved. I moaned into Lori's cunt. Her silky hairs rubbed at my face. I pumped the dildo faster and faster into her asshole. We were all moaning. All sounding like we were on the verge of cumming.

"I love this dildo!" gasped Hannah. "Holy shit, I have to get one."

"And fuck Lori with it?" I asked.

"Yes!" she moaned.

"Oh, yes, yes, fuck me with it!" Lori whimpered. Then I heard sucking.

"Yes, yes, nurse on my clit!" gasped Helen. "That's amazing. Oh, you naughty, wicked girl. You're going to make me cum.

I shuddered, licking up and down Lori's pussy slit. I didn't teach the girl to suck on a clit. That was all her. She was growing her lesbian skills. This strange pride shot through me, feeding the delight churned up by Hannah's thrusting dildo.

The climaxes started with Helen. "Oh, fuck, yes, Lori!" my boss moaned. "You're such a good pussy licker. Drink it. Drink my cream!"

"Yes, Officer Reynolds," the girl moaned, wiggling her hips. She smeared her furred muff into my face.

I jammed the vibrator deep into her bowels and stirred it around in her by gripping the base. She whimpered, her pussy clenching about my tongue. I fucked it in and out of her cunt, loving the spicy flavor of her.

She squealed. Her pussy convulsed around my tongue. Hot juices gushed into my mouth. The spicy delight spilled over my lips and poured down my chin. I fluttered my tongue up and down her snatch, licking up all that yummy cream.

"Yes, yes, yes!" Lori moaned. "So good. I'm cumming! I'm cumming, Hannah!"

"Awesome!" the girl moaned, fucking my pussy hard.

My cunt drank in the friction. The heat of that shaft plowing into my twat rippled through me. I squeezed down on it, my asshole clenching about the butt plug. Its presence added that naughty spark to what I was doing. The heat rushed through my body, bringing me closer and closer to that moment of eruption.

"Yes, yes, yes!" I groaned into Lori's pussy. "Ooh, that's good. That's delicious. Make me cum!"

"You got it!" Hannah hissed and grabbed the handle of my butt plug.

She ripped it out of my asshole.

My anal ring spread wide in a flash. The burst of hot pleasure shot down to my cunt being plundered by her dildo. She slammed it back into my twat. I gasped into Lori's pussy. The pleasure burst through me.

Waves of rapture washed out of my spasming snatch. My bowels, feeling so empty, convulsed. The ecstasy swept through my body. It spilled over my thoughts. I groaned as it smothered my mind in euphoria.

"Oh, god, yes!" I moaned into Lori's pussy. I drank more of the cream flowing out of her.

"That's so hot!" howled Hannah. She buried her dildo to the hilt in my cunt. "Fuck, yes!"

My pussy convulsed around the toy as she bucked. Her body's shudders stirred the dildo around in my snatch as I heard her crying out in rapture. We were all moaning, our passion echoing through the room. It was such a heady rush to have this foursome with the two hot girls and a fellow MILF.

"Oh, my fucking god," my supervisor purred. "Oh, Lori, you're such a naughty girl. Mmm, you know how to eat pussy."

"It was so yummy to do," moaned Lori. "I just did what Officer Beverley did to my pussy. She was amazing but... but... That vibrator in my asshole."

More juices gushed out of the girl as she came a second time. I licked them up as I trembled through my own orgasm. I hit the peak of pleasure, reveling in the spicy cream spilling down my chin, my large breasts swaying beneath me.

The four of us groaned and panted. I pulled the vibrator out of Lori's asshole and turned it off. We all stood up. Kisses were shared. Helen's tangy pussy tasted wonderful on Lori's lips. I shivered as I handed the blonde girl back her vibrator.

"This is allowed on the airplane," I told her. "You know how to use it properly. It's not a threat."

"Only to other women's pussies," giggled Hannah.

Lori gave a shy smile.

We all dressed after that. We couldn't keep having our fun. The girls had to get to their flight. The vibrator vanished into Lori's carry on. I donned my uniform. It was another wonderful search. I felt ready to get back to my shift.

"We're going to get so much pussy, aren't we," I heard Hannah say to Lori as the two girls headed out of the screening room. "Just going to have a dyke orgy in our hotel room."

"Yes," Lori said, though she sounded like she was blushing. "Yes, we are."

Hannah laughed as the door closed.

"Now, you, Shanisa," Helen said, my boss adjusting her belt, "need to call me whenever you have one of these 'naughty girls' to search. I have to be here to make sure that you do it properly."

"You don't think I can make those girls cum?" I asked, arching an eyebrow.

"I'm your supervisor," she purred. "It's my job to watch and evaluate." She cupped my face. "I need to make sure you do every step right."

She kissed me on the mouth. I closed my eyes, melting into the

White MILF's hot lips. I knew that we would be having so much fun screening the passengers who came through our airport. A hot shiver ran through me.

I loved being a lesbian MILF working security.

* * *

The lesbian wish continues to spread from those naughty MILFs. On airplanes, passengers travel across the world, bringing the effects of the wish to new communities. More and more sexy girls are turning on those hot and mature older women.

And they are returning the delights to those nubile, young things in their lives.

To be continued in Ruth's story...

# About the Author

Reed James is a thirty year-old guy living in Tacoma, WA. "I love to write, I find it freeing to immerse myself in a world and tell its stories and then share them with others." He's been writing naughty stories since high school, furiously polishing his craft, and finally feels ready to share his fantasies with the world.

"I love writing about women who want to be a little (or a lot) naughty, people expressing their love for each other as physically and kinkily as possible, and women loving other women. Whether it's a virgin experiencing her/his first time or a long-term couple exploring the bounds of their relationships, it will be a hot, erotic story!"

You can find Reed on the internet at the following places:

Twitter: https://twitter.com/NLPublications
Facebook: https://www.facebook.com/reed.james.9231
Blog: http://blog.naughtyladiespublications.com/wp
Newsletter: http://eepurl.com/4nlN5

Made in the USA
Monee, IL
05 July 2023

38721711R00157